Lord

of

Innis Torr

I0612739

A GameLit Adventure Series

(BRIDGE QUEST Book 3)

pdmac

Trimble Hollow Press

Lord of Innis Torr is a work of fiction. Though actual locations may be mentioned, they are used in a fictitious manner and the events and occurrences were created/invented in the mind and imagination of the author, except for the inclusion of actual historical fact. Similarities of characters or names used within for any person – past, present, or future – are coincidental except where actual historical characters are purposely interwoven. The actions, thoughts, and dialogue of the historical characters featured in this story are fictional and not meant to reflect actual personalities and behavior.

Published by Trimble Hollow Press, Acworth, Georgia

ISBN: 978-1-946495-21-1
eISBN: 978-1-946495-20-4

Cover design by Trimble Hollow Concepts
Cover art by James Esquivel

for Terri Lynn
my Soulmate and Best Friend

Marbeck

Abeloft

Stonekirk

Westhaven

Helkirk

Durness

Statmyr

Odryssa

Torgue

Contyn

Eglyn

Avnoch   Kinlich

Abynee   Glenloc

Krief

Dinwahl

Hulgard

Tarrytown

Tal Olea

Hillfurt

erismo

Strathwick

Beally

Ozgul

Ryath-sari

Braghurk

Banvie

Zag Nurgal

Rigar Khar

Lyster

Krugrodh

Innis Torr

Contents

Chapter 1

It was dark as Karl became aware of his surroundings, dark and raining. *This is the most beneficial place?* Light from the streetlamps at the end of the alley flickered, providing enough light for him to see Caryn standing next to him.

"This sucks," she muttered.

Karl stared at her for a moment. Despite the bedraggled wet hair, she was very pretty, and he easily remembered what she looked like in real life. Then he noticed she had her bow and he looked down at his hip.

"I'm wearing Orc's Bane," he said then checked his belt. "And I've still got all my stuff."

"What'd you expect?"

"I don't know. I figured Orc's Bane would be the last place I was... which wasn't here. Let's go find out where 'here' is."

As soon as they emerged from the alley, Karl huffed an exasperated sigh. "We're in Talbet." He looked up and down the deserted street. "Let's find Evnan."

Leading the way, he passed a tavern, half tempted to get a cold pint. Arriving at the gate to Evnan's walled compound, Karl banged on the door. When no one answered, he banged again, louder.

The door's peephole slid open, and a man's eyes filled the space. "What do you want?" he snapped.

"Open the door, Darren. We're wet and hungry."

The man focused on Karl only a moment before exclaiming, "O my God, it's you, your Lordship. We thought you might have been taken prisoner. Where have you been? M'Lord Evnan has been worried about you. All of us have."

"Darren," Karl smiled despite the rain, "I'd be happy to share my story after we have dried off."

1

"Of course, m'Lord, I'm so sorry, my apologies." The door swung open, and Karl and Caryn ducked in then through the courtyard, empty of animals and petitioners. Closing the door, Darren led them to Evnan's main house opposite the gate and inside where a stunned Beitris nearly dropped the tray laden with tonight's dinner.

"My Lord," she said in reverent tones, dipping a brief curtsey.

"Good to see you too, Beitris," Karl acknowledged with a smile.

The maid beamed that the king not only remembered her but remembered her name. She ticked her head towards the door to the dining room. "He's in there, m'Lord."

"Who else?" Karl asked when he noted there didn't seem to be a lot of food on the tray she held.

"No one, m'Lord. He says he needs time to think, but he's been thinking this entire time since you've been gone, especially these past two weeks now that some man called Kevin declared himself king."

"Kevin?" Karl startled.

"Yes, m'Lord."

Karl shook his head and turned to Caryn. "So this is what they meant when they said we had to get back."

Caryn's lips tightened. "What's he look like?" she asked Beitris.

"I don't know, m'Lady," she shrugged, tray in hand. "All I know is that he's some stranger who is now king. I don't understand any of it, m'Lady."

Karl folded his arms and exhaled a long breath. "If it's who I think it is, we got ourselves a big problem."

"I know," Caryn grimly replied. "I remember you telling me about him. Wonder how he made it across the bridge."

"And past everything else to get here," Karl added with furrowed brow then turned back to Beitris and Darren. "Tell no one we are here."

"M'Lord?" Darren said, puzzled

"Once we have talked with Lord Evnan, we were never here, and you never saw us."

2

"As you wish, m'Lord. My lips are sealed," Beitris asserted.

"Darren?"

"Yes, m'Lord. Of course," Darren affirmed with a dip of his head.

"Good," Karl said, reaching up to take the tray from Beitris. "Here, let me take this."

"M'Lord?" Beitris' eyes grew wide, first at the thought that the King would lower himself to a servant's work then secondly that she would be chastised for letting the King do her work.

But Karl forced the tray for her hands. "It's OK, Beitris. This is merely to have a little fun."

Without waiting for an answer and the tray held high, he butted the door open and announced, "Dinner is served, m'Lord."

Evnan looked up when the voice did not match the woman who had served his household for almost thirty years. When Karl lowered the tray and revealed his face, Evnan leaped out of his chair.

"By the gods, you're alive... and Lady Caryn with you. Where have you been? The kingdom is in peril."

"So I heard," Karl said, placing the tray down on the table.

"Beitris, bring more food and ale for our king and Lady Caryn," Evnan commanded. Seeing Darren, he thrust a finger at him. "Alert the garrison captain that the king has returned."

Darren remained rooted and shifted a glance to look helplessly at Karl.

"Hold that order for the moment," Karl said. "We need to talk."

"Is that wise, Sire?" Evnan warned. "Spies abound even more now."

"So I imagine," Karl said taking the seat next to Evnan's place. Caryn slid out a chair beside him. Looking back over his shoulder, he smiled when Beitris returned with two steins of ale. "Haven't had good ale since we left."

"Where *did* you go, Sire?" Evnan asked, resuming his seat. "I heard you were there one moment and the next you vanished into thin air."

"Sorcery," Karl lied. "We were whisked away to fulfill a quest."

Evnan's eyes brightened and his interest perked. "By the gods, where?"

"Far, far away from here," he evasively answered, his mind scrambling for a convincing story.

"What was the quest?"

"Rescue a damsel in distress," Caryn replied, taking a sip of ale and peering at Karl over the rim.

"By the gods," Evnan blurted, his appetite and thirst suddenly returning. "What happened? How did you manage it?" He swallowed a gulp of ale.

"With weapons so magical," she explained, "that you can see an enemy kilometers away, set up an ambush, and continue watching as he approaches, he doesn't even know you are there."

"By... the... gods," Evnan replied in wonder. "This sorcery must be powerful."

"Very," Karl nodded in agreement.

"Did you see what he or she looked like?" Though focused on Caryn, he waved a hand at Beitris to hurry up with the food.

"Yes. There were two of them, the head sorcerer and his assistant."

"What did they look like?" Evnan's ale mug hovered below his lips.

Caryn glanced over to Karl who leaned forward and whispered, "Just like you and me."

"By the gods. And the woman?"

"Stunning," Karl replied with a grin, rolling his eyes for emphasis then feeling a not so gentle kick beneath the table.

The tale paused when Beitris returned, carrying a tray laden with fresh bread, cheese, and sliced cold meat then resumed when she left.

"Tell me about what has happened while we were away," Karl said, changing the topic. "Who is this Kevin character?"

"We all thought he was one of your retainers, for he claimed he was part of your closest advisors. He came through here with several others, one who looked like you," he said, looking at Caryn.

"An elf?" she exclaimed.

"Yes."

"Did he have a name?

"Not that I remember," he shrugged as apology. "They weren't here for very long."

"What did he look like?"

"I don't know. I wasn't here when they came through," he replied, "but I was told he was a warrior like you. He was reserved and kept to himself."

"The others?" Karl asked.

"There were three others, all men: one a Ranger like Lady Raquel, a sorcerer, and a Berserker like Lord Dieter, though not quite as big."

"And the only name you know is Kevin?"

"I didn't find that out until I discovered he was king. But more importantly, Sire, the rest of your followers are imprisoned in Avnoch."

"I assumed as much," he replied.

"Actually, not all are imprisoned," Evnan said. "Lady Sakura is not among those imprisoned."

"I'm surprised Annabeth didn't manage to wrangle her way out," Caryn said.

"It was three against one," Evnan said, "from what I heard. Lady Annabeth had to contend against Caillic, Finella and the new sorcerer." He then peered intently at Karl. "Why is it you wish no one to know you are here, Sire?"

"Like you said, spies abound. I can't afford to be recognized before I make my move. That doesn't mean I want you to be idle. Caryn and I are going to disappear for a while, but we will still be close. I need time to recon and plan. When I am ready, I will return here."

"What do you want us to do?"

Pushing the plate aside, Karl picked up the knife to use as a pointer. "I want you to sound out all those who can be 100% trusted. Do not let anyone know we have returned. Not yet. Is Annys still the commander up in Abynee?"

"Yes," Evnan nodded with satisfaction. "She is doggedly loyal to you, as is Rhan. Those are two whom we can depend on."

"Good. That's a start. In the meantime, I'll need food for a week for Caryn and me," Karl said. "Hopefully we should be back before then," he added when he saw Evnan's puzzled face. "That should give you enough time to see who we can depend on."

That evening, Karl asked for a small piece of oak wood and a private place where he would be left alone to meditate. Darren led him to a remote room down the corridor from Evnan's personal chapel. The room was large, the size of the dining room, hung with tapestries and filled with dark heavy chairs and bureaus ornately carved with plant designs. Three gothic arched windows filled the outer wall that overlooked the gardens.

Waiting until Darren lit the tapers of several candles, Karl barred the door when Darren left then returned to the center of the room to sit on a thick cushioned armchair, pulling out his knife to carve F-R-E-Y-A into the piece of oak. As soon as he finished, he sheathed his blade and stood.

"I call upon the Goddess Freya, mighty and benevolent ruler in Vanir, to come to me from your abode above, now to this place in time and space, appear to me face to face."

Silence settled for only a moment before a sensual voice said, "I was beginning to wonder if you had forgotten me. What? No summoning circle," she teased

Freya materialized, her long flowing blond hair held back with a garland of flowers. She smiled at him, the intense gaze of sky-blue eyes making him feel no one else in the world existed. Her diaphanous dress, billowing in the windless room, accentuated her curvaceous body and Karl was momentarily distracted.

"Do try to stay focused," she chuckled before glancing down at the runes. "You're getting better, though your 'Y' needs a little work. What is it this time?"

"I need your help."

"Like the last time?"

"It's different this time."

"That's what they all say," she sighed.

"I need help regaining my kingdom," he explained.

"You haven't even started yet," she retorted. "You interrupt a busy goddess like me to intercede in something that hasn't even begun. You're wasting my time."

"But you don't understand –"

"I understand perfectly," she calmly answered. "Your arch enemy Kevin has taken over your kingdom while you were gone, which points to the obvious question of why were you gone in the first place?"

"I had no choice," he replied.

Ignoring him, she continued, "Now you're faced with defeating him and his friends while rescuing your own friends. My, my... your irresponsibility seems to have complicated things."

"I said it wasn't my fault," he fussed.

"That's what they all say." She placed a hand in front of her mouth to cover a yawn.

"Are you going to help me or not?" Karl fumed.

"What's to help with? You're certainly not in life-threatening peril and as far as I can tell, you don't need any help."

She started to disappear.

"What the hell?" Karl burst. "What's the point in having a patron Goddess if all you do is say 'take care of it yourself'? I thought you were supposed to actually do something."

"Now, now," Freyja retorted, her body solidifying, "not so testy."

"But what's the point? I was told having a patron goddess was supposed to be some wonderful benefit that would help me in time of need. And here you are, again, telling me to handle it."

"There you go," she said with a benevolent smile. "You yourself see the foolishness of your summoning me at this moment, for, like you just said, I would help you in time of need. What is your need at this very moment? Are you in danger? Is your life threatened?"

Karl's jaw clenched and he let out and exasperated sigh. "Obviously I'm in no jeopardy at this exact moment, but I will be once I leave here."

"Then call me when you are in need. Until that time, stop pestering me."

"Pestering you?" he shouted.

"Yes," she snapped. "Look at you. You're a level 25. Your enemy Kevin is only a level 14. Your friend Caryn is also a level 25. Between the two of you, you can kick ass all the way to the next bridge." She abruptly stopped and giggled. "Did I just say 'ass?'"

Karl frowned at the realization. "What about Kevin's other friends?"

"Kevin is the highest among them and that's all I'll say at the moment."

Karl's eyes blinked wide. "You know what's going on but you won't tell me?"

"It's not my place."

"Not your place?" he barked. "What the hell? You're a goddess who knows stuff that can help me and it's not your place to tell me? Tell me again why I need you?"

"You don't," she said, biting off the words, "which is my point all along. You summon me when you don't need to. I'm reminded of that fable of the little boy who cried wolf."

"I get it," Karl fumed. "Look. If you're not going to help me at least you could help Annabeth deal with the three sorcerers."

"I'm your goddess, not hers," she tartly responded.

"This is crazy," he bristled. "What's the point of having a goddess if all she does is – nothing? So if I was in dire straits and you appeared and condescended to actually do something, and I said help someone else, you'd say, 'sorry, not my job?'"

"Pretty much," she grinned.

Karl flipped the piece of wood with the runes in the air behind him.

"You might want to be careful with that," she warned. "That wood is now imbued with magical summoning powers. If it falls into the wrong hands, it might be to your detriment. If you're finished with it, either secure it or burn it."

With a huff of pique, Karl turned and retrieved the carved piece of wood. When he turned around, her gossamer form was beginning to fade as was the voice who called out, "Think before you call me again. The next time will be the last time if it's like this time. Fare well, Viking."

She vanished, leaving Karl frustrated and angry. Yet she did provide one bit of comfort. If Kevin was the highest player at level 14, then he and Caryn would be in a far better position to impose their will. Now all he needed to do was find Sakura.

Karl and Caryn were on the road at first light, dressed as simple laborers, the drab hooded capes pulled up over their shoulders and heads against the rain, as well as covering their weapons, though Caryn carried the unstrung bow in her hand, the bowstring tucked safely away to stay dry. Though focused on the task at hand, Karl couldn't help but cast the more than occasional glimpse at his co-wanderer, the reverie of last night's frolicking playing over and over in his memory. This truly was a first – sex with an elf.

"Why do you keep looking at me?" she asked with a frown. "Do I have spinach in my teeth or something?"

"No," he grinned. "Just thinking of last night and trying to assimilate the Caryn of two days ago with the Caryn of last night. Except for the pointed ears... and the completely different body... you're still *exactly* the same."

"Look who's talking," she replied with a laugh.

"Touché."

"On another note, I'm still confused as to why we're backtracking through Mann all the way to the elf city in the orc kingdom. Seems to me that we're going in the wrong direction."

9

"I need a safe place for the moment," Karl replied. "I know it's not exactly on the way, but this will give us time to organize and plan. We can keep track of what's going on by way of your animal and bird friends."

"Still seems counterproductive to me."

"I understand," Karl said. "The problem we face here is that, knowing Kevin, he will have spies running all over Odryssa and there are enough citizens here who would be more than willing to help him."

"Leri for example," Caryn pointed out.

"Wouldn't surprise me if she's out conducting business as usual. The point is, you and I stand out as it is. Anyone sees us and we're fighting for our lives, even if we are level 25s. We need time to regroup, check out what's going on."

"How do we do that if we're all the way over in the orc kingdom?"

"Like I said, you're a ranger. You can communicate with animals and birds. We use them to help us."

"Not as good as people," she countered.

"Of course not. Which people would you suggest?"

Caryn thought a moment then shrugged. "Point taken. We can't exactly use folks as counter spies until we know what's going on."

"So we lay low for the time being."

"You think a week's enough?"

"Probably not," Karl answered, "but I don't see us carrying a month's worth of vittles on our backs. We're gonna have to raid some places on the way."

"Sounds like fun," she grinned.

For the first half hour, the road ran in a straight line towards the forest, dipping and rising in gentle curves. Verdant farms spread wide on both sides of the road, smoke curling out of the chimneys of the solidly built homes. Morning traffic on the road began to pick up with the occasional merchant wagon passing them on the way to the border, the drivers too preoccupied with getting the merchandise to market to offer more than a simple lifted hand or grunt in greeting, which was fine with Karl who wanted little attention.

By the time they were well into the forest separating the two kingdoms, Karl felt something was off. The rain had stopped and the thick clouds were starting to thin with the promise of sunlight. Every now and then he would look behind him, taking note that no one else was on the road, which struck him as odd.

"Something's not right," he said, looking once again over his shoulder. "We've been out for more than an hour. It's too quiet, even for where we are. There ought to be the occasional merchant wagon headed one way or the other."

Caryn turned to look behind them just as movement in the distance where the trees swallowed up the road caught her attention. "Someone's coming. Fast."

Without a word, they ducked into the forest and hunkered down within a thicket of shrubs. They had not long to wait when four riders came charging up then slowed to a walk before stopping in the middle of the road. They wore long robes with the hoods back now that the rain had stopped.

"You sure you saw them?" a woman complained, standing up in the stirrups and twisting around to stare back the way they came then twisting back around to focus up the road. Her long blond hair was held in place by a woven headband.

"I swear I saw something," the man beside her replied. He urged his steed forward a few steps before he too stood in his stirrups and stared up the road.

"Maybe we spooked them," a man with close cropped hair suggested, slowly scanning the surrounding forest.

After a moment, the last man in the group, a middle-aged man with a thick auburn beard said, "Maybe you saw a deer or some animal."

"I know what I saw," the first man tersely replied. He turned his horse and came up beside the woman. "The road's too wet to track them. We know they're on the road into Eglyn. If we did spook them, let's turn around and head back to the forest edge and wait for them to think we've gone.

Give 'em more of a head start this time. They're gotta go through Eglyn, probably spend the night there. We can take them there."

"Why not just head to Eglyn now," the bearded man said, "and take 'em when they get there? That way we can get dry at least."

"And have an ale," the short haired man grinned.

The first man dismissively shook his head. "That assumes they haven't seen us or won't see us. If they do, they'll just avoid Eglyn altogether. Besides, we hang around Eglyn too long and someone's bound to get suspicious."

"You really think *we* can take them?" the short haired man scoffed. "If it *is* the Viking, he's probably got that sword with him."

"He's just a man," the first man testily replied. "All the others are locked up in Avnoch."

"That's not what I heard," the bearded man said. "They say the assassin went missing and then there's the elf ranger not been seen either."

"So how *are* we gonna take 'em?" the short haired man asked.

"It's called drugs," the woman coldly answered, reining her horse back around. "Fyras is right. We give them another head start then take them in Eglyn then hand them over to Lord Kerr."

"Wonder why he wants 'em so bad?" the bearded man mused aloud.

"It's not Kerr who wants them," the woman answered, urging her mount forward, the others falling in behind.

"Who then?" Fyras asked, frowning in thought.

"Think, man," the woman sniffed in disdain at the man's obtuseness.

It was a moment before the epiphany hit and he uttered, "Kevin?"

The woman said nothing, merely shaking her head as they rode away.

Karl and Caryn waited until the riders were well beyond earshot then edged to the road, peering out when the last rider disappeared.

"That was fast," Caryn sourly stated. "We're barely out of the city and already everyone knows were here."

"Only three people knew of our return," Karl stated, "Evnan, Beitris, and Darren. Evnan would not betray us."

"Which leaves Beitris and Darren," Caryn finished for him. "Between the two, I trust Beitris over Darren."

Karl looked up the road where the riders had gone. "We need to put some distance between us and them. You up for some double time speed?"

"We staying on the road?" she asked as they took off at a jog.

"As long as they're heading back that way, it gives us a good head start. At this pace, we should hit Eglyn by early evening."

"Providing we can keep this pace for the next eight hours," she reminded him.

"Point taken."

As they jogged up the road, Karl pulled up his stats. "Y'know, being a level 25 gives me some nice benefits. Despite still not having a clue as to what most of these things mean, like Mana for instance, my stats have drastically improved."

"Mana has to do with your ability to use magic," Caryn said.

"I know. I read the same definition. I just don't understand why the need for Mana. If I can use a spell only once, why not just say so? If I can use a spell more than once, why not just let me instead of adding this Mana stuff?"

"Maybe it's to cause you to use your magic wisely and only when you need to?"

Karl remembered his disappointing visit with Freyja. *What's the point of having friends in high places if you can't exploit them when you want?*

"What's weird is that even with my level at 25 now," Caryn said, scrolling her skills, "all my skills have pretty much stayed the same. The only difference, as far as I can tell, is the duration or intensity. For instance, I've this skill called 'Pace-breaker' where I can increase my pace by fifteen feet per second. If I combine it with the "Tireless Travel' skill, I could outrun and outlast the horses chasing us."

Karl frowned as he focused on his own skills. "All my skills fall within strength, wisdom, and knowledge, though I now have magical skills." He paused and scrolled. "Huh. I have the 'Pace-breaker' skill under my Strength skill and 'Tireless Travel' under endurance, which is a subset of Strength. Sheesh. How can anyone keep track of all this stuff? No wonder Annabeth complains all the time."

"She's not a complainer," Caryn countered, though not pleased that an object of Karl's affection was mentioned. She liked having him to herself.

"You're right," Karl acknowledged. "She's always upbeat."

"Why not use our skills," Caryn said, not wanting to hear any more about Annabeth, "and pick up the pace?"

"Sounds good."

In one instant they went from just under ten kilometers per hour pace to effortlessly flying along the road at over twenty-six kilometers per hour.

"At this pace," Karl said, breathing comfortably, "we should hit Eglyn in a little more than an hour. Let's bypass it and head on down along the coast wards Banvie. We could get there in twelve hours at this pace."

"You really think we can maintain this pace for the next twelve hours?" Caryn chuckled.

"Eh," Karl smiled back, "probably not."

Caryn nodded and smiled. "Still, don't you wish you could do this in real life?"

Their pace slowed as they approached Eglyn and instead of staying on the road leading to the town, they worked their way along the edges of the forest edging the farms, which surrounded the town of Eglyn in the center.

Once around the town and farms and back on the main road, Caryn placed her hand on Karl's arm to stop him from resuming their pace. "We were lucky on the road here that we didn't see anyone. I'm not so sure we'll be that lucky from here to Banvie. I need to employ some of my other skills."

Pausing, she tilted her head back and closed her eyes. Looking up, Karl was about to ask her what she was doing when he saw an eagle high above them, cresting the currents in lazy circles.

"We're good," she announced, opening her eyes. "We have a lookout for us."

Karl glanced back up to note the eagle had moved away, headed in the direction of where the road split to go to Banvie. "I keep forgetting all the powers everyone has. After all this time in the game, I'm still too much of a linear thinker."

"We all are," Caryn sympathized. "He says it's clear up ahead."

They resumed their pace, the eagle forced to push its own speed to keep up. Twice they had to stop and duck into the forest when a farmer's wagon trundled past. An hour later, they approached a small village called Torgue and Caryn bid the eagle a heartfelt 'Thank you' and sent it on its way.

"Do we stop in town?" Caryn asked.

"We could use a rest and something to eat," Karl admitted. "Hopefully, no one should know us here."

Their pace back to a leisurely stroll, they walked into the hamlet, a collection of shops, homes, and a tavern. Karl glanced at Caryn's ears.

"I wonder if you could hide those somehow."

Caryn shook her head to loosen her hair, running her fingers through it and covering her ears. "I have a feeling we're going to get more than our fair share of attention anyway. After all, you're not exactly the lowly laborer type."

"Unfortunately, you're probably right," he acknowledged. "Well... let's go see what the natives are like."

Side by side, they walked into the village and entered the tavern. Though the town was small, the tavern was half filled with locals, mostly old men and a few younger idlers wanting to avoid work for a while. Their heads turned in unison as Karl and Caryn entered.

"Good day to all here," Karl greeted them, though they all stared at Caryn. Glancing rapidly around the room, he realized that except for the two serving girls, Caryn was the only woman in the tavern. Curiously enough, while the men ogled Caryn, the two serving girls, both in their late teens, cast amorous eyes at Karl.

"Good day to you," the taverner smiled. "What can I get you?" He was a middle-aged man with a receding hairline and a bulbous nose, but his smile was genuine.

"Two ales and something to eat," Karl answered, heading for a table near the far wall.

"Sit here," a patron, an old man with a bushy grey beard and wrinkled skin, said, pointing to a table close by him. "Tell us who you are. Don't get many new folks comin' round here these days."

Karl slid out a chair while Caryn propped her bow against the edge of the table.

"Where ya comin' from and where ya headed?" another voice asked.

"Give 'im a chance," the old man retorted.

"My name is Karl, and this is my wife, Caryn." As Karl watched the disappointment on the faces of the serving girls and a number of the men, he did his best to unobtrusively position his sword so that no one would notice it. "We are from Abynee."

"Abynee?" another old man frowned. "Never heard of it."

"Ain't that over in Odryssa?" the old man asked.

"Yes," Karl said as the taverner brought over two pewter steins of ale.

Caryn sipped the contents and gave an appreciative nod. "This is very good."

"Thank you," the taverner replied with a confident grin. "Got some venison stew with fresh bread and cheese. You won't be disappointed."

16

"He's tellin' the truth," the old man acknowledged. "Bin comin' here every day fer the past fifteen years. Food's better'n my wife used to cook, the gods rest her soul."

"Sounds good," Caryn said.

The taverner turned back to one of the serving girls, a pretty girl with curly blond hair, and held up two fingers indicating stew for the two strangers.

"How'd ya end up here?" an older man sitting at another close by table asked. He was bald on top with wisps of hair above the ears. His skin was the tanned brown of someone who worked outside all his life.

"Just passing through," Karl said, sipping his ale.

"Where ya headed?"

"We're thinking of heading south to Glenloch," Karl answered. "Heard there might be work available for the likes of us."

"Whaddaya do?" the old man asked.

"I'm a fighter, a warrior," he began.

"We all could tell that the moment ya walked in," the old man interrupted.

"Yes, well, my wife is a hunter without equal. We figure between us we should be able to make a living."

"What's wrong with where ya lived?" the bald older man asked.

Karl shook his head with a sigh. "The kingdom is divided between two houses of the same family, both wanting to rule alone. They spend so much time fighting each other that neither side cares about the common folk. The roads are no longer safe and even the hard-working farmers have to have escorts just to bring in the grains and other food to market."

"Sounds like you two had no problems gettin' jobs," the old man observed.

"That's the problem," Karl said. "Sure, I could easily find work as a soldier, but that meant killing people who belonged to the same kingdom, innocent people who all they wanted was to lead a quiet and happy life. I can understand fighting enemies of the kingdom, but I can't tolerate choosing sides in a family."

His response met with grunts and nods of approval.

"So tell me," Karl said with a half-smile. "I heard Mann was a quiet place where they only worried about the weather."

"Haw," the old man barked a laugh. "Wish it were so, young fella. Ever since the king's daughter returned, the witch has been beside herself."

"Witch?" Karl repeated, eyes wide.

"She ain't a witch," the bald man argued. "She's a sorceress."

"Same difference," the old man retorted.

"The king has a sorceress?" Karl asked with a frown of concern.

Caryn laid a tender hand on Karl's arm. "Honey, it's just like back home with Kerr and Fraster. They have sorceresses too."

"Who are they?" the old man asked.

"Those are the two rulers who constantly fight against each other," Caryn explained.

"Ah," the old man nodded. "Don't know how good them sorceresses are, but this one's mighty powerful. Her name's Eleris. She can turn a man into a lizard. You sure don't wanna cross her."

"My word." Karl's frown deepened and he turned to Caryn. "Maybe we should look elsewhere."

"I was thinking the same thing," she somberly replied.

As Karl turned back to the old man, the blond curly haired serving girl brought their stew. She gave Karl a longing stare as she slowly placed the bowl in front of him.

Giving her a polite smile, Karl spoke to the old man. "You said something about his daughter returning. Where was she?"

"They all thought she was dead," he answered.

"Dead?" Caryn said. "What happened to her?"

"Don't know," he shrugged. "Lots of stories, most don't make no sense. One that seems most likely was that she was kidnapped long ago when she as a baby."

"So the king never saw his daughter in all that time?" Caryn asked.

"Nope. Then she shows up with a whole bunch o' unusual folk. One o' them was this giant of a man. Another was a beautiful sorceress. And then the one everyone's lookin' for, that fella wearin' the sword called Orc's Bane."

Karl tilted his head to frown at him. "Orc's Bane. From the name of the sword, it's meant to kill orcs. Did he kill a lot of orcs?"

The old man narrowed his gaze at Karl. "Ain't you never heard of the prophecy?"

"What prophecy?" Karl's frown deepened.

"The one that says the man who wields Orc's Bane will rule the land and there'll be a hundred years of peace."

"It's a thousand years," the balding man corrected.

"A hundred, a thousand, who cares?" the old man sniffed. "The point is that the man who wields the sword is the true king."

"And you believe that?" Karl said, cocking an eyebrow.

"Why not," the old man shrugged. "And even if I think it might be a tale, the witch believes it and if she does, there must be something to it."

"How do you know she does?" Caryn asked.

"'Cause ever since the daughter come back, there's been a change. I can feel it. We all can." The rest of the patrons nodded agreement. "We get the occasional strangers come through here, but they ain't like you two. You can tell the difference. Usual they just come in here, look around, pretend to be just passing through, but askin' a lot o' questions 'bout whether we seen anyone unusual."

"Who are they looking for?" Caryn said.

"Why they're lookin' fer the fella with the sword," the old man replied, the answer obvious.

"I thought he was in Glenloch," Karl said with a puzzled look.

"He was, but he escaped. As did all those with him, at least that's what we heard." The old man glanced at Karl and Caryn and then their stew. "Ya may wanna eat that before it gets cold.

Karl chuckled and took a spoonful of stew, noting the nice sized chunks of venison. "This is superb," he complimented then addressed the old man. "I see why you come here for your meals." He swallowed another portion then said, "If this man who wields Orc's Bane is supposed to be the king, what about the king already in place and his daughter? Wouldn't that make her next in line for the throne? I'm sure they can't be happy this man with the sword is around."

"Ach," the old man said. "Not meanin' to be rude, but m'name's Alick. That one there with the contrary tongue is Rabbie." He ticked his head at the balding man.

"Well met," Karl responded with a warm smile.

"But to answer yer question, sure the king's a might put out... well," he laughed, "maybe more than a might, but the truth of it is that the witch is the one with the power. The king does what she tells him."

"Aye, that's true," Rabbie emphasized. "Everyone knows that. The way I heard it was that since the girl come back, he won't let her out if his sight, or," he tapped his nose, "that's what they say. Course, no one's seen much of her. The way I figure it –"

"Ach, Rabbie," Alick interrupted, "You and you wild tales. Next you'll be havin' the witch flyin' over the kingdom lookin' for the sword man."

"She don't need to," Rabbie countered, "what with all the spies she's got."

"Still," Karl interrupted, "if the prophecy is true, does it mean that this man or any man who takes up the sword can become king. What's to stop someone from simply killing this man, taking the sword and declaring himself king?"

"That's just it," Rabbie said, shooting a 'you-re-not-as-smart-as-you-thin-you-are' look at Alick. "The sword will only yield to one person."

"What do you mean?" Caryn asked, intrigued.

"There's something about the sword that makes it so only one man can wield it. It won't do anyone's else's bidding. Only him."

"That way you'll know fer sure," Alick added.

"I thought you didn't believe in the prophecy," Karl gibed.

"Let's just say I've an open mind about it," Alick answered. "I wanna believe but it sounds too grand."

"Don't let 'im fool ya," Rabbie grinned. "He just pretends to doubt. Once the king shows up, he'll be first in line to shake his hand."

Karl laughed. "Might I buy you a pint? In fact," he leaned back and caught the taverner's attention, "a pint for all in here, including yourself and your staff, Master Taverner."

An immediate cheer erupted as Caryn gripped Karl's arm. "Sweetheart," she said, her eyes intimating it wasn't such a good idea.

"We'll be OK," he reassured her, patting her hand.

Noting the exchange, Alick said to Karl, "Now, now. Don't do something you might regret later."

"Wise advice," Caryn agreed.

"Darling," Karl replied with a longsuffering sigh. "We can afford this. It's not like we're destitute. These are genuinely good people, the kind we always said we wanted to live around."

Flattered at the praise, Alick said, "You're a good judge of character. You won't find any better than those of Torgue."

"So it seems," Karl readily agreed. He reached into his belt bag and retrieved five gold coins, placing them on the table. "Will this be enough?"

"That's too much," Alick said, his eyes blinking wide then giving Karl a curious stare. "You ain't who you seem to be."

"What do you mean?"

"No one ever comes in here and don't know how much a round of ale and mid-day meal cost. You ain't common folk."

"Never said we were," Karl replied, taking another spoonful of stew. "This is really good."

"Who are you then?" He leaned forward and focused a hard stare at him.

"You already know who we are."

Alick leaned back. "All we know is yer names."

"A name can tell you a lot," Karl parried. He slowly looked around the room, noting the position of each patron, those by the door and those close to the kitchen door. "For instance, I told you my name was Karl. That alone should tell you volumes about me."

"It tells us nothin'," Rabbie argued.

"Then you need to think about it a little more," he teased then turned to the taverner. "How much for a round of ale for these good folks and our lunch?"

"One gold and twelve coppers."

Karl placed three of the gold coins back in his belt pouch. He dipped his head at the two remaining coins. "The extra is in appreciation for the excellent food, ale, and conversation." Placing the spoon in his empty bowl, he drained the rest of his ale then stood. Caryn followed his lead.

"Thank you for a wonderful meal. My wife and I agree that you have a lovely town. We will be back through here very soon. We look forward to seeing each of you again."

The room descended to awkward silence as Karl and Caryn weaved their way around the tables and out the door. Once outside, Karl did a quick glance around and said, "We head out on the road to Glenloch then retrace our steps back to the road going to Banvie. I'm sure someone is watching us."

"No doubt. I'm not sure I want to run quite yet though," she said, patting her stomach.

"Call one of your friends and see if we can find out who might be lurking behind us."

Looking up, Caryn saw a sparrow and held out a hand to it. The bird swooped down and landed on her finger. After a brief exchange in a language that Karl did not understand, the sparrow flew away, soon joined by several other sparrows and then by a small flock that swirled and chatted and watched the road.

Inside the tavern, Alick's frown of concentration suddenly broke. "By the gods," he blurted. "His name is Karl. Did you see the size of him? He was big enough to be a Viking."

Rabbie was the first to understand. "Say it ain't so," he marveled.

"Haw."   Alick slapped his knee in delight then immediately understood the repercussions. Taking in the room he said, "You all know what just happened here is somethin' we gotta keep our yaps shut about. That means everyone." He shot a meaningful stare at the two serving girls and the taverner. "Unless we want the witch and all her evil creatures comin' here, nothin' happened and we don't know nuthin'."

Rabbie stood and jammed his hands on his hips. "Alick is right as rain in this, and you all know it. We all keeps our mouths shut and wait. Agreed? One person opens his or her mouth and we're all screwed."

Rabbie looked around the tavern and realized some had no clue as to who Karl was or why they had to keep their yaps shut. His first instinct was to explain then thought better of it. They'd figure it out eventually.

As Karl and Caryn strolled the road to Glenloch, she playfully bumped against him.

"You're wife, hmmm?"

"It made the most sense," he said, already beginning to wonder how this was going to play out with Annabeth and Raquel.

"Oh, I agree," she said with a mischievous smile. "It *does* make the most sense."

A sparrow flew close, and she lifted her hand for the tiny feet to grip her finger. After a few cheeps and chirps, it flew away.

"She says that there's no one following us," Caryn remarked. "We can head back to the other road."

As they veered north into the forest, Karl said, "It just occurred to me that Kevin will be expecting us back, he just doesn't know when. I think the longer we can avoid detection, he'll start to relax. At least those who are spying for him will begin to lose their edge."

"You never did tell me much about him."

Karl's face hardened. "The man has no redeeming qualities. He's a traitor and a coward."

"I know all that," she said. "But why does he anger you so much."

Karl stopped and turned to her. "Former First Lieutenant Kevin Bristow was a team leader in bravo company of the 4th Battalion of the 25th SF Group. Because he was a traitor to his country, I lost my best friend, Lieutenant Colonel Christopher Lovell."

They resumed walking in silence before Caryn asked, "What did he do?"

Karl paused before answering, "During the Tiwanaku War, 4th Battalion was operating south of La Paz. When they entered Calamarca, they were ambushed by the Cochabamba Cartel. They were ambushed because Kevin sold them out. He had passed the battalion's orders to the Cartel. Just before the battalion entered the city, he mysteriously disappeared, leaving his team, the men and women who trusted and depended upon him, to die. Not only was his team completely eliminated, the battalion was nearly annihilated. The Cartel had enough time to booby trap the entire place, to include the planned escape route. When they hit the 4th Battalion, it was the mother of all ambushes. Incendiary grenades, roadside bombs, you name it, it was there."

"How many survived?" she asked.

"Eleven," he coldly replied.

"He was court martialed?

"Life in prison without parole," Karl answered, "at least that was what was supposed to happen. He spent less than six months in jail before some fancy pants lawyer got him off on a technicality, something about chain of control for evidence. My guess is that the Cartel paid big bucks to a lawyer in appreciation for the failure of the mission."

"I'm surprised no one took him out after he was released," she wondered. "I certainly would have."

"He dropped out of circulation. My guess is that he went south for a while, under the protection of the Cartel. What I don't understand is how he got into this game."

"Probably should have asked Felix or Landon when you had the chance."

"Didn't think about it then. I was too busy tracking down someone's girlfriend."

"Amongst other things," she impishly grinned.

"Amongst other things," he agreed with a smile.

They came upon the road to Banvie, and Caryn once again called upon her feathered friends to keep watch while she and Karl accelerated their pace and were soon zipping along at twenty-six kilometers an hour. Conversation stopped as they focused on the road ahead

It was dusk when they approached the outskirts of Banvie.

"Do we press on or stop for the night?" Caryn asked.

"We still have our supplies from when we left Talbet," Karl observed. "I don't want to press our luck. While no one should know us, I have a feeling old Alick had more than a clue and I don't want the same to happen here… yet."

"So we press on?"

Karl pulled up his screen map. "We're not that far from the border. We should be in Ryath-sari in a couple of hours at the pace we're going."

"Works for me."

Thankfully the night was clear and dry. By the time they arrived at the no man's land between the two kingdoms, night had settled with a half-moon providing light.

"It looks different," Karl sighed, "especially in the dark and from the other side. You still got that Augury Stone?"

"Yes," she replied pulling out a smooth solid black onyx stone about the size of a softball from her belt pouch. "Don't know if we'll be able to read it though, out here in the dark."

"Eh, try it anyway. Ask it if we're close to Ryath-sari."

Caryn shook the stone and asked, "Are we close to Ryath-sari?" then turned it over. The answer glowed in green letters. "Yes."

For the next half hour, they used the stone to maneuver inside the elven forest until it answered the last question, "Is this the tree?" with a glowing green 'Yes.'

Karl felt around the tree for the branch knob and twisted it, activating the door. Stepping in and closing the door behind them, he felt it was the blind leading the blind as he groped for the handrail of the circular staircase.

When they arrived at the top and opened the door to the platform leading to the city, the moon was high, and they easily made out the outlines of the ancient elven houses rising above the wall.

"Hopefully the silverware is still in place," Karl mumbled as he led the way across the narrow boardwalk, feeling the not-so-subtle swaying of the bridge. Once across, they came to a wall of intertwined branches, in the center a stout thick wooden door that was slightly ajar.

Once inside through the long gateway and inside the city walls, green lights adorning walls and walkways cast a dim luminescence and giving soft shape to the dark buildings. They entered onto a street, solidly made of packed earth on top of boards. In the middle of each intersection, the telltale 'breadcrumbs' of silverware pointed the direction for them to get to the citadel.

An hour later they arrived at the citadel and unpacked their vittles in the kitchen then headed for the buttery.

"I could use a nice glass of wine," Caryn sighed contentedly.

Karl twisted the spigot of a large wine cask and poured wine into two glasses.

Accepting the glass, Caryn inhaled the bouquet then tasted the wine. "This is good. This one tastes more like a Merlot than a Cabernet."

"So you're a wine connoisseur too?" he asked, impressed.

"Not like Noble. I like my wines, but I'm not a snob."

"Noble's a snob?"

"That's not what I meant," she replied. "How about we pour another glass and munch on something before we settle in for the night."

"I could use a bath, too," he said. "Care to join me?"

"Of course," she answered with a wink. "I'll even let you scrub my back."

Chapter 2

Karl was the first to awaken and he headed down to the kitchen and began searching through the cupboards.

"What're you looking for?" Caryn asked.

Karl turned to see her standing in the doorway. She was barefoot, wearing a long gossamer silk shirt that ended mid-thigh, accentuating her shapely legs. The shirt did little to hide her perfect body, especially the large firm breasts. Her long blond hair cascaded down her back and sides. The effect was innocent and sensual.

Karl sucked in his breath and stared at her, marveling how wonderful she was, even though her body was a lot like Annabeth's and Raquel's.

"You're staring at me again," she said, raising an eyebrow.

"Nice shirt."

"Like it? I found it in one of the closets in my room." She held her arms out and slowly turned around, the fabric gently folding to the contours of her body. "With the amount of clothes they left behind, you'd think they left here naked."

Karl stood rooted, unable to break his gaze from her. "You're gorgeous."

"That was sweet," she replied, finally sauntering in. "What *are* you looking for?"

"I was hoping to find some coffee."

"Ah, yes, the very elixir of life. Let me help you."

Though Karl pretended to search, most of his attention ended up on Caryn and snatching glances on what lay beneath the silken shirt.

"Eureka," she exclaimed, pulling out a jar with coffee beans in it.

While Karl stoked up the wood stove, Caryn crushed the beans and soon the aroma of freshly brewed coffee filled the kitchen.

"What's on the agenda for today?" Caryn asked.

"I think we ought to explore more of the city," he said. "There may be more stuff we can use."

"I like that," she smiled. "It's almost like shopping."

"I suppose," he replied with a curious frown.

The afternoon's search proved uneventful, and they returned to the citadel for the evening. Karl found a small cask of wine and carried it into the living chamber with the two fireplaces. Arranging the furniture with a view to look over the city, he propped the cask on a low table and poured two glasses.

Caryn returned a few minutes later, wearing a sheer dress that gathered at the waist and ended just above the knees. The scooped neck dipped low, revealing plenty of cleavage, the bodice tight against her bosom.

"Nice view," Caryn complimented, walking over to stand beside him then lifting her glass in toast. "I could live here."

"Nice dress," Karl said, leering at the body beneath it.

"I think you're supposed to wear something underneath it, but what fun would that be?" She winked.

Karl continued taking in the sensual woman, occasionally reminding himself that she *was* a deadly killer. Yet that thought quickly faded in the reverie of their time together in real life and now here.

"Ya know," he said, forcing his gaze to shift up to her eyes. "I'm still trying to understand how you and Frank got together. The first time I met you two, I could tell he was a jerk from the get-go."

"Yeah, well," she shrugged, "I thought it was a good idea at the time. You know how it is in the beginning of relationships; all you see is the good side, the wonderful parts. And then when he agreed to come into the game with me, I thought it was the beginning of something serious. Besides, he was great in bed... though not as good as you," she reassured Karl, gently placing a tender hand on his arm. "But as time went on, I began to have my doubts as to why he came into the game with me. Initially, I thought it was solely because he wanted to be with me. But as time went on and little hints dropped here and there, and then the whole controlling thing." She rolled her eyes.

"I just couldn't picture you two together," Karl replied.

"Eventually, neither could I, which made my choice all the easier when you showed up."

Karl chuckled. "Me and the little woman."

"Julie was fun, in a nagging sort of way," she teased.

A groan emerged behind them, and they leaped up and twirled around to witness a body coalescing and solidifying. Before it was finished, Karl blurted, "Raquel."

Raquel was on her hands and knees, gasping for breath. A hand went to her throat followed by a deep breath of relief. She twisted her head to see Karl and Caryn staring at her.

"You're back," Raquel said, sitting back on her haunches, blithely unconcerned that she was naked.

Karl and Caryn were instantly beside to her, helping her stand on shaky legs.

"What happened?" Karl asked, gripping her elbow to steady her.

Inhaling a deep breath, she said, "Kevin showed up." She shivered then frowned at them. "Where have you been? When did you get back?"

"We got back yesterday," Caryn answered, with a fleeting glance of disappointment that her time having Karl all to herself was over.

Raquel noticed then did a slow appraisal of Caryn's attire. "Sorry I didn't have time to put on my best dress."

"Lemme go find something for you to put on," Caryn quickly parried.

"That's OK," Raquel said. "I can manage. I'm sure there are some clothes in my bedroom."

"Don't' change on my account," Karl deadpanned.

With a half-smile, Raquel shook her head and headed towards the door.

"Nice butt," Caryn whispered to Karl.

"I heard that," Raquel said over her shoulders as she disappeared through the door.

Karl's first urge was to follow her to find out what happened, but he twisted his head to glance at Caryn who was still staring at the door.

"Wonder what happened," she muttered. "On the plus side, that makes three of us now."

When Raquel returned, she wore a tight and supple leather corset that covered just enough of her large breasts so that her nipples didn't show. Her narrow midriff was bare, revealing a toned stomach. The supple tanned leather leggings disappeared into calf-high leather boots that gripped her muscular legs. She had combed her thick auburn, shoulder length hair and washed her face so that she looked somewhat refreshed.

"This better?" she demurely asked, spreading her arms.

"I liked the way you looked before," Karl teased, "though this is a nice look."

"I'd say 'me too'," Caryn grinned mischievously, "but we probably should leave well enough alone." Though aware her own choice of clothing did little to hide her intentions, or her body, she decided that it was time to assert her place and intimacy with Karl.

"What *did* happen?" Karl asked, returning to the most important matter.

Noticing the cask of wine and two glasses, Raquel said, "I'll take a glass of that if you don't mind."

"Here,' Caryn said, handing her a glass. "Take mine. I haven't had it yet. I'll get another glass. Don't tell anything until I get back."

As Caryn bustled through the door and headed towards the kitchen, Raquel sipped the wine, sighed then shifted a look at Karl. "Looks like you two have been enjoying yourselves?"

"Yes, we have," Karl answered, knowing the intention behind the question.

Raquel nodded slowly, taking another sip of wine and gazing out the window. "She's very pretty. Always thought so."

"Yes, she is."

Raquel's hand again went to her throat, and she tenderly rubbed her smooth skin.

"Why are you massaging your throat?" Karl asked.

Raquel's lips tightened as Caryn walked in with another glass. "It's because he slit my throat."

Caryn jerked to a halt, her jaw clenched. "That bastard."

"Tell us from the beginning," Karl said, his thirst for vengeance exploding within.

While Caryn twisted the spigot and filled her glass, Raquel downed the rest of her wine. In one smooth motion, Caryn handed her the filled glass, taking the empty and filling it.

"After you left, things were a bit unsettled as we had to explain why you weren't around," Raquel said. "The longer you were gone, the harder it was. People had no problems being good when you were here because everyone bought into the prophecy thing. But when you disappeared, that's when the problems started."

Caryn's brows creased. "We weren't gone that long."

"Close to two months," Raquel pointed out.

"Two months?" Caryn's frown deepened.

"Remember the time dilation thing Felix talked about?" Karl said.

"Who's Felix?" Raquel asked.

"The man whose girlfriend we had to rescue," Caryn answered.

"Two months is a long time," Karl said. "What else happened?"

"Well, like I said, at first it wasn't too bad, but then that Gerard fella became quite the pain in the ass. At first, he kept repeating that he was going to disappear at any moment, but the longer those moments became, the less sure I was that he was going anywhere. When he realized that something wasn't quite right, he started on this 'the only reason you're in this game is because of me' crap. When that didn't get a rise from us, he started the 'I know the real reason why you're here, and then he blurted the fact that none of us were ever really sick.' She narrowed her gaze at Karl.

Karl returned the stare then said, "It's true. Caryn and I learned the truth when we went back."

Raquel's frown deepened into anger. She tilted her head back and drained the glass. She was about to refill it when Caryn simply exchanged glasses with the one she had yet to taste.

"Those bastards," Raquel spat. "They took my life from me. They stole my children from me." Tears brimmed her eyes. She walked over to the window and stared at the brightness of the day. A lone hawk crested the winds in lazy drifting.

She chugged half the glass of wine. "If there was nothing wrong with you, why did you come back?"

Caryn walked up to stand next to her, their shoulders nearly touching. "It's not the same anymore. The world as we knew it no longer exists. The world is run by AI now. The rest of the world's a ghost town, like some post-apocalyptic novel. Though a few hold outs remain, the rest of the world is immersed in a game of some kind. There are thousands upon thousands of games appealing to any interest or perversion you can think of. In the long run, they might have done you a favor."

"A favor," she snapped. "Taking my kids away from me?"

"Would you want your kids here with you now?"

Raquel pondered the thought and let out a slow sigh.

"Think about it," Caryn continued. "Would you have chosen this game from the start?"

"No,' Raquel admitted.

"Have you had fun, though?"

Raquel silently pondered the question then admitted, "I've had a great time. This is something I never would have imagined."

"What about your kids? Is this the game they would have chosen?" Caryn turned to face her.

"Probably not," Raquel replied. "My son was into cars, all sorts and kinds: racing, drifting, vintage, you name it. The kid could disassemble a 'Vette engine when he was four years old."

"Your daughter?" Caryn asked.

"Dragons and horses," Raquel chuckled.

"Would you have wanted to be in either one of those worlds, especially when your kids reached the age where they wanted to be on their own? Not that they don't love you, but it's now their time to move on in life."

Raquel twisted to face her, peering intently into her eyes. "So you're saying my kids are probably happier on their own?"

"It's not that they stopped loving you," Caryn softly answered. "It's just that they have their own lives to live. It would be the same even if we were back in the real world."

Raquel gazed at her a moment. "How'd you get so smart?"

"My folks died when I was six," Caryn answered. "I went to live with my aunt and uncle who had no kids. They were wonderful folks, but I always felt I was in the way. They had chosen not to have children and now they were stuck with me. I was more than a handful at the time, but they were patient and loving. I came to think of them as my real parents. But when I was eighteen, I decided I knew it all, needed my space, and moved out. I think they were actually relieved. Not that they didn't love me, but now they could do what they wanted without having to look after me."

Raquel silently absorbed Caryn's insight, wanting to know more about her for this was the most she had ever revealed about herself. Come to think of it, though she was closest to Annabeth, she really didn't know her, let alone any of the others.

Giving Caryn an affectionate smile, Raquel said, "I think Annabeth may be right. Life for us is here and now and we need to make the most of it."

"Back to Kevin," Karl interrupted. "You were saying about Gerard?"

"Yeah, the man is a total jerk. After telling us that none of us were sick, he then went on about how we all were supposed to be training to be an assassination team."

"Then what happened?" Karl asked, side stepping the topic of assassination teams.

"The man was all mouth," Raquel complained. "Then I see he's a Level 1, a Level 1 mind you. He's a Level 1 nothing as in merely a human with no special skills or talents, other than a talent for being all mouth."

A loud groan followed by a heavy thud that reverberated throughout the entire house. In unison, the three ran upstairs to witness Dieter coalescing in the bedroom he shared with Elena. He lay on his side, back facing them, panting, catching his breath. They waited until he solidified then rolled onto his back.

Raquel's gaze drifted to between his legs, and she uttered a soft, "Oh my," grinning wickedly at Caryn who was likewise fixated on that part of Dieter's anatomy.

"You two are so bad," Karl muttered, shaking his head. "C'mon and help me get him up."

Dieter heard them talking and turned his head. Seeing Karl, he weakly smiled. "Boss. You're back." His countenance morphed to a cold scowl as he waved them away and stood up. Inhaling a slow deep breath, he straightened to full height.

Raquel's and Caryn's gaze never went above his waist.

"Get dressed and meet us downstairs," Karl said, heading back out the door, only to stop and cock an eyebrow at Raquel and Caryn. "C'mon you two. Show's over."

"I probably should change," Caryn commented.

"Why?" Raquel said, casting an approving gaze at her. "You look very sensual."

"Yeah, well, it might be alright with just you two, but it's starting to get crowded around here." She peeled off and slipped into her room.

Raquel stopped in the hallway, deciding to wait for her. Turning to Karl, she smiled thoughtfully. "You both realize that she has to share now."

"You'll notice I'm not complaining," he said with an innocent smile.

Pretending to ponder, she crossed an arm over her stomach and perched the other elbow on it as she gently tapped her lips. "Of course that would mean I'd have you every other night. Not sure I want to wait that long. Maybe we ought to do both of us each night and work up to three when we reconnect with Annabeth. That way we can enjoy you every night."

Karl's smile disappeared when he realized she might be serious.

Caryn reappeared, dressed much like Raquel, complete with the tight corset that covered barely enough. "There," she grinned at Raquel. "Now we can be twins."

"Twins... hmmm." With a bawdy grin, Raquel flicked her eyebrows at Karl.

Karl shook his head and rolled his eyes. "C'mon. You can finish telling us the rest of your story."

"Did I miss something?" Caryn asked as they headed down to the living chamber.

"I was telling our handsome Viking," Raquel commented, "that instead of us having him every other night, we'd just double team him. And then when Annabeth finally returns, we'd do three at once."

"Uh..." Caryn muttered, frowning until she realized Raquel was teasing.

"You were telling us about Kevin," Karl huffed, ignoring the joke.

Raquel turned somber. "We should have eliminated Fraster and Kerr... permanently, along with the two sorceresses... well, make that two sorceresses and a sorcerer. But I get ahead of myself. The best I can figure out is that Kevin quietly showed up in Avnoch and managed to ingratiate himself to the two sorceresses, most likely with the help of his sorcerer. You remember Greg?"

"Greg," Karl blurted. "Greg's with him? The one he killed because he joined us?"

"The same," Raquel sighed. "Apparently they buried the proverbial hatchet and are buds again. He's got three others with him. One you'll remember. His name is Chet."

"Chet?" Karl grimaced. "And to think I saved his ass back in Tarrytown."

"Then there's the barbarian called Charles. The man's rather slow-witted. Kevin calls him 'Chuckie-poo.' Still, he's supposedly an excellent fighter."

"And the last one?"

"An elf named Frank."

"Frank?" Caryn sputtered. "An elf ranger, arrogant and full of himself?"

"Yeah," Raquel answered. "You know him?"

"Only too well," she groaned. "Remember me telling you about the jerk of a former boyfriend?"

"You poor thing," Raquel commiserated.

"Tell me about it," she said, rolling her eyes. "Our parting was not the best. If I remember right, his last words as he stalked out the door were, 'If we ever meet again, watch your back you little whore.'"

"Charming fellow," Raquel deadpanned.

"Then what happened?" Karl inquired.

"Before anyone even knows Kevin is here, Greg managed to sway the two sorceresses, Caillac and Finella, though I don't think it took much effort. Never did trust those two. Anyway, the two bitches convinced Annabeth to play a little game and she's now confined in the dungeons below the castle in Avnoch. Those two put spells on the door and she can't get out."

They stood by the window in the living chamber as Dieter stormed in.

"I'm going to rip his heart out," the berserker raged.

"Slow down, big fella," Raquel soothed. "I'm almost finished with my tale of woe." As Dieter paced, she resumed her explanation. "Once Annabeth was out of the way, Kevin convinced Fraster and Kerr to join him. The fools actually believed he was going to restore the status quo. One by one, Kevin had us arrested. It happened all in one day. Noble was the easiest as he's not a fighter. I only realized what was happening when I couldn't find anyone, and no one would tell me where they were."

"We got tossed into individual cells," Dieter chimed in.

"How was it that you didn't know Kevin was behind all this?" Karl said, asking the obvious question.

"Because he didn't show up until the very end," Raquel answered. "Chet showed up and we welcomed him with open arms. And when Greg arrived, we were pleased to see him. Then Frank and then Charles... by then, Kevin had already worked out the details of his coup. We were taken like lambs led to the slaughter."

Karl stared up at the big man. "How did they manage to subdue you?"

"Drugged ale," he snarled. "One minute I'm having dinner with Elena, the next I wake up flat on my back, spread-eagled on a table, my wrists and ankles chained." He paused, his nostrils flaring as his lips tightened. "They bring Elena in and begin abusing her, laughing as I struggle to break my chains. Finally, Kevin leans over and says, 'Say goodbye to your lover. You'll never see her again." He turned his head to stare out the window. "Then he slit my throat." His hand went to his throat. "All I remember is Elena sobbing and crying before it all went blank."

He clenched his hands and growled, "I'm gonna rip him apart."

"What about Sakura?" Caryn asked.

"She disappeared as soon as Chet showed up," Raquel answered.

A heavy silence filled the room before Karl said, "Though I don't like what happened to you, I am glad you're here. It'll make regaining the kingdom easier."

Dieter turned around. "You have a plan, Boss?"

"I've been giving it some thought," Karl answered. "I think the key to it is gaining control of Rhyeem first."

"Rhyeem?" Raquel repeated. "If I remember correctly, the last time we were there we had to escape a prison and beat feet out of there all the way to Odryssa."

"The key to it is Eleris," Karl replied. "If we can find a way to defeat her, we can gain control of the kingdom."

"Easier said than done," Raquel said with obvious doubt.

"Wish Annabeth was here with all her magical talents." Dieter opined. "She'd be a big help."

"Unfortunately she's not, so we'll have to come up with another way," Caryn said.

It was then that Raquel noticed. "My God, you both are level 25. How'd you manage that?"

"A reward for being sucked out of the game," Karl shrugged.

"So why were you taken out of the game if you weren't cured?" Dieter asked.

"We had to rescue a damsel in distress," Caryn replied then related the story of the kidnapping and rescue.

When she finished, Raquel gave her a meaningful stare. "You going to tell him?"

"Tell me what?"

Caryn mused for only a moment. "There's one more thing you should know. None of us was sick or dying. It was all a ruse to get us into the game."

Expecting Dieter to blow up, they were surprised when he quietly absorbed the news.

"I'm actually glad they put me in this game, regardless of their method." He gazed at each of them. "I've had more fun than all the years of my real life put together. And I found Elena. I've never been this happy... well this present moment doesn't count. But it's like I have a purpose, a reason to live. At the moment, it's to rescue Elena, restore the kingdom and kill Kevin... maybe not in that order. But, the bottom line is that I've been given an opportunity like no other. I'm going to live forever, and when I rescue Elena, it'll be with the one I love. So, they actually did me a favor."

Karl eyes brightened and he turned to Caryn. "You have the Augury Stone, right?"

"Yes." She frowned at him, wondering what brought that to mind.

"Then let's find out which way to go," he triumphantly exclaimed.

Caryn withdrew the stone from her belt pouch and unwrapped the cloth protecting it.

"First question," Karl said. "Should we conquer Rhyeem before we return to Odryssa?"

Caryn repeated the question, shook the stone, and flipped it over. "Yes." She grinned in understanding.

Without waiting for Karl to ask the next question, she said, "Will we be able to defeat Eleris?" She shook the stone and again flipped it over. "Yes." Her excitement bubbled over.

"Will I rescue Elena?" Dieter asked.

Caryn paused and narrowed a stare at him. "Are you sure you want to know the answer?"

Dieter hesitated, immediately understanding the anguish he would experience if the answer was not what he wanted to hear.

"No," he softly answered. "I take it back."

"A wise decision," she said.

"Pity all it gives us is 'yes' or 'no' answers," Karl said, folding his arms. "It'd be nice to have a solution provided for us."

"What about that Goddess of yours?" Raquel asked.

Karl tilted his head back and shook it, rolling his eyes at the same time. "Useless. I've tried twice to get her to help and all I got was the 'you'll figure it out.' What's the sense of having a goddess who's supposed to be there when you need her and all she does is complain that you're wasting her time? And don't even think of asking her to help someone else, like Annabeth for instance. I tired that once and got the 'I'm your goddess not hers' response."

"Why don't you ask it if there's coffee made," a voice from behind them asked.

Startled, they turned to see Noble standing in the doorway, dressed, casting a lascivious stare at the two Rangers.

"How did you get here?" Raquel greeted him with a broad smile.

"Probably the same way you did," he casually replied, walking up to them. He looked at Raquel then to Dieter. "I told him my respawn spot was in my bedroom at the castle. I guess you guys said the same thing." They both nodded. "He was angry when it turned out that it wasn't true, especially after Dieter disappeared. Talk about pissed off. He demanded I tell him where your respawn spots were and I said, 'How the hell do I know? I just assumed they changed theirs like the rest of us did.' In a fit of pique, he slit my throat." He laughed though his hand went to his throat. "I can only imagine his shock when I don't show up."

Noble twisted around to gaze out the window. "Anyway, I respawn here, and I get dressed and when I come downstairs, I hear voices and it was you guys." He turned to Raquel and Caryn. "You two look very fetching." He flicked his eyebrows then focused on Caryn. "When did you guys arrive?"

"Yesterday," Caryn answered, ignoring his overt leer. "We can tell you all about it later. Right now, we're figuring out our plan to take back what rightfully belongs to us."

"By asking that thing?" he chuckled, pointing to the stone.

"Yes," Karl replied.

Noble nodded and smiled. "Any coffee made?"

"In the kitchen," Caryn answered.

With a flip of a hand as a wave, he spun around and strode off to the kitchen.

"I see he's somewhat stressed," Raquel deadpanned.

Karl watched him walk away, wondering how the thief could be so nonchalant after experiencing the excruciating pain of respawning.

"Let's get back to business," Dieter suggested. "Ask it if we should go to Glenloch first."

"Why?" Caryn asked with a frown.

"I don't know," he said and shrugged. "I just thought that if we're going to defeat Eleris, we need to go to Glenloch."

"Should we go to Glenloch first?" Caryn asked. Flipping the stone over, she said, "No."

"Should we stay here?" Karl asked.

"Yes," Caryn said, peering at the stone.

"That doesn't make sense," Dieter fussed. "How are we supposed to do anything if we stay here?"

Karl sensed the big man's frustration. "Don't worry, Dieter. We'll find her."

"That thing's like playing 20 questions," Noble chuckled, walking in, one hand over the top of the coffee mug. "It'll take you forever to figure out what to do."

"You got a better idea?" Raquel asked.

"Yeah," he replied. "Skip Mann altogether and head to Avnoch. That's where the problem is."

"Then what?" Karl inquired, studying the thief.

"Then we rescue Annabeth and Elena and get rid of Kevin and company."

"How?" Raquel cocked her head to the side to stare at him.

"I don't know. That's your department." He sauntered over to a plush chair by the window and stretched out his legs.

"You're no help," Raquel said, dismissing the thief's input. "Besides, the stone already said to conquer Rhyeem before we go to Odryssa."

"That's if you believe in that silly stone," Noble dismissively replied.

"If you've nothing worthwhile to contribute," Caryn tersely said, "then you can keep quiet."

"Oooh, touchy are we?" Noble shot back.

Karl straightened to full height and strode over to stand in front of him. "What's your problem?"

"Me?" Noble replied with innocent eyes. "I don't have a problem."

Karl studied him for a moment then folded his arms. "What did he offer you?"

"What?" Noble stiffened.

"Kevin," Karl said with a cold calmness. "What did he offer you to betray us?"

The other three surrounded the thief, the initial friendliness evaporated, replaced by stone hard stares.

"I don't know what you're talking about," Noble tartly answered, squirming under their glare.

"What did you tell him about here?" Karl demanded, suddenly aware that their safe place might not be so safe anymore."

"I didn't tell him anything. I swear." Noble leaped up and turned to face them. "What's got into you all? It's me, Noble, the same old loveable thief."

Karl shifted his attention to Raquel and Dieter. "You all were in difference cells, weren't you."

"Yes," they replied in unison.

Karl turned back to Noble. "You were surprised to see Caryn and me... but you weren't surprised to see Raquel and Dieter. You expected they would be here. Why is that?"

"I don't know," he evasively replied and shrugged. "I just figured someone might be here."

"You're lying," Karl acidly said. Without taking his eyes of the thief, he said, "Dieter, how about beating this one to an inch of his life. After that, we'll throw him to the orcs."

"With pleasure, Boss." Dieter grabbed the thief by the shirt and lifted him off the ground.

"I'm telling the truth, I swear," Noble pleaded as he flew through the air to crash against the far wall.

Dieter was on him before he could rise to his knees.

"Why are you doing this?" Noble begged as he was lifted high then hurled down upon a low sofa table. He groaned in agony as Dieter grabbed him by the ankles. "Stop. Stop," he cried out. "OK. OK. I admit it. You're right."

Karl held out a hand for Dieter to stop. "I'm right about what?"

"I'm... I'm working for Kevin," he gasped, pain wracking his body.

"Why?" Raquel demanded.

Noble paused, his breath labored, and shot a quick glance at Karl. "I... I didn't think he was ever coming back." He lay flat on his back, his eyes closed, thankful the agony was beginning to subside and reminding himself that respawning hurt worse. "Kevin was in control and if I wanted to have a decent chance at survival, I had to agree." He inhaled a deep breath. "Look at me. I'm not like you," he said reminding them of his character choice, though the tone sounding like he blamed them. "You're all big and strong and can take care of yourselves. Me? I'm just a little thief who's always in the way. When you're not around, who's gonna take care of me."

"What a sad story," Caryn said, her tone dripping with melodrama. "I'm all choked up. Where're the violins to add pathos to your terrible tale?"

Karl withdrew Orc's Bane and pressed it against Noble's throat. "The next question is, what did you tell him about here? Choose your words wisely. Remember the pain of respawning. If I think you're lying to me, you get to play the respawn game... over and over and over."

Feeling the point of the blade at his throat, Noble gazed up at Karl with nervous eyes, the pain of respawning still fresh. "I told him the truth, that it was an elf city, that I didn't know how to get here."

"What else?" Karl demanded.

"Nothing else, I swear."

"Did you tell him about Ben?" Raquel asked.

"Oh, uh yeah, I did tell him about Ben, but I told him Ben wasn't playing with a full deck."

"What did he say?" Karl replied.

"He asked where Ben lived, and I told him that I hadn't a clue. I merely went where you all led."

"And?"

"And what?" Noble silently prayed they would grow tired of this game and Orc's Bane would slip back into its scabbard.

"What about the weapons' room and the chests of gold?" Caryn challenged.

"Hell no," Noble sniffed. "I may be stupid sometimes, but I ain't dumb. It's hard enough sharing all that gold with you all. Last thing I want to do is add more claims to the pile."

"That's about the most honest thing you've said so far," Raquel dryly commented.

An epiphany burst with in Caryn. "So he killed you to send you back here."

Noble swallowed hard.

"Why did he do that?" Karl demanded, the blade still at Noble's throat.

Noble's hand went to his belt pouch and withdrew an Augury Stone.

Caryn snatched it out of his hands and ran out of the room, returning a few moments later with is wrapped in a kitchen towel.

"Why did you do that?" Dieter asked.

Caryn cast a penetrating glare at Noble. "He knows why, don't you." It wasn't a question.

When he didn't answer, Caryn explained, "The Augury Stone is more than a stone to tell you your future. It is also a means of communication... to other augury stones. My guess is that his stone is connected to another stone, which means Kevin or one of his minions has a stone." She gave him a not so gentle prod with her foot. "Who's at the other end?"

Noble's entire body settled in defeat. "Kevin. Kevin has the other stone. Greg found this one, but Kevin demanded that he give it to him."

Dieter looked over at Caryn. "Does this mean that the stone you have is connected to Kevin's stone?"

"I don't know," she replied.

"Can you tell if it's connected to another stone?" Raquel wanted to know.

"Again," she shrugged, "I don't know. And I'm not sure we want to try at the present moment."

"Good point," Raquel readily agreed.

"Still," Karl pensively said, "how was Noble going to help Kevin get here, if all he could do was talk to him?"

"Here," Caryn said, "Lemme read what I have on it." She pulled up her screen and scrolled to Augury Stone. She then read aloud:

"The Augury Stone is usually an onyx stone, though black agate and malachite are also used. It is both a divination and communication device. Divination is restricted to questions requiring 'Yes' or 'No' answers. Questions may concern present and future conditions. Questions on past conditions may be answered only insofar as they relate to present circumstances. In other words, one may ask the stone if 'X' crossed the bridge yesterday.

The method for receiving an answer is to: 1) ask the question, 2) shake the stone for at least several seconds (asking a question without shaking the stone may result in an incorrect answer), and 3) turn the stone over so that the answer is revealed at the bottom flat part of the stone.

While the stone only provides 'Yes' or 'No' answers, there may be occurrences where no answer is provided. Often this is because more than one question is asked at a time, or the question posed is not correctly phrased.

The Augury Stone is also a communication device, much akin to the Palantir Stones in Lord of the Rings. Though one may discover an Augury Stone, it does not necessarily mean the stone is connected to any other stone or stones. Communication requires initial connectivity. To accomplish this, two or more stones desired for connection must be placed no less that a meter apart. Stones may be closer but may not touch. Each stone will be asked the following question: Will you allow me to connect to this stone (or these stones). See the above paragraph for the proper methodology of inquiry. If the stone agrees, you will see an electrical discharge occur between/among the stones. Wait for the conclusion of the discharge. The stones are now connected.

However, a stone may choose not to connect, in which case, the divination properties will still work.

For those stones successfully connected, the operator of the stone simply commands: "Connect," and the stones are now operational. From that moment forward, the stones are always connected, regardless of who owns/controls the stone/s, and regardless of the distance of separation. However, communication is restricted to a single island. Thus, while the stone may go with you to the next island, unless the connected stones also go to the next/same island, the communications link is temporarily disabled until such time as the connected stone/s arrive on the island. Divination properties remain consistent regardless of communication status.

To communicate via the stone, both (or more) parties must be present. One cannot leave messages or 'emails', or any other notification. It is recommended that the Augury Stone be wrapped in an opaque cloth when not in use as the stone is always 'on' meaning that if one stone is unwrapped, *anyone at another connected stone will see and hear what passes in front of the unwrapped stone. Wrapping the stone in an opaque cloth effectively shuts it 'off.'"*

Caryn closed the screen as she finished.

"It says nothing about tracking," Raquel observed. "It's either divination or communication."

"So how was he going to use it?" Dieter wondered.

They all looked at Noble who shook his head and shrugged. "All he told me was to take this stone and report on what was happening here. He knew that Raquel and Dieter would be here."

"He probably knows that Caryn and I are here," Karl said. "If he has a stone, all he has to do is ask it if we are here."

"Fortunately," Caryn said, "he doesn't know where 'here' is, at least not yet."

Karl sheathed his sword and stared down at Noble. "He's expecting a call from you, isn't he?"

"Yes."

"When?"

"As soon as I saw who was here."

"Damn," Karl mumbled. "He wants to make sure we're all here. Noble can't lie because the stone will reveal the truth and Kevin will know he's lying, which means that Noble has betrayed him. If he tells Kevin we're all here, Kevin will thus know for sure that Caryn and I are back, but it will keep Noble in his confidence. If Noble doesn't use the stone, Kevin will know something is wrong and again suspect Noble."

"What do you wanna do, Boss?" Dieter asked.

Karl flashed a stern stare at Noble. "Well? Whose side are you on?"

"If I say 'yours' would you believe me?" Noble grunted and pushed himself to sitting.

"Probably not," Karl answered. "But you have a choice to make. And trust me, after this, there are no second chances."

"I know you don't believe me," Noble stated, "but I truly thought you were gone for good. Kevin managed to eliminate our team and take control. All I was doing was looking out for my future."

"You said all that before," Caryn sneered. "My violin's still playing."

"Save the excuses," Karl admonished. "What's your answer?"

"You're back," Noble said with a crooked grin. "I prefer to be on the winning side."

"That doesn't answer the question," Raquel tersely stated.

"I'm with you, OK?" Noble huffed. "Is that plain enough?"

"I still don't trust him," Caryn said.

"Neither do I," Raquel added.

"Nor me," Dieter growled, giving the thief a cold glare.

"None of us do," Karl reiterated, peering intently at Noble, "which means you're going to have to prove we can trust you again."

"How do I do that?"

"We'll come up with something," Karl answered. "For the moment, I think you need to let Kevin know you're here. Tell him that Caryn and I are here."

"You want to tell him that?" Raquel objected.

"He's merely telling him what he already knows," Caryn pointed out then turned to Noble. "When are you supposed to talk with him?"

"Tonight, after everyone is asleep."

"What did he offer you," Dieter asked, staring coldly at the thief, "that made you willing to endure the pain of respawning?"

Noble hesitated. "He said I could have anything I wanted in Avnoch and that he would protect me in exchange for keeping him informed with what was going on here and in Mann."

Dieter's glare intensified.

"You just don't get it, do you," Noble snapped. "He doesn't view me as a threat like he believes you all are. I still can't figure out why he killed you two. It makes more sense to keep you chained up and out of the way. He has to know you're gonna come back for Elena. At least this way I'm far away from him. He doesn't know where I am and after a while I'll conveniently forget to use the stone and hopefully he'd forget all about me."

"And you'd be safe on your own," Dieter said.

"Exactly."

"He does raise a good point," Raquel said. "Why did he kill you and me? Noble's right. It would've been smarter to keep us locked up." She shifted a glance at Karl. "Well?"

Karl thought for a few moments. "If he knows that Caryn and I are back, he also has to know that I'm going to go back and reclaim my throne. He's sent you two to make sure that happens, knowing that I would be more confident, or over-confident in his estimation, if I had you two with me."

"Why not Annabeth then?" she asked.

"She's a sorceress," Karl pointed out. "She has more magical powers that are harder to defeat." He abruptly grew quiet.

"What?" Caryn said, observing his look.

"I wonder if we can get her back here," he mused with a half-smile then turned to Noble. "But first things first. We will be in the shadows when you talk to Kevin tonight. I expect a performance from you worthy of an academy award. You will tell him that Caryn and I are here. If he asks what our plans are, you can tell him the truth that you don't know yet. You can ad lib from there. Under no circumstances are you to tell him that Caryn has a stone. Do you understand?"

"I've already said I was part of your team again," Noble grumbled.

"And we all said we still don't trust you," Caryn responded. "You still have to earn our trust again."

"Fine," he said through tight lips.

Karl turned to Caryn. "We need to find out if that stone of yours is connected to anyone else, especially Kevin."

"I have an idea," she answered. "I'll set it up then show you."

It was almost midnight when Noble, in the dim light of a single candle in his bedroom, positioned the Augury Stone on a small table and unfolded the cloth covering it.

Kevin's visage burst on the stone. "Where the hell have you been?"

"Shhh," Noble admonished in a whisper. "Not so loud. You want to blow my cover?"

Kevin lowered his voice, but his cold demeanor remained. "Well? Report."

"Raquel and Dieter are here, like you intended. But the big news is that Karl and Caryn are here. They arrived yesterday."

Surprise flashed across Kevin's face, quickly replaced by the cold hardness. "Damned stone wouldn't answer my questions. No matter. What else?"

"Nothing else," Noble replied.

"What're their plans?"

"Don't know yet. Karl's still debating what he wants to do, but he seems to be leaning towards sneaking back to Avnoch and surprising you."

A wicked smile spread across Kevin's lips. "Perfect. I expect you to let me know as soon as he decides."

"Of course." Noble suddenly jabbed a finger to his lips and jerked is head towards the door.

The seconds tipped by in silence. Noble quietly stood and tiptoed to the door, hunched over, and pressed his ear close to the door, listening for what or who might be on the other side. Kevin's visage on the stone shifted across the smooth surface, following the thief as he made his way to the door.

After a few more tense moments, Noble relaxed and returned to his place before the stone.

"Whoever it was is gone," he whispered.

"Report to me again tomorrow," Kevin commanded.

"I will," Noble acknowledged.

Kevin's face disappeared and silence ruled Noble's room as he wrapped the stone in the cloth.

Karl emerged from the corner shadows and held out his hand and Noble gave him the stone. "That was well done. I liked the listening at the door part. Well played."

Noble bowed with mock humility. "Thank you."

"Let's go see how Caryn fared."

Karl led the way to Caryn's room and lightly tapped on the door.

Raquel opened it and motioned them inside.

The Augury Stone sat on an end table brought up from the living room. A makeshift curtain shielded most of the stone except for a portion that faced a mirror. Caryn was in the process of lighting a candle.

"Well?" Karl asked.

"Nothing," Caryn replied with a relieved sigh. "It doesn't mean I'm not connected to someone else, but at least it's not Kevin."

"Good," he nodded and handed her Noble's stone. Stifling a yawn, he said, "Let's all get some rest."

"Suits me," Noble said and headed out the door to his bedroom.

An awkward silence filled the room as Raquel and Caryn gazed at each other then at Karl who wanted simply to go to sleep.

"Why don't we all just go to our own bedrooms," he suggested, "and get a good night's sleep."

Caryn gave Raquel a sympathetic smile. "It's probably a good idea for us all to get a good night's sleep. You can have him tomorrow night."

"That's very sweet of you," Raquel said, returning the smile, "but you have just as much right to him as Annabeth and I do.

"Yeah, but I've had the fun of having him to myself for the past two plus weeks. It wouldn't be fair to say you have to wait another day."

Raquel studied her and smiled, leaning in to kiss her on the cheek. "Welcome to the club. You're an official member now."

"Thank you," Caryn, said with all earnestness. "That means a lot to me."

"So," Raquel ventured, "I was thinking of my suggestion earlier."

Caryn stared at her. "Which was?"

"About both of us at once," Raquel impishly grinned.

"Um… sounds interesting," Caryn answered, unconvinced. When Raquel winked at her, she grinned in understanding. "Of course we'll need a big enough bed for all of us to sleep in."

"I think the bed in his bedroom is big enough," Raquel opined.

"Now that I think about it, you're right," Caryn nodded.

"You both realize I *am* standing here," Karl groused.

"Ignore him," Raquel said with a nonchalant grin. "He gets like this when he's tired."

"I've noticed that," Caryn nodded then grinned at Karl.

"I'm going to bed," he grumbled and strode out, wishing he had heeded Dieter's example and gone to bed when he was tired.

Back in his bedroom, he peeled off his clothes, layering them carefully on an upright chair and crawled into bed noting that it seemed bigger than usual, far bigger. He realized that this was the first time he was in a bed without Caryn for at least two weeks. While it might be OK being able to stretch out, he wasn't sure he liked sleeping alone. Besides, he liked having Caryn with him… and Raquel… and Annabeth… and yes, even Julie. But if he were being honest, there was something about Caryn that was different. Was it that she shared his combat experiences, that she was proficient as a soldier and leader? Sure, that was part of it, but it was her personality. She was fun to be around… and ravishing in bed. Wonder why she hooked up with that loser Frank? What was the attraction? Desperate? He couldn't see how. She was gorgeous in real life. She had a quick mind and a quick sense of humor.

While Karl tried to settle, Raquel and Caryn had remained in the hallway.

"Now that you've had him all to yourself for so long," Raquel said, "it's going to be hard sharing."

"I'll adapt," Caryn stoically replied.

"I was half serious about double teaming him," Raquel said, awaiting a reaction.

"I don't think I'm not ready for that," Caryn said, shaking her head. "Anyway, he's not really tired. Why don't you go ahead and welcome him home. I'm sure he'd like the company. I'm going to bed."

Giving Raquel a patient smile, she headed to her room, sighing quietly that this was her life now. She would have to be a team-player and share. One of these days that was gonna have to change.

Raquel watched her until the door closed behind her, a slow smile curling the corners of her lips, pleased to have Karl to herself for the evening. After the intimacy drought of these past two months, it was nice to be able to relax and curl up next to the Viking.

Karl's drifting thoughts were interrupted when the door opened and light from a three stemmed candelabrum poked through.

"You asleep?" Raquel asked in a low voice, walking in.

"I was working on it," he answered with a quiet resigned sigh, "but no, not yet."

"Good," she answered, approaching the bed.

Placing the candelabrum on the nightstand, Raquel faced him and slowly undressed, ensuring Karl had a full view of her body.

Pulling back the covers, she slipped in beside him, her warm smooth voluptuous body snuggling close.

"How am I supposed to sleep?" Karl asked, though not disappointed.

"You're not," Raquel said, turning his face to give him a deep passionate kiss. "At least, not yet."

Chapter 3

For the next three days, Karl kept them busy with exploring the city, becoming familiar with the numerous streets and what were once family homes, businesses, and other venues. They were surprised at the amount of things left behind, clothing mostly, personal items, kitchen wares, furniture, and even children's toys and the occasional weapon.

"It's almost as though they were expecting to return," Caryn observed, absentmindedly pushing around some papers on a desk in a library in a home several streets away from the citadel. "Wish I could read these, but they're all in elvish."

"I thought you could read other languages," Karl said, coming up to stand next to her.

"She and I can only read other languages if they concern magic and spells and stuff," Raquel answered, standing in the doorway. Noting Karl's raised eyebrow and added, "Yeah, I know. Why the difference? Seems to me if I can read the language at one time, I ought to be able to read it all the time."

"I bet Annabeth can read these," Caryn said, "not that it would really matter. I'm more curious than anything else. Wonder what this place was like when it was a real city, active with daily life."

"Maybe one day we'll know," Karl replied. "In the meantime, we're gonna need some more food. I thought you two might like a little diversion, stretch your legs. We'll get some coin out of the chests in the weapon's room."

"Noble's not gonna like that," Raquel observed.

"Noble's not gonna like what?" Noble announced as he and Dieter entered the study.

"We need food," Karl explained, so I'm sending Raquel and Caryn to get us some."

"Why should I mind about that?" Noble replied with a frown.

"We need money so we're taking it from the pile in the weapon's room."

Noble looked at Karl then at his belt. "Don't you have money?

Karl smiled and stared knowingly at the thief. "Yes I do."

Noble blinked a few times then sheepishly grinned. "I'm not that bad, am I?" When no one responded, he lamely shrugged and explained, "I can't help it. It's in my genes as a thief."

"Whatever," Raquel answered, heading out the door and leading the way back to the citadel then to the weapons room to stand before the door.

"Who's gonna open it?" Noble asked, his eye bright with anticipation.

"Go ahead," Caryn offered.

Noble's mouth slacked open as he abruptly realized he didn't remember the pattern. "It's got something to do with some guy shaving and getting a haircut."

"You're hopeless," Raquel teased and knocked the pattern on the door, which promptly swung open.

The early afternoon sunlight slanted through the two tall and wide barred windows of frosted glass, illuminating the armory, a large high-ceiling room. Elven swords, bows, arrows, axes, helmets, armor, chainmail lined the walls, all neatly arrayed and lined up.

"I still say they expected to come back," Caryn said, her voice quiet.

Ignoring the wonder of all the weapons, Noble made a beeline for the two chests tucked against the far wall. His legs spread apart like he was preparing for battle, he interlaced his fingers and pushed them forward, audibly cracking the joints then separated his hands, wiggled his fingers, and shook his arms.

"What are you doing?" Raquel asked with a chuckle.

"Getting ready to open the eighth wonder of the world," he gushed then flipped the clasp up and slowly lifted the lid.

His hands slid into the mass of coins, and he uttered a long sigh of contentment.

Watching him, Caryn grinned. "It's like you're on drugs. Noble's catnip."

Ignoring Noble's display, Karl reached into his belt bag and withdrew a handful of coins, telling Caryn and Raquel, "Take what you think you need, but don't overdo it. My guess is that too much gold in one place and tongues will wag. We don't need to draw attention to ourselves. And make sure you're not followed."

"Yes, Dad," Raquel replied, shooting a mischievous glance at Caryn.

"I think we can handle this," Caryn replied with emphasis.

"Uh, sorry," Karl sheepishly answered. "I know you can. Get us enough for another week or two."

"We're staying here for another two weeks?" Dieter said, an angry frown crowning his face.

"Probably," Karl replied, giving him a meaningful wink, and ticking his head at the still absorbed Noble lost in the sensation of gold coins.

"OK," Dieter responded with a nod, immediately understanding,

"Don't be too long," he counseled the two rangers.

"Don't worry," Raquel said with a sly grin. "Wouldn't want you to get lonely."

"C'mon Catnip," Caryn teased Noble. "It'll still be here tomorrow."

"Yeah," Noble wistfully replied, withdrawing his hands. "I suppose." Turning to Karl, he groused, "Why'd you bring me in here just to tease me when you had the money all along?"

"Just a reminder of whose side you're on," Karl replied. Curving a hand at the contents in the room, he said, "Kevin knows nothing about this, but we do."

He turned and led the way out, leaving Noble to ponder what he meant.

Caryn and Raquel returned as night descended, much to Karl's relief. "What took so long?" he complained.

"Had to evade a couple of overly interested young men fresh off the farm," Caryn grinned while Raquel rolled her eyes.

"One would think they'd never seen a woman before," Raquel added, shaking her head.

"Not like you two," Noble complimented.

Raquel narrowed a curious glance at him. "You're really sucking up these days. You may want to tone it down a notch."

"Just trying to blend in," he replied with a smile.

"Well try a little less," she replied, "and go pick out a wine for dinner. We're having venison."

Noble saluted and sauntered off, leaving her to sheepishly look at the others. "Anyone know how to cook this so it won't taste like leather?"

Caryn and Karl both shook their heads.

"I can," Dieter said

"You can?" Caryn said, doubt in her eyes.

"Yeah. Remember my lady is the cook? She's shared a lot of cooking secrets with me."

Much to their surprise and satisfaction, the venison was cooked to perfection, balanced off with a red wine that Noble said was like a Pinot Noir.

Conversation slowed as they directed their attention to the meal on their plates until Caryn tilted her head at Noble, a wry smile curling her lips.

"Looking forward to your call with Kevin tonight?"

Noble uttered a pained sigh and shook his head. "The man is becoming a royal pain in the ass. You've heard him. He spends most of the time yelling at me that I'm not giving him enough, like I'm supposed to have discovered some earth-shaking news in the twenty-four hours since the last time we talked. This is getting real old."

"You're doing fine," Karl encouraged. "We want his frustration to expand. The longer he has to wait, the more that frustration grows and cause him to make a mistake."

"Like what?" Noble grumbled.

"We'll know it when we see it," Karl answered.

So it was that Noble found himself in the usual spot at midnight in his room, the Augury stone before him.

"What's the hold up?" Kevin demanded.

"How the hell should I know?" Noble shot back. "And keep your voice down."

"Don't tell me what to do you little cretin," Kevin snapped.

"Do you want me to find out what's going on or not?" Noble shot back, his voice barely above a whisper. "Because if you do, you need to keep your voice down."

Kevin glared at him though he obediently lowered his voice. "What about the others?"

"It's like I told you before," Noble sighed. "Dieter is like a caged animal. He wants to get back to rescue Elena. By the way, what did you do with her?"

"None of your business," Kevin growled.

"It's not a question of my 'business,'" Noble retorted. "If I knew where she was and what she was doing, I could use that to play upon his anxiety."

Kevin thought for a moment then nodded and smiled. "You're right. Truth is, she's a damned good cook so she prepares all my meals."

"That's it?" Noble said, disappointed.

"Yeah," Kevin chuckled, "that's it. I figure no sense in making an enemy of the big guy. When he comes back, he'll see that she was well taken care of, and I can pry him away from Karl."

"Huh," Noble grunted. "That's a good idea."

"What else?" Kevin urged.

Noble shrugged. "It's the same story. We spend our days exploring the city and come back here. While Dieter stalks around the place wanting to get back to rescue Elena, Karl and Caryn and Raquel are frolicking in his bedroom."

"Together?" Kevin said, his eyes popping wide, though not without a hint of envy.

"Naw, not together. Still, while they're enjoying themselves, Dieter and I are left to fend for ourselves. Karl sent the two women into some town today to get food with the intention of staying here for a while."

"What?" Kevin snarled. "What town, where?"

"I don't know. They didn't say."

"Did you ask them?"

"No. I didn't want to raise suspicions."

"Find out." Kevin ordered.

"I will," Noble calmly replied, "when the time is right."

Kevin pursed his lips in irritation then said, "What's Karl got in mind?"

"It's like I've said before, I'm not quite sure yet, but now he talks about wanting Annabeth here, that if they had her, he'd feel confident enough to start back."

"I will *not* give him the sorceress," Kevin tartly replied.

"Have it your way," Noble said. "All I'm doing is telling you what he said. My guess is that if she was here, it might cause a little discord."

"What do you mean?"

"Though the two women are willing to play along, I don't think they're quite as happy as they let on. It's not overt, but the two women snip at each other. My guess is that if Annabeth was here, it would get even worse. You can imagine how three women would be all wanting the same guy. Karl would have to move on just to keep them occupied."

"I won't give him the sorceress," Kevin said.

"You said that already. I'm just relaying what I hear."

"Anything else?" Kevin said with finality.

"No."

"Tomorrow night then. Find out where the town is."

Kevin's stone went blank and Noble wrapped his in the opaque cloth.

Karl emerged from the shadows. "Good job. Sleep well."

For the next week, Noble's reports remained the same. Kevin's anger manifested itself when Noble was unable to produce the name of the town where Caryn and Raquel once again went food shopping.

"Why not?" Kevin demanded, barely controlling his frustration.

"Because they said the damned town didn't have a name," Noble snapped.

"That's impossible," Kevin stated. "Every town in this game has a name."

"Listen," Noble replied, his own frustration mounting, "I'm telling you what they told me. If I keep pestering them, they're gonna begin to wonder about me. For the last time, all they said was that it was a small village with a smithy, a butcher, two taverns and a bunch of homes, somewhere in Mann."

"That doesn't help," Kevin huffed.

"Yeah, well that's all I got." Noble folded his arms and with a grimace of pained irritation, said, "This is getting old. At least Karl has the two women to play with. I'm stuck here twiddling my thumbs waiting for the man to get off his ass and do something. I'm beginning to think he'd be content to stay here for the next ten years."

"Do something then."

"Like what?" Noble disdainfully replied. "It's not like he's going to listen to me."

"What about Dieter?"

"Dieter is loyal to a fault," Noble said, shaking his head. "Even though his beloved Elena is back there, Dieter will not cross Karl and will support him in everything. I give the man credit. He's a man of his word, regardless of circumstances."

"What's that supposed to mean," Kevin said, staring at him with cold hard eyes.

"It means just what I said," Noble answered, wondering what had suddenly upset Kevin. "The man will not budge unless Karl tells him it's OK."

"And the two women?"

Noble splayed his hands. "The same."

"Dammit all," Kevin groused. "What's wrong with him?"

"He's distracted," Noble answered. "He's got two babes with him here. Why should he move on when he has all he needs right here?"

"That's not like him," Kevin observed.

"I know you said you wouldn't send Annabeth back, but I think you're making a mistake."

"Why?" Kevin's face hardened.

"Look at it this way," Noble reasoned. "With Annabeth here, the only person left in Avnoch is Elena. Karl can't justify leaving her there, especially when the rest of the team is here. He'll have to go back just to get her. How could he look Dieter in the face and say, 'we're gonna stay put.' Besides, add Annabeth to the mix and you know we're gonna have to move. Further, once we get going, it'll be only a matter of time before I can find out where we are and report back to you."

Kevin silently stared at him. "Two days. We'll talk again in two days."

Two days later, Noble reported the same repetitive report. Kevin angrily terminated the link before Noble could finish.

Noble didn't report in for the next three days. When he finally did, Kevin was not happy.

"Where the hell have you been?"

"Right here like usual," Noble replied, the answer obvious.

"Why didn't you report in?" Kevin's glower had the look of someone who hadn't slept well for a couple of days.

"Didn't see the sense to it," Noble indifferently replied. "All I do is tell you the same thing over and over again, and all you do is get mad that nothing's changed, like it's somehow my fault that Karl hasn't done anything."

"That's not your place," Kevin flared, "to decide when to report. You do it like I ordered you to."

"Ordered me to," Noble sneered. "You can get off your high horse. I'm not some lackey to be pushed around. I'm doing this because I see personal gain from it. In fact, I could terminate this whole business and you'd be up shit's creek not knowing what's going on. How'd you like that to happen?"

"What?" Kevin exploded.

"Keep it down," Noble snarled. "Yell at me all you want, but if you compromise me, we're through. Get it? Through."

Noble forcibly suppressed a laugh watching Kevin simmer, his eyes bugged out in apoplectic anger, jaw clenched.   After a long silence filled the room, and Kevin regained control of his emotions, he narrowed a hateful stare at Noble.

Wanting to reach through the stone to throttle the little bastard, he instead restrained himself and asked, "What's the status?"

"Pretty much the same," Noble replied. "We're learning the city quite well. I think he's decided to make this place our home base, sort of his new capital. He's talked about positioning weapons at strategic spots while scoping out the locals to see who can be trusted to bring into the city."

Kevin's jaw dropped. "Dammit all." Then in one quick burst of words, he said, "Two days from today. Report." And the stone went blank.

Surprised at the rebuff, Noble wrapped the stone as Karl stepped out of the shadows.

"That was well done," Karl complimented. "Let's see what happens."

What happened occurred the next day. Karl purposely kept everyone in the citadel. He had Noble make a listing of the wines in the buttery, and Dieter was put to inventorying the weapons while he and the two Rangers waited in Annabeth's room, seated comfortably in cushioned chairs brought up from the living room.

"I wonder if one of us ought to wait in your room," Raquel said, standing.

"Probably a good idea," Caryn agreed.

No sooner had Raquel stepped into his room that she called out, "She's coming."

Karl and Caryn raced back to his room to witness Annabeth amalgamating in the middle of the room. Like Raquel before her, Annabeth solidified on her hands and knees, facing away from them.

Her transformation complete, she sat back and gasped a deep long breath, her hand probing her throat. She startled when Raquel softly asked, "Are you OK?"

She turned her head to stare up at them, her face unmasked in a pain that penetrated her soul. Tears coursed down her cheeks, and she struggled to stand, oblivious to her nakedness.

The others stormed over to lift her up. Once on her feet, she looked briefly at each of their faces before erupting into a well of tears and throwing her arms around Raquel, to sob uncontrollably.

Feeling a bit awkward, Karl watched and waited.

Finally regaining control, Annabeth pulled away from Raquel and wiped away the tears with the heels of her palms.

"Sorry. I'm sorry," she repeated, inhaling a deep breath.

"Nothing to be sorry about," Karl soothed.

"I didn't realize it would hurt so much," she explained, wiping the last bit of dampness from her cheeks. "But it was when he stood before me, a razor in his hand and the look in his eyes. I... I've never been so scared in all my life. I couldn't even defend myself because Caillac and Finella were there casting spells and counter spells." She raised a hand and tapped a finger to the side of her head. "In here I knew I would come back here, but at that moment, all I felt was the terror of dying. I was so scared that I froze."

Staring at Karl and Caryn, she blinked and suddenly remembered. "When did you get back?"

"About a week or so ago," Caryn answered.

"I'm glad you're back," she said with heartfelt emotion. "Is anyone else here?"

"Dieter and Noble are also here," Raquel said. "We thought it might be better if they were elsewhere when you arrived." Her eyes traveled the length of Annabeth's naked body as way of explanation.

"Thanks." Annabeth replied then frowned. "You knew I was coming?"

"It's a long story and we'll tell you all about it after you get dressed," Raquel said.

"I don't have any sorceress clothes here," Annabeth said.

"You'll have to wear Ranger clothing for now," Caryn answered. "I'll get you some."

While Caryn left to rummage up some suitable clothing, Annabeth caught Karl's eyes lingering on her gorgeous nakedness.

"See," she smiled knowingly at him.   "That's the difference between a player and an NPC."

"What is?" Raquel asked, puzzled.

"The way they look at you when sex is on their mind," Annabeth smirked, starting to feel her old self.

"Speaking of which," Raquel said, "Caryn now has dibs on the Viking too."

"I kinda figured as much," Annabeth said with a nonchalant shrug. "I like her."

Raquel leaned in and stage whispered, "We've talked about double-teaming him at night. With you here now, we can triple team him."

Annabeth cast a playful glance at Karl and flicked here eyebrows. "You randy fellow you."

Karl responded with a long-suffering sigh but said nothing.

Caryn returned with an armload of clothes and plopped them on the bed. "I think these should fit." She turned and leaned against the bedpost and flashed a mischievous grin at Annabeth. "Mind if I watch?"

"She's getting dressed not doing a strip tease," Karl said with a frown.

"You just have no imagination," Annabeth teased. She sashayed over to the bed in slow sensual steps.

Karl's gaze lingered on every part of her exquisite body.

Picking up a top in each hand, she languidly turned and held them out to her sides, exposing her voluptuous body, the large firm breasts, narrow waist, toned legs and shaved-smooth flesh.

"Which one do you like better?" she innocently asked then narrowed a carnal gaze at him.

Feeling like he had just been caught as a voyeur, Karl shook his head and huffed, "Come downstairs when you're ready."   Spinning on his heels he strode out, sounds of giggling following him.

The three men were in the living room when the three ladies walked in. Annabeth looked the part of a Ranger, giving Karl an idea.

"For now," he said to Annabeth, "I think you should remain a Ranger so that no one knows we have a powerful sorceress with us."

"If I'm so powerful," she countered, "why couldn't I defend myself?"

"Three against one is tough to beat," Noble consoled, "especially when you don't know who your friends are." He gave a meaningful glance at Karl.

"You're getting better," Karl acknowledged.

"I miss something while I was gone?" Annabeth said, noting the exchange.

"We'll talk about it later," Karl said, wanting to move on, but Noble preempted him.

"I'm, or was, a traitor," he said matter-of-factly. "When I saw that the team was either gone or in prison, I had to make a choice. I chose to throw my lot with Kevin so that I wouldn't end up like you all. I made the wrong choice and am now trying to earn my place back on the team."

Annabeth stared at him then asked the obvious question. "Why would you do that?"

"Because I'm not a sorcerer or a ranger or a Viking or a berserker," he sourly replied. "I chose to be a thief and that is what I am stuck with. Had I known then what I know now, I'd have chosen anything other than thief."

Annabeth's frown remained then dissipated. Turning to Karl, she asked, "What's the plan?"

"We wait another couple of days then we begin." He turned to Noble. "Your part in this is critical. Are you up for it?"

"Yes," he replied without hesitation.

"Good." Addressing the group, Karl said, "Everyone spend time in the armory. Take your time and find the right weapon or weapons for you. You too," he said to Noble. Then addressing the two Rangers, he said, "I wonder if you two can track down Ben."

"You want us to go into orc territory?" Caryn said, wide eyed.

"No," Karl answered with an understanding smile. "I want you to call up some friends to do it for us."

"Oh yeah, duh," she sheepishly replied. Leaning over to Raquel she whispered, "Remind me to think before I open my mouth."

"Likewise," Raquel whispered back.

"Are you going to tell us what the plan is?" Noble asked.

"Not until after your talk with Kevin." Noting Noble's lips tighten, Karl explained, "When he asks you if you know our plans, you can tell him the truth and should he use the Augury Stone to double check..." He didn't need to finish as Noble immediately understood.

"You can talk to Kevin?" Annabeth asked, her face grim.

"I'll let Raquel explain," Karl replied. "For now, let's get busy."

In the late evening, Karl and three ladies sat in the living room sipping on a sweet white wine and discussing the events of the past several days. Noble, glad to be able to go to sleep without having to wait up for a call to Kevin, had followed Dieter out the door and upstairs to their rooms.

Caryn gave Annabeth a sympathetic look. "You look tired."

"I am." Lifting the crystal wine glass up, she noted it was still half-filled. "This will be it for me tonight."

Caryn shifted her eyes to peer intently at Raquel. "Did I show you that one blouse I found in my closet?"

Raquel furrowed her brow and blinked, wondering why that was so important at the moment when epiphany struck. "No, you haven't," she answered, downing the rest of her wine.

Standing, she held her hand out to Caryn who likewise tipped her glass back and drained the rest of her wine. Without further comment, the two Rangers walked hand in hand out the door, leaving a confused Karl as to the sudden interest in a blouse.

Annabeth uttered s soft sigh and smiled. "That is so sweet."

"What is?" Karl said, raising an eyebrow, wondering what he had missed.

"They gave you to me tonight," she explained, her eyes misting. "That is just so sweet."

She placed the half-filled glass of wine on the sofa table and stood, reaching out for Karl who quickly emptied his glass. Pressing against him, she luxuriated in the strength of his arms.

"I just need you to hold me, to feel your arms around me… to know that I am safe."

Lifting her up in his arms, he carried her to the threshold then up the stairs, her head buried in his shoulder, her tears moistening his shirt.

The following night, Kevin was in an apoplectic rage, the veins in his temple throbbing, when Noble expressed surprise that Annabeth was supposed to be there.

"What do you mean she's not there," Kevin exploded.

"Just what I said," Noble replied. "She's not here," which was the truth, because she wasn't 'here' in his bedroom.

"Then where is she," Kevin angrily demanded.

"How should I know," which was also the truth, because Annabeth could be anywhere in the citadel. "Are you sure you sent her back?"

"Of course I'm sure you moron," Kevin snapped.

"Maybe her bind spot was someplace other than here," Noble suggested, 'here' being in his bedroom.

"Just dammit all," Kevin fumed. "Find her. I know she's somewhere back there. You find her or you're in deep shit."

Instead of anger, Noble calmly replied, "You insult me and now you want me to do you a favor?"

"Remember who you're talking to, little man," Kevin threatened.

"Oh," Noble replied with mock terror, holding up his hands in front of his face, "I'm so scared." Lifting the opaque cloth, he said, "See this? This is the curtain that holds your future. Now you see me. Now you don't." He draped the cloth over the stone then lifted it and repeated, "Now you see me. Now you don't." Again he draped the cloth over the stone. He waited a few seconds then lifted the cloth off the stone to see Kevin's face purple with rage.

"You want me to work for you, but you insult me. Here's the deal. Before, I was content to accept the price you set. But not anymore. Now I want part of your kingdom. I want to rule a city. I want to be lord of some well-established good-sized city, like Contyn or Statmyr."

"But those are domain capitals," Kevin sharply replied.

"Exactly," Nobel benignly nodded. "You want to rule a kingdom and I want to rule a domain. The only way you can do that is if I lead Karl into your hands. Therefore, the way I see it, you need me. We need each other. Are we agreed?"

Kevin's face morphed to cold calculating before answering, "Agreed."

"Good. I will find our missing sorceress. Give me five days. I will report back in five days."

"Why five?" Kevin said with a snarl.

"Because I'll need time to search the city," Noble said with mild irritation, "that is if she's even here. This place is bigger than you think. I'm thinking that if she is here, there's a possibility that her bind spot is still at the house by the rear gate, the first house we were in with Ben."

"Fine," Kevin said through tight lips. "Five days then. You better –" he began before Noble cut him off by draping the cloth over the stone and wrapping it securely.

Soft clapping sounded behind him as Karl stepped out and laughed. "That was a performance worthy of an Oscar. I tip my hat to you."

"Thank you," Noble acknowledged with a deep breath. "I'm committed now."

"I know," Karl said walking up to him, his hand outstretched. "Welcome back to the team."

"Ben's on his way here," Raquel informed Karl the next morning. "He should be here probably around noonish."

"Go ahead and meet him and bring him here," Karl said.

"There's one more thing," Caryn said. "The orcs are on the move. They've been raiding the border towns and villages of Mann for the past three days."

"Can you find out what the Mann response is?" Karl asked, suddenly feeling a sense of urgency.

"We'll send out scouts when we're finished here," she replied.

Karl nodded. "See if you can get info as close to Avnoch as possible."

"Will do," she said, "but it will take some time."

"I know," he reassured her.

It was early afternoon when Raquel arrived back at the citadel, Ben in tow, who was more than impressed with her knowledge of the city. His admiration grew for the team when he saw their comfort in the citadel.

"Day-um," he said, marveling at the efficient operation Karl had emplaced. He sniffed the air as his mouth watered. "Is that venison I smell?"

"Yes," Raquel replied, heading towards the dining room. "We're just in time for lunch."

"That Elena's one hell of a cook," he said, rubbing his hands in expectation.

"Elena's still in Avnoch," Caryn explained. "Dieter's handling the cooking duties until we get her back."

"Dieter?" Ben's anticipation dwindled.

"Relax," Karl chuckled. "Dieter's almost as good."

Ben was indeed surprised at Dieter's culinary skills, but his focus soon shifted as to why he was there.

"Something big is happening," he announced between chews. "Orcs are on the more. Haven't seen them like this before."

"When you say, 'on the move,' what do you mean?" Karl asked.

"In the past, they'd go on patrols, occasionally raid the border towns on both sides of their kingdom," Ben explained. "They were content to be pains in the ass. But now? Now they got whole companies roaming the borders, like they're probing for weak spots. I got a feeling they're getting ready for something big, and my guess is that they're getting ready to expand their kingdom."

"So why'd you come here?" Noble wondered.

"'Cause it's getting a little harder to do my job, which is killing orcs." His brow furrowed and he turned to Karl.

"What're you guys doing here anyway? I thought you were gonna deliver that little lady to the House of Rhyeem."

"We did," Karl replied. "It's a long story. Right now, we're plotting our future because of a certain PC named Kevin, an assassin. He's in Avnoch at the moment. You didn't see him pass though?"

"Nope. Haven't heard or seen anyone but you guys."

"Wonder how he made it through the orc kingdom without being seen," Noble mused aloud.

Ben paused eating and counted heads. "You're missing that assassin woman. What's her name?"

"Sakura," Annabeth answered.

"Yeah, Sakura. Where's she at?"

"Don't know yet," Karl said. "I suppose we ought to catch you up to speed." He then related the entire tale from the time they left Ryath-sari, delivered Julie, escaped Eleris, conquered Odryssa, got yanked out of the game and returned and now here they were.

"Day-um," Ben chuckled. "You been around these past months. So your plan is to go back to Odryssa and reclaim your throne?"

"That's the plan," Karl replied, "and I'd like you to be a part of it."

"Me? How?"

"However you want," Karl said. "You enjoy killing orcs. Help us kill orcs so we can get to Avnoch and deal with Eleris."

Ben silently pondered the proposal. "Do I have to leave here?"

"Why would you want to stay?" Annabeth asked. "There's got to be more to life than killing orcs."

Ben was about to say, "Like what?" Instead, the furrow in his brow deepened as he thought about where he lived and compared it to where Karl and the others were living, here in the citadel with wines and food and no worries. Suddenly his thirst for vengeance didn't seem all that significant. Maybe it was time to try something new. If it didn't work out, he could always come back here.

"OK," he replied with a slow nod. "I think I may take you up on your proposition."

"Excellent," Karl said, pleased to have another fighter with them.

"You might want to find some new clothes," Caryn suggested.

"And a bath," Annabeth added with a sweet smile.

"OK, OK," Ben laughed. "I get it. A new me."

When Ben returned later that evening, his appearance shocked even the normally staid Dieter. He had cut his hair to just about his shoulders and shaved his beard. Wearing the clothes of an elf Ranger, he looked the part, lean, wiry, and strong.

"My God," Raquel blurted. "I don't recognize you."

"Yeah, well," he awkwardly replied, "it's the same old me with a new coat of paint."

"Wait 'til the barmaids and other hot babes get a look at you," Caryn complimented.

Ben reddened and waved a hand. "Now you're talking nonsense." Wanting to divert attention, he turned to Karl. "So what's the plan?"

"We assemble an army and defeat the orcs," Karl confidently replied.

Ben mutely stared at him before saying, "That's your plan?"

"You'll see," Karl grinned.

After breakfast the following morning, they assembled in the living room. Karl stood by the window while the others settled in chairs or leaned against bureaus.

"It's time to begin the next phase," Karl said. "The reports are that Mann is sending contingents of soldiers to the various border areas affected by the orc raids. We are going to join one of those contingents, specifically the one sent towards Banvie. With that unit, we will defeat the orcs then carry the battle into the orc kingdom of Krug. We want to throw the orcs off balance enough for them to pause their operations long enough for us to consolidate our position in Mann."

"That means going to Glenloch," Caryn said, "at the head of an army.   That's the only way we're going to defeat Eleris."

"That's where you come in," Karl said to Noble.

"Me?" he squeaked.   "How?"

Karl leveled his gaze at him and smiled.   "You're going to steal the Delf Stone."

Chapter 4

Avoiding the roaming orc patrols, Karl and company made their way in a circuitous route to finally arrive at the outskirts of Banvie where a company of Mann soldiers was preparing to scout the border.

Karl boldly strode through the assembled warriors towards the captain, the men and women parting like a torn curtain. The warriors marveled and pointed at the new arrivals, especially the giant berserker who hefted an elven battle ax. Excitement rippled through the company and the captain felt it, only to look up and see a tall Viking and even taller berserker flanked by Rangers, a sorceress, and a... smaller man.

"You are the captain?" Karl asked with the air of authority.

"I am," he replied. The captain was a tall, powerfully built man who exuded a no-nonsense air.

"I am Karl the Viking, and these are my friends. We have come to help you."

"Karl the Viking," the captain repeated. "I have heard of you. You brought back the King's long-lost daughter."

"*We* did," Karl said, emphasizing the rest of his team.

"I also heard that you fell out of favor with the King and his witch." The captain gazed at him with unemotional eyes.

Karl noted the choice of words... not sorceress, but witch. "That I did," he calmly answered. "If you know this then you know why."

The captain glanced down at the sword on Karl's hip. "They say you wear Orc's Bane. If it is true, your presence here would greatly help us."

Karl withdrew the sword and held it out to the man. "Take it and see."

"I do not need to… my Lord," he replied. "I know it is you. I saw you when you arrived in Glenloch. I know the prophecy. I also know you are the rightful king."

"Finally," Annabeth said with a loud sigh, "someone who understands what's going on."

The captain flashed a smile then resumed his professional demeanor. "I am called Maddoc, m'Lord. I am the commander of the Eagle's Claw Brigade. We are spread across the border, too thin, I fear. I am here checking on this company."

"How many do you have here in Banvie?" Karl asked.

"I have 150, m'Lord."

"Battle tested?"

Maddoc paused then said, "Most, but not all."

"Then let me explain what I have in mind," Karl said with a confident smile.

An hour later, Karl had an additional 100 warriors with him, while Maddoc sent word for the rest of his brigade to hold the line.

"We should be back in a couple of days," Karl told Maddoc. "Send word to those you trust. But only those you know can keep a secret."

"Yes, m'Lord. Good hunting."

As Maddoc left to resume command, Karl called together the subordinate leaders of the Mann contingent, along with his own team.

"We march on Righul Khar first. Our ultimate objective is Ozgul. Along the way, we kill every orc we can find." He then elaborated the movement plans and the battle plans. "Two final things. We torch the cities in reverse order, starting with Ozgul. Secondly, rear security is as important as forward security. We cannot afford to be surprised, nor do we want to have to fight our way back."

He paused then mumbled. "Wish I had Uafas and Sakura here."

With the aid of their feathered scouts circling both high in the sky and amongst the trees, Raquel and Caryn led the way into the thick forest toward Ryath-sari. A half hour into the forest, they met Ben, nonchalantly leaning against a tree.

"How many we got?" he asked, looking at the soldiers behind Karl.

"100 more than we started with," Karl replied. Turning around, he was pleased to see the soldiers spread out and hunker down to be out of sight, as well as establishing perimeter security. He motioned for the five section leaders to come forward. Three women and two men, masking their excitement of hunting orcs, hustled to where Karl stood with Ben and the others of Karl's inner group.

Karl turned back to Ben. "What's the status here?"

"Patrols are increasing, none larger than ten to fifteen. Activity is also increasing at Righul Khar with most of the traffic coming from Braghurk."

"How big is Righul Khar?" Caryn asked.

"A couple hundred," Ben said, "including women and children. The city's laid out in a sort of square. There's probably a hundred buildings, all single story, made of stone. The roofs are thatch so are susceptible to fire. The clan chief's house, bigger than the rest, is in the center. The entire city is surrounded by a stone wall of varying height, the highest being about chest high. There are two gates to the city at opposite ends. Only one road leads out of the main gate then splits, one branch going towards Braghurk, the other to Krugrodh."

"What's the rear gate for then?" Annabeth asked.

Ben shrugged. "Don't know. Possibly an escape route in case of attack. I've scouted it out a number of times but have never seen anyone come through it."

"What about activity here in the forest?" Karl asked.

"Like I said," Ben answered, "not much other than patrols." He leaned in. "On the plus side, they're lazy and they don't send out patrols after dark."

"Good," Karl nodded, dropping to a knee. Clearing a space on the ground, he motioned for Ben to join him while the others gathered around. Drawing a square, he said, "Here's the city. Where are the gates and roads?"

"There's a gate here and here." Ben drew an 'X' on two opposite sides of the square. "The road leads from this gate then splits here." He drew a line out from one gate then split it into a 'Y'. "This branch goes to Braghurk and this one goes to Krugrodh."

"Alright," he addressed the others, "listen up. We attack at midnight tonight. Before that, we set up booby traps at the back gate. Annabeth is responsible for that. Once the traps are set, Caryn and Raquel and all archers will surround the city and launch fire arrows into as many houses as possible. The object is to cause as much confusion as we can. Once the fires are raging, and upon my command, we attack. We kill every orc we find."

"Women and children too?" one of the section leaders asked, though it was more of a statement than a question. He was a robust muscular man with a scar across his bicep.

"Especially women and children," Caryn answered. "Little orcs grow up to be big orcs. We either kill them now or have to deal with them later."

Another section leader, a woman of athletic build with long auburn hair tied in a ponytail, said, "I thought you said we were gonna torch the cities in reverse order."

"I did," Karl nodded, "but I've reconsidered. We need the element of surprise, which means we take out orcs on the way to Ozgul so that no one knows where we are or how big our force is."

"But what if someone discovers what we did to Righul Khar?" she asked.

"The road splits here," Karl said, pointing to the ground. "The only way it would be discovered is if someone from Krugrodh stumbled upon it. It is close enough to the border to make them think it was a raid. By the time they report back to Krugrodh, we'll have laid waste to Braghurk and Ozgul. While part of me would like to continue on until we get to Beally and connect up with the forces there, I want the orc kingdom off balance enough for them to retract their forces to the mountains around Krugrodh for the time being. What that means is that when we finish with Ozgul, we faint like we're going to Krugrodh then beat feet back to Mann. Questions?"

When no one replied, Karl stood. "Let's move out."

Ben led the way through the woods. By the time they reached the edge of the elven forest, deep in orc territory, it was late afternoon. Forewarned by ravens, they had avoided two orc patrols who stuck to a routine well-worn path, returning the same way.

Once beyond the elven part of the woodland, their progress slowed as they came closer to their objective. Raquel and Caryn sent the birds out to scout the surrounding area, learning that orc patrols were heading back to Righul Khar and that the road between Righul Khar and Braghurk was clear, as was the road leading to Krugrodh.

"Wish we had more time to set up booby traps," Karl quietly said to Caryn.

"Annabeth will give us what we need," she replied.

"I heard my name," Annabeth whispered.

"Just saying you've got some great booby traps," Caryn answered.

"Oh, booby *traps*," Annabeth innocently repeated. "I thought you said I had great boobs."

"Those too," Caryn grinned. "What traps are you going to use?"

"The same ones I used on the way to Abynee, a long narrow ditch with spikes in it. Remember though, the spell lasts for only an hour, so we need to attack as soon as the spell is set. I'll also use Trap Ivy spell that will snare any and all who come close to it. I'll place that on both side of the booby trap.

"How long does that last?" Caryn asked.

"An hour to creep and hold and another hour before it releases. Also, remember, the ivy doesn't discriminate. If you get too close, it'll take you too." She placed a gentle hand on Caryn's arm. "I'll cast a Night Vision spell on you and Raquel again, like the last time. Then," she brightened, "I get to play with fire. I've got a spell called Fireworks Burst. It's like the 4th of July gone horribly wrong."

Seeing the childlike excitement in her friend's eyes, Caryn snickered. "Try not to have too much fun."

"I'll do my best," she cheerily replied.

Dusk settled upon the forest and Karl motioned to press on. Ben again led the way, stopping when the light from the outside cooking fires rimmed the city walls. Karl sent the two Rangers to scout the walls, looking for opportune spots to conduct the attack.

Returning after night had darkened the area, Raquel reported, "The wall is just like Ben said. The highest parts are at the two gates then drop down to around gut high in the middle of the other two walls."

"Guards?"

"Two," Raquel replied. "One patrols along the wall, the other meanders in and around the houses. It doesn't take them long and they pause in the open not far from the lower part in the wall. It'll be an easy shot."

"Excellent. We take them out first," Karl said. "I'll leave that to you two."

Karl then arrayed his force, concentrating on the lower parts of the wall and the main gate. Caryn, Raquel, and Annabeth were positioned with two Mann sections on one side while Karl, Dieter, Noble, and two more Mann sections on the other. The remaining Mann section was placed outside the main gate.

"OK mighty sorceress," Karl said to Annabeth. "Go do your thing. We attack once you get back. Noble, you go with her."

"Me?" the little man squeaked. "I'm not a mighty warrior like you guys."

"Yes, but you're a thief, a silent one who can make sure no one catches her unexpectedly."

"Uh... sure," he replied.

Twenty minutes later, Annabeth returned and whispered, "All set. Don't go near the back or you'll get snared in the vines."

"Good job," Karl complimented. "Go ahead and tell Caryn and Raquel to take out the guards then do your thing to as many roofs as possible."

"Oh boy," she replied with a devilish grin.

Annabeth stealthily made her way to where Raquel and Caryn waited with the hidden Mann soldiers.

"It's time," she whispered to the two Rangers.

Nodding in reply, Caryn and Raquel each notched an arrow and repositioned themselves, waiting for the guards to come together. Their patience was rewarded when they saw the two orcs approach each other.

"What's that make so far?" one orc said to the other. He carried a falchion, resting it on his shoulder.

"Damned if I know. Wasn't countin'," the other replied. He carried a sword, but it was sheathed, the leather securing strap wrapped around the handle. "How long we gotta do this?"

"Yeah, that's what I say," the first agreed. "I'm tired. This is the third day in a row we been out here. All a waste of time. Ain't nuthin' gonna happen. They all knows that. Ever since they came here and told us to start raidin' 'cross the border, Mister hoity toity clan chief here decides he's gonna show them he's in charge and what's he do?"

"Sticks us out here patrolin' while he's sleepin' like a baby," the other sneered.

"Damned right," the first one said. "Why isn't his sorry ass out here patrolin' some of the time?"

"Why patrol at all?" the other wisely responded. "Like you said, this is a waste of time."

The first orc cast a quick glance around then leaned in. "I say we find a spot to catch a few winks. No one's gonna know."

"Yeah," the other eagerly replied.

Raquel leaned over to Caryn and whispered, "I got the one on the left."

Caryn nodded and they took aim and fired.

Their arrows hit the marks at the same time, puncturing the temples and ramming through the other side, the fletchings partially protruding from the impact point.

The orcs fell like dropped sacks of flour.

Caryn turned to Annabeth. "OK, good-lookin', your turn."

With a fiendish grin, Annabeth stood and began hurling small fireballs onto the roofs of the houses close by. Once the thatch began to catch flame, she moved along the wall, tossing fireballs at other homes. By the time she reached the other side of the village, flames roared in the roofs of over one half the homes.

It took a few moments before the first orcs burst out of their burning houses. Caryn, Raquel, and the archers from the Mann sections quickly dispatched the unfortunates. By the time Annabeth had finished, almost the entire village was in flames, making targets easier to hit for the archers. Those orcs trying to get to the wells were cut down, buckets in hand.

Karl glanced over at Dieter whose restlessness indicated he was ready to get in on the action. Shifting his gaze back to the burning village, he saw other orcs organizing, weapons in hand as they searched out the cause for the conflagration.

"Now," Karl shouted at the top of his lungs, leading the way and leaping over the wall.

For his size, Dieter's agility was surprising as he cleared the wall in one jump and was already engaging orcs with wide sweeps of his broadax.

Like ants swarming over a hilltop, Karl and his small army hurled themselves over the walls of Righul Khar and assaulted every orc they found. While Annabeth took to hurling fireballs at individual orcs, Caryn and Raquel and other archers, felled rampaging orcs attempting to break out.

One of the last to fall was the clan chief, a bigger orc than the rest. He was barefoot and wore only leather breeches though he carried a sword and buckler. Dieter saw him at once and cleared a path to challenge him. While the fires and battle raged around them, the orc and Dieter squared off.

The bloodlust raged in the berserker, and he took the battle to the orc who stood his ground then leaped high, swinging his shield outward to ward off counterblows while simultaneously striking overhand and slicing down. Dieter easily parried the blow, twisting to the left and forcing the orc past him before spinning around to the right, his double axe blade slicing the orc across his side. Blood immediately began flowing from the long thin gash on the orc's bare flesh.

Surprised he had been wounded so soon, the orc angrily spun around to face the berserker, his eyes hard with anger. Ignoring the pain, he focused his attention on his larger opponent, gazing at his eyes, but keenly aware of his ax and posture. Impervious to the dwindling battle around him, the orc charged.

Instead of falling back or dodging, Dieter met him head on. Ax and sword and buckler clashed with loud viciousness. They repeatedly shared and deflected blows, yet with each strike of the berserker's axe, the orc felt the raw power behind the man's blows and was soon forced to parry and dodge as best he could. Yet the berserker seemed to grow stronger as their duel continued.

And then the orc did not respond quickly enough and his arm holding the buckler was not in position when Dieter's axe crashed against it. The orc felt the snap at his elbow and his arm flopped to his side, the buckler sliding from his grip. The orc looked up just in time to dodge another swipe from Dieter's axe.

While blood oozed out of his wound and down his hip, the orc's confidence suddenly wavered as he felt his strength and stamina ebbing. The berserker paused and stared at him, and the orc chief quickly looked around to realize the fighting had dramatically slowed and some of the humans had the arrogant confidence to pause in their slaughter to watch the fight. Fires continued to rage in the individual homes.

Realizing his town was both defeated and destroyed, his momentary anxiety passed into anger as he accepted he had nothing left to lose other than to die an honorable death.

Ignoring those humans silently waiting his fate, he once again charged.

Instead of waiting for him to attack, Dieter carried the force of his strength against him, driving him back, causing the clan chief to stumble over the body of a dead orc. Deciding he had already spent too much time on this one opponent, Dieter leaped forward and swung his great axe in a whirling arc, the blade sweeping towards the orc's head.

And then it was finished.

Dieter stood over his opponent. The severed head lay on the ground close by the body, which quivered in spasmodic death convulsions.

While Dieter's bloodlust settled, Karl and his soldiers swept through the village, finishing off wounded orcs, searching the few homes not yet burning and dispatching several women and children who had fled to safety. When Karl arrived at the back gate, it was open.

Calling Annabeth to him, he asked, "Can you give me some light here?"

She did a quick scroll of her skills. "I can do a Shining Light spell. It's like having five Coleman lanterns overlapping their light, but only lasts two minutes."

'That's good enough," he replied.

"If you're going to walk around back there," she warned, "remember the vines,"

"You're coming with me," he said.

"I knew that," she grinned then held up her hand and cast the spell. Immediately, five lanterns like those used by night watchmen dangled in a straight line in the air before them, each about three meters away from the next. The light spilling from each lantern was enough to clearly see that Annabeth's traps had worked, quite effectively. About a dozen orcs were impaled on the spikes in the ditch, while half a dozen lay entrapped in vines, choked to death when the tendrils wrapped tightly around their necks.

They were about to turn away when something caught Karl's eye. Off to the side, an orc sat on the ground, vines wrapped around one ankle and a wrist. Severed vine tendrils lay scattered close by. The orc was still alive and, hoping to escape notice, had paused in his struggle to free himself when the two strangers emerged out the gate.

"That one's still alive," Annabeth said, disappointed, staring at the orc who returned her stare with icy hatred.

Caryn and Raquel walked up and before Karl could respond, Caryn sent an arrow into the orc's chest while Raquel shot the orc through the head.

"That settles that," Annabeth blithely announced.

"How we doing?" Karl asked the two Rangers.

"Surprisingly, quite good," Caryn answered. "Two wounded, not serious, and that's it. We were lucky."

"I agree," Karl nodded. "Let's hope our luck holds out."

One of the Mann section leaders appeared in the door. She was a tall, muscular woman with short blond hair. "Pardon, m'Lord, but we found something interesting."

"What?"

"Slaves, m'Lord."

Frowning, Karl walked towards her, as she waited to escort him. "Status of your section, Gwenno?"

"All present and accounted for, m'Lord," she answered as she directed him towards the center of the village. "No injuries or wounds... well except one who twisted his ankle when he tripped over himself in all the excitement."

Karl chuckled then turned somber when he approached a group of his soldiers standing guard at a house surprisingly untouched by the flames.

One of the soldiers opened the door and Karl stepped into a large open room, followed by Gwenno, the two

Rangers and Annabeth. Along the edges, shackled at their wrists and necks, a dozen women, dirty and unkempt, stared up at him in hope and fear. One woman tried to crawl to him, but the chains stopped her.

"Who are you?" he asked.

"We are the lost girls of Mann," another woman boldly answered. She was a slender woman with dark eyes and coarse brown hair. Cleaned up, she would be pretty.

Karl twisted his head to frown at Gwenno.

"Every so often, one of our children disappears," Gwenno explained. "We call them 'Lost Children.' We naturally assume that either wild beasts or orcs have killed them." She ticked her head at the chained women. "This is the first instance we have that some are still alive."

"Unchain them," Karl commanded.

"We can't, m'Lord," Gwenno sighed. "No one knows where the key is, and the chains are too thick for our resources."

Karl shifted a glance to Annabeth who shook her head. "Sorry. These aren't magical."

"Get Noble in here," he ordered then turned to the women. "Why are you chained?"

"Though we are slaves, my Lord," the woman answered, "and bound to obey the beck and call of these horrid beasts, none of them wants a human slave living in their quarters for fear of being murdered in the night."

"Every night we are brought here," another chimed in, "and in the morning we are unchained to cook or sew or clean whatever they want."

Noble stepped in and cocked an eyebrow at the women who appeared out of place in an orc village.

"I need you to unlock their chains," Karl said.

Without a word, Noble stepped forward, withdrawing his thief tools as he approached the first woman whose pleading eyes caused him to pause for an instant. In a matter of minutes, Noble had freed all the women who now stood, rubbing their wrists and throats.

"Will you protect us, take us home?" the dark-eyed woman begged, tears in her eyes.

"We can't," Karl said, softening his voice. "We have orcs to kill and if we turn back to take you home, the opportunity will be lost. But you need not fear. There are no orcs between here and Mann. Wait until almost daylight and head back. You'll be safe."

"Please," another pleaded, fear in her eyes.

An alert popped up in Karl's screen.

Congratulations: You have freed -

With a snarl, he swiped it away before reading the rest. "I thought these damned things were turned off," he grumbled.

"Please, my Lord," the woman begged. "We have been here for so many years. I myself have been a prisoner for eight years. We need your help. Please."

"Stay here," he commanded and stepped outside. "Section leaders to me," he called out. The five leaders assembled around him. "I need two volunteers to take these women back to Mann, preferably someone who's nonessential, it you get my drift."

"I have two I can donate," one section leader replied. She was an athletic woman with long black hair held back in a ponytail. "They're good lads, but a little scatterbrained sometimes."

"Can we trust them to find their way home, Alva?" Karl said with a smile.

"Aye, m'Lord," she said, returning the smile.

"Good. Fetch them and give them their mission, which is to lead these women back to Mann. Tell them to report to Maddoc."

"Aye, m'Lord."

Karl stepped back inside. "You will have two warriors to escort you back to Mann."

"Just two?" another woman whined.

"Two are all you need," Karl said, his voice firm. "I have already stated that the path is free of orcs between here and Mann. You will leave at first light."

The dark-eyed woman stepped towards him and kneeled. "Thank you my Lord, for saving us."

"What is your name?"

"I was once called Eveen, my Lord."

"Stand Eveen," he regally commanded. Addressing the women, he said, "Eveen is in charge of your little group. You will do what she says until you are back in Mann. After that, you are free to return to your own homes. Is that understood?"

They responded with nods and 'yes, m'Lord."

"You leave at first light." He was about to turn when Eveen spoke.

"My Lord, if it please you, I'd like to come with you instead. I am not from Mann. I am from a small vil near a town called Beally on the other side of the orc kingdom."

"I know Beally," Karl said.

Eveen's eyes widened in surprise. "You do?"

"Yes. How is it that you are here?"

A sly smile curled the corners of her mouth before turning grim. "I was known as a problem slave. I have been a captive for six years. During that time, I was bought and sold eleven times, each time moving me farther away from Beally."

"Why didn't they just kill you and be done with it?" Caryn asked, not without sympathy.

"Because I am a scholar," she proudly answered, "one who understands words and the importance of them when making covenants." Seeing her doubt, she said, "I was four and twenty when I was taken."

"Doesn't answer my question," Caryn pointed out.

"Orcs are a querulous and contentious bunch –"

"'Querulous,'" Raquel repeated with a smile. "Nice word."

"When they found out I could read and write, they decided to use me to write out binding contracts to which they never paid attention and broke them as soon as it suited one or the other," Eveen said, shaking her head.

"How did you end up here?" Annabeth asked.

"Losers have a way of making life difficult," Eveen replied, "especially if they're stronger than the winner. In order to stop inner-clan wars, the clan chief would sell me to another clan. Like I said, I was sold eleven times, and here I am."

"And that's what made you a problem slave," Raquel said, nodding in understanding.

"Yes."

"How long have you been here?" Caryn asked.

"About a month," Eveen said then turned back to Karl. "I've been listening to them, especially when they think we're all asleep or too stupid to understand them. From what I can piece together, they're planning some sort of an invasion into Mann."

"When?" Caryn interrupted.

"A week or two," Eveen replied, "maybe a little more. They've been stockpiling weapons at various locations along the border between the sea and the mountains to the south of here."

Karl looked pensive as he came to a decision. "Alright, Eveen, you may come with us, but understand that we only go to Ozgul before returning. You will have to make a decision whether to return with us or chance it on your own to make it to Beally."

A flash of disappointment crossed her face, immediately replaced by resolved determination. She was about to tell Karl that she would take that chance when Ben spoke up.

"I'll take her back."

"You will?" Eveen said, her gratitude obvious.

Karl momentarily frowned at his prized orc-killer deserting at a critical time, but then rationalized that Ben's presence here was by mutual agreement and that Ben could leave anytime he wanted. But more importantly, he noticed the way Ben looked at the woman and realized his motivation was not purely altruistic.

"This is Ben," Karl said by way of introduction. "He lives here in Krug."

"You do?" a shocked Eveen said. "Why?"

"I'm an orc hunter," Ben explained. "I like to kill orcs. I figure the easiest way to do that is live right here among them."

"And they never suspect you're here?" Her look was one of incredulity.

"Not yet," he grinned with confidence.

"Don't you miss people, good food and ale, and other comforts?"

Ben was about to answer, 'Nah,' but thought again. "Oh sure, but it's the price I have to pay to deal with these evil monsters."

Leaving the two in conversation, Karl addressed the remaining former prisoners. "Eveen will be coming with us. The rest of you will leave at first light." He turned to the five section leaders. "Plunder what you can but divide it equally.

Make sure each of the ladies here receives a fair share. It's the least we can do after all the suffering they've endured."

Startled at the bounty, the former prisoners reached out to hug him, several in tears.

Awkwardly prying their arms away, Karl stepped away. "Get some sleep. You've a busy day ahead of you."

Karl's small army was halfway to Braghurk when the ravens brought back the news that a large force of orcs along with half a dozen wagons were headed on the road to Righul Khar.

"How large a force?" Karl asked Raquel.

Raquel spoke the raven perched on her arm. "She says less than half the number of us."

"Then we set up an ambush," Karl announced.

Positioning his forces on both sides of the road as well as a cut off force at both ends, Karl created a kill zone box to contain the orcs and prevent them from escaping. Now it was just a matter of waiting.

The front end of the orc troop plodded into view, their security nonexistent. Those with falchions wore them sheathed, while those carrying halberds carried them loosely on their shoulders. The troop moved with little hurry. In the middle of the force, six bored orcs drove large, wheeled freight wagons, a team of oxen hitched in front.

Waiting until the rear part of the troop passed his position, Karl gave a yell and attacked.

The carnage was swift and complete. The orc drivers were among the first to go, impaled by arrows shot from both side of the road. At the same time, arrows impacted those in the front and rear of the orc troop. A few orcs were quick enough to take cover beneath the wagons, requiring a temporary halt to the flight of arrows while Dieter and Karl and a few Mann soldiers flushed them out and cut them down.

The ambush lasted less than three minutes. By the time the last arrow found its mark, the road was strewn with dead orcs. While the archers walked amongst the dead, yanking out arrows and wiping off orc blood from the arrowheads, Karl looked over the side of the first wagon to see falchions, halberds, maces, flails, and battle axes all neatly arranged. Each following wagon contained the same cargo.

"There's enough weapons here to arm an entire battalion," Caryn observed, wiping an arrow on the leather vest of a dead orc. "What do you wanna do with it all?"

"Good question," Karl frowned. "We can't take it with us, and I don't want to leave it all here for them to use later. We can't just torch them for fear of revealing we're here."

"There's a river close by," Eveen said.

"How do you know that?" Caryn asked.

'I came through here once, remember?"

"Once," Caryn replied, raising and eyebrow "and you know the entire landscape?"

"Orcs have maps too," Eveen answered, unfazed, "good ones. I know where we are." She pointed to the right into the forest. "There's a river about 600 meters that way. It winds its way away from the road but eventually comes back so that this road here will have to cross it as the river makes its way to the sea."

"She's right," Ben chimed in. "Been over this neck of the woods a bunch of times." He shifted a sympathetic glance at the woman. "Wish I woulda known you were coming through here. I might have been able to do something to help, had I known."

"That's sweet," she replied, gently touching his arm.

Karl surveyed the road, the wagons, and the dead orcs scattered around, recognizing that they would lose valuable time while turning the wagons around and detouring to get rid of the weapons. He glanced behind him to see his berserker.

"Dieter."

"Yes, Boss?"

"What would it take to destroy a bunch of these weapons?"

Dieter leaned over the wagon side, his brows furrowed in thought. "All we need to do is bend the sword blades, break the halberd shafts –"

"Why not just use your sword?" Annabeth asked. "It cuts through everything."

Karl shook his head in sheepish acknowledgement. "I guess that would make sense." Seeing Alva organizing security, he called to her. "Alva?"

"Yes, m'Lord," she replied, hustling over.

"Get me some folks to unload all this stuff."

"Yes, m'Lord."

Shifting his attention to Raquel and Caryn, he asked, "What do our scouts report?"

"Nothing yet," Raquel said.

"We'll be here for a little longer. Let's make sure we're not surprised."

For the next half hour, Karl sliced through falchions, halberds, axes, and the rest of the weapons, much to the amazement of Mann's soldiers and giving added weight to Karl's right as the king. The bits and pieces of the broken and splinted weapons were scattered around the bodies.

"Do we unhook the oxen?" Alva asked.

"What are your thoughts?" Karl responded.

Pleased that the king thought her input worthy, she said, "I don't like leaving the beasts here in the hope that someone finds them. At the same time, we don't need them traipsing along the roads arousing curiosity. I can send some soldiers to lead them to the river and leave them there. That would get them off the roads and they would have water. Once they got hungry, they would wander around, long enough for us to do what we need to do."

"I like it," Karl replied, dipping his head. "Make it so."

As Alva ran off to implement Karl's order, Caryn observed, "That's one happy camper. You just made her day."

"She's a smart and dependable woman," Karl answered. "We'll need her smarts when we get back to Mann."

"She's pretty too," Caryn added with an innocent smile.

"Not even funny," Karl said, rolling his eyes and shaking his head.

An hour later, the oxen were gone, the soldiers returned, and Karl's army was again on the march. They were still two hours away from Braghurk when Karl noted some soldiers beginning to lag. Calling a halt, he called up Ben and Eveen who now traveled together.

"We need to stop and rest before tonight's operation. You two know the area. Where's a good spot?"

Ben and Eveen shared a glance and a smile before Ben answered, "Another two kilometers there's a spot away from the road we can bed down for a while. It's the site of another elven city, a lot smaller than –"

"Other ones," Caryn quickly interrupted, causing Ben to frown at her until understanding pierced his preoccupied brain.

"Ah, yes, yes, other ones," he awkwardly nodded. "This one is interesting in that there is an obvious elven curse on it, very oppressive, even for friends of elves. In the past, a few orcs wandered in there and never back came out, so orcs bypass the place for the most part."

"How do you know this?" Caryn asked.

Ben shrugged. "Like Eveen, I listen to them."

Two kilometers up, Ben paused and pointed to barely visible cobblestones in the ground off to the right. "Here we are."

"Here?" Noble said, frowning, for aside from the hard to see cobblestones, what confronted him was forest, thick with trees and dense underbrush.

"Yes," Ben grinned. "Here."

"How'd you know where to find it?" Annabeth asked.

"Like I said," he shrugged, "I listen to 'em. Came here once to check it out."

"Did you spend the night?" Raquel asked.

"Naw," he indifferently replied. "Place gives me the willies. Ready?" Without waiting for a reply, he plunged into the woods, Eveen beside him.

Nature had long since taken over the once busy thoroughfare. Oak, chestnut, birch, and ash trees had thrust their way through the worn cobblestones to spread wide their branches, intertwining enough to filter the sunlight. Butcher's Broom, wild privet, and holly filled in beneath the tree limbs.

Ben led with sure step in and around the various shrubs and they soon stood before a solidly built stone city, surrounded by tall walls covered in thick vines. The city gates were open wide, one door dangling on the top hinge while the other lay flat on the ground requiring one to walk upon it if one wanted to go into the city.

"This place is creepy," Annabeth said with awe.

"Yup," Ben acknowledged. "I think they made it on purpose, to keep the varmints away, varmints being mostly orcs." He stepped across the door and entered the city.

"I thought elves usually built their cities in the mountains," Caryn commented, purposely omitting the Ryath-sari. She followed Ben and Eveen through the gate.

Inside the walls, the city loomed ominous. Though solidly built of stone, time had made its presence felt and the omnipresent vines covered the buildings, the occasional stone dislodged onto the streets, which were surprisingly clear of anything else. Unlike Ryath-sari, whose occupants seemed to have left in a hurry, this city appeared deserted as though methodically emptied of all trace of habitation then abandoned to the creeping grip of time.

Though shafts of afternoon sunlight slipped through the canopy of trees and numerous stone archways crossing over the streets, the place was dark, and Karl felt a foreboding presence.

Motioning the five section leaders to him, he said, "Tell everyone to spread out, but stick close to the main gate here. Send some scouts out to check out the local area." He then pulled up his screen and discovered there was a paragraph about the city where he and his force now encamped.

"Where are these things when you need them?" he complained with a frustrated sigh.

Onith-ari, an ancient city of the Alari-dona clan, was built and occupied fifty years before Ryath-sari. In exchange for imbuing dwarven weapons with elven magic, the mountain dwarves of the Crannoc Kingdom carved and hauled stones to the city site, Onith-ari, assembling and constructing the city. As a result of the arrangement, trade and commerce between the two races commenced and both the city and the dwarven kingdom prospered. Onith-ari assumed an elevated importance as the capital of the Alari-dona Kingdom. Three hundred and thirty-three years later, as the elven kingdom expanded to cover the areas from the edges of the mountain kingdom of Crannoc to the seas on both sides of the island, peace was forever sundered when Ronagg the Lame, King of Crannoc, became jealous of Alari-

dona's imposing strength and determined to put an end to elven power. As the headwaters of the river that coursed through parts of the city descended from a mountain lake in the dwarven kingdom, Ronagg had a sorceress place a deep slumber spell on the water in the lake, which caused all who drank the cold clear water to fall into a deep sleep that lasted seven days. Though the occasional dwarf forgot and succumbed to the spell, the effect on the Onith-ari was devastating as the city was plunged into chaos as almost the entire city fell victim to the curse. Only after they had abandoned the city did they learn the truth and by then the island wars had overtaken the island. Yet to this day, the curse remains.

Startled to action, Karl called out, "Don't drink the water." But it was too late as a scout team returned, carrying two soldiers who were sound asleep.

"Damn it all," Karl barked.

"We found them on the bank next to the river not far from here," one worried soldier explained. "They're not dead, but they won't respond."

"They're asleep," Karl grimly replied, "because the water has a curse on it." Turning so all could hear him, he intoned, "Do not drink the water from the river. It is cursed with a sleep spell."

"How long does it last, Sire?" Gwenno asked.

"Seven days,' he grimaced, "seven days of having to drag them around with us."

"It's not their fault, Sire," Gwenno pointed out. "They didn't know."

"I'm not blaming them," Karl replied, "but it does impact our operation." He turned to Ben who ambled up, Eveen tagging along. "Why didn't you tell us about the water here?"

"Didn't know about it," he shrugged.

"Me neither," Eveen added.

Karl frowned at Ben. "How could you not know? You would have got the info when you accessed your game data."

"Aw," he chuckled, "haven't done that in so long, I forget it's there."

"What about all the pop-ups?"

"I just ignore 'em," he blithely answered. "Besides, with all the time I been here killing orcs, didn't really get a lot of pop-ups."

"What are pop-ups?" Eveen asked.

"Uh," Ben hesitated. "Sort of difficult to explain, but it's the way we figure out some stuff." Seeing her puzzled look, he scratched his head and said, "Some of us have special powers, and..."

"And he can explain it later," Karl interrupted. "Right now we need to get organized." He turned to tell Caryn to check the perimeter when a thought emerged. Glancing back at the team leaders who had been attentively listening to Ben's comments, Karl asked, "How many water flasks does each soldier carry?"

"Two, m'Lord," Gwenno answered, surprised that he didn't know that already.

Ignoring her, Karl muttered to himself, "Pity we turned the oxen loose."

"What are you thinking?" Caryn asked, recognizing the look.

"The water," he said. "We need to take as much of it with us as we can."

"For use on the orcs," Gwenno commented in understanding.

"No," Karl said with a sly grin, "for use on certain folks back home."

"You want to poison *our* people?" Gwenno blurted, her eyes wide.

"Not necessarily," Karl evasively replied. "I'll know when the time comes. In the meantime, I want every other soldier to carry one flask filled with the river water. We move out at dark, so get some rest. Rotate security." Turning to Raquel and Caryn, he said, "We need eyes on the road. We have to assume more orcs will be travelling between Braghurk and Righul Khar. We don't want to lose our element of surprise."

Caryn cleared her throat and caught Karl's attention. Ticking her head to the side, she indicated that she wanted to talk with him in private.

Understanding, Karl addressed the others. "Give us a minute but stay here."

Karl and Caryn stepped away far enough to be outside of eavesdropping. Caryn cast a brief glance ensuring they were far enough away.

"I don't think it's a good idea to have everyone carry a flask of this river water," she said.

"Why not?" he replied with a flash of irritation.

"First, each soldier only carries two flasks. Requiring them to fill one with poisoned water effectively reduces their water intake to one flask. When the next battle comes, they won't have enough to drink."

Karl blinked as he listened. "The second reason?"

"The second is think about who we have here with us. We already have two soldiers asleep for the next seven days. Just imagine in the heat of battle when more forget which flask is safe to drink from."

Karl stared at her, immediately recognizing the logic of her advice as well as her method of delivery. She specifically chose to do it in private.

Pursing his lips, he slowly nodded. "You're right." Giving her an appreciative smile, he walked back to where the others waited.

"Cancel that order to carry the river water from here," he announced. "Saner heads have prevailed. We don't need more distractions, but we will need to find safe water sources. Ben? Eveen?"

"There are plenty of other rivers we can use," Ben replied.

"Suppose there are more orcs coming?" Raquel asked, curious as to what Caryn said that changed Karl's mind. "What do we do?"

"Depends on the size," Karl replied. "Too large a force then our mission is blown and we E&E back across the border."

"E&E?" Raquel repeated, puzzled.

"Escape and evade," Caryn answered.

"Any force we can take on, we do so and eliminate it," Karl added. "I want to put the orc kingdom off balance until we can get the rest sorted out."

"What about those two?" Caryn asked, jerking a thumb at the two reposed warriors.

"Leave 'em," Karl said.

"What?" Gwenno exclaimed.

"They'll only slow us down," Caryn interrupted, immediately understanding Karl's position. "This place is relatively safe from orcs. We leave a guard or two with them to keep unwanted critters away."

"Exactly," Karl agreed with a nod. "We're going to come back this way and we'll pick them up on the way back."

"Yes, m'Lord," Gwenno replied, recognizing the wisdom of the order, but not looking forward to designating two "volunteers," knowing no one would want to stay behind and miss the action.

In the early afternoon, Raquel shook Karl awake.

"What?" he grunted, rubbing his eyes.

"Two wagons headed this way."

"How many orcs?"

"Just four."

"Tell Alva to set an ambush."

"You want some or one of us to go along?"

Karl paused for only a moment. "No. She can handle it." Seeing Raquel's unconvinced look, he added, "They were killing orcs long before we showed up."

"Are you sure?" she replied, raising an eyebrow. "This is only a game, remember."

"So we're all repeatedly told," he sourly responded. "The way I see it, real life isn't all that different. Now go tell Alva."

Forty-five minutes later, Alva returned and reported to Karl.

"It was a supply train, m'Lord," she said, as more of her unit carried casks of ale, grain sacks, and crated meat into the campsite. "I figured we could use the food. I unhitched the oxen like the last time and sent them on their way. We were careful not leave a trail to here."

"Well done," Karl complimented. "Distribute the food and ale amongst the units."

"The ale, m'Lord?" she questioned.

"Yes," he said, "even the ale. They may drink what they wish, but I expect them to be clear-headed and ready to move out when dusk arrives."

Alva straightened to full height. "They will all be ready, m'Lord."

Chapter 5

The attack on Braghurk mimicked the attack on Righul Khar and was accomplished just as quickly even though Braghurk was a bit larger. And just like at Righul Khar, they liberated a group of slaves, eight men and women captured from the bordering lands. Two of the men were from Beally.

The moment Eveen saw them, she burst away from Ben and leaped into the arms of a former slave, crying out, "Filib."

Ben awkwardly stared at the two as they hugged and showered each other with kisses, and not the kind one would give to a sibling or close friend.

Pausing to catch her breath, she remembered Ben and curled her hand for him to come over, all the while clinging to the man, a tall slender man in his early 30s.

"Oh Ben," she exclaimed with radiant joy. "This is Filib, my husband."

"Your hu... husband?" Ben stammered.

Turning back to Filib, she said, "I thought you were dead."

"As I did you," he solemnly replied. He gazed at Ben with cautious appreciation. "Thank you for saving her." Yet his appreciation disappeared when he turned his ardor back to his wife, effectively ignoring Ben

"You're welcome," Ben replied, his face a mask of indifference. Awkwardly turning, he headed back to where Karl was directing the follow up activities.

"There will be other opportunities," Karl commiserated.

"Why didn't she say she was married?" Ben groused.

Karl shrugged. "Who knows? It's moot now. Besides," he said, "I think it's time we headed back."

Ben looked back over his shoulder to briefly watch Eveen and Filib in animated conversation and the joyous celebration of their reunion. "Guess I'll head on out then."

"No," Karl stated. "I need you with us. Besides, I've someone I want to introduce you to."

"You do?" His eyes brightened. "Who?"

Karl waved him away. "That's all I'm going to say for the moment. I don't mean to be cryptic, but I have my reasons."

Ben's brows furrowed as he studied him a moment. "You making this up just to get my mind off of that?" He jerked a thumb towards Eveen and Filib.

"Not really," Karl replied. "I've had it in mind for a while, but when you and Eveen seemed interested in each other, I held my tongue. Now I don't have to. However, I don't want to give you false hopes, and I'd rather if anything develops that it happen naturally. Now that's really all I'm going to say about it."

Ben folded his arms and chewed his lip. "OK. But what about her and him?" He ticked his head at the engrossed couple. "Promised I'd take her back to Beally."

"I'll take care of that."

Assembling his force and the newly liberated slaves, he addressed the combined group.

"We've accomplished far more than I expected. As such, there is a change of plans. We're heading home to asset our rightful position and authority." He noticed a visible relief and excitement in the Mann soldiers. Addressing the former captives, he said, "You have a choice. Some of you are not from Mann. You are free to return to your own homes. However, my army and I will return to Mann. If you choose to return to Beally or any other town on the other side of the orc kingdom, you will proceed on your own. I will not provide escort anywhere other than back to Mann."

"But he promised to take me back to Beally," Eveen protested, gazing intently at Ben.

Before Ben or Karl could reply, Filib interrupted, "What's there to go back to? We've been gone so long that no one cares anymore, and we'd have to start again whether we were there or in Mann." He gazed affectionately at Eveen. "I say we start a new life in a new town." Receiving a loving nod of agreement, he turned to Karl. "We'll go with you to Mann."

"Good." Karl circled his finger in the air. "Let's get ready to move out. Same order of movement. I want a good steady pace. Let's get back to Mann as quickly as possible."

With the detour to pick up the two sleeping soldiers and their guards, Karl and his army found themselves dragging their feet and still in orc territory by the time dusk arrived.

"We need to stop and rest," Raquel said as they trudged along the road to the border. "Everyone's bone tired. The slaves are having trouble keeping up."

Karl turned to Caryn on his other side. "Your thoughts?"

Caryn did a quick glance up and down the road at the marching soldiers whose discipline showed. They marched steadily though they were exhausted.

"I agree with Raquel. If we were attacked now, we'd be hard pressed to fight our way out."

"Everyone's been awake for two days," Raquel pointed out. "They're not like you two. They need rest."

Karl felt the not-so-subtle sting in her retort and wondered if part of it was from jealousy. Regardless, they were getting close to Ryath-sari and could use the oppressiveness of the forest to help with security.

"We'll set up camp at Ryath-sari," he said. "I want tight perimeter security. No campfires, no unnecessary noise, the whole nine yards of making sure no one knows we are there."

"Yes, sir," Raquel answered and moved off to tell the others.

"She's not very happy right now," Caryn observed.

"Not my fault," he answered.

"But it is," she replied with a wry smile. "She's got it bad for you and she has to share you with two other women. And then she was once your dependable second in command until I showed up."

"You have experience where she doesn't," he said by way of explanation.

"That's not my point," Caryn said. "She feels she's been demoted, shunted to the side because of me."

"It can't be helped," Karl indifferently answered.

"Easy for you to say. You're not the one in her situation."

"So what do you suggest?" Karl was growing tired of placating so many personalities.

Caryn studied him for a moment then shrugged. "Eventually you're going to have to make a choice. While this harem approach is interesting, at some point in time, someone is going to want you all to herself."

"Like you?" He said it before he had a chance to think about it. But if she was offended, she hid it well.

Instead, a slight smile curled the corners of her lips. "I better go check on security."

"Remind each of our team to remain silent about what's above us," he said referring to the elven city.

"Of course," she replied.

Karl watched her saunter away, knowing she was right, yet unwilling to decide. Besides, there were more important things to worry about now.

Once the perimeter was secure, Karl called the leaders and his team together. "Our mission now is to liberate the Kingdom of Mann."

"How?" Gwenno asked.

"We march on Glenloch."

The effect was instant, but not what he wanted for instead of steely determination, their faces revealed their apprehension.

"Is it the sorceress Eleris you fear?" Karl asked, knowing the answer.

"Yes, m'Lord," Alva answered for the group. "She is powerful... very powerful."

"She can turn a man into a beast," Gwenno added.

Karl remembered his last incursion into Eleris's lair when he went to retrieve his sword. "That beast is dead. I killed it." *Though to be fair, he filled himself.*

"I knew it," Alva exclaimed. "Rumor spread that the beast was dead, but no one wanted to believe it. But I knew it was true because my cousin is stationed in Glenloch and he said she was really angry when you all escaped and the beast dead."

"That doesn't mean she can't do it again," Gwenno pointed out, "turn a man into a beast."

"You forget," Karl said with subtle pride, "that we have our own powerful sorceress. You saw her in action here."

"I ask your patience m'Lord," Gwenno ventured, "but wasn't she also a captive with you?"

"Touché," Annabeth stage whispered with a chuckle.

"But we did escape," Karl countered, "and here we are kicking orc ass. We will do the same to all who stand in our way. Now get some sleep. We leave at first light."

As the Mann leaders went to check on their troops, Annabeth sidled up beside Karl. "Very inspirational speech." She grinned impishly at him.

Shaking his head, he grinned back. "Get some sleep." He then glanced around for a place to settle himself, silently verifying his team's positions when he discovered he couldn't find Ben.

"Noble," he quietly called out.

"Yes?" The thief raised himself up from leaning against a tree and ambled over to stand before Karl.

"Yes."

"Ben's missing. I have an idea where he is. Would you mind checking upstairs?"

"Upstairs?" Noble frowned at him.

"Yes," Karl said, lowering his voice and repeating, "upstairs."

"Oh... ah, yes, I get it. I'll be back shortly."

Karl found a tree and sat down to get comfortable. He was just beginning to doze when Noble woke him.

"He said he'll be back in time."

"Was he where I expected?"

"Yeah. Quite comfortable too."

Karl shook his head, imagining a nice soft bed. "We'll get our chance to sleep when we get back into Mann."

"I was half-tempted to find my own bed."

"I need you here with us," Karl said with a yawn.

"And not Ben?" Noble questioned, raising an eyebrow.

"He's not as important to the mission as you are," Karl answered.

Flattered, Noble nodded. "Anything else you need?"

"No. Thanks."

"Any time," he replied with a half-smile and wandered back to his spot by the tree to curl up and sleep.

Karl's gaze briefly followed him as he walked away until the darkness swallowed his form. He then slowly scanned the surrounding area, listening intently for any sound revealing their presence. Satisfied, he settled beside a tree and for some reason Sakura came to mind and he wondered where she might be, which morphed into him wondering why she wasn't part of the 'spend a night with Karl' game. Not that he wanted additional partners. It was getting to the point where he really did need to make a choice. Still, Sakura was certainly attractive.   What was it about her that didn't generate the same arousal in him as with the others?   Loner. She was a loner, someone who preferred doing things her own way. Of all the members of his team, she had the innate ability to take care of herself.

The next thing he remembered was being shaken awake by Ben.

"They're lookin' for us," Ben announced.

Karl awoke to his surroundings and jerked up to standing. "How do you know?"

"I been out doin' some scouting."

"I thought you were asleep upstairs," Karl replied, scanning the proximity.   The forest was oppressively dark and he could barely make out the outline of those close to him.

"I was, but I got a wild hair and decided to do some lookin' around.   Figured I could get some sleep when we cross the border into Mann."

"So what's the status?"

"They got some good-sized patrols workin' the entire border and the roads headin' up to Krugrodh.   We got 'em good and scared, especially when they found all the weapons cut in half."

Karl frowned and stared at him. "How'd you learn all that?"

Ben tapped his nose with his forefinger. "I listen to 'em talkin'.   We're good here for the moment, but I wouldn't be surprised if they came up through here, even if they find the place spooky."

"We better alert the perimeter security."

No sooner had he spoke the words that Raquel appeared.

"There's a patrol about half an hour distant heading this way," she reported.

"I thought you were asleep," Karl said, walking over to waken Caryn who was already awake when she heard the voices.

"Couldn't get comfortable," Raquel answered. "Figured I'd scout around."

"What's up?" Caryn asked.

"Orc patrol heading this way," Karl replied then turned to Raquel. "How many?"

"Probably around thirty," she replied.

"Anything else?"

"They're noisy," Raquel dismissively answered. "I think they don't expect to find anything here."

"Or maybe they do and hope that by making a lot of noise, they'll scare off whoever is here," Caryn said. "Regardless, it works to our advantage."

Alva and Gwenno arrived, as did the rest of Karl's team.

"What's the plan, Boss?" Dieter asked.

"Part of me wants to eliminate them, while another part says to let them pass. If they believe nothing is here, it will add to their frustration in discovering where we are. Input."

"Let them pass," Caryn agreed. "We're too close to the border. We fight them now and they'll know we were here."

"I agree with her," Raquel said. "Besides, it's dark and a pitched battle in here might result in deaths on our side."

"And we have freed captives to consider," Annabeth added.

Karl turned to Sakura and Ben. "Your thoughts?"

"I know it's smarter to let them pass," Raquel said, shifting a glance at Ben, "but I can't help but want to commit mayhem on them."

"Ben?"

"Let 'em pass. We can always come back and give 'em hell."

"Noble?"

Startled that he was asked for input, the thief cleared his throat. "I'm all for whatever is safest for our folks."

"You two?" Karl said, turning his attention to Alva and Gwenno.

"We follow you, m'Lord," Alva replied.

"I know," Karl said, "but I want your input."

"Avoid contact," Gwenno said.

"Agreed," Alva said.

Karl slowly nodded and turned to Ben. "I need you to monitor their position and progress and get word back to us. We reposition based upon what you tell us." He then addressed the others. "If we are discovered, we attack without mercy. Annabeth will create enough light to give us an advantage. Position forward elements in a semi-circular defensive position, captives in the middle. We move and flow as one in relation to the patrol. Remember, we do not want to be seen. Annabeth in the middle with me, Raquel and Caryn on the flanks, Dieter in the middle, Noble in the center with the captives." He addressed the thief. "I need you to make sure our guests keep their yaps shut."

"Roger wilco," Noble said and saluted.

"Positions then," Karl commanded.

For the next half hour Ben flitted back and forth between monitoring the orc patrol and the base camp. Three times, they had to move their position to avoid the patrol, each time moving closer to the border.

At one point, they were close enough to hear the patrol.

"… don't like this place," a voice grumbled.

"Me neither," another voice mutely agreed.

"Shaddup, back there,"

Karl twisted his head at Annabeth and placed both hands to the side of his face and tilting his head imitating sleep.

Immediately understanding, she rapidly cast sleep spells on three of the orcs causing them to collapse on the ground in a deep slumber.

"What the hell," a voice burst as an orc tripped over the body and fell headlong into the orc in front, while two more orcs stumbled over the reposing patrol members.

"Halt," a commanding voice growled. "What goes on back there?"

"It's Burgash," a voice answered. "He's asleep."

"What?" the commanding voice snapped followed by the commotion of the head orc working his way back to the problem.

Two more voices called out, "Cagnok is too." "So is Urnoth."

"This place is cursed," other voices chimed in.

"Shaddup all of ya," the commanding orc ordered followed by silence as he prodded the prone orc with his foot. "Git up."

"I tried that already," the one orc peevishly said.

"Git up Burgash," the commander barked at him then ordered the one who had tripped over him, "Wake him up."

'I already tried, Voltog," he retorted. "You can see he's asleep. I tell you, this place is cursed. The sooner we leave here the better."

Karl tapped Annabeth on the shoulder and held up three fingers.

Annabeth muffled a snicker then cast three more sleep spells.

"By the gods below," an orc exclaimed, leaping away as the commander slumped to the ground, asleep.

"Let's get outta here before we're all cursed," yet another voice urged.

Karl was half-tempted to have Annabeth put spells on the entire patrol but knew the spells wouldn't last long enough. He held up three more fingers and Annabeth obliged.

Three more orcs slumped to the floor.

"I'm outta here," a voice cried out.

"What do we do with them?"

"Leave 'em."

"We can't leave 'em," a voice of reason spoke out. "Grab 'em and drag 'em outta this place."

For the next few minutes, a flurry of activity ensued as those of the patrol still standing grabbed feet or hands and dragged the nine away out of the offending forest. Annabeth was about to launch another set of spells for good measure when Karl grabbed her hand and shook his head, though smirking. As the voices and grunts diminished, Karl waited until Raquel and Ben returned with the news that the orc patrol was slowly making its way back to Righul Khar.

"Well done everyone," Karl said, "and a special thanks to our very own sorceress."

A quiet murmur of agreement floated in the air as Karl noted that the night was giving way to beginning morning nautical twilight.

He walked over to the two Mann commanders. "Alva. Gwenno. Get ready to move out."

By the time they arrived at the border zone, BMNT was giving way to civil twilight. Karl sent scouts north and south of the zone, ensuring the main body would cross undetected. When the scouts returned and reported 'all clear,' Karl lined up the entire unit within arms' length of each other. At his command, they raced across in one wave and reassembled on the other side.

Karl gathered the leaders in an impromptu planning session. Taking a knee, he cleared a space on the ground and drew a rough map with a stick

"We're here," he said, jabbing the stick in the ground. "Banvie is here." He jabbed the ground close to the indentation of their present position. "Alva and Gwenno. I want you to connect with Maddoc and assemble whatever forces he has at Banvie. Everyone here needs some rest, so we delay operations until tomorrow. But we move out tomorrow. Clear?"

"Yes, m'Lord," they responded together.

"Good. Take charge of your units and I'll see you tomorrow. I and the rest of my team will be in Banvie."

The Mann forces quickly disappeared, leaving Karl alone with his core team.

"I could use a beer," Noble commented.

"Me too," Ben brightly agreed. "Been too long since I had good ale."

Karl shifted his glance to see Caryn, Raquel, and Annabeth approach.

"Pick a number between one and a hundred, but don't tell us yet," Annabeth said.

"Why?" Karl asked, frowning.

"Just do it," Raquel coaxed.

"OK," Karl sighed, suddenly realizing where this was going. "I got one."

"Twenty-five," Annabeth said.

"Fifty-three," Raquel answered.

Caryn paused and measured the man. He looked tired and probably could use a good night's sleep. "One hundred," she replied, hoping he'd recognize that she was offering a peaceful night of sleep.

"It was ninety-seven," Karl announced to the disappointment of both Annabeth and Raquel. If Caryn was pleased, she didn't show it.

Smiling at Caryn and kissing her on the cheek, Annabeth said, "He's all yours." Turning to Raquel she hooked a thumb at Noble and Ben. "C'mon. Let's go get a brew with these two."

"Not so fast," Karl admonished. "We need to determine where we're staying. And Noble has a job to do tonight."

"Aw man," Noble moaned. "I'd forgotten all about him. Do I have to?"

"Yes," Karl firmly replied. "We'll talk about what you should say. Let's go find a place to stay."

As they headed to Banvie, Raquel scooted over next to Caryn. "We forgot about the Augury Stone thing. You can have him tomorrow night then."

"Or we can triple-team him," Annabeth said with an impish grin.

Caryn smiled sweetly at them. "Y'know, one of these days he just might say 'enough is enough' and tell us all to take a hike."

Annabeth leaned back to peer at Raquel whose look said she had already thought about that. "Naw," she reassured her. "It'll never happen."

At midnight, in the dim candlelight of the bedroom, Noble unwrapped his Augury Stone and set it on the table. In an instant, Kevin's haggard face popped into view.

"Where the hell have you been?" he snapped.

"I've been busy," Noble calmly replied, "and keep it down or you'll blow my cover." Noble frowned at him. "Dude, you look pretty rough. What's going on?"

"This damned kingdom is harder to control that I thought," he admitted. "Some jerk named Evnan controls the east half of the kingdom."

"What about Fraster and Kerr?" Noble asked. "I thought they were supposed to help."

"Those two?" Kevin sneered. "They're about as useful as a one-legged man in an ass kicking contest."

Noble snorted a laugh. "Doesn't Fraster have a monster or something?"

"Oh jeez, don't get me started," Kevin huffed. "All it is is a dead warrior that Fraster's necromancer sorceress brought back to life. It's not like he has any magical powers. You probably could even take him."

"Thanks for the vote of confidence," Noble sourly replied. "What about the rest of the PCs? They gotta be a big help."

Kevin leaned forward so that his face filled the orb. Lowering his voice, he said, "Can't trust 'em. Ross is OK. But Frank is so full of himself that I have to watch my back. The others are so-so. And this Gerard character is one whiney wuss. I'm half tempted to move on."

"Why don't you?"

It was if someone suddenly flicked a switch. "What the hell are you talking about," Kevin snarled. "Gimme your report."

Taken aback, Nobel quickly collected himself. "Not much *to* report. We've been out killing orcs."

"What?" Kevin frowned. "Where? Why?"

"In the orc kingdom," Noble shot back, "where else? As to why, the orcs have been raiding the border area of Mann, so Karl decided to help."

Kevin's frown deepened. "What game is he playing?" he muttered.

"Dunno," Noble shrugged. "He seems quite content to hang around here, building up support among the common folk."

"He's wasting time," Kevin mused. "Why...?"

"Like I said before, he doesn't exactly confide in me, or anyone else for that matter. He keeps things pretty close to the chest until he's made a decision and we do what he's decided."

"Where are you now?"

"In a little town called Banvie. We're hanging out here for a while, sort of resting for a bit after the recent orc affair."

"Then what?"

"Not really sure. There's this guy named Maddoc. We're waiting for him to show up."

"Why?"

"How the hell do I know? I told you already that he keeps things to himself. I'll let you know once I find out."

Kevin nodded pensively. "What about the others."

"They're still pretty mad at you. In fact, I'm still not sure the pain of respawning was worth the hassle of this whole 'keeping track of Karl' scheme."

"You'll get your reward," Kevin reminded him.

"That's what I'm afraid of," Noble mumbled.

"What?" Kevin scowled.

"I said, what about the others?"

"What others?"

"Those back there with you," Noble pointed out. "What have you promised them?"

"None of your business," Kevin shot back. "You just do what I tell you."

"For the record," Noble stated, "I expect a whole lot more than they get. I'm the one running all the risks."

"Don't worry, you're gonna get what's coming to you," Kevin replied. "Contact me when you get more information."

Noble's globe went blank, and he wrapped the cloth around it as Karl and Caryn emerged from the shadows.

"Good job," Karl complimented. "The man's getting desperate. My guess is that the others are getting bored hanging around."

"Frank can be a pain in the ass regardless of location," Caryn reminded him.

Karl turned to Noble. "Get some sleep. We're leaving in the morning."

"Where to now?" he complained.

"Glenloch," he smiled. "You've a magical stone to steal."

It was midmorning by the time Maddoc arrived with the rest of his Eagle's Claw Brigade. Karl called the leaders into a war council and explained the mission.

"My team and I will act as a sort of silent and unseen advance party. Maddoc and his forces will follow half-a-day behind. Initial rally point is Lyster day after tomorrow." Gazing directly at the brigade commander, he said, "I want everyone to know you are marching on Glenloch, so make it as obvious as possible."

"But that will announce your intentions and most likely give away your position, m'Lord, Maddoc counseled.

"Yes, I know," he said then turned to Noble and Annabeth, "which means you have a short window of opportunity to accomplish what we need."

Noble swallowed hard and shifted a worried glance at Annabeth who seemed quite unaffected.

"My team will move out at dusk," Karl said to Maddoc. "You and your regiment will leave tomorrow at first light."

"Yes, m'Lord."

Karl dismissed Maddoc and his subordinate leaders and turned to his team. "Get whatever additional rest you need. I want to be at Lyster while it's still dark."

"Why the secrecy?" Ben asked.

"Noble and Annabeth have a special mission," Karl answered, "and we need to give them all the help we can."

Ben was about to ask, 'What secret mission,' but decided he'd find out soon enough. Besides, there was an ale with his name on it in the nearby tavern.

The trip to Lyster was uneventful as honest folk were either at the pubs or relaxing in their homes, leaving the road to Lyster deserted. When they arrived, they discovered Lyster consisted of about three dozen homes arranged around a crossroad. Further scouting revealed a single two-story tavern. As dawn was still an hour away, Karl sent Raquel to find a way into the pub. She returned twenty minutes later.

"Back door to the kitchen is open," she reported.

"It was unlocked?" Noble blurted.

"I didn't say that," she replied, turning to lead the way.

Once inside, she led the way through the kitchen to the tavern proper. A dozen tables with chairs stacked on top were arranged in the room. A large fireplace sat opposite the main door. A door close to the fireplace led to the rooms upstairs. Another door off the kitchen led to the taverner's lodgings.

"Nobody's upstairs," she whispered to Karl. "There are eight rooms, two large ones with eight beds apiece, and six smaller ones with single beds."

"Wonder where the serving girls sleep?" Ben muttered.

"Not our problem," Dieter answered.

"Find a room," Karl ordered, "and be quiet."

Raquel again led the way upstairs. Deciding to keep the company in one room, Karl opted for one of the large rooms, one with a window that overlooked the back of the tavern.

"Settle down and find a spot to rest," he said. "Rotating shift. I'll take the first shift. I'll be downstairs."

"Need company?" Caryn asked.

"Not yet. I'll wake you when the time comes."

Leaving them to get comfortable, Karl headed back down the stairs and scoped out the tavern and the relation of the front door to the kitchen and upstairs doors. Walking over to the bar counter, he retrieved a mug from the shelf then held it under the spigot on an ale keg. Pouring a frothy brew, he took a sip, nodding in appreciation of an excellent ale though wishing he had a cup of coffee instead. He then headed over to a table in a corner, scooted out a chair and sat, his back to the wall.

Dawn had long rimmed the shuttered windows when he heard rustling in the kitchen and the bouquet of coffee wafted beneath the kitchen door. The door opened and the taverner, a stocky middle-aged man whistling a drinking song, ambled in, a mug of coffee in his hands.

"Smells good," Karl commented, causing the man to yelp and drop his mug which bounced on the floor, spilling its contents.

"Whaddaya want," the frightened man exclaimed. "I got no money and what I got ain't here."

"Relax," Karl said standing, causing the man to tremble even more. "I and my friends need your help."

"Your friends?" he said, glancing around the otherwise empty tavern.

"They're upstairs asleep." Karl walked over to the bar counter and placed two stacks of gold coins on top. "The first stack is for the lodging and food. The second stack is for ensuring no one knows we are here."

Staring at the coins, the taverner's fright evaporated. "It will be as you desire, good sir."

"We will stay out of the way and upstairs. There are seven of us. Ensure there is plenty of food and ale sent up. Is there another way down from upstairs without coming through the tavern here?"

"No," the man replied, scooping up the coins before the tall Viking changed his mind. "But I can arrange for a ladder to be placed by the window."

"That will suffice," Karl said then gave him a cold smile. "A warning, good friend. If word gets out that we are here, it will go ill for you and those who reveal our presence. Understood?"

"Perfectly," he said, bobbing his head. "Um…" he grinned solicitously. "Perhaps a little more, you know… to help guarantee the rest of my staff see the wisdom in maintaining their silence."

"How many are we talking about?"

"Well, there's the cook and the four serving girls."

Karl looked around the room. "You're that busy?"

"We get business form Glenloch on a regular basis," he assured him.

"That's five," Karl said and counted out five gold pieces. "Warn them."

"Of course, my Lord," he replied with an avaricious grin.

"Remember," Karl intoned, "your neck is on the line if they fail."

The taverner heard the threat and swallowed his smile.

"How far is it from here to Glenloch?" Karl asked.

"Not more than a two-hour journey."

"Good," Karl nodded. "When is breakfast served?"

"Breakfast begins at nine," he replied, "but as soon as the cook arrives, I'll have her prepare something for you and your friends."

"Leave it a nine," Karl said then leaned forward and locked his gaze on the man. "There's an extra five gold for you if your silence lasts until the day after tomorrow."

The taverner's eyes brightened. "You can count on me, m'Lord."

Satisfied he made enough of an impression, Karl climbed the stairs to the back bedroom. Attempting to open the door, he found it locked from the inside.

"Damn."

Before he had a chance to head back downstairs for a key, Caryn opened the door.

"Figured it was you, but you never know. When I heard the 'damn,' I knew it was you. What's the status?"

"Breakfast at nine for those who want it, to be served up here," he replied with a yawn, glancing around the room at the rest who were in various poses of repose. "No one leaves here or goes downstairs." Yawning again, he rubbed his eyes. "Get some sleep."

"I'm awake," she said with a nonchalant shrug. "You go ahead."

Unwilling to argue, he shuffled over to an empty bed, unhooked his sword and belt, and stretched out on the bed, the sword and belt next to him, while Caryn sat on the floor and leaned back against the door.

An hour later, a knock on the door startled Caryn and she jerked up to standing. "Yes?" she cautiously said.

"Breakfast," came the reply from the other side of the door.

"Leave it on the floor in front of the door."

"Are you sure?"

"Do it."

"OK."

Caryn listened and waited. When she heard the muted footsteps lessen then disappear, she pried the door open. A mixed bouquet of coffee, hot bread and sausage spilled into the room.

"Need help?" Annabeth softly called out.

"You're awake," Caryn replied with a smile, glancing back over her shoulder.

"I'm a light sleeper," Annabeth replied, walking over. "When I heard the knock, I had a spell ready just in case."

"Appreciate you having my back," Caryn answered, reaching down for one of the trays.

"Least I could do for a friend," Annabeth said with a mischievous grin. "We're gonna need more coffee," she opined when she saw the size of the urn.

Between the two, they carried the three trays of food, cups, plates, utensils, and coffee urn to a small table by the window at the far wall.

The aroma of coffee penetrated through the somnolence of the others and soon everyone was awake and up, mug in hand, waiting for their turn at the urn. Annabeth filled two mugs and handed one to Caryn who already had a mug of her own.

"For our imperial leader," Annabeth grinned, ticking her head at Karl who sat on the edge of the bed, rubbing his eyes.

Surprised that she willingly relinquished that little act of intimacy, Caryn gave her a warm smile and headed over to Karl.

"With the compliments of our sorceress," she said, shooting a quick smile at Annabeth who raised her mug in salute.

Whatever exchange was happening between Annabeth and Caryn was lost on Karl who simply took the proffered mug and imbibed a satisfying sip then another.

"Ah, the elixir of life," he cooed. Realizing everyone was up, he said, "Here's the game plan folks. We all stay out of sight, which means we hang out in the room here today. In the meantime, we need to get Annabeth and Noble into the city this afternoon, undetected."

"You ain't gonna do that with the way they look," Ben commented.

"Exactly," Karl agreed, "which means they need to look like everyday folks."

"Which means we need different clothes," Annabeth added, "hopefully ones that fit."

"Wait here," Karl said and headed out the door and down the stairs. As it was still early, the tavern was empty. The taverner was taking the chairs off the tables when he heard the door open.

Karl curled a finger at him.

"Yes, m'Lord."

"I need your help. Come upstairs with me."

"Yes, m'Lord," he replied with a solicitous smile.

Once inside the bedroom, the taverner smiled, his eyes lingering over the women before blinking wide when Dieter stood up, the top of his head close to the ceiling.

"We need clothing for her and him," Karl said, pointing to Annabeth and Noble, "clothes that will fit."

The taverner sized up the two. "The man will be easy. The lady a bit more difficult, if you know what I mean." He winked and curled his hands over his chest.

"Do your best. We need them by lunch time."

"Lunch time?" he exclaimed.

Karl reached in his belt and pulled out a small bag of coins and poured out a handful. Counting out ten, he dropped them into the taverner's outstretched hand. "Remember –"

"No one shall know, m'Lord," he answered, bobbing his head.

The man was back before lunch, carrying two sacks. "The man's clothes were easy," he explained. "We just looked for a lad his size."

"Hey," Noble objected.

"Small does not mean less powerful," the taverner spoke then rolled his eyes. "My former missus was a little one who could put the fear of the gods in those three times her size."

"Yeah, whatever," Noble huffed, opening the bag and pulling out a scruffy pair of leggings and urchin's smock. Holding up the smock, he curled a lip. "I gotta wear this?"

"Yes," Karl replied. "What about you?" he said to Annabeth who held up a peasant's skirt and blouse and cloak.

"It's the best we could do, m'Lord," the taverner apologized. "The cloak should hide her well enough."

"It'll have to do," Karl said with a nod. "Now we need that ladder."

"At once, m'Lord."

Karl waited until the taverner left then said, "Let's do it."

There was an awkward pause as both Noble and Annabeth stared at the others.

"Oh well," Annabeth said with a shrug and promptly began removing her clothing, momentarily stunning the men to overt voyeurism when she removed her top.

Karl cleared his throat and turned to Noble. "C'mon. The clock's ticking."

Noble did a quick glance around the room before heading to a corner and facing it so that the rest of the team could only see his backside, unaware that the rest of the team was still watching Annabeth.

By the time the sorceress and thief were dressed, the ladder leaned against the tavern.

"OK," Karl said. "You both know what to do."

"Are you sure this is such a smart idea?" Noble replied, unconvinced.

"We need the stone and you two are the only ones who can get it," Karl said. "Stay out of sight until you know it's time."

"Easy for you to say," Noble groused.

"Quit cher bellyachin' and c'mon," Annabeth said, hands on her hips. "If you're good, I might let you take a peek at the girls again." She thrust her chest out at him.

"Lot of good that'll do when she turns us into monsters," he griped, though staring at her chest.

"That's why she's going with you," Karl admonished. "Listen to her. Now get going."

Chapter 6

Annabeth and Noble melded into the throng of merchants, peasants, farmers, and other visitors working their way in and out the main gates. Four guards posted at the outside entrance scrutinized individuals, their intense stares occasionally falling on someone who, to them, looked either too suspicious or overly calm and relaxed. Naturally, their attention soon diverted to the two newcomers, a short peasant accompanying a tall slender woman whose ample figure was not well hidden by the cloak.

"You there," a gruff thick-bodied guard called out. "Come here."

Annabeth turned to the guard and pointed to herself. "Me?"

"Yes, you," he firmly replied, "and the little man too."

"We're toast," Noble muttered under his breath.

"Of course," Annabeth politely replied with a circular wave of her hand, causing the guard to slump to the ground, fast asleep. "C'mon," Annabeth urged, grabbing Noble by the elbow as the other guard burst "What the hell?" and dropped to his knees. The other two guards forced their way through the crowd, giving Annabeth and Noble sufficient time to work their way through the gate house and into the city proper.

"That was too damn close," Noble complained, sucking in a deep breath.

"We're here," Annabeth reassured him. "Let's find a place to roost, preferably not the same as the last time we were here." She flashed a grin and led the way through the main streets and then the back ways until she came to a small inn called 'The Stag's Head' with the requisite stag's head carved in the sign.

"This will do," she said and pushed through the door, tripping a bell attached to a trip bar. Beyond the dull ringing of the bell, a thick silence greeted them as they stepped inside. The inn's main tavern room was deserted. The number of tables and chairs and the length of the bar counter was a silent reminder of what was once a thriving business. Though dust layered most of the tables, there was a neatness to the room with everything in its place, the ale mugs on the shelves behind the bar in orderly rows, the chairs tucked and arranged under the tables in symmetrical design. It looked as though whoever owned the place simply walked off and no one had entered since.

"You sure?" Noble said, curling a lip.

The door to the kitchen opened and an attractive diminutive woman, a little taller than Noble, stepped out, a small bucket in hand

"Good day to you," she said with a charming smile. Her voice was warm and inviting.

The moment Noble saw her, he was smitten. She appeared to be a smaller version of Annabeth, well-proportioned with long black hair.

"You don't seem to be very busy," Annabeth said, glancing around the empty room.

"That's because everyone has been warned away," she said, stepping behind the counter and taking up a damp rag and wiping the counter.

"Why?" Noble asked, walking over to stand on the opposite side of the counter where she cleaned.

"Because I angered a certain witch," she replied, her lips tight, "when I refused to bend to her demands."

"What happened?" he said, brushing off a stool and sitting.

The woman tilted her head and stared at them. "I'm surprised you made it past the spell."

"What spell?" Annabeth asked, frowning that she didn't detect any spell when they entered.

"The one surrounding my inn, the one that Eleris placed on it warning no one to enter."

Annabeth summoned a quick Detect Magic divination spell and found nothing. "Are you sure the spell is still working?"

The woman's shoulders slumped, and she shook her head. "Perhaps not anymore. No sense to prolong the inevitable. By now, most people know to avoid my inn."

"Looks like you used to be a busy place," Noble remarked.

"We were," she ruefully replied.

"What happened?" Annabeth asked, sitting beside Noble.

"There was a time when my husband and I experienced all the joys of a prosperous business."

"You're married," Noble said, disappointed.

"I was once," she said, her voice turning hard, "until she came."

"Eleris?"

"Yes," she snipped, "may she rot in hell where she belongs."

"What did she do?" he asked.

The woman paused as she ruminated her past. "She destroyed my life is what she did."

"How?"

The woman stared intently at him. "But I forget my manners and my responsibilities. My name is Aylish. I have no ale, but I do have wine. And I can fix you something to eat."

"I'm not hun –" Noble began when Annabeth elbowed him in the side.

"That would be wonderful," she sweetly said. "Noble here is a wine connoisseur."

"Ah," Aylish smiled. "My husband, may he rest in peace, was likewise. Wait here."

While Aylish disappeared into the kitchen, Noble looked up at Annabeth. "What did you hit me for?"

"You really are clueless aren't you," she sniffed, shaking her head. "Men. Can't you see the woman's lonely?"

"What do you expect me to do about it? She's still mourning her dead husband."

"Find out more," she said, lifting her hands towards the door. "Get to know her. She's quite attractive."

"That she is," Noble readily agreed. Looking back over his shoulder, he said, "Wonder what she did to piss off the witch?"

"Why don't you find out?"

"I'm gonna. Just gimme a chance."

The door opened and Aylish returned, carrying a tray with three glasses.

"Thought I might as well join you. Here, tell me what you think." She set a glass before Noble then handed one to Annabeth.

Noble lifted the glass, gently swirled the liquid then inhaled the bouquet. "Hmmm... has the nose of a Bordeaux, hints of blackberry, coffee bean and something else." Taking a sip, he savored the taste, his eyes widening. "By the gods, this is awesome. Better than –"

Annabeth elbowed him again.

"Ow," he winced. "Stop it. I was gonna say better than the wines in so many other places we've been."

Aylish studied the two, giving them more than a curious glance. "Why do you keep hitting him?"

"Because sometimes he needs a little prodding," she sighed, "like most men do."

Aylish laughed then pointed a finger back and forth at them. "Are you two...?"

"Good God no," Annabeth replied, immediately understanding. "We're partners not lovers."

"Only in her dreams," Noble remarked, irritated at her quick dismissive response.

Aylish rewarded him with smirk. "So what brings two partners to my lowly tavern?"

"Just passing through," Annabeth answered.

'Just passing through," Aylish repeated. "Of all the inns and taverns in Glenloch, my little out of the way place suited you best."

"Yes," Annabeth replied with a smile.

"You were gonna tell us about how Eleris destroyed your life," Noble interrupted.

Aylish turned somber and sipped her wine, silence reigning.

"If you'd rather not," Annabeth began.

"No," Aylish said, "it's OK. The witch has spies throughout the kingdom and especially in the city here. What would it matter if she heard my angry words? She already ruined my life. What more could she do?"

Taking a deep swallow, she said, "I was married to the most handsomest man in the kingdom. His name was Nycol. We shared a love like no other. We were happy and prosperous. Though we had no children, this tavern became our joy and we worked hard to make it work. Believe it or not," she said taking in the room, "this place used to be filled with laughter and song. We had eight serving girls and the rooms upstairs were always filled. Our cook was the best in Glenloch. Even the ale and wine were the best."

She downed the rest of her glass and refilled it. "Then she came."

"Eleris?" Noble said.

Aylish nodded. "She saw my love and decided she wanted him for herself. But he was true to me. She sent him presents, found ways to get him alone, but he never yielded to favors, beautiful as she was. In time, she heard the gossip, the titters, the quiet mocking that said she wasn't as beautiful as she thought, that true love was something she couldn't overcome, and it made her angry. By now, she was the king's sorceress, his witch, though everyone knew she ran the kingdom. So one day she summoned my husband and right there before the very eyes of the palace guards, transformed him into a hideous monster. His only salvation was if he confessed he loved her more than any other and yielded to her bed. This he could not do. But she already knew that and so condemned him to a life of torture."

"Did you ever try to see him?" Noble asked.

"Every day. Though his appearance had changed, his soul had not, and I loved him all the more for it." She took another swallow. "Finally, when she saw her machinations had failed, she decided to curse me as well by destroying the one thing he and I had worked so hard for." She waved a hand at the interior of the tavern.

"What happened to your husband?"

"Not long ago, a Viking appeared with his band of followers. They said he carried a magical sword, the sword of the rightful king. I never saw him or the sword, but I heard that she had him and his friends imprisoned. They say that she tried to take the sword, but no one can lift it except the true owner. I heard that the sword lay on the floor in her chambers and no one could pick it up, not even her with all her sorcery. Even more shocking is that they escaped, the sword with them. I then learned that my husband was dead, killed by the Viking. At least that is what the witch said happened. If so, then he did my husband a favor, for death was his only release."

Annabeth and Noble shared a knowing glance that did not go unnoticed.

"And now you two arrive, quite unexpectedly," she mused. "I think there is far more to you two than you are willing to reveal."

"We're just looking for a quiet out of the way place to spend the night," Annabeth said with a polite smile.

"Then you've come to the right place," Aylish remarked. "Eleris's place is not more than five minutes from here. I can show you the quickest way."

"Who said we were going to Eleris's place?" Annabeth challenged.

"No one did," Aylish replied. "I was merely making an observation."

"Ah," Annabeth nodded and smiled.

"Another observation is that there seems to be an increase in the number of guards patrolling around her dwelling, but they are easily bypassed as they tend to stick to routines and specific routes."

"Another interesting observation," Annabeth said, looking at Noble, "don't you think?"

"I think all the time," Noble joked, "one of my many bad habits." He turned to Aylish. "This place needs a little sprucing up, don't you think? How about the little lady here and I help you clean it up a bit?"

"You are guests," Aylish firmly replied.

"No," Noble interrupted, cutting her off. "We are friends." He stared intently at her. "And friends help friends."

Aylish returned his gaze. "I would rather my friends help me in other ways."

"We'll see what we can do," he cryptically replied.

"I thought so," she acknowledged, taking his wine glass from him. "You should not be fuzzy when you decide to help me."

Momentarily disappointed at not finishing this excellent vintage, he smiled when she said, "I'll have plenty more for you when you return."

"How do you know we're going anywhere?" Annabeth objected.

Aylish flashed a knowing smile. "I'm not a fool. Both of you are not what you pretend. Take you for instance." She narrowed her gaze at Noble. "You're obviously not a peasant, nor a merchant, nor a commoner. Few people can discern a wine like you did. Likewise, except for the very rich, few can afford the wine I offered. And then there's you," she said, redirecting her gaze at Annabeth. "You are far from a commoner. You are beautiful and mysterious yet have the aura of one in complete control. You remind me of her."

"Eleris?" Noble blurted.

"Yes," Aylish answered, staring at Annabeth.

Annabeth blithely smiled at her. "For now, the less you know, the better. However, we will take you up on the offer to lead us to her place."

"It will be my pleasure," Aylish replied.

It was midnight when they stood in the murky shadows across the wide street from the colonnaded edifice that housed Eleris's quarters. Two sets of guards patrolled the perimeter, passing each other at regular intervals.

"You probably should head back now," Noble whispered to Aylish, his protective attitude obvious.

The inn keeper nodded then gently touched him on the arm. "Will I see you again?"

"You can count on it," he confidently replied. "You promised me another glass of that wine."

"I'll have it waiting for you." She squeezed his arm. "Be careful."

"I will."

Their eyes locked on each other and for an awkward moment, neither moved.

Aylish broke the spell by reaching out and placing a tender hand on his face. "Good fortunes to you both." She then scooted back and silently moved off into the shadows.

With a longing sigh, Noble watched her disappear into the night then turned to the task at hand, his confidence suddenly waning. "You know it's probably got a spell protecting it," he nervously warned Annabeth.

"That's why I'm here with you," she reassured him. "We've been through this before."

"Yeah, yeah, I know," he sighed in frustration. "Just wanna make sure you know you gotta check it out first."

"We have to find it first," she reminded him. "I'm going to cast Spider's Touch on you. I don't know if you'll need it, but it might come in handy."

"Thanks. What about you?"

"I've got other things I want to try," she grinned.

"Now?" he blurted.

"With the Spider's Touch spell. You ready?"

Noble took a deep breath and nodded.

They waited until the two sets of guards passed each other just outside the main doors. They paused to chat.

"Not now, damn it," Noble grimaced.

Fortunately, they didn't pause long and resumed their rounds. It was when they disappeared around the sides of the building that Annabeth and Noble raced across the road and up the steps.

The main doors to the building were locked, causing Noble to mutter a curse. "They're expecting us," he whispered. "The last time we were here, the doors were open. Remember?"

"That was then," Annabeth whispered back with a nonchalant shrug. "But these doors aren't magic. You're the thief. Hurry up and open them before they come back and discover us here."

Noble grimaced but yielded, withdrawing a small leather case from his belt bag. Opening it, he pulled out a lock pick set and tension tool, inserting them into the keyhole. Five seconds later he twisted the handle.

"That was fast," Annabeth complimented.

"Let's hope the rest is as easy," he replied.

Pushing through the doors, they tiptoed into the large wide wood-paneled room with a tall arched ceiling, silently closing and locking the door behind them. At this hour, the room was empty and oppressively silent. Moonlight filtered down through the wide ceiling skylights, casting a soft illumination to the entire room.

The waiting area by the wall with its four rows of ten chairs each was empty. Annabeth walked over to the pedestal podium at the front of the waiting area and flipped up the number on the small take-a-number dispenser.

"We're number 62," she grinned.

"Real funny," Noble whispered back, ready to be done with this whole affair. Quietly padding over to the doors leading to Eleris's quarters, he tried the door handle. "Damn. Locked."

"C'mon master thief, this is child's play for you," Annabeth teased, gliding silently to stand next to him. She waved a hand at the door. "It's not magically locked."

Out came Noble's lock pick set and again, five seconds later it was unlocked. He shot a hand up as warning. "Remember what Karl told us about the time he was in here?"

"That's because she had his sword," she reminded him. "There's nothing in there now."

"Famous last words," he said, his face betraying his doubt.

Gingerly opening the door, he poked his head through to see the dying embers from the two hearths cast flickering dim light, enough light for him to see the rest of the vast empty room. At the rear was the raised dais with the throne chair in the center. Straining to see in the hazy darkness, he finally discerned the single door to the left side of dais.

Cautiously entering, he was jolted to anxiety when Annabeth breezed by him and strode to the center of the room. He quickly closed the door behind him and locked it.

"There's nothing in here," she whispered, "though I can feel the presence of magic-that-once-was. Come. We've little time to waste."

At that moment the far door creaked and Noble leaped away from the door and crawled up the wall, wedging himself into the shadows in the corner of the ceiling. Looking down he was glad that he remembered to lock the door. Yet when his eyes went to find Annabeth, she was nowhere to be seen.

The door creaked again and opened, and two guards entered. One was a half a head taller than the other.

"I coulda swore I heard talkin'" the taller guard said.

"I didn't hear nuthin'" the shorter one replied with obvious boredom. "This has got to be the most mind-numbing assignment I ever did. Ever since she heard about that Karl fella, she's been on edge."

"You'd be too if'n he was comin' to take your kingdom. We better look around."

"What's to see?" the shorter one complained. "The damned place is empty."

"Let's check the door."

The shorter guard uttered a pained 'this-is-a-waste-of-time' sigh but followed. Striding reluctantly across the room, he stopped at the door where the guard twisted the handle.

"Locked," the taller guard announced.

"Duh," the other responded. "We locked it ourselves a couple o' hours ago."

"Wonder if we should check the outer doors to the building," the taller guard said, beginning to unlock the door.

Noble's tension mounted as he worried trying to remember if he had relocked the main doors to the building.

"What for?" the other guard argued. "We're unlocking a door to go check to see if another door is locked. That's stupid. There ain't nuthin on the other side of this door except the waiting room."

"There's doors leading to the other offices," the taller one countered.

"So what? There's nuthin in them either. And what do you suppose would happen if we go through this door and she happened to wonder where we are. She comes in here and we ain't here and you know there'd be hell to pay." He shuddered. "And I sure as hell don't wanna be turned into some gross monster like Nycol. Poor bastard."

The taller guard's hand jerked back from the doorknob. "Good point." He turned around and did a quick scan of the rest of the room. "Nuthin here."

"Like I said all along," the shorter guard affirmed. "Let's finish the round. I got a pork sandwich back in the office callin' my name."

As they leisurely strolled back to the door by the dais, the taller guard said, "Wonder why she's got us patrolling the hallways around her bedroom. Ain't never done that before. It was always good enough just to walk the perimeter."

"She's probably scared he's gonna sneak in here and try and kill her."

"She's a sorceress," the taller one replied. "What's she gotta be scared of?"

"You believe the prophecy?" the shorter guard asked, reaching for the doorknob.

The taller guard lowered his voice. "I'd be real careful about sayin' stuff like that, especially around here."

The shorter guard mumbled a "Yeah, you're right," as the door closed behind them.

Noble remained perched in the corner, until Annabeth materialized in the middle of the room.

"You can come down now," she whispered.

Climbing down off the wall, he tiptoed over to her. "How'd you do that?"

"Invisibility shield," she replied. "I have to hold it in front of me, but it picks up the background so that I'm invisible. When I hit level 4 skills, it becomes a cloak that I can wear and move around better. But that will be a while," she smiled, "especially if we're staying on this island the next thousand years."

Noble pulled out and unfolded the hand drawn map, holding it close to scrutinize. "Once we're through the door there, we head off to the right." He held it up for her to see.

Annabeth studied a moment. "A right, two lefts and a right again, and we're there."

"Yeah," he fretted, "and the hallway goes on to the guard room."

"We hit there first and I'll put the sleep hex on them."

Noble gazed up at her and frowned. "You're pretty calm for all this."

"This is kinda fun," she answered with a smile.

Noble stared at her a moment longer then simply shook his head. "You are one strange lady. C'mon."

His lock picks were out before they reached the door and the door lock yielded to his finesse.

"Voila," he whispered.

"Viola?" she replied with an impish grin.

Ignoring her, he poked his head through and checked up and down the hallway, curling his fingers at her, telling her it was all clear.

Initially leading the way, Noble's jitters increased when Annabeth passed him and picked up the pace and he found himself double-timing to keep up.

"What's the rush?" he hoarsely whispered.

"We're taking too long," she replied, not slowing down. "Get in, get out, as quickly as possible. That's what Karl said to do."

"Well Karl ain't here," Noble sourly answered, "and my legs aren't as long as yours are."

Annabeth stopped when they came to the corner. "Do your best," she said, slowly sliding her head around. "Clear."

Noble again found himself jogging to keep up.

Two left turns later, they were in the hallway that passed Eleris's bedroom. At the far end, the hallway intersected another hallway. Light spilled out from the open door to the guard room at the intersection.

Annabeth shifted a glance to Nobel and held a finger to her lips.

Noble returned the look and silently mouthed, "Duh."

Annabeth took off again, breezing by Eleris's door on the right, the lone disruption in the entire smooth walled hallway, Noble racing to keep up. She slowed down as they approached the intersection, stopping and checking the connecting hallway before slipping across to stand and listen outside the door.

They were talking, the one guard commenting on the price of pork these days. Annabeth waved a hand, casting a sleep spell. She heard a thump and a grunt.

Poking her head around the door jam, she saw them at a small table in the center of the room. The taller guard had fallen off his chair and lay curled up asleep on the floor. The other's head rested on the table, his arms draped by his side, the pork sandwich on the floor, having slipped from his hand. Both softly snored.

Turning, Annabeth flicked her eyebrows. "It's show time."

Heading back to the lone door in the hallway, Annabeth quietly commented, "I doubt she put magic on this door. Guards gotta be able to barge in when necessary."

"Or they could just knock," Noble argued, "which means there could still be a hex on the door."

Annabeth shook her head. "There isn't. I cast a Detect spell and I get nothing, at least not here."

"That's not very reassuring," he griped, pulling out the lock picks. To his surprise, the door opened in only a few seconds. "This ain't right. If she's supposed to be so paranoid, this is too easy."

"Maybe you're just real good," Annabeth encouraged.

"Yeah, but not like this. Something don't smell right."

"C'mon. We got a job to do."

Noble opened the door and light from the hallway spilled into the room.

Annabeth noted the layout of the room was just like Gwen's in Westhaven, even down to the positioning of the furniture. At the far end of the room, to the side of the grand hearth was the door to Eleris's bedroom. Her first thought was to wonder if Eleris had a secret entrance in the mirror like Gwen. Her second thought was that she prayed the evil sorceress was asleep.

Silently gliding up to the bedroom door, she felt the presence of magic grow as she approached, but it was not in the door.   Trying the handle, the door was not locked. Offering a silent prayer that Eleris was in undisturbed sleep, she conjured up and cast a deep slumber spell.

Opening the door, she led the way.

Embers rippled in the hearth, casting a low light throughout the room.   She noticed a bed large enough for four to sleep comfortably together. *Focus, Annabeth*, she grinned.

Eleris lay on her back in the center, her head on a pillow, her arms outside the covers.   Her chest moved in the slow rhythm of one in a deep sleep.

Annabeth scanned the room, searching for the Delf Stone.   Her searching paused on a large wall mirror opposite the bed then stopped on a small picture hanging on the wall beside the bed.   Creeping around the bed, she came to the picture and gently pried it away from the wall, noting the combination lock to a wall safe.   With a frown she knew it would take both her and Noble to open it.   It was then she had her epiphany.

Silently placing the picture back against the wall, she padded over to the mirror and slid a hand into it, grinning in triumph as it passed through the mirror.   Curling her fingers at Noble, she led the way into the mirror and onto the small platform enclosed by the stone of the castle.   To the side, a set of spiral stairs descended into darkness, the weak light coming through the mirror the only light in tiny anteroom.

Only then did she notice that Noble was not with her. Stepping halfway through the mirror she grabbed his arm and yanked him through, jamming a finger against her lips as warning.

As she prepared to descend, Noble grabbed her arm and shook his head, jabbing a thumb back to the room.

Annabeth nodded her head in response that she understood, but insisted they continue. Without waiting for a response, she began the familiar descent into the darkness that was pushed away by a soft glow emanating from the stone wall by the steps creating a dizzying corkscrew.

They continued in silence until they hit another platform with a thick iron door to the side. It was barred and locked on this side.

"Where are we going?" Noble whispered.

"To get help," she answered.

"Huh?" he frowned.

"I'll explain in a bit," she answered. "Wonder where this leads." She pointed to the barred door then continued the descent to finally arrive in the middle of a large circular room, lit by the same low glowing stone lights at the edges where the ceiling and walls met.

"This is just like Gwen's place," she said with confidence.

"What are you talking about?" he huffed. "How did you know about the mirror?"

"Like I said, it's just like the one at Gwen's place."

Noble glanced around, his worry growing as there were at least a dozen doors recessed in the wall surrounding the stairs.

"All except one are false doors," Annabeth explained. "Take the wrong door and you're screwed."

"What?" Noble burst.

"They all lead to traps and a lingering death."

"How the hell do you know which door is the right one?"

Annabeth stood at the bottom step and faced the door directly opposite them. She then executed a left face and faced the door to the left of the stairs. Marching towards it, she stopped two paces away and pointed to the next door to the left. "This is the door. You make a left and a left."

Noble looked unconvinced.

Annabeth stood at the bottom of the stairs and repeated the steps.

"C'mere," she said and motioned him closer. "There's small smooth spot on the stone here. It's warm, almost hot, but only in the spot where you touch. Move an inch away and the stone is cold. You know this is the right door by the hot stone."

"Easy for you to say," Noble complained. "You'll notice I can't reach that high."

"Trust me," she smiled and slid the bars back, opening the door to a tunnel paved and lined in the same stone as the castle. The air was dry and cool. As soon as they stepped inside, a series of lights set in the stone walls rippled down the tunnel.

"It's pretty much a straight shot to the other end," Annabeth said. "There are two places where you have to pay attention."

"How did you know this was here?" Noble marveled as they walked.

"When we were in Westhaven, Gwen had the same setup. We used it to defeat what's-his-name's army. This will eventually come out outside the city."

"Why didn't we just steal the gem like we were supposed to?

"Because that only solves part of the problem," she said. "We need to defang Eleris to the point where she can't interfere. If all we do is take the stone, she's still a level 20 sorceress."

"So what're we gonna do?"

"You'll see," she evasively answered. "The point here though is that it's gonna take both of us to open the safe and I have a feeling even with the spells off it, it'll still take you some time."

"What kind of safe was it?"

"It had one of those dial things on it."

"That's not so hard," he frowned.

"You ever done one before?" She slid a sideways glance at him.

Noble paused then admitted, "Not yet."

"Exactly. We need time for us to work."

They came to an intersection leading left and right.

"We go left," Annabeth said. "Remember – left out, right in. You always go left when you go out and right when you come back in."

"I don't intend on coming back here by myself," he stated. "Where does that way go?"

"More traps," she answered. "C'mon."

Past another intersection later, they came to a door leading to a dimly lit circular room with a dozen doors, an imitation of the room at the other end. A set of winding stairs ascended in the middle of the room, disappearing into the darkness above.

"This one is just like the first room," Annabeth explained, reaching up. "Just like before, you can feel the smooth warm stone and know it's the right door. When you come back down the stairs, you turn to your right and then pick the door to the right."

"That does me no good, unless you can give me permanent spider fingers," he grumbled.

"Unfortunately, no can do," she said with a shrug. "Follow me. If it's like Westhaven, it's not much further."

The climb was much shorter than the descent at the castle and Noble found himself following Annabeth thorough a heavy door held together with iron straps then into an empty room with a single door at the opposite end. The room was lit by moonlight that illuminated the ethereal walls and roof of what was a small cottage.

"We're about half a kilometer beyond the outer walls," Annabeth said with an excited grin.

Mystified, Noble did a slow circle around the room, peering through the shimmering walls at the hazy forms of trees and shrubs that occasionally pierced through the translucent roof and walls.

"How is this possible?" he asked, filled with wonder.

"My guess is that it's one of Eleris's spells," she replied. "You can see out, but no one can see in."

"Can someone walk though it?"

"Not unless you know the spell is here," she said. "Whenever anyone comes close, they think there's this huge mass of thorny shrubs and go around it."

Noble went over to the door through which they had entered the cottage and tested the wood. "This seems real enough."

"It is," she chuckled. "It's the only real thing here."

Noble opened the door and saw the small platform and the descending stairs. Closing the door, he looked around and behind it and saw nothing but the hazy forms of trees and underbrush.

"This is awesome," he marveled, shaking his head. "How do we know where to come back to?"

"If it's like Westhaven, I know exactly where it is. C'mon, let's go find Karl."

"And no one can see us standing here, even in the daytime?"

"Nope."

Noble remained rooted for a moment. "So when we take down Eleris, this all disappears?"

Annabeth furrowed her brows in thought. "I don't know. Once a spell is cast, it's out there. I don't know if a spell like this requires maintenance or something like that. I guess we'll see."

Karl looked up when they walked in. By the look on their faces, he knew something was up. "Well?"

"She still has it," Annabeth answered, "but we found a way to get it."

"What happened?"

Noble elaborated their attempt and the location of the combination safe within the wall, finishing with, "Then we walk into this mirror."

Karl's interest perked up, especially when Annabeth informed him of the tunnel.

"Everything's just like Westhaven," she grinned.

"Weird," he mused as he began pacing the room. "My first thought is that it's a trap of some kind, but then you both made it out easily enough. Why would the designers repeat the tunnel concept?"

"In order to know about it," Annabeth pointed out, "you had to help Gwen defeat Cyril. Kevin chose not to do that. Our thief friend here didn't know about it either."

"Hey," Noble objected, "I'm a thief not a hero."

"It wasn't a put down," Annabeth consoled. "It was merely an observation. My point is that the successful quest on the first island helps us in this quest here."

"You may be right," Karl slowly nodded. "Regardless, we need to act."

"I have an idea," Annabeth said. "We get it tomorrow morning."

"In the daytime?" Noble exclaimed. "You crazy?"

"I don't think so," she replied, smiling at him. "My idea is that Karl and the army surround the city tomorrow like they're going to assault it or something, you know, like Cyril did, and then demand they surrender. Hopefully Eleris will come out to see what's going on."

"And if she doesn't?" Noble objected.

"Then he demands to see her," Annabeth said and shrugged. "One way or another, we need to separate her from the stone, get her out of the bedroom."

"Suppose she has the stone with her," Noble argued.

"Geez, you're just full of problems, aren't you," she huffed.

"Though he does have a point," Karl said. "But for the moment, let's say it's still in the safe. Then what?"

"Well," Annabeth continued, "Me and Noble and the rest of our team sneak in through the tunnel and we get the stone."

"Then what?"

"We either come back out or we wreak havoc while we're there. I really hadn't thought much beyond getting the stone."

Karl folded his arms across his chest and tilted his head then turned to the others. "Input."

"It's a good plan," Caryn replied, "provided the stone is where we want it to be. If our object is to overthrow Eleris, then we need to do it now when we have the strength."

"If this stone enhances powers," Raquel pointed out, "perhaps it will give our own sorceress enough power to defeat Eleris."

"I was thinking that already," Annabeth agreed.

Karl listened then turned to Dieter. "Your thoughts?"

"Your call, Boss," he shrugged. "I'm open to anything that will get us back to Avnoch faster."

Silence settled until Noble piped up, "What about me?"

Karl narrowed his gaze at him. "You are the key to this whole operation. You don't open the safe, we're screwed."

"No pressure," Annabeth teased.

Noble swallowed hard. At least this time he'd have Dieter and the others to help.

"OK," Karl announced. "Here's the plan."

Karl stared up at the battlements where Gordyn, surrounded by the leaders of the city stood, taking in the army spread before its walls.

"So, you've returned Viking," Gordyn sneered. "I see you've managed to sway some of the malcontents in my kingdom." His voice rose as he projected it as best he could. "Listen my people. Do not be fooled by this charlatan claiming to be your king. You have a king, and he stands right here before you. Go back to your homes and leave this pretender to me."

"Why should they listen to you?" Karl taunted. "They know you are not the real king, the real ruler who governs this city or this nation. Where is she? Where is the witch who makes you crawl on your hands and knees, the one who commands you to obey her whims? Come Gordyn, where is the woman who has bewitched you?"

Gordyn's face twisted in rage. "I am the king. No one tells me what to do. Eleris is *my* sorceress. She does what I tell her."

Karl barked a mocking laugh. "Now that's funny. Tell me Gordyn, does she still have your daughter locked up?"

"That's a lie," Gordyn snapped.

"Then show her to us," Karl demanded. "Show us that you are the king. Show us your daughter then bring forth your witch. Beckon her to obey your command. Let's see who's really in charge."

Karl watched as Gordyn twisted his head to issue the command to a youthful messenger.

Gordyn then leaned over the edge and sneered, "You have condemned yourself, Viking."

"We'll see," Karl replied.

Several minutes later, the contrite messenger appeared. His report caused Gordyn to explode.

"She said what? Now is not a convenient time? Tell her to get her ass here, now or I will have her head, and yours too."

"Trouble in paradise?" Karl mocked.

Ignoring him, Gordyn pointed to a commander and barked an order, causing the man to bustle off.

"Sending an armed escort?" Karl jeered. "I thought you were the king."

"I am, damn you," Gordyn yelled back.

"I guess we'll find out."

Gordyn's impatience grew as time passed and Eleris did not appear. Karl continued a flow of taunts and mocking. Finally, when even the city elders were deciding whether it was in their best interests to drift away and ensure their own affairs were protected that a small canopy appeared over the battlements as Eleris regally appeared. The canopy, supported by four servants shielded the sorceress from the sun.

Eleris was a beautiful willowy woman with long silky white hair and the milky skin of an albino. She wore a flowing white dress with long sleeves covering her slender arms. She squinted and blinked in radiance of the day, despite the awning above her.

"I see someone's not used to being out in the sun," Karl scoffed. "Vampires have the same problem."

"You demanded to see me, Viking?" Eleris coldly asked.

"You mean you're here because I asked you?" Karl said, feigning surprise. "I thought you came here because King Gordyn told you to report here. After all, he supposedly is the king."

"I am here nonetheless. Why do you encamp outside our city with an army of our own subjects?"

Karl grinned. "I like the way you said, 'our subjects.' So, you do admit that it is you who rule the nation, not Gordyn."

"Gordyn is the king," she stated.

"You didn't answer the question."

"You didn't ask a question," she retorted.

"OK, I'll rephrase it," Karl said. "Who rules this nation, you or Gordyn?"

"Gordyn is the king," she repeated.

"Again, you haven't answered the question."

"But I have, Viking. Gordyn is the king. Now is that all you wanted?"

"All I wanted?" Karl chuckled. "Aren't you here because Gordyn commanded you to be here?"

Eleris's jaw clenched. "Yes."

Karl shifted his attention to Gordyn. "If she is subject to your will, command her to take off her clothes. Let's have a look at that beautiful body of hers."

Eleris's eyes flared. "How dare you. I will not stand here to be humiliated by you or anyone else." She turned to leave.

"Wait a minute," Karl called out. "You're here at the behest of the king. You can't leave until he tells you to. How about it Gordyn? You going to prove you're in charge?"

Eleris slowly turned back around, cold hatred filling her face.

"Well, Gordyn?" Karl said. "Tell her to take off her clothes."

"I will do no such thing," Gordyn snapped. "I will not publicly humiliate her or anyone else in my kingdom."

"See?" Karl announced. "She's in charge."

"You are wasting our time, Viking," Eleris sneered then suddenly stiffened, her eyes bolting wide as she jerked her head towards Gordyn. "You damned fool," she exploded and whirled around, the bearers carrying the awning racing to catch up.

While Karl mocked and jeered at Gordyn and Eleris, Annabeth led the others through the tunnels and up the stairs to Eleris's bedroom, pausing before arriving at the small platform on this side of the mirror. Poking her head just above the floor level, she gazed through the mirror into the bedroom she and Noble had recently scouted. Seeing no movement, she carefully edged up until she was standing off to the side of the mirror. Suddenly Eleris breezed by on the other side and Annabeth watched as the sorceress swung around the bed and pulled back the picture covering the wall safe, her head twitching to the doorway, making sure she was unobserved.

Eleris twirled the lock and opened the safe, withdrawing a small necklace of finely crafted gold chain. Attached was a tear-drop shaped pendant about seven centimeters long of polished lapis lazuli. She started to place the necklace over her head then abruptly stopped as her head jerked to the left. In one quick motion she thrust the stone and necklace into the safe, slammed the door close and spun the dial before adjusting the picture.

"What is it?" she loudly fussed as she stormed around the bed.

Annabeth cast a quick Detect Speech divination spell.

"The king requests your presence," a male voice said.

"I'm busy," Eleris snapped.

"You pardon, m'Lady, but he was insistent."

"You tell that damned fool that now is not a convenient time."

"But m'Lady –"

"Go, damn you."

A leaden silence ensued, and Annabeth was tempted to poke her head through the mirror to see if the sorceress was still in her chambers when the woman in question suddenly stood in front of the mirror. Jerking back and to the side, Annabeth watched as Eleris peered at herself, adjusting her clothing, and arranging her hair, casting an occasional covert glance back at the picture covering the safe.

Stepping away from the mirror, Eleris stood in indecision, scowling in frustration. Her musing was interrupted by a knock on the door.

Gritting her teeth, she disappeared from Annabeth's view.

"What is it this time," Eleris fumed.

"I'm sorry m'Lady," the same male voice said, wanting to be firm, but the tremor in his voice betraying is fear. "Please, m'Lady. He said he'd have my head if you didn't come."

"Who does that fool think he is," she fussed. "Fine. Let's go."

Annabeth waited until she heard the door close. "C'mon. Let's move."

She and Noble hustled to the wall while the others filed in behind them and positioned themselves throughout the suite and on both sides of the front door. Annabeth removed the picture and placed it on the floor then stared at the safe, puzzled.

"That's odd. I don't detect a spell on it," she said, furrowing her brow.

"You sure?" Noble studied the dial, fingers hovering above the dial, noting the relation of the numbers on the dial to the opening index.

"As sure as I can be," she replied with a shrug. "Now that I think about it, I didn't feel a spell on it when we were here before. I wonder if she…" Her hand shot up. "Wait a minute." Closing her eyes, she bent her head close to the safe. "There is a spell. It's a warning spell."

She stood back and peered intently at the thief. "You're gonna have to be fast. Once you touch the dial, an alarm goes off and she's gonna be back her in a flash."

"Alarm?" he exclaimed, his hand jerking back.

"It's not that kind of alarm," Annabeth reassured him. "She's the only one who will know. It's a good thing we didn't try to open it last night. She'd have been on us in an instant." Noting him waiting, she urged, "Get a move on. We're running out of time."

Licking his lips, Noble sucked in a deep breath and examined the dial once again then lightly placed his ear against the safe, his hand delicately twisting the knob to the right then left then right again then back to zero. Feeling the tumblers drop, he twisted the dial one last time and opened the safe.

"You're a genius," Annabeth boasted, much to his satisfaction when she planted a kiss on his forehead. Reaching in, she snatched the sole contents of the container – the Delf Stone, and slipped the necklace over her head.

No sooner was she adorned with the necklace that the front door to the apartment burst open and Eleris stormed in.

Annabeth reacted by conjuring and launching a ball of sticky mud, but Eleris's reaction was fast, and the ball impacted harmlessly on a hastily formed protective shield. Yet the shield only partially covered her, and Annabeth cast a fireball at Eleris's feet, simultaneously casting a sleep spell.

However, Eleris was not without her own devices and countered with fire bolts of her own while fighting off her drowsiness and stamping out the flames licking at her feet. Annabeth quickly enacted an Electric Shield abjuration, causing the fire bolts to ricochet off and impact on furniture and curtains, catching them on fire.

Eleris summoned a giant scorpion that drew Dieter, Raquel, and Caryn into the fight, and they quickly distracted and slew the beast, while the fire spread to the rest of the apartment.

Smoke billowed and rolled within the room as the two sorceresses dueled. Annabeth felt her powers and confidence growing, courtesy of the Delf Stone. "Arrows," she called out to Caryn and Raquel while casting an Arrow Division spell. Now each arrow the two Rangers fired was duplicated and Eleris struggled to duck, her powers weakening.

Annabeth now cast Acid Bomb and hurled them at Eleris's head and feet. One small orb broke on impact near the sorceress' feet and splattered on her leg, causing her to yelp in pain. Her defenses dwindling under the onslaught, Eleris ducked one acid bomb at her face and the set of arrows Raquel aimed at her heart but missed the duplicate arrows

Caryn s directed at her head and the impact sent her reeling back into the flames, which caught her clothing on fire.

All too quickly, the flames swallowed her body and despite her pitifully desperate efforts to find relief or assert her powers, fire consumed her, and she collapsed in a heap. They watched as her life and mana bars shifted color to red then disappeared.

"Let's get out of here," Caryn ordered.

Eleris's charred corpse lay near the door as Caryn led the way out of the inferno consuming the apartment. The alarm had already sounded, and servants and guards were rapidly transferring water buckets and hurling the contents onto the fire.

Karl knew his team had succeeded when Gordyn turned to an agitated messenger and the heads and faces of the city's nobility abruptly disappeared. A moment later, the gates swung open and Dieter strode out.

"It's all yours Boss," he grinned.

"Anyone hurt?" Karl asked, walking up to the berserker.

"Just the witch," he replied. "She's dead." He grinned mischievously. "There was a slight fire. I think they've got it under control."

"The others?"

"They're rounding up the rest of the city leaders." He glanced back over his shoulder. "In fact, they're here now."

His face grim, Gordyn, marched up, the burgomaster, and other city notables beside him. Surrounding them, Caryn, Raquel, Annabeth and Noble, along with a growing crowd of citizens whose obvious relief spilled over into cheerful faces, approached the new ruler of Glenloch.

Ignoring Gordyn, Karl turned to a middle-aged man with a head of thick black hair cut fashionably short. He wore the chained medallion of office.

"You're name?" Karl said, giving him a regal nod.

"I am Baldur, my Lord," he respectfully answered.

"How long have you been burgomaster," Karl inquired.

"Seven years, my Lord."

"And how did you become burgomaster?"

"King Gordyn appointed me, my Lord," he candidly replied, all the while keeping his eyes on the commanding Viking before him.

"Gordyn is no longer King," Annabeth cheerfully pointed out.

"Wait just a damned minute," Gordyn began before Karl's look of cold justice stopped him.

Turning his attention back to the burgomaster, Karl said, "Do you know who I am?"

"Yes, my Lord," he said, dipping his head. "Everyone knows who you are."

"Karl," a woman's voice cried out as the former servant girl, now king's daughter, thrust her way through the crowd and charged forward to leap into his arms.

"Oh no," Annabeth moaned, glancing at Raquel and rolling her eyes.

Prying himself from Julie's arms, Karl quickly scanned the surrounding crowd and settled on a young fair-complexioned soldier, tall and well-built, with blond hair and chiseled jaw. "You. Come here."

The young man ran up and dropped to a knee. "Yes, m'Lord?"

"Your name?"

"Dayle, m'Lord."

"What position do you hold in the army?"

"I am a squadron commander, m'Lord."

"Good. Squadron Commander Dayle, I want you to take Lord Gordyn and his daughter and place them under house arrest."

"What?" Gordyn snapped.

"What?" Julie whined, crestfallen.

"Just until I decide what to do with your father," Karl soothed.

"But I want to stay here, with you," she pouted.

"Later," Karl said. "I need you to go with him so that I can be sure you're safe while I finish here."

"But –" she began then saw his determined look. "OK," she sighed, her dreams momentarily crushed, especially when she saw Annabeth's smile.

Karl spoke again to Dale. "I hold you personally responsible for their welfare. I want them treated kindly."

"Yes, m'Lord."

'You can't do this," Gordyn growled in anger. "I am the king."

"Not anymore," Karl coldly intoned. "Be thankful I don't stuff your head on a pike outside these city gates."

Startled that Karl would make good the threat, especially after learning about Eleris's death, Gordyn clamped his mouth shut and silently began plotting how to regain his throne.

Once Dayle escorted Gordyn and Julie back into the city, Karl turned back to Baldur. "See this man here?" He pointed to Ben.

"Yes, m'Lord."

"He is now in charge as the Lord of Mann. Though I am king, he will rule in my stead as my vassal." He leaned over to Ben and whispered out the side of his mouth, "You OK with that?"

"Me a lord?" Ben grinned. "Day-um."

Karl stepped back to take in as much of the crowd as possible. Then in a loud voice, he said, "I am King Karl, the rightful king of Mann. This," he pointed to Ben, "is Lord Ben. He will rule this kingdom in my place as I unite Mann and the Kingdom of Odryssa. Be pleased that Lord Ben is your ruler, especially as this kingdom's borders are harassed by orcs. Know this. Lord Ben is the greatest slayer of orcs in the history of this nation. He has killed more orcs than I and my army combined. He is wise and kind. But do not try his patience."

He then directed his focus on Baldur. "You serve at the pleasure of Lord Ben. If he chooses to remove you or remove your head, that is his privilege. Do you understand?"

Baldur swallowed hard. "Yes, Sire."

"Good. Now leave us and attend to your duties. Clear out Gordyn's lodgings and have them ready for Lord Ben by the time he and I are finished."

Baldur's eyes popped wide, and he bustled off, praying that Karl and Ben would linger for some time.

"I know I didn't talk to you about this," Karl said to Ben. "Thought it might be a nice surprise."

"Bet your ass I'm surprised." Ben's grin widened. He glanced around the city and thought of the possibilities as well as the comfort. "Sure as hell beats living in caves."

"There's one more thing you'll need to do," Karl said with a sly smile.

"Oh?"

"You remember that lovely creature who threw herself at me?"

"Julie?"

"Yes."

"What about her?"

"I want you to think about possible matrimony."

"To her?" he spouted.

"Yes. Hear me out. First, she's not bad looking. In fact, she's a babe."

"Yeah, but she's got the hots for you," Ben objected.

"That's only temporary."

"Not from what I saw."

"She'll get over me, especially with the suave Ben now in charge. Secondly, it would be a smart political move to unite the House of Rhyeem to yourself. Sort of gives you an even more legitimate claim."

Ben mused a bit. "Yeah, but... married?"

"You don't have to do it right away. After all I'm supposed to rule for a thousand years. You got time."

"But why me?

Karl peered intently at him. "Because I trust you."

Though flattered, Ben pointed out, "What about the others? They could rule here just as well, and I could go with you."

"True, but there are mitigating circumstances that make you the best choice. First, you're devilishly handsome and Julie is sure to fall in love with you."

Ben cocked a skeptically eyebrow. "Now you're teasing me."

"Not at all. Second, you're the best orc fighter here. The kingdom has a problem with orcs. Who better than you to deal with them? Third, you know what's going on and how to rule."

"I know nuthin' about ruling," he argued.

"You'll learn"

"Uh," Noble interrupted. "I'd sort of like to stay too."

"You do?" Karl frowned at him, not liking the idea of the thief running rampant in Glenloch.

"There's a certain lady," Annabeth explained.

Karl raised an eyebrow. "This all happened since yesterday? That was quick."

"Do you mind?" Noble said.

"No practicing your trade," Karl said with heavy emphasis.

"I can be good," Noble grinned.

"Let me think about it," Karl answered. "It's not so much your chosen profession as it is your talents for getting us out of tight spots." He watched with satisfaction as Noble preened at the compliment. "I don't know what to expect when we get to Avnoch. In the meantime, go enjoy yourself. If I need you, Annabeth knows where to find you."

"Thanks," Noble gushed and ran off before Karl could change his mind.

"I think we'll be fine without him," Caryn observed as Noble disappeared into the crowds.

"I agree," Karl answered. "We need to get the augury stone from him before we go. Why don't you and Annabeth retrieve it before he forgets he has it."

"C'mon," Annabeth said with a confident smile, tugging at Caryn. "She's got some great wine."

Karl reached out and placed a gentle hand on Annabeth's arm. "Well done by the way. I owe you."

"You can demonstrate your appreciation later," she said with an impish grin, flicking her eyebrows.

"I look forward to it." The words slipped out before he realized what he said. Caryn's smile briefly disappeared then returned as though forced. "Meet back at Gordyn's lodgings."

"Roger dodger," Annabeth said and saluted.

Dinner finished, Karl and his team, now called the 'Inner Circle,' sat at the dining table in what had become Ben's residence, savoring digestifs of Sambuca and amaretto. Noble was absent as he had chosen to help Aylish whose business suddenly became the place to be when Karl and the Inner Circle made it an overt display of favor and walked through the city, bypassing other inns and taverns to settle on the Stag's Head Inn and Tavern. The attention did not go unnoticed and Aylish was immediately overwhelmed, her meager supplies quickly vanishing.

Noble rose to the occasion, dispensing his precious gold and managing to corner ale and wine merchants, and bakers and butchers who were more than happy to oblige, especially when they saw the King's preference for the place.

Karl and the Inner Circle headed back to Ben's new accommodations leaving Noble to rescue Aylish who, despite being overwhelmed, was euphoric at the change of her fortunes. Karl also noted that Aylish was more than attentive to Noble, and it pleased him, for Noble would be content here with her.

"What do you want to do with Noble's augury stone?" Caryn asked, bring him back to the moment.

"Haven't decided yet," he replied, sipping his Sambuca.

"Why not use it to help Noble?" Annabeth said.

"How?"

"Convince Kevin that Noble is dead."

Karl furrowed his brows. "Again, how, and for what purpose?"

"Like I said," she answered, "to help Noble. Right now, he's probably the happiest he'll ever be. He's got a lady who seems to reciprocate his interest. And do we really need him to go after Kevin? Seems to me that he'd just be in the way, especially when the fighting begins."

"OK," Karl mused, "point taken. How do you propose to do that?"

Annabeth grinned, her eyes half lidded. "Use the stone. Then have someone dress up as some intimidating person, mysterious and threatening… someone like Caryn."

"Me?" Caryn startled.

"Yes," Annabeth affirmed, "you. He doesn't know you, nor has he ever seen you. He's seen the rest of us. You contact him at midnight, tell him Noble is dead and that you now control the stone, and that Kevin now works for you."

Karl sat up straight. "What a great idea. It would confuse the hell out of him."

"Are you sure?" Caryn frowned, unconvinced.

At midnight, Caryn, dressed in a black hooded robe that hid most of her face, sat at a small table in the darkened bedroom. A single flickering candle close by cast dull shadows. Unwrapping the cloth from the stone, she was momentarily surprised to see Kevin's looming face.

"What the hell are you doing?" he demanded, thinking Noble was getting melodramatic.

"Shut up, fool," she snapped, her voice low and threatening. "Your little friend has told me all about you... Kevin."

"Who... who are you? Where's Noble?"

"Noble? That little worm of a creature? He is no more for he was useless to me."

"Who are you?" Kevin's apprehension mounted.

"I will tell you when I deem you worthy enough to know my name. Until then, I expect obedience."

"Obedience?" Kevin repeated, waffling between being indignant and concerned. "Who the hell do you think you are?"

"Silence," Caryn seethed, "you pathetic maggot." Small flare bursts, courtesy of Annabeth, erupted behind her. "When I want your input I will beat it out of you."

Kevin obeyed and his mouth clamped shut.

"Now listen, you miserable cretin, I am searching for Karl the Viking. Tell me where he is."

"What?" Kevin exclaimed. "Noble was with him. He's gotta be there where you are."

"If he was," Caryn growled, "do you think I would waste my time talking to you?"

"But... but," Kevin stammered, "I don't understand. He was with Karl."

"That is not true, you liar. Just before I exterminated him, he told me Karl was with you. Now tell me where he is, and I just might spare you."

"I don't know where he is," Kevin wailed. "I swear it."

"Stay there," Caryn commanded, "while I consult my other stones." Wrapping the cloth securely around the stone, she idly counted to 100 then unwrapped the stone. Kevin was still there. "You are a liar, and I will seek my vengeance. The stones tell me the truth that Karl is close by." She suppressed a snicker for that was the truth. "I ask one last time. Where is he?"

"I don't know," Kevin whined. "I swear it."

"Then you are dead," Caryn intoned. "Do not think that Avnoch is far enough away for me not to find you. And do not think your assassin skills will save you. And your pathetic followers? I know each of them." She laughed an evil cackle. "They are not as loyal as you believe. They will sell you out when your back is turned. In fact," she pretended to muse, "I expect one will accomplish your elimination before I get there."

She wrapped the stone, cutting off Kevin's protestations.

"That should keep him occupied for a while," she said with a chuckle.

Chapter 7

Landon stood next to Felix, as they both stared out the window in Felix's office to the golf course across the river. With no one left to care for the course, the fairways were overgrown, sand traps sprouted weeds, and kudzu carpeted the clubhouse and most of the trees separating the holes.

"I never played that much," Landon observed. "Though I found the game interesting, it was the mindless natter of the others in the foursome that I couldn't put up with. Their purpose on the course was either to get away from their wives and kids or personal advancement via networking. The game was incidental to their quest for making more money." He twisted his head to smile at Felix. "Nothing wrong with money, you understand."

Felix offered a sympathetic smile in return. "Pity we never got the chance. I think it would have been an enjoyable time. Alyson is quite the player."

"Speaking of Alyson," Landon said, turning and walking over to an overstuffed chair and easing down onto the thick cushion, "reminds me of what are we to do with Gerard? His predicament in Bridge Quest has been fun, especially with his inability to progress beyond the first level, but I have a feeling that the others will end up feeling sorry for the fool and ease his plight."

"I've given thought to that," Felix said, picking up a decanter of a 20-year-old oloroso sherry. Filling two white wine glasses halfway, he handed one glass to Landon. Lifting his glass in a salute, he said, "We bring him back."

Landon swirled the liquid in the glass then inhaled the bouquet. "Bring him back?" he said with a frown that smoothed out when he tasted the smooth Moscatel sweetness.

"Yes," Felix replied, "but with a twist. He comes back but now cannot enter another game. We write a global protocol effectively shutting him out from the future."

A satisfied grin curled the corners of Landon's lips. "I like it. It condemns him to living his life in the real world."

"And prohibits him from interfering in the game world," Felix added.

Landon raised his glass. "This is good sherry."

"Thank you."

"I think we ought to bring him back just in time to see us immerse. He will truly be on his own then."

It was late afternoon when Karl called a halt. It had taken almost a week heading west from Glenloch by the time Karl and his army reached the border of Odryssa. Another day's march and they would be at Abynee. Calling a halt, Karl waited for Maddoc to position his forces in perimeter security then hustle over.

Kneeling on the ground, Karl cleared a spot and picked up a stick, scratching a line in the dirt. "We're here," he said, jabbing the stick into the ground on the side of the line. "Abynee is here." He moved the stick to the left about half a meter. "It'll take us a day to get there." He then directed his attention to Maddoc.

"Annys is the commander in Abynee. She is loyal and a good soldier and leader. Odryssa is her kingdom as Mann is yours. In this instance, I ask that you temporarily subordinate yourself to her while we are in Odryssa."

"I understand, Sire," Maddoc replied. "We will have no conflict between our armies."

Karl nodded in appreciation. Maddoc was a professional soldier and would not allow personal jealousies to get in the way.

"Once we unite the armies, we march on Avnoch," Karl continued. "However, to the best of our ability, I want our presence in Odryssa kept secret." He looked pointedly at Caryn and Raquel. "Figure that Kevin has probably increased the number of his spies, which means we need as many spies and scouts as possible."

"Got it," they replied in unison.

"We move out a first light."

Karl's concerns thankfully evaporated when he and his army encamped outside Abynee. Upon seeing the King returning, Annys burst through the city gates and ran to him, dropping to her knees before him.

"You are back, Sire," she exclaimed, her joy overt, especially seeing the rest of his Inner Circle and the accompanying soldiers.

Though pleased, Karl was somewhat surprised at the public display of devotion. "Good to see you too, Commander. Rise. What's been happening since the last time I was here?"

"Rumors abounded that you were dead and your followers imprisoned," she said, standing. "This fellow who calls himself Kevin assumed the throne, yet we all knew something wasn't right. Lord Evnan refused to yield to him as did the rest of us in his domain."

At that moment, Brin emerged from the gates and bustled over. "Sire," she burst, her face a mixture of joy and relief. "Thank the gods you are safe and back." She kneeled.

"Stand please," Karl encouraged.

"We must talk, Sire," Brin said then looked past Karl's shoulder at the array of forces. "It is good you have brought an army, though they appear unfamiliar."

"These are soldiers from Mann," Karl said then pointed at Maddoc. "This is Commander Maddoc, commander of the Eagle's Claw Brigade. We're fortunate to have them as most of them were with me when we invaded the orc kingdom, killing hundreds of orcs."

Brin's eyes widened in pleasure. "Then they are doubly welcome, Sire. We will ensure their needs are met with satisfaction. May we talk, Sire?"

"Of course." Turning to Maddoc and Annys, he said, "You two get to know each other. Get your forces together and work out the kinks. We leave first thing in the morning. The rest of you," he said addressing his Inner Circle, "come with me."

Once seated in the Burgomaster's large dining room, Brin waited until Karl sat. "Would you like refreshment, Sire?"

"Whatever my soldiers are having would be find with us," he replied without thinking.

"Sire," Brin replied. "You soldiers will be well cared for."

Karl looked at the others who seemed unconcerned with what they ate, preferring to find out what lay in store. "Fine. Whatever is handy. What's going on?"

Brin motioned for the servants to bring in food and ale, waiting for the platters of meats and cheeses and bread to be placed on the table as other servants filled the ale steins, before launching into her report.

"The kingdom is in turmoil, Sire. Kevin rules through intimidation and fear. Though Kerr and Fraster are nominally in charge of their respective domains, their sorceresses, Finella and Caillac, remain with Kevin in Avnoch, as does Fraster's monster. Finella has conjured another monster."

"What's this one look like?" Annabeth asked.

"He has the head and tail of a bull and the body of a man," Brin solemnly replied.

"A minotaur?" Karl said, cocking an eyebrow. "What is it with the Greek mythology in this game?"

"Sire?" Brin said with a puzzled frown.

"Long story. What else?"

"Kevin's spies are everywhere, even here."

Karl's face hardened. "Who?"

She flashed a sly smile. "Our former burgomaster Graer has found his true calling. Fortunately, he is as inept in that skill as he was as burgomaster. We feed him enough false information to add to the confusion in Avnoch."

"I do not want Kevin to know we are here," Karl sternly replied.

"It's already taken care of, Sire," she reassured him. "Graer had quite the taste for ale when he was burgomaster, demanding ale merchants provide him with their best before he would grant licenses, which he had renewed on a quarterly basis. That kept him well supplied and well tipsy, though never too much. However, with his demotion and the elimination of quarterly licensing, his supply of ale has run dry. He has taken to frequenting the local pubs, one in particular called the Lazy Boar where he is now passed out."

"Lazy Boar?" Karl said with a chuckle.

"It's a play on words, Sire," she explained. "The taverner said most conversations in pubs were thoroughly boring."

"Got it," Karl said with a smile. "Anything else?"

"Bandits again plague the kingdom. Lord Evnan copes as best he can, but he has his hands full with the domain. Though Kevin has placed Kerr back as Lord, he has little support among the people."

"Any more good news?" Caryn interjected.

"Isn't that enough?" she answered.

Karl turned to the Inner Circle. "Thoughts?"

"Seems to me we don't have much of a choice," Caryn opined. "We need to cut the head off the snake."

"I agree with Caryn," Raquel said. "I think now's the time to advertise that the king has returned. Let Kevin know. Let the people know. My guess is that Kevin and his company will soon find themselves deserted."

"We're still gonna have to fight him and the others," Annabeth pointed out. "He still has two sorceresses and two monsters plus the other PCs. We may have an army, but he's got some pretty powerful support."

Karl looked at Dieter. "Your thoughts?"

Dieter shrugged. "You know how I feel, Boss. I intend to commit mayhem on anyone and everyone until I get Elena back. And if anything has happened to her, they 'll wish they were never born."

Karl nodded and took a slow sip of cold ale. "This is very good," he complimented.

"It's my own brew," Brin said, pleased.

"Well done," he said, raising his stein. "Now to business." He leaned forward. "I agree with Raquel. Now is the time to advertise. Let's get the word out. Send out runners, especially to Avnoch. It's time for Kevin to know the game is up."

Karl led the way into the town and headed for the tavern. The door opened just as he reached for it, surprising a merchant, a man not quite into middle age, wearing brightly colored shirt, vest, and trousers. His boots were shined to a high gloss.

"My apologies," he said, dipping his head and holding the door open, giving them the once over at the same time. "You're not from around here."

"We're from Abynee, on the way to Avnoch," Karl answered.

"Ah," the merchant nodded, stroking his clean-shaven chin. His brown eyes, bright with inquisitiveness searched the faces of the newcomers, especially the giant of a man in the back. "Come in and enjoy the finest food and ale this side of Avnoch. I was just about to head there myself, but there's no rush. Mind if I join you?"

"We don't want to interfere with your day," Caryn replied.

"Not at all. We get few visitors these days and it's nice to see new faces, even when... um, I mean, especially when they're strangers."

They walked in and the man waved for a barmaid. "The best table for my friends," he grandly announced.

"Ach," she laughed. "Take yer pick."

Karl looked around the tavern. Of the approximately twenty tables in the tavern, only one table was occupied, and the man there appeared to have fallen asleep, slumped over with his head resting on his hands.

"Don't mind him," the merchant whispered. "He likes to snooze here after a long night."

"What does he do?" Raquel asked with a smile.

"He's the night watchman for the vil. I'd tell him to go home, but he's a good paying customer."

"You're the owner?" Karl asked, knowing the answer.

"In the flesh," the man grinned then swept his hand and bowed. "Lomen, at your service."

"What table do you suggest?" Caryn smirked.

"One far away from inquiring eyes," Lomen said with a wink.

"That should be easy," Caryn said then pointed to a table in the far corner.

Once seated, the barmaid, a slender teenage girl with strawberry blond hair and freckles, came over carrying three mugs of ale. "The ale's the best this side of Avnoch," she said, bored with the need to repeat the mantra. "If you want anything else to drink, you're outta luck 'cause ale is all we got."

"But it's good," Lomen added with a frown, playfully swatting the girl on the butt then leaning in to whisper as she walked away, "my daughter. She's a handful."

"Pretty girl," Karl remarked.

"Ach, that she is." Lifting his mug, he held it up in toast. "To your health and future."

"And to yours," Karl replied, sipping the cold brew. "This *is* good," he complimented. "Some of the best I've had between here and Abynee."

"I know," Lomen grinned, though pleased with the compliment. "Hungry? My wife is the best cook –"

"This side of Avnoch," Annabeth chuckled, finishing for him.

Lomen's smile widened. "There's venison stew with fresh bread and hard cheese."

"Sounds delicious," Karl replied, his mouth watering.

Lomen leaned back, tilting his head towards his daughter who stood behind the bar counter, bored. "Tell your mother we have five for midday meal." As his daughter silently pushed through the door to the kitchen, he turned back to the newcomers. "So," he said, giving them an appraising glance, "what business does a Viking, an elf warrior, a giant, a sorceress most likely and a Ranger have in Avnoch?"

Caryn's hand instinctively went to her ear.

"It wasn't that," he assured her. "You have the look of an elf."

"A lot of elves come through here?" Karl commented.

"Just one," Lomen answered, "a male elf."

"Did he have a name?"

"Don't remember him providing one. In fact, none of them did."

"Them?" Karl politely said.

"Six of them," Lomen replied as his daughter set down bowls of steaming stew and a cutting board with bread and cheese, "an elf like I said and five others... a lot like you all."

"Did any of them have names?" Karl asked.

"Not then, but I did learn the name of the leader of the group. Oddly enough, he's our new king... Kevin." He peered intently at Karl. "Sort of makes one wonder what happened to the previous king, the one we all thought was going to institute a reign of peace... or so he promised."

"Sometimes promises get delayed," Karl responded.

Lomen gazed at him a bit longer. "Are you back for good then, Sire?"

Karl paused mid-chew.

"I was in Avnoch when you assumed the throne," Lomen explained. "I was glad someone with some sense was going to rule. Then the next thing I know is you're gone and no one knows where you went. A little while later, Kevin and his friends come through here and the next thing I know, he's declared himself king... And then word come through here just yesterday saying that the king has returned."

"When was the last time you were in Avnoch?" Karl asked him.

"A week ago," Lomen replied, sipping his ale. "The mood is worse than I've ever seen. Apparently your return has upset his plans. Until the news of your return came through, he was imposing new taxes on merchants and farmers then giving a large portion to the soldiers and military, causing a rift between the military and everyone else."

"Divide and conquer," Caryn said, pursing her lips. "Keep everyone at each other's throat. Rule by intimidation."

"He was like this in real life," Karl said.

"You know him, Sire?" Lomen asked, surprised.

"Yes. I've had dealings with him before. He is not an honorable man."

Lomen gazed at him a moment before asking, "Why did you leave, Sire?"

"We got called to another quest," he answered.

"By whom?" Lomen frowned, curious a king would so easily leave a kingdom to go on some foolish quest.

"Sorcery," Caryn interjected.

Lomen's eyes bolted wide.

"No," Caryn said, shaking her head, recognizing his fear, "not the ones here. These were two powerful sorcerers. The sorcery here is but child's play compared to them." She snapped her fingers.

"And the quest?" Lomen asked with reverent tone.

"A huge success," she replied. "We rescued a woman important to one of the sorcerers."

Lomen frowned in thought. "If they are as powerful as you say, enough to whisk you away from here, why couldn't they rescue the woman themselves?"

"We wondered the same thing," Karl said. "The woman was held by men immune to the sorcerer's magic."

"My God, really?" Lomen's daughter blurted, for she had come around the bar and edged closer as the story unfolded.

Unaware she was privy to the conversation, Lomen jerked his head to glare at her. "Don't you have work to do?"

"Aw Da," she whined. "There's nothing to do right now. Everything's clean."

"Then go help your Ma."

"But Da," she moped.

"Let her stay," Caryn said, giving the girl a sympathetic smile.

Without waiting for approval, the girl yanked a chair out and sat down.

Rolling his eyes, Lomen turned back to his guests. "What happened? How did you manage it?"

"With stealth and magical weapons," Caryn explained.

Lomen shook his head in wonder. "This sorcery must be powerful."

"Very," Karl nodded, hoping he and Caryn would remember the story and keep it the same.

"What did the sorcerers look like?" the daughter asked, enjoying the tale.

Caryn glanced over to Karl then leaned forward and whispered, "Just like your Da."

"O my God," she exclaimed, twisting her head to stare at her father with newfound wonder. "And the woman you rescued? What did she look like?"

"Stunning," Karl smirked, sliding his eyes to look at Caryn then Raquel and Annabeth whose return looks told him they didn't think him funny.

"What happened after you finished the quest?" the daughter asked.

"We were returned to Talbet," Karl answered.

"Why not back in Avnoch?" Lomen asked.

"We were told that the kingdom was in trouble, and we decided the best way to deal with it was to not let anyone know we had returned," Karl replied. "This way, Kevin and his lackeys would be caught by surprise." He narrowed his gaze at Lomen and his daughter. "My army is encamped to the east of town. It would be best if you and the rest of the vil stayed here in town for the next few days."

"We understand, Sire," Lomen firmly asserted. "We are your loyal servants."

Caryn scooted her chair back and walked over to the man asleep at the table. "What about you? Can we trust you?"

"He's asleep," Lomen assured her.

Ignoring his declaration, she focused her attention on the man. "I'll ask you one more time. Can we trust you?"

Karl watched her unfold her arms, her right hand sliding down to rest on the hilt of the dagger in her belt. Then in one quick motion, she grabbed a headful of hair and jerked the man's head back, her blade at his throat.

"You move and I slit your throat," she growled. "Drop the blade."

"My God," Lomen burst, seeing the stiletto in the man's hand fall and clatter on the floor. "He's one of us… at least we all believed he was. He's got a wife and kids."

"How long has he been here?"

"Years," Lomen answered, staring at the man whose cold eyes were filled with hatred.

"Get a rope or something to tie him," Caryn commanded, causing the daughter to leap up and race to the kitchen. She quickly returned, a spool of cord in her hands.

As the girl helped Caryn secure the man to the chair, Karl stood and walked over to stand before him. Keeping his focus on the man, he spoke to Caryn. "How did you know?"

"I could tell he wasn't asleep as soon as we walked in."

Karl turned to Lomen. "How long has he been here today?"

"A few minutes before you came in," Lomen replied, "but he always comes in around this time."

"No he doesn't, Da," his daughter corrected. "He never comes in 'til after midday."

Lomen frowned then nodded. "You're right. He was early today."

"Which meant he expected us," Karl said to Caryn. "Time to find out what he knows, which means this tavern is closed for a little while."

Lomen crossed the floor and bolted the door. The kitchen door opened and attractive woman wearing a chef's apron emerged. She had strawberry blond hair like her daughter.

"What's going on here?" she demanded. "Nellie came into the kitchen demanding rope of some sort then dashed out. Why on earth is Cambul all tied up?"

"He's a spy," the daughter gushed.

"By the gods of course he is," she huffed, walking over.

"He is?" Lomen said, shocked.

"He's been spying for that new king ever since he came here."

"How do you know that?" Lomen asked, irritated his wife withheld news like that.

"I saw him one morning a while back talking to some stranger at the edge of town. He handed him a scroll of papers. I saw the same stranger on a regular basis after that."

"And you never saw fit to tell me?" Lomen fumed.

"What was there to tell?" she shrugged. "It was obvious that Cambul was passing on some sort of secrets, but it had nothing to do with us and the less we knew the better. Better to leave things like that alone and go on about our own business."

"You two can talk about that later," Karl interrupted. He bent down and retrieved the stiletto, studying the pommel and handle. "This is marked with runes." He held it out for them to see then handed it to Annabeth. "Can you read these?"

Annabeth scrutinized the writing then pursed her lips and glared at Cambul though speaking to the rest. "The blade is imbued with some sort of poison spell that immobilizes a victim. All one has to do is nick the victim." She looked up at Karl. "This was meant for you."

Karl tilted his head and studied Cambul whose cold demeanor hadn't changed. "I have a feeling we're not going to get much out of him. But, I think we'll give it a try anyway." He looked up at Lomen. "You say he has a wife and kids in town?"

"Yes."

"How many kids?"

Lomen frowned and looked at his wife. "Elspa dear? Four?"

"Four," she answered. "The oldest is twelve, the youngest three."

Karl leaned down to stare into Cambul's eyes. "We'll start with the youngest first. Their screams usually hurt the worst because the pain is insufferable, and we'll draw it out so your wife will hear every cry and whimper. We'll make sure she gets to witness each child's torture. Then will save her for last so she can share her final pain with her husband."

Tears formed in Cambul's eyes. "Please."

"Please what?" Karl sneered. "You're in no position to petition for mercy. You were quite content to condemn us to our deaths and now you want mercy?"

"I was only doing what I was commanded to do," he pleaded.

"By whom?"

Cambul hesitated.

"Go on man," Lomen's wife urged. "Why are you stalling? Save yourself and your family." She pointed to Karl. "You know who he is. Do the right thing. He just might forgive you."

"Do not commit me," Karl said, his voice firm, "unless I say so."

"I'm sorry, m'Lord," she contritely replied.

"Well?" Karl said, staring at Cambul.

"Before you returned, King Kevin passed on orders to me to keep watch in this town and the surrounding countryside. All I was to do was report on what was happening here, if there was any sedition. But there was none, so I had nothing to report."

"What changed?"

"You returned, Sire."

"Who gave you this mission?"

Cambul shrugged. "It came from the same man who I gave the reports to. He gave me the blade. Neither of us could read the runes, but he said it came from one of the sorceresses."

"Which one," Annabeth demanded.

"He didn't say, m'Lady. All he told me was that should the king come through here I was to use it on him then send word to Avnoch."

"How long would the poison work?" Lomen interrupted.

"I don't know," Cambul answered. "I swear. I never wanted to do it, but the man said if I didn't, they would kill my children."

Elspa stared at the man with a mixture of pity and disappointment. "To think that we trusted *you* to keep us safe."

"How were you to get word to Avnoch?" Raquel asked.

Avoiding the condemning eyes of the wife, Cambul replied, "By carrier bird."

"Where do you keep them?"

"At my home. The children care for them." He shuddered at the thought of his children. "I am a dead man anyway. Kill me," he pleaded, "but let my family go. They know nothing of this. It's all on my own head."

"You should have thought of that when you accepted this commission," Karl chided. "While I might be magnanimous, your superiors won't be so forgiving. When does the man come for your report?"

"He doesn't anymore," Cambul said. "The last time was when he gave me the blade. He said that riding out here was a waste of time, that from now on I was to send reports by bird."

"When is the next report?"

"I sent it yesterday."

"And the next report?"

"I wasn't supposed to send anything unless something important happened."

"Like the King showing up?" Raquel taunted.

Cambul did not reply though his look of guilt was answer enough.

Ignoring him for the moment, Karl turned to Caryn and the others. "We dodged a bullet this time, but we can't count on being so lucky the closer we get to Avnoch." Shifting his gaze to Lomen, he asked, "What's the road like from here to Avnoch?"

"Easy travel," Lomen answered. "Farms on both side of the road for an hour, then a wide road through the forest for seven and a half hours then farms for another hour and a half until you come to the city. Lots of small towns like ours along the way."

Karl thought for a moment then announced, "We leave tonight."

"But, Sire," Lomen protested. "The road is safe during the day, but who knows what lurks there during the night."

"We'll take our chances."

"What do we do with him?" Caryn ticked her head at Cambul.

"Release him."

"What?" Caryn blurted, giving Karl an 'are-you-crazy' stare.

Karl turned his focus to Cambul. "Where is your loyalty, Cambul?"

"To you, Sire," he replied without hesitation.

"And you believe him?" Caryn scoffed.

"I swear on the heads of my children," Cambul asserted.

"Those are all just words," Caryn sneered. "As soon as we're gone, you'd be tossing that bird in the air telling the world where we are."

Ignoring her, Cambul focused his attention on Karl. "I can help you, Sire. I know Avnoch like the back of my hand. I was born there. I grew up learning the back-alleys and hiding places."

"Now you're really laying it on," Caryn mocked. "First you want to kill us and now you want to endanger your own life to help us. Puh-lease. Someone get me a bag before I throw up."

Suppressing a grin, Karl said, "She does have a point. Why are you so accommodating now?"

Cambul paused, his gaze solemn. "My Lord, if I can help you regain your throne, would you release me from having to spy on my neighbors and friends?" He twisted his head to look at Lomen. "I always reported nothing happening here, even when you brought in that wagon of black-market ale."

Lomen flushed and swallowed hard. Even Elspa suddenly grew quiet and introspective.

"I did the same for others," Cambul continued. "I kept everyone's secrets."

"Then why the poison blade, here and now?" Caryn accused.

"Because they demanded something to prove I was worth their trust," he answered, his confidence growing. "I saw you all in the distance when you suddenly appeared as if from nowhere. I could tell from his size that he was not local, so I grabbed the blade and came here to wait, figuring you would come here."

"So what stopped you?"

"When I heard Lomen call him 'Sire.' I knew then who you were. I was hoping that you would leave so that I could put that away." He nodded at the blade in her hand.

Caryn studied him. "You weave a good tale."

"I tell the truth," he stated.

"You mean like spying on your neighbors and friends," Caryn retorted, "that kind of truth?"

"I cannot undo what has been done," he responded. "Yes, I kept hidden who I was, but I never betrayed my friends and neighbors."

"Untie him," Karl said. When they hesitated, he bent down and began untying the knot until Lomen stepped in and took over.

Once free, Cambul rubbed his wrists and stood. "To prove my trust, Sire, you can take one of my children and place them in Lomen's care. If I fail in my word, he can do with the child as he wishes."

"That's no pledge," Caryn ridiculed. "Lomen would never hurt the child, no matter what you did."

Cambul turned to Karl. "I have nothing else to offer other than my word."

"Which doesn't mean squat," Caryn noted.

"OK, OK," Karl intoned. "We're getting nowhere here. You," he said to Cambul. "Tell me about the city. Can we get into the city after the gates are closed?"

"Yes, Sire. I know a way."

"I don't believe this," Caryn moaned. "You're actually going to trust him?"

"Yes, I am," Karl replied. "Now can we move on?"

Recognizing she had lost the battle, Caryn begrudgingly nodded.

"Good. I want you to find out what you can from him while I see if I can contact our mutual friend."

Caryn frowned in confusion then remembered. "As you wish."

While Caryn interrogated Cambul, the others watched Karl close his eyes as though going to sleep.

Uafas? Are you out there?

"What's he doing?" Lomen asked.

"Shhh," Caryn fussed. "Don't interrupt him."

Uafas? Can you hear me?

Yes, faintly. Where are you? Where did you go?

Long story. Where are you?

I'm in the forest half a day's walk from the city you call Avnoch.

Which side? Karl asked.

Which side?

Yes. Sunrise side or sunset side?

Sunrise side.

Good. We are too.

We?

Caryn, Raquel, Annabeth, Dieter and I.

There was a pause before Uafas said, *Let me guess. You're going back to Avnoch.*

Yes.

Uafas paused again before sighing and asked, *Where do you want me?*

Standing by, but I need to know exactly where you are. We're in the small town called Kinlich midway between Contyn and Avnoch.

Except for the place you call Avnoch, I don't know where any of those places are.

Hold on a minute. Opening his eyes, he caught Caryn's attention. "I need you to send an eagle or hawk or something to track down Uafas and bring him here."

"Where is he?"

"Somewhere between here and Avnoch."

Caryn turned to Elspa. "Is there a back door to the kitchen?"

"Yes, follow me."

The two women headed to the kitchen, the daughter tagging along.

"Who is Uafas, Sire?" Lomen asked when the kitchen door closed.

175

"My friend," Karl answered, "a wolf."

"The giant wolf that now roams free?" Cambul said. "I was told to keep a lookout for him, though it seems foolish to do so. By the time I told anyone, the wolf would be long gone."

"Still, he would be rather hard to miss," Lomen said. "How do you know where he is?"

"I don't," Karl replied. "That's why I've asked Caryn to send someone."

"She can talk to birds?" Lomen asked, his eyes filled with wonder.

"And more," Karl added.

The kitchen door opened, and the three women returned, the daughter bubbling with excitement.

"O Da," she exclaimed. "You shoulda seen it. This big hawk comes down and lands on her arm. And she talked to it."

"I told him to get some help. Hopefully they'll spot him."

Karl closed his eyes again. *Uafas.*

Yes.

We've sent some hawks to find you. Go somewhere safe but visible.

Easy for you to say, Uafas replied.

Let me know when they find you.

Karl opened his eyes and glanced around the otherwise empty tavern. "You may want to resume some sense of normality."

"I was hoping you'd say that, Sire."

Shifting his attention to Cambul, he said, "You too need to resume your normal behavior. We leave when it gets dark."

"Yes, Sire. I was just telling Lady Raquel here that we'll need to make speed if we're going to get into the city before daylight."

"You don't have to worry about us," Karl replied.

"What's the plan?" Caryn asked then turned to Lomen and his wife and daughter. "This might be a good time for you three to let us plan in private. The less you know the better."

"Understood," Lomen said with a smile then headed to the door, unlocked the bolt, swung the door open and poked his head out. "I'll be glad when someone we all know is back where he belongs. This latest fella is bad for business."

Uafas showed up midafternoon, far enough outside the town to be unobserved. Karl went to meet him, leaving Caryn in town to keep an eye on things.

It's good to see you again. Karl scratched the wolf's cheek and chin.

I know, Uafas chuckled. *Where have you been?*

Caryn and I were whisked away by two sorcerers, Karl said, already feeling guilty for concocting such an outlandish story then having to repeat it, even to NPCs who had become friends.

Ah. I understand. Well... you have three of them to deal with now. I escaped just in time before they put a hex on me.

What happened?

You were gone and Raquel was in charge. Things seemed to settle down, so I decided to leave the city to hunt for my own food for a change. I communicated with both Annabeth and Raquel. I like Annabeth. I like them both, but she has a sense of humor.

Then what happened?

I was tracking down a buck when I felt the commotion. Annabeth warned me to stay as far away as possible. I left off hunting and headed deeper into the forest. I've been there ever since. Annabeth said they were caught by surprise by a man called Kevin. He had managed to free the sorceresses who were now helping him. There is one name you will remember, the man you called Chet.

Yes, I know, Karl replied with a scowl.

You should have let me eat him when I had the opportunity.

Karl nodded. *You're probably right*
What's the plan?

For now, I want you to remain outside the city acting as a scout. I've got an army close by. The five of us are going to sneak into the city and open the gates so that when Kevin wakes up in the morning, he's in for a surprise. In the meantime, I need to know what's going on beyond the city area so that we're not surprised ourselves.

Easily done.

Thanks. Be careful.

I usually am. Uafas gave Karl a gentle bump of affection and trotted off.

Dusk has just begun to sift across Kinlich when Cambul led Karl and the others to the edge of town before setting off on a brisk pace. He was more than surprised when he realized that Karl and his team could easily move faster.

Two hours out from Kinlich, with the moon full and the night clear, Karl guesstimated they would arrive in Avnoch in another two to three hours, giving them plenty of time to sneak into the city and work their way to the main gates. The forest edging both sides of the road gave it a tunnel-like feeling, moonlight illuminating the way.

They moved in silence, their senses on edge as they swept the landscape around them. The road curved gently shortening the distance they could survey. As they rounded a wider spot in the road, Uafas let out a deep throated howl.

There's a roadblock ahead with four guards. Their attention is probably on me now.

Thanks.

Karl spread his hands and stopped the team. "Roadblock ahead," he whispered. "Four guards." He pointed to Annabeth who grinned with immediate understanding.

Two minutes later, there were four guards sound asleep.

Giving Cambul no time to marvel at Annabeth's powers, Karl urged him on. Thankfully there were no further obstacles and they made good time, arriving outside the city walls little after midnight. Cambul pointed to the sentries making their rounds high above behind the crenelated walls. They moved in perfunctory motion, bored with the monotonous repetition of walking the rounds in the middle of the night, especially when the city gates were locked tight.

Cambul curled his fingers motioning the others to follow as he led them around the city towards the cattle pens where livestock were kept prior to slaughter. Weaving through the numerous fenced off areas of pigs, sheep, lambs, and a few steers, he worked his way towards the caretaker hut, a small, single story, two room affair where the watchperson stayed during his or her assigned times. A chute of wood fencing bypassed the hut and ended at a small portcullis within the city wall.

Karl frowned at Cambul. "We're supposed to go in through here?"

"Nobody's watching it on the other side. It leads to the slaughterhouse."

"There's no winch here to raise it," Karl pointed out.

Cambul ticked his head at Dieter. "I bet he can lift it."

Dieter strode over to the iron grating and grabbed a bar. With a grunt, he pressed the gate up, surprised that not only did it make no noise, it lifted rather easily.

Caryn and the rest pushed through, Karl bringing up the rear to hold up the door for Dieter then silently lowering it into place.

"How'd you know about the door?" a suspicious Caryn asked Cambul.

"I used to sneak out this way all the time," he said with a smile. "They grease the door grooves so it's pretty quiet." He took a step off to the side, bent down and lifted an oak stave about half a meter in height. "It's still here. I used to use this to hold the door open when I snuck out. It's oak, so it's pretty solid. It gave me enough space to crawl under."

Caryn gaped at the stave that seemed too brittle now to holdup anything. "You were either young or stupid."

"I was both," he agreed. "But that was long ago. Come."

He led them past the interior pens, the butchering tables and meat hooks. Flies swarmed the offal left in the butchering pits. Annabeth held her hand over her mouth and tried not to breath in the rancid air. It wasn't until they were outside the slaughterhouse that she sucked in a deep breath of air.

"How can anyone breathe in there?" she complained.

"You get used to it," Cambul replied.

"Yeah, right," she answered, unconvinced.

Cambul stepped over to Karl. "With your permission, Sire, I think it best that I not be here in the morning. I wasn't here last night, and it wouldn't take long for folks to figure out that I had a part in this. It would also add to the mystery as to how you got in."

"I agree," Karl answered.

"You're going to let him go back?" Caryn objected.

"I know what you're thinking, M'Lady," Cambul stoically replied, "but you all are going to win. What purpose would it serve me to interfere for a losing cause? I have given my oath and loyalty to the King."

"Just like you did to Kevin," she parried.

"No, m'Lady," he quietly answered. "There you are wrong. I never gave my oath or loyalty to Kevin."

"Yet you were willing to follow him," she retorted.

"That's enough," Karl interjected. "We don't have time for this. Dieter. Help me lift the gate for him."

"Sure Boss."

In only a moment, Cambul was gone.

"I can't believe you're letting him go," Caryn said, shaking her head.

"He has nothing to gain," Karl said. "Besides, he'd only be in the way. C'mon. We got a front door to open."

He had yet to take a step when a body materialized before him. "Dammit Sakura," he griped though pleased to see her. "I hate it when you do that."

"Sakura," came the enthused response from the others. "Where've you been?"

"I've been hiding, waiting for you. When I heard that you all were no longer in prison, I knew it was just a matter of time before you came back here." She grinned at Karl. "When did you get back?"

"A little while ago," he said. "We were in the elf city to start then worked our way here. I'll explain later. At the moment, we're headed to open the gates and let my army come in."

"Works for me. I do have one request though."

"Yes?"

"I want Kevin."

"As far as I'm concerned, I don't care who kills Kevin, but that's not the end result we need at the moment. I don't want him respawning to create more havoc. If I knew where his respawn spot was, I might be persuaded otherwise. In the meantime, let's get an army in here."

"What do we do with the guards on top of the walls?" Dieter asked.

Karl smiled at Annabeth.

"I know, I know," she replied, pretending annoyance. "One of these days I wanna use something other than a sleep spell, something pure fun."

"You'll get your chance," Karl soothed. "Remember, there are some sorcery folks here that need reminding of who's in charge, especially in the sorcery department."

Annabeth fingered the Delf Stone around her neck. "Trust me," she coldly replied. "I haven't forgotten."

This time Sakura led the way. They travelled unseen and unheard as she crept down dark alleyways and back paths avoiding the roving city patrols. Forty-five minutes later, they approached the gatehouse.

"We need to work quickly," Karl softly reminded them. "Maddoc and the rest of them should be here in an hour or two. Annabeth will take out the guards and give us the heads up when Maddoc gets here. Raquel, you go with Annabeth. Stay partially visible so that other guards can see there are still two guards on top of the gate house. In the meantime, the rest of us will deal with some gate guards."

While Annabeth and Raquel climbed the stone steps to take care of the two guards, Karl led the way to the gatehouse, which he was surprised to find empty.

"That's odd," he commented, gathering everyone inside the small room containing a thin legged table and two chairs. "There should be two guards here."

"They're not always that diligent," Sakura said. "Some guards will stay here, while others who live close by will sleep at home until an hour before they have to open the gates. There's an older guard who's been here so long that it doesn't matter who is on guard with him, he always goes home to sleep. No one seems to object."

"How do you know that?" Caryn asked.

"People talk," Sakura deadpanned, "and I listen. And I've seen him shuffle off home once the gate is closed. I didn't see who was on duty tonight, but my guess is that they're not going to be back until they have to open the gates."

"All the better for us," Karl said.

"How *did* you manage to evade Kevin?" Caryn asked.

"As soon as I heard he was in town, I knew it wasn't going to be good," she said, though looking at Karl. "You and Karl were gone, and the odds were suddenly stacked against us. There were just the four of us against the six in Kevin's group plus the two sorceresses. I decided to split while I could."

"Why hang around here then?" Caryn wondered aloud.

"I may be a bit of a loner," Sakura replied, "but I am a loyal teammate. I figured something would happen sooner or later and I wasn't going to abandon you all." She shook her head. "Then I find out that you're all gone, disappeared. When I learned the truth, I knew it was just a matter of time before you all ended up here again."

"So you've been in the city the entire time?" Karl asked.

"Yes," she replied, "looking for opportunity to level the playing field. I could've taken out some of those who were with Kevin, but I figured their respawn spots were here, and it would alert him to my presence here. So I did my best to stay out of sight, gathering intelligence."

"Like what?" Karl's interest suddenly perked.

"Like not everyone gets along," Sakura explained. "They all stay in the citadel here, even the NPCs and monsters, but there's bickering within Kevin's group, especially with the one elf ranger."

"Frank?" Caryn chuckled.

"Yeah. That guy's got an ego problem. He believes he should be the leader. More than once Kevin has told him to 'take a hike' if he's not happy here, otherwise, 'shut up' and remember his place. Then there's a guy named Chet, a berserker, who seems to be out of place. It's like he's with them, but he's not, like he he's looking for an excuse to take off on his own but worries that Kevin is going to stab him in the back." She pondered for a moment then laughed. "Then there's this guy named Charles, a barbarian, who seems to be a bit clueless. Kevin calls him Chucky-poo and it doesn't seem to register with the guy."

"What about the sorceresses?" Karl asked.

"Now that's interesting," Sakura said. "They supposedly belonged to the former lords Fraster and Kerr, but they immediately transferred their loyalties to Kevin."

"What happened to Fraster and Kerr?" Karl asked, knowing the answer but wanting to verify.

"They're still supposedly in charge of their domains, but they don't do anything without Kevin's approval, especially since he has their sorceresses with him here."

"What about the monsters?" Dieter asked, more out of curiosity than concern.

"There are two of them," Sakura replied. "One is a dead guy, a former mighty warrior, raised back from the dead, and the other is a man with a bull's head and tail, almost as tall as our Dieter here."

Karl nodded then said, "We have our hands full. My guess is that once Kevin discovers we're back, he's going to pull out all the stops, which means monsters and sorcerers and sorceresses and anything else he can use."

"What about Elena?" Dieter said, interrupting Karl.

"She's fine," Sakura answered. "Kevin made her his personal cook. She's not allowed to leave the castle and has to have others get the food and stuff. I decided not to let her know I was here because I didn't want to get her hopes up. But I've checked on her a couple of times and other than missing you, she's fine."

"Getting back to the immediate mission," Karl said with a patient smile. "We've got a city to capture and a kingdom to conquer. Dieter, you can have the minotaur while I take on the dead man. Sakura, I'll need you to keep Kevin occupied while Annabeth deals with the sorcery folks." He turned to Caryn. "That leaves you handling everyone else."

"A walk in the park," she sniffed with mock disdain.

Karl turned back to Sakura. "What time did you say the gate guards returned?"

"Usually between an hour and a half hour before required opening time, which is usually a half hour after sunup, though," she smirked, "I've seen them running late on more than one occasion."

"Looks like we got a few minutes," Karl said. "Find a spot if you can and relax. I'm going up top to brief Annabeth."

Karl slipped out the door and headed up the stairs to the platform above the gatehouse where Annabeth and Raquel stood guard over two slumbering guards.

"I'll need to hit them with another spell in half an hour," Annabeth said.

"I think we can let them wake up and persuade them that it is in their best interests to cooperate," Karl advised. "Anything going on out there?" He nodded in the direction of the forest in the distance.

"Not yet," Raquel said

No sooner did she speak that Uafas interrupted.

They've arrived. They're just inside the forest edge.

Thanks. "They're here," he said to the two women. "Both of you come with me."

"What about them?" Raquel pointed to the sleeping guards.

"Leave 'em for now. We'll deal with them once I get the army inside."

Once back down in the gate house, Karl and Dieter slowly cranked the portcullis winch, doing their best to be as quiet as possible considering the iron bars were scraping against stone. Sakura and the others stood in the shadows outside the gatehouse and surrounding houses, ready to prevent interference.

With the portcullis raised high enough and locked down, Dieter lifted the gate-bar off the two doors and pushed them open while Karl lit a lantern then stood in the gateway and swung the lantern side to side.

A minute later, he saw movement on the road as Maddoc's forces silently swarmed towards the city, passing through the gates and spreading out onto the surrounding streets and alleyways. Closing the gates behind them, Dieter and one of Maddoc's warriors reversed the portcullis winch and lowered the iron bars back into place.

"How are your soldiers?" Karl asked Maddoc.

"We're ready, Sire."

"Good. We attack the citadel now. We want as few people as possible hurt."

"Understand, Sire. They already know."

"Let's move out."

Sakura noiselessly led the way, followed a short distance by Raquel and Caryn, with another ten meters between them and Karl, Dieter, Annabeth, Maddoc, and the rest of the force, tucking in behind them, moving without a sound.

Halfway to the citadel, Sakura came upon a roving patrol. Her first inclination was to eliminate them, but remembering Karl's injunction, she struck with a karate immobilizing knife hand to the neck, rendering them unconscious. The speed of her attack was so fast that no one knew the danger had been eliminated until they passed by the two guards crumpled on the ground.

Yet the closer they came to the citadel the number of roving patrols increased. Karl initially thought to simply swarm over the patrols and bypass them until he discovered that they had no loyalty to Kevin, especially when they discovered the real King had returned. By the time Karl and his forces stood outside the citadel, Kevin's supposed early warning system had been absorbed into Karl's army.

"Well, well," a sneer emerged from high above. "Look what the cat dragged in. Did you really think you could keep your sneaking in here a secret?"

Raising their eyes to the upper stories of a guard tower, they could see the outline of a person, framed within a narrow window.

Then to their surprise, the tall twin oak doors to the edifice swung open and Cambul was thrust out the opening, tripping then careening down the steps to the bottom before pushing himself to his hands and knees. His head twisted to gaze up at Karl, his look like that of a beaten cur.

"Apparently there is another way into the city," Caryn scorned.

Ignoring Cambul, Karl redirected his gaze up to Kevin. "I see you're still hiding as usual, Kevin," he taunted. "You always were a coward."

"Coward?" Kevin snapped, his temper flaring. "We'll see about that. Attack."

From out of other windows high above, small balls of flame hurled down on the army. The warriors jerked shields up and braced themselves when to their astonishment, the flaming balls swung wide, many of them reversing course and heading back up to explode on the walls and windows of the citadel.

Annabeth strode into the open space between the army and the castle steps. In a loud and firm voice, she called out, "Remember me?"

"We handled you before," a voice from the upper windows mocked, "and we can do it again. What's one puny sorceress against three of us?"

"I recognize that grating voice, Caillac," Annabeth sniffed with disdain. She pulled the necklace away from her chest, the stone dangling before her. "See this?"

"Yeah. So what?" another voice replied.

"Ah. Is that you Greg?"

"Yeah."

"And here I thought we were friends," she said with feigned disappointment. "This, as your two friends might know is the Delf Stone."

"Liar," Caillac yelled with sudden nervousness. "Eleris wears the Delf Stone."

"Eleris is dead," Annabeth retorted. "I killed her."

"Liar," Caillac repeated though less convinced.

"We shall see, won't we," Annabeth threatened.

"So what if you wear the Delf Stone?" Greg haughtily replied.

"Don't be a damned fool," Caillac snapped. "If true, we three are no match for her."

"I never really wanted to be a part of this," another voice interrupted.

Annabeth snorted a laugh. "Finella, is that you?"

"You know it's true," Finella replied. "You remember. I said to leave you alone."

"You have a selective memory," Annabeth replied. "You were the first one to cast the spell imprisoning me."

The doors opened once again and two beings emerged, a Minotaur, claymore in hand, and a broad-shouldered warrior whose stiff legged walk and cadaver appearance reminded those watching that this once powerful warrior was even more powerful in death. He held a short sword in one hand and a buckler in the other.

A momentary shock of fear rippled in the ranks that was soon suppressed when they saw Karl's bold indifference.

"Looks like we're on, Dieter," Karl said. "Maddoc. Time to finish this. You know what to do."

Staring down form the tower window, Kevin startled when he saw Karl's forces swarm past Karl and Dieter opposing his two monsters to burst into the castle.

Standing behind him, Gerard began wringing his hands and whined, "What're we gonna do?"

"We're gonna get out of here," Kevin retorted then whirled around thrust a finger in Gerard's chest. "I protected your sorry ass when you needed help. Now it's payback time. When you finally get out of here, you take me with you. You got that? I don't care how you do it, but you get me out of this game."

"OK, OK," Gerard whimpered, "I will. I promise. But what're we gonna do *now*?"

"Follow me," Kevin said, taking long strides to the door, snatching the Augury Stone along the way. "Remember. There's more than one way out of this city."

"What about the others?" Gerard asked, scampering to keep up as Kevin led the way down the circular staircase."

"What others?" Kevin shot back over his shoulder. "There are no others. There's only you and me."

At the bottom of the steps Kevin nearly bumped into Charles, a battle ax in his right hand.

"What're you doing here?" Kevin demanded. "You're supposed to be out down there fighting."

Charles cocked an eyebrow and stared at him. "Where're you guys going?"

"That's none of your business," Kevin snapped. "Get your ass down there and help the others."

"What others?" Charles coldly replied. "There are no others. There's just you and me. Remember?"

"Listen Chucky-poo," Kevin riposted, placing a reassuring hand on his shoulder up near his neck. "I'm not sure what you heard, but it's not what you think."

"You don't know what I think," Charles growled, "and I've had it with you calling me 'Chucky-poo.'"

Before his ax was halfway raised, Kevin struck first, gripping the back of Charles' neck and jerking him forward while plunging a stiletto into his gut, twisting the blade. As the axe fell from Charles' hand, Kevin whispered in his ear, "You always were a damned fool, Chucky-poo."

Charles expression of surprise, morphed to anger. "You... son of... a..."

Kevin wasted no time watching Charles slump his knees and roll over to his side. "C'mon," he urged Gerard. "We gotta move."

"Poor bugger," Gerard mumbled, stepping around him. "Wonder where his respawn spot is."

"Not our problem," Kevin said, hurrying down the hallway.

While Maddoc and the army burst into the castle, they found little opposition for once the guards saw the might arrayed against them, they laid down their weapons. It was then a question of mopping up operations.

As Maddoc's soldiers disarmed the guards, Caryn and Sakura raced through the hallways, searching out two specific men. As she scoured the numerous rooms and hallways, Caryn wondered what it would feel like to confront a man who had been a former lover, especially with the intent to kill him. Yet their prey eluded them.

In one of the hallways behind them, Annabeth strode with confident purpose, making her way to the upper levels where her nemeses had gathered to collectively defend themselves. Entering the top level, she proceeded down the hallway, standing to the side as she pushed open the door. The first three doors revealed empty rooms.

It was at the fourth door that she found them. Pausing, she cast a Detect Thoughts spell through the door and smirked at the angst and nervousness of the three inside the room. Their surface thoughts were a mixture of impulse and anticipation.

Annabeth smiled at the idea that had germinated and now developed. Standing before the closed door, she cast a Passionate Desire spell on Greg followed by an Implant Idea on Finella then forcibly controlled her mirth when she heard the commotion in the room.

"What the hell are you doing?" Caillac demanded. "Get away from me."

"Come to me my ravishing beauty," Greg gushed.

"Look at me," Finella exclaimed. "I can fly."

"Stop it," Caillac fussed then burst, "Get down from that window. She's doing this to us. Can't you see?"

"Who cares," Greg dreamily responded, "as long as I have you."

"Let go of me, you damned fool," Caillac snapped.

Annabeth cast a Summon Pest spell.

"Spiders," Caillac sneered, flicking her hand at the imaginary spiders. "You think I'm afraid of spiders?"

"You're right," Annabeth quietly agreed, casting another Summon Pest spell then smirked when she heard Caillac scream as.

"O God, rats! Get them off me."

"I'll help you my love," Greg said.

"I'm going to fly away for help," Finella joyfully announced.

Annabeth opened the door just in time to see Finella leap from the window and plummet out of sight. To the side, Caillac was spastically dancing, swatting and flicking at imaginary rats crawling up her legs and swarming over her body while Greg tried his best to kiss her.

Ten paces separated Karl from the dead warrior. He had yet to press the battle when a body dropped between them, smacking the cobbled stones in a bone crushing thump. Frowning, Karl looked up at the open window a good four stories up then back down at the crushed and crumpled sorceress, twisted grotesquely in death.

Assuming Annabeth had the situation well in hand, he twirled Orc's Bane in his hand and moved to position himself to attack. The dead warrior, monitoring Karl's movement moved accordingly. A roar to Karl's right caused him to shift a quick glance to see Dieter and the minotaur trading blows.

Seeing Karl's attention diverted, the dead warrior leaped forward to attack only to have his blade sliced in half.

Karl then spun around and dropped low, swinging his blade in a wide arc and severing the left leg between the knee and ankle. The warrior wavered for a moment before toppling forward.

Yet this set back did not stop him as he propped himself on his knees and continued the fight. Still, a dead body however much reawakened was no match for Karl's speed and it was less than a minute later that the warrior's head tumbled off to the side and the corpse collapsed.

By now, the castle had been cleared and Raquel, Caryn, and Sakura were back, Ross in tow, hands tied behind him.

Karl watched Dieter and the minotaur circling and gauging each other, both huffing form their exertions. "Want some help?"

"No," Dieter shot back, the berserker rage just beginning to erupt.

"Dieter," a voice cried out and Karl turned to see Elena standing in the doorway.

Thankfully the berserker fury was pouring out and the giant man heard nothing as his focus was on the beast before him. Raising his battle ax, Dieter attacked, driving the minotaur backwards towards the door where Elena now stood in frozen terror.

Karl raced across the gap and plucked the young woman out of the way before the minotaur tripped over the steps and fell backwards through the doorway. Giving no mercy, Dieter's axe swung in a blurred circle and impaled itself into the monster's chest, burying itself almost to the handle.

The monster stared up at him, the anger in its eyes sloughing away in layers of realization that death was about to overtake it. Letting out one last groan, the creature breathed its last and settled onto the cold stones of the anteroom floor.

The battle over, Dieter's berserker lust dissolved, replaced with the quest to find his love. He was brought up short when he heard his name.

"Dieter."

Spinning around, he saw her and opened his arms as she rushed to be crushed by his adoration and affection.

Leaving them to enjoy their reunion, Karl walked over to where Ross stood.

"He's the only one we can find," Caryn said. "No one else is around, except Greg who Annabeth has under control."

"They can't be far."

Hello Karl.

Yes?

There's an elf man running as fast as he can past me.

Stop him.

Can I eat him?

Karl laughed. *Sure.* Turning to the others, he explained, "Apparently Frank took off before we got in here. Uafas is… um… detaining him. He should be respawning soon."

Caryn snorted a laugh. "This should be interesting."

"Kevin is still missing," Sakura pointed out.

"As are Chet and Charles," Raquel added, "and that annoying Gerard guy."

"Chet's in prison," Ross glumly said.

"Why?" Karl asked, giving him a cold stare.

"Kevin didn't trust him," Ross replied with an indifferent shrug. "Thought he'd try and sneak out to connect up with you."

"Unlike you, who he could trust," Caryn retorted.

"It is what it is," Ross replied, returning her gaze with equal force.

Karl glanced up at the sky that was beginning to brighten with dawn's light. Turning to Maddoc, he said, "Release all the Avnoch soldiers and return their weapons."

"Sire?" Maddoc replied, raising a concerned eyebrow.

"We're not enemies," Karl reminded him. "We've accomplished what we set out to do." Glancing around, he realized that Cambul was missing. "Find Cambul, the man who was pushed out the doors. Send someone to fetch Chet from the gaol then send out joint patrols to track down where Kevin, Charles and Gerard are."

"Yes, Sire," Maddoc crisply said.

"What're we gonna do?" Caryn asked.

"We're going to go inside and set up shop," Karl said with a satisfied smile.

Felix walked down the empty hallway, his footsteps echoing as he passed vacant offices and cubicles. Knowing they couldn't take it with them, the former occupants left their personalities imprinted in each space – pictures, photos, and baubles of memories, the debris of former lives.

Two weeks ago, the last employee had immersed, leaving Felix the sole proprietor and caretaker of Immersion Technologies. For the past two weeks Felix arrived at his usual time, parked in his usual spot, paused to survey the empty parking garage before plodding up the front steps to activate the palm scanner to open the front doors. For two weeks he had settled into his office, like he always did, the comfort of routine giving him a sort of grounding. Yet scarcely had thirty minutes elapsed before he took to prowling the corridors, yearning for human interaction.

And here he was again today, ambling the same corridors, his boredom sinking to ennui. His traveling had taken him to the bowels of the building to places he never would have visited before. What impressed him was the efficiency of the place, computers synchronizing the lighting, room temperatures, humidity, and even the ambient music.

Retracing his steps led him back to his office where he would stare out the window at the empty golf course across the river, the fairways overgrown as nature reclaimed the former pristine place.

His distracted thoughts startled when his earphone buzzed. He was even more startled when he heard Mister Landon's voice.

"Good morning, Felix. I'm at your front door. I'd appreciate you coming down to let me in."

"Yes, Sir. I'll be there shortly."

Surprised that Landon had actually left his lair, though thankful for the company, Felix impatiently waited for the elevator to settle on the first floor and the doors open. Bursting through, he strode across the wide foyer floor and pressed the inside palm scanner, allowing the rotating door to slowly arc forward. Mister Landon stepped in and was inside the building before Felix had a chance for an appropriate greeting.

"What a pleasant surprise," he said with a smile.

"Yes," Landon replied, taking in the tall ceilings and windows of the foyer, "I suppose it is. It's been a long time since I was last here." Turning around, he gazed out through the windows overlooking part of the parking lot next to the river. "And that's the golf course across the river that you and Alyson play on. Must have been a nice view from your office."

"It was, though now Alyson and I don't play much there as the fairways and greens are overgrown."

Landon silently stared for a moment. "Alyson says you are quite the golfer."

"I used to be," Felix allowed, "I suppose, though don't really play much these days." He had tried, along with Alyson, but after the third time of playing an 18-hole round on an otherwise empty golf course overgrown with kudzu and other weeds, it wasn't quite the same.

Landon shifted a knowing glance at him. "I imagine you're ready to pick up the game again."

"I've thought about it," he confessed.

"That's why I'm here," Landon stated. "It's time."

"Already?" Felix blurted.

"Yes," Landon soothed. "We're a few of the last ones remaining who have not immersed. Once we immerse, I believe there are perhaps a hundred worldwide who have yet to… take the plunge." He grinned at his own joke.

"I've heard there are thousands of holdouts who had fled to the hills to avoid immersing."

"Not really our problem," Landon dismissively replied. "Drones will find them soon enough. Besides, given time, they'll eventually die off. What game have you decided?"

"PGA Grandmaster," Felix said with a sheepish smile.

"You enjoy the game that much," Landon said, cocking an eyebrow, "to spend the rest of eternity playing golf? What is there to it other than the game itself?"

Felix chuckled. "That's just it. There's far more to it than that. The game is designed so that you progress from one course to the next based upon skill level. But all the variables are in the game from wind speed and direction to sand traps, water holes, chip shots and anything else you can think of. Then there's over 10,000 courses, from Saint Andrews to Augusta to Royal County Down to so many others."

"I get the picture," Landon, said with a sympathetic smile. "And Alyson is going with you?"

"Yes," he replied with a sheepish smile. "Though to be honest, I'd go wherever she wanted, and we might look at other games after a while. What about you? What game are you going into?"

"Rarities and Collectibles." Noting Felix's puzzled look, he explained, "It's a game based upon the acquisition and exchange of rarities and collectibles. Things like the T208 Honus Wagner baseball card, which sold for $5.2 million the last time. Or Gustav Klimt's first Portrait of Adele Bloch-Bauer, which recently sold for $274 million. It's a quest to collect and own the most desirable of man's history. The pity of it all is that they're not real."

"And Meghan is going with you?"

"We share a passion for the finer things in life," Landon replied with a pleased smile. He starred out across the river. "Anyway. I wanted to give you a head's up and I wanted to do it in person. Let's shoot for the day after tomorrow. That way we can all enjoy our last meals together and prepare for our futures."

Two days later, Landon stood by Felix at the control console in ITL's immersion room, his arms folded. "Your thoughts?"

"Part of me wants to leave him there," Felix replied with an impish grin. "The problem is that he serves no purpose other than being an irritant. Now that Kevin has escaped, I think it's time we retrieve him and exile him from the gaming world all together. That will leave Kevin as a continued threat in the game while effectively condemning Gerard to the real life."

"He can always immerse into a rogue game," Landon mused, "though the protocols and safety nets are suspect."

"As long as he is prevented from accessing global games, it really doesn't matter what happens to him. Besides, we're making effective progress in finding rogue games and spiking them. It would just be a matter of time before his rogue game was discovered and wormed."

Landon nodded agreement. "Go ahead and bring him back while I go get the girls."

"Yes, Sir," Felix answered, tapping the keyboard.

Gerard awoke to a headache and thick tongue, causing him to wonder if he had too much to drink the night before until awareness settled and he realized he was back in real life, in the immersion room. His head throbbed and he snarled that he was getting damned tired of playing this silly-ass game of messenger boy.

Pushing himself to sitting, he blinked at the brightness of the room, turning his head when the door opened and Felix walked in.

"How're we feeling?" Felix greeted him.

Instead of replying with what he wanted to tell him, Gerard glared at him. "When are you going to stop this nonsense and leave me alone?"

"You're in luck," Felix said with a smile. "That was the last time. Looks like you're good to go from now on."

"So Karl has finally dealt with Kevin?" Gerard said, scooting to the edge of the table.

"Not quite," Felix replied, "but it's just a matter of time."

The door opened and Meghan and Alyson walked in, followed by Landon who remained in the doorway

"What's going on?" Gerard asked, frowning.

"Time for us to move on," Felix cheerfully replied.

"Looks like you'll be the last man standing," Landon said, "but you won't be alone."

"Pardon?" Gerard's frown deepened.

Landon stepped aside and another woman entered, though from the awkward gait Gerard knew it to be a robot.

"Meet R-237," Landon said with a smile. "She and hundreds of other robots will be manning the Landon empire while we're gone. They will assist you when you are ready to depart."

Gerard's mouth gaped open. "When did this all happen?"

"We've been working on it for some time," Landon breezily replied. "Anyway, enough chitchat. It's time for us to get going." He turned to Felix. "It has been a distinct pleasure having you by my side. I shall miss our discussions and your companionship."

"I was honored to have had the opportunity to share your time," Felix replied with humble gravitas.

Landon turned to Alyson. "He is a lucky man to have your devotion and affection. For a brief time, I was blessed to have that same devotion, protecting me and organizing my life. I can't imagine what my life would have been without you. I now wish you both a bounteous future."

There were tears in Alyson's eyes and all she could muster to say was, "I shall miss you." She stepped to him and hugged him followed by a hug for Meghan.

Felix shook Landon's hand and gave Meghan a hug one would give to a not so close relative.

Landon turned to Gerard. "It's going to be rather quiet very soon. While the robots are pleasant company, I'm sure you'll be wanting to re-immerse rather quickly. Good luck to you."

Gerard started to extend a hand, but Landon ignored him and headed to an immersion table, the others following and settling themselves. R-237 breezed past him and went to each table and adjusted the electrodes before heading to the center console.

Landon sighed with contentment turning his head to Felix one last time. "By the way, our friend here is in for a big surprise. Well done."

A look of abject terror encased Felix's face just as R-237 flipped the switch. "But I thought you –"

Though having no clue to Landon's cryptic statement Gerard sat mesmerized as he watched the exalted Landon and the others immerse as the life energy in the four bodies departed and what remained were lifeless corpses, limp and settled as in death.

"Would you like to immerse?" R-237 asked him.

"Not yet," he replied with a yawn. "Think I might like to wander around for a bit before I go."

"As you wish." She flipped the switch turning off the power and closed the destination screen on the computer. "The transfer staff will be here momentarily." She then stiffly ambled to the door.

Once alone, Gerard waited briefly then scooted to the door, silently opening it, and poking his head out. With the hallways clear, he strode over to the console and flicked the power switchback on and powered up the computer. Waiting for the restricted access prompt, he typed in his personal code then typed 'Bridge Quest' in the 'Game Selection' box. Scrolling through the player names, he clicked on 'Kevin Bristow.' A pop-up window opened with various options, and he clicked on 'Return to Real Life.' Clicking the 'Are you sure?' box, the 'Select a bed' option appeared.

Gerard surveyed the four possibilities before him and snickered thinking of Kevin's reaction if he awoke in a woman's body. Deciding that despite the humor in Kevin's shock, there were smarter ways of accomplishing what he wanted and there was one body on the table who was perfect. Making his choice, he clicked the bed number.

The response was instantaneous as life and breath returned to Felix's body. Gerard moved over to the side of the bed, watching as Kevin/Felix's eyes blinked open.

"Who the hell are you?" he gruffly demanded, his voice hoarse.

"Gerard," came the reply. "You're back in real life."

"About damned time," Kevin snapped. Pushing himself to siting, he frowned when he saw the other bodies. "Who are they?"

"Just some folks who recently immersed."

Kevin rubbed his face and sucked in a deep breath. "Glad to be out of that abomination. I was getting damned tired of having to watch my back." He placed a hand at his jaw and twisted his head, cracking his neck. "So what's the plan? What other games are available?"

"Do you want revenge first?" Gerard tempted.

"Damned straight," Kevin huffed, pushing himself to standing.

The door opened and four robots, identical to R-237, entered, each one pushing a gurney. They paused when they realized there were only three bodies to remove.

"There are three of us, not four," Gerard haughtily stated, hoping to confuse them.

"But we were told there were four," one robot meekly replied.

"Well as you can see, there are three here, are there not?" Gerard said with arrogant authority. "Two of us are obviously not quite ready yet." Flipping a hand at them, he added, "Take these others and be done with it. I'll let you know when he and I are ready."

"Yes, sir," the robot respectfully answered.

In short order, the bodies of the three dearly departed were loaded onto the gurneys and pushed out and down to the cryogenic freezers in the vast underground storage floor where thousands upon thousands of freezers stacked ten high in long rows that stretched the entire length of the storage floor. Gerard knew from experience, only the wealthy or connected or the physically beautiful and healthy made it to the freezers. The rest were dumped into the recycle chambers to be cast upon the winds.

"You were saying?" Kevin remarked as the door closed.

"You want revenge, right?" Gerard half-lidded his eyes and curled his lips in a smug smile.

"I've already said I do," Kevin retorted. "Get to the point."

Gerard grinned and leaned in. "We're gonna kill Karl."

Kevin's first demand was making a detour to the bathroom. His, "I gotta take a piss" was followed by a loud "What the hell," when he didn't recognize himself in the mirror. Forgetting his immediate need to urinate, he whirled around to face Gerard. "What the hell did you do to me? Who is this?" He spread his arms in anger.

"I didn't have time to get your own body," Gerard retorted. "I had to make the most of an opportunity."

"Opportunity?" Kevin snapped. "You could have just trotted down and retrieved me. It would've taken all of ten minutes."

"On what excuse?" Gerard demanded. "Nobody knows you're back... at least not yet. And there's one other little point you've forgotten. I can't retrieve a body from the freezer without proper authorization."

"Well get it," Kevin bristled.

"I can't. What you don't know," Gerard calmly replied, "is that you and I are the last ones alive in this company. I need someone higher up for authorization."

"What?" Kevin exploded. "You mean I'm stuck in this guy's body?"

"Think of it as a loaner," Gerard chuckled. "Besides, does it really matter what body you're in now, especially since we're going to immerse in a little while?"

"It matters to me," Kevin fumed.

"Relax," Gerard said with a sly grin. "When I said that I can't, I didn't say that you couldn't."

Kevin gave him a hard stare. "Cut the bullshit and get to the point."

"The body you are in happens to be Felix Hubach, the CEO of Immersion Technology, the very man who can give us access to the freezer zone."

Kevin turned to look at himself in the mirror. He looked to be in his early 40's, short wavy auburn hair, brown eyes, and somewhat trim and fit. He wore slacks and an open collar, short-sleeve shirt.

"At least the guy's not out of shape," he commented with a resigned sigh.

"Hurry up and do your business,' Gerard urged. "We got work to do."

Once finished and heading down the hallways, Kevin followed Gerard to the elevators down to the cryogenic floor, passing several robots along the way who gave deferential nods to Kevin/Felix. Entering the elevator, Kevin waited, expecting Gerard to press the button for the freezer floor.

"This elevator will only go down as far as the lobby floor unless you give the authorization," Gerard explained. "See that screen there?" He pointed to a small touch screen above the floor buttons. "That's the authorization screen. Press your thumb against it and tell it to descend. The access is both thumb print and voice activated."

"What's it called'" Kevin asked.

Gerard frowned at him. "A security screen."

"No, the floor we're going to. What's the proper name?"

"Oh," Gerard replied. "It's called the Cryogenic Zone."

Kevin pressed his thumb against the screen and said, "Cryogenic Zone."

"Good day, Mister Hubach," a female voice crooned inside the elevator as it began its slow descent then picked up speed. "I'm surprised that you are still with us. Latest data states that you were immersed not more than twenty-six minutes ago."

When Kevin didn't respond, Gerard nudged him. "Why are you back, Mister Hubach?" he said in slow emphatic words. "Isn't it because there were a few last-minute details to attend to?"

"Uh… yes, yes," Kevin chimed in. "Just some last-minute things I wanted to check on before I depart."

"I imagine Miss Whitmar will be disappointed you are not with her," the voice said.

"I'm sure she is," Kevin replied.

"Is she an avid golfer like you?" the voice asked.

Kevin scowled at Gerard for help.

"Yes, she is," Gerard answered for him. "She's quite the pro."

There was an awkward silence before the voice said, "That's odd. There is nothing in her data records to indicate she is a professional."

Gerard quickly backtracked. "That's not what I meant. When I said she was a pro, I meant she golfed like a pro, not that she was one."

"Ah," the voice replied. "I understand. It is an expression of admiration."

"Yes, that's it exactly," Gerard said as the elevator slowed then stopped.

The elevator stopped but the doors didn't open.

"What's going on?" Kevin whispered.

"I'm sorry Mister Hubach, but there is some confusion concerning your presence. According to Immersion records, an electronic signature identified as Felix Hubach was immersed into the Golf Pro game approximately twenty-seven minutes ago, along with Alyson Whitmar."

"Well there's obviously a mistake," Kevin bluffed, "because here I am. I'll look into it as soon as I finish here. Now open the doors."

The seconds ticked silently, and Gerard shot a nervous glance at Kevin.

"Yes, Mister Hubach," the voice replied as the doors opened. "R237 is at the Immersion room verifying the data and awaits your return."

"Thank you," Kevin said.

"We gotta move," Gerard growled in a low tone and grabbed him by the elbow and forcibly hurried him into the outer room.

"What's going on?" Kevin demanded, yanking his arm away.

"R-237 is up in the Immersion room. It's just a matter of time before she recognizes what transpired. C'mon."

Gerard led the way though the outer room then through the opaque doors and into the main storage unit.

Kevin jerked to a halt, overwhelmed at the vastness of the storage area. Before him, twin rows of cryogenic pods stacked ten high, a frozen body in each one, stretched into the disappearing distance. A narrow maintenance path bisected each row   Ceiling lights, four stories above the floor, cast dull shadows on the drab concrete floor.

"How the hell are we going to find him?" Kevin muttered.

Gerard ticked his head to the left where several golf carts sat parked in front of the Registration and Location office. Off to the side were half a dozen forklifts.

"Follow me," he grandly announced and led the way into the office, past the vacant desks and to the main control room and to the desk with the main computer, flicking on the power. In moments, the access screen popped up.

"Damn," Gerard snarled. "I forgot you wouldn't have his password."

"Then let's get outta here," Kevin replied, immediately recognizing the impossibility of finding Karl.

"Not so fast," Gerard countered. "I guaran-damn-tee you there's a paper back up somewhere." He gazed around the office then crossed the floor towards a side door. Opening it, he flicked on the light and grinned. "Voila."

Kevin poked his head in and saw a large windowless room with old library index card cabinets lined floor to ceiling against three walls. "Are you serious?" he scoffed. "They used this?"

"It's not as silly as it appears," Gerard answered, walking into the room and identifying the alphabetical arrangement. "While it might take a little longer than a computer, it does have its advantages."

"Like what?" Kevin mocked.

"Computers crash," Gerard said.

"And paper burns," he retorted.

"Whatever," Gerard shrugged. "Karl's last name is Hanson."

"And Caryn?"

"We don't have time for her." He pulled open the 'Hal-Han' drawer.

Kevin grabbed his arm. "We'll make time."

Gerard saw his determination. "Why?"

"Let's just say screwing with her screws with him."

"Then why not unplug Raquel and Annabeth too," Gerard huffed, "and the rest of them?"

"Naw," Kevin said, shaking his head. "He's got something more for her."

Gerard stared at him for a moment then said, "Her last name is Allen."

Kevin spun around and headed to the first cabinets while Gerard flipped through the cards.

Gerard found Karl first. "He's in row F-4-6."

"Caryn's in F-2-2," Kevin announced.

"Excellent,' Gerard said with a wicked grin. "That means they're practically next to each other and close to the front here."

Kevin paused then walked over to another section and pulled open the 'Bra-Bur' drawer.

"What're you doing?" Gerard fussed.

Ignoring him, he flipped through the cards. "I'm also in row F, F-3-8."

"We don't have time to change you back," Gerard tersely reminded him. "We can always come back when we get things settled. C'mon. We gotta move it."

Kevin yanked the card out, folded it and stuck it in his pocket.

They hustled out of the office and jumped into a cart, Kevin driving. He looked up at the large aisle signs and saw that they were at aisle GG. Flicking on the electric starter, he pressed the fuel pedal and turned the wheel and headed towards the far side of the warehouse. In short order, they arrived at row F and exited the cart.

Kevin looked up at the aisle sign – a large 'F' with '1-5,000' with an arrow pointing left and '5001-10,000' with an arrow pointing right. In the middle between the two rows of pods was the narrow maintenance aisle. Protruding from the back of each pod were the power cords; temperature, pressure, and climate gauges; liquid nitrogen tubes; regulators; and the status computer pad.

"This should be easy," Kevin chuckled, walking down the maintenance aisle and stopping at the second row and turning left. He counted two pods up. "Go around to the front," he ordered, "and make sure I got the right one."

Gerard cocked an eyebrow at him. "Just access the damned screen in front of you."

"Just do it," Kevin snapped.

Instead, Gerard stepped up next to him and touched the screen, turning it on to reveal a name – Caryn Elizabeth Allen – followed by a ten-digit alpha-numeric identification code. "See?"

"You sure it's her?"

"Of course I am," Gerard huffed. "She was one of the first ones in the game. Are we gonna stand here wasting time or can we get on with this?"

Turning to the array of cords and tubes, Kevin grinned. Flipping off the locking bars to the power cord, he said, "Here goes" and yanked the cord away.

Suddenly an alarm horn blared, and the dim lights brightened to illuminate the warehouse as if an incandescent bomb had exploded. Sirens then added to the cacophony.

"We gotta get out of here," Gerard clamored.

"No," Kevin shouted back. "We have to destroy Karl first."

"Too late," Gerard shot back, hustling towards the cart. "We're toast unless we get out of here now. They know where we are."

Kevin wavered in indecision then, with a frustrated "Damn," turned and leaped into the cart that was already moving away.

Instead of heading to the front, Gerard sped towards the rear of the warehouse.

"Where are you going?" Kevin shouted above the din.

"There's always an emergency exit, even in places like this. Government regulation." He slowed and pointed to a fire station containing a hose, extinguisher, and an axe. "Grab the axe."

Obeying, Kevin added the metal extinguisher for good measure.

A mile later, they were still passing stacks of pods.

"How far does this place go?" Kevin scowled in frustration. He was ready to be outside in the open air and far away from here.

"There's 10,000 pods per row divided in half," Gerard said, displaying his knowledge. "So that's 5,000 pods at, say, a meter wide each."

"That's five kilometers," Kevin said shaking his head, "more than three miles."

"Let's hope there's nothing waiting for us at the other end," Gerard observed.

"Like what?"

"How should I know?" he shrugged. "More robots?"

The noise continued unabated, the volume never diminishing as they arrived at the far end of the vast warehouse where they were greeted by ten cargo and equipment elevators with the doors open. Gerard drove the cart into the closest elevator, leaping out and rapidly assessing the quickest way out of the building and slapped the ground floor button. The doors closed and the elevator began its ascent.

"This should take us to the maintenance garage," he said, "I hope."

When the doors opened, they were relieved to find they were in the part of the building that housed the vehicle part of the maintenance department, containing forklifts, golf carts, vans, trucks, sedans, and other company vehicles. Gerard drove the cart out of the elevator and headed towards the far end where he saw the tall outside garage doors that gave access to the repair part of the shop. His heart sank when he saw several robots stocking and organizing various vehicle parts. They looked up at him and Kevin as they approached. Recognizing Felix, they paused in their work and nodded their respect. Gerard stopped the cart and approached one of the robots who seemed quite indifferent to the mayhem in the immersion room as well as the muted alarms throughout the rest of the building.

"Don't you hear the alarm?" he chastised.

The robot looked at him then addressed his answer to Kevin/Felix. "Yes, we were notified that a breach had occurred in the immersion room. Per ITL regulation governing post immersion accountability, nonhuman caretakers are restricted to their specific duties and will not interfere with the actions of another caretaker unless asked to do so."

"And you have not been asked to do so, is that correct?" Kevin asked assuming the role of ITL CEO.

"Yes sir."

"Very good." He turned to Gerard. "See? I told you the directives were effective." He turned back to the robot. "Now let's see how well everything else is, shall we? I'm going to select a sedan and take it for a drive. I expect they will be fully charged and maintenance performed."

"They are," the robot answered with a hint of pride.

Kevin walked over to the row of sedans and leisurely strolled along the line then stopped and pointed to a cream colored two-door Mercedes Benz. "That one. Get me the keys to that one."

The robot turned and called out to a robot near the key rack. "Bring the keys to M-11 and open the bay doors."

Gerard watched as the robots hustled as best they could and just in time he and Kevin were out the garage and turning left onto Amnicola Highway.

"Where we headed," Kevin asked.

"Far away from here," Gerard grinned and exhaled a sigh of relief. "We need to find another immersion point. Head down towards Atlanta."

Had they paid attention, they would have noticed the drone high above them, following their twists and turns until they got onto I-75 heading south. By then, the interstate cameras monitored their flight.

Chapter 8

Karl leaned forward on the throne, an elbow planted on the armrest, the other hand jammed on his side, and calmly stared at the five players, Kevin's former allies, and a contrite sorceress standing before him. Except for Frank whose haughty arrogance said he was above all this nonsense, and Ross whose cold anger revealed he still hadn't forgiven Karl for giving him a respawning experience, the other three PCs seemed genuinely contrite, especially Chet who stood apart from the other four. Caillac was another matter.

Karl shifted his glance to encompass the rest of the room. Close behind the prisoners stood an entire platoon of Avnoch's finest warriors, a sort of temporary imperial guard used now to enforce Karl's will. Behind them stood the elite of the city and other parts of the kingdom, curious onlookers waiting to hear the king's decision. Outside the walls of the citadel, Maddoc's combined forces continued their search for Kevin and Gerard. Maddoc himself stood to Karl's left, along with Sakura, Dieter, and Elena. Caryn, Raquel, and Annabeth stood to his right.

"Some think we should let you go, live and let live." Karl said. "But I don't trust you. Anyone who would follow a worm like Kevin has no place in this kingdom or on this island."

"How was I to know you were still alive," Chet objected.

"Why should that matter?" Karl replied. "You had the opportunity to do what was right. Still, from the looks of it, your presence in the gaol said you had second thoughts. So there is that in your favor."

"Dude," Frank sniffed in disdain. "You're pretty full of yourself. What gives you the right to pass judgment on us? This is all just a game. You kill us and we'll be right back to get our revenge. So watch your back."

Karl narrowed his gaze at him. "Thank you for making my point. Yet you misjudge me. I do not intend killing you over and over again. Unfortunately, since you have not leveled up high enough to cross the next bridge, I am stuck with you for a while. Some," he shifted his gaze at Chet, "I will reconsider and allow them to resume their place in the kingdom, if only to assist them in leveling up."

Turning to the platoon commander, he pointed to Ross and Frank. "Take those two and toss them in the dungeon until I decide what to do with them."

Frank curled a lip and snarled at Caryn. "Don't think I won't forget this, bitch. Revenge is gonna be so sweet."

Caryn shook her head and rolled her eyes. "I'm so terrified."

"You were lousy in bed anyway," he shot back as they led him and Ross away.

"Sounds like somebody's mad because I wouldn't let him wear my underwear," she quipped.

There was an audible gasp and not a few titters as the crowd snickered at Frank.

"That's a damned lie," he shouted before he was hustled through the door.

Raising an eyebrow, Karl twisted his head to gaze at Caryn who returned his gaze with innocent aplomb. He hesitated to ask if it was true.

Seeing his curiosity, she leaned in and whispered, "Just think of the reputation he's gonna have to deal with."

Smirking, Karl turned his attention to the remaining three players. "Chet. Come and stand before me."

Chet moved to stand in front of Karl.

"Do you here and now swear allegiance to me and my friends, to always support one or all of us at all times?"

Chet paused before he spoke. "I do. You have my loyalty. I'm not a PK, remember?"

"Preacher's kid?" Karl said with a grin.

Chet flashed a smile.

"Preacher's kid?" Caryn mumbled.

"Private joke," Karl commented. "I'll explain later." He then looked at Charles. "It appears you have been on the receiving end of Kevin's treachery."

"That son-of-a-bitch killed me," he snarled. "When I get the chance, I'm gonna return the favor."

"In the meantime, I will ask you for the same allegiance I offered Chet."

"You have it," Charles answered, "as long as you don't call me Chuckie-poo."

"I wouldn't disrespect you like that," Karl affirmed.

"Then you have it. I give my word."

"That's good enough for me," Karl nodded. "That leaves you two." He narrowed his gaze at Greg and Caillac. "I'm going to let Annabeth decide your fate."

Annabeth stepped forward, folded one arm across her slender stomach and propped the elbow of the other arm while she fingered the Delf Stone dangling from the thin gold chain around her neck.

"Truth is," she said, peering intently at them, "I don't trust either of you."

"They made me do it," Greg protested.

"Oh shut up," Caillac sourly snapped. "We didn't have to do anything to convince you. You were a willing accomplice."

"That's only because you two put spells on me."

"Oh puh-lease," Caillac sighed, rolling her eyes. "All we had to do was intimate that we'd have sex with you, and you did whatever we asked. You're pathetic."

Annabeth twisted her head to gaze at Karl. "The problem is that they both still retain their sorcery powers. We can eliminate one of them like what happened to Finella."

At the mention of Finella, Caillac's eyes popped wide. "I'll be good. I swear it."

Ignoring her, Annabeth continued, "But we're still left with one who can respawn and still cause havoc. For now, we probably ought to restrain and confine them until I can come up with a better solution."

"I swear it," Caillac repeated. "I promise to do whatever you want me to."

Annabeth slowly turned to face her. "So if I put you in prison for a few days, you'd promise not to cast spells on the guards and try to escape."

Caillac paused only a moment before bobbing her head. "I promise."

"She's got her fingers crossed behind her back," Greg blurted.

Annabeth shook her head and chuckled. "Really? Like crossing your fingers somehow invalidates what you said? And you said *he* was pathetic?" Annabeth waved her hand and directed an Obedience spell at Caillac. "You will allow yourself to be led to prison."

"Yes, m'Lady," Caillac replied with a deferential smile.

"You go along with her," Annabeth said to Greg, "before I turn you into a toad."

Greg's mouth slacked open, and his eyes widened and he quickly caught up to Caillac as she was led away by several guards.

"I probably should go along and put a spell on the cell," Annabeth mentioned, "like they did to me. The spell I put on her only lasts an hour. Don't do anything exciting until I get back."

Karl redirected his attention to the two players before him. "You two are free to go and accomplish what you need to do to level up. I suggest you head west where there is a portion of the island still untamed."

"And if I want to stay here?" Chet said, rubbing his wrists.

"If you stay," Karl warned, "you are expected to become a valued member of this team, which means there is still an orc kingdom to conquer."

"I'd like to stay too," Charles chimed in, shifting a gaze at Raquel.

"Then so be it," Karl regally announced then motioned for Maddoc to come closer. "I have a feeling Kevin and Gerard are heading towards the bridge to the third island.

They're gonna have to level up to cross, which means Gerard will be hanging around this island for quite some time."

Maddoc stared blankly at him and Karl realized the man had no clue what he was talking about. "They're headed west to the far tip of the... uh, they're headed west, most likely towards Statmyr."

"I'm on it, Sire," he deferentially bowed and headed back through the crowd to resume the search for Kevin and Gerard.

"For everyone else," Karl said, speaking with a regal tone, "let's get back to normal, to a prosperous life." Turning to Raquel, he started to explain how he wanted to consolidate the two kingdoms before cleaning out the orcs when the room suddenly darkened then disappeared.

"Damn it all," Raquel erupted as both Karl and Caryn fizzled and vanished, "not again."

A stunned hush fell upon the crowd.

"Don't worry," she encouraged though sighing. "They'll be back. In the meantime, let's get things back to normal around here." She repositioned herself and sat on the throne.

The rest of Karl's team closed ranks around Raquel, as did Chet and Charles. Chet leaned in towards Dieter. "What's going on?"

"I'll explain later," he replied with a grim smile. "It's all good. We just keep doing what we're supposed to do."

"What're we supposed to do?"

"Unite two kingdoms."

Karl's initial torpor gave way to the feeling of overwhelming heaviness, a feeling that even opening his eyes would require an exertion beyond his strength. The second awareness was his heartbeat and the realization that he had been, once again, brought out of the game. This was quickly followed by anger *I'm going to rip somebody's heart out as soon I get my strength back.*

The coalescing of light and shape momentarily invaded his fixation on brutal punishment. He blinked his eyes to focus, staring briefly at the ceiling before slowly twisting his head, recognizing the immersion room where he and Caryn had last emerged.

Caryn. Is she here too?

He shivered and inhaled a deep breath. Feeling pulsed throughout his body and he lifted a stiff arm, seeing the electrodes on the tips of his fingers fall away as life returned to his body. Rolling over onto his side, he struggled to sit up.

"Please allow suitable time to regain strength and equilibrium," a female voice cooed.

Licking dry lips, Karl frowned as he looked around the room for the speaker. His gaze wandered from the control panel to a platform bed where a woman was resurrecting from a game. Expecting to see Caryn, he was disappointed as he did not recognize the woman.

His mouth felt parched, and he managed to give voice to his immediate need. "Water."

"There is a water bottle on the table next to your bed," the female voice relied.

Karl again glanced around the room yet saw no one except the woman who had awoken and struggled to sit on the edge of the bed.

The woman saw him and smiled. "Hey."

Karl stared at her. She wore shorts and a loose t-shirt, her legs dangling over the side of the bed. She was very pretty, reminding him of a shorter version of Felix's girlfriend, Alyson, extremely fit, good-sized firm breasts, narrow waist, toned smooth legs, thick blond long hair, flawless skin, pert nose on a captivating face, and bright eyes that, at the moment were a mixture of puzzlement and bemusement. She scratched her head and ran her fingers through her hair.

"Wonder what it is this time?" she said with a chuckle, noting the water bottle by the bed. Reaching for the container, she lifted it to her lips and squeezed the sides, squirting the colorless liquid into her mouth.

"You've been here before?" Karl politely asked, unscrewing the lid to the water bottle and tilting it to his mouth.

The woman cocked an eyebrow at him. "You suddenly lose your memory? We were here not all that long ago to, as you put it, rescue a damsel in distress."

Karl blinked as he stared at her. "Uh... and who would that have been?"

"Alyson," she frowned. "Are you OK?"

"I'm fine," he replied. He stared at her a moment longer then said, "Who are you?"

The woman stiffened and cocked her head, irritated and concerned at the same time. "It's me, Caryn."

"Caryn?" It was Karl's turn to startle and raise an eyebrow. "As in Bridge Quest Caryn?"

"Who else?" she demanded, her frown deepening.

"You look different," he said, "not the same. What happened to the old Caryn?"

"What?" Her head jerked back then shifted to look down at her body. "What the hell?" She yanked up the bottom of her t-shirt, exposing herself. "They're bigger... nice shaped, but bigger."

Leaping off the table, she held her arms out as she studied her body. Her head jerked up and she gave Karl a pained look. "Is my face different?"

"Yes."

"Bad?"

"No," he replied shaking, his head, "just different, still very pretty though."

Caryn's eyes shifted around the room. "Where are they? If this is their idea of a joke, I'm gonna kill someone."

"To go to the ladies room," the female voice sweetly said, "exit this room and turn left. It is three doors down on your left. You will see the universal sign for woman on the door."

"I'll be back," Caryn called over her shoulder as she rammed the door open and disappeared.

Karl stood and looked down at his own body clad in only spandex shorts, recognizing the physical shell was still who he once was. Yet something wasn't quite right. Where were Felix and Landon?

"Where are you?" he called out.

"I'll be there in seventeen seconds," the voice replied.

Karl counted off the seconds and seventeen counts later, the door opened and a woman strode in. At first, Karl thought the woman might have a physical impairment because of her awkward stride, but as she drew closer, he realized her limitation was because she was not human. The latex skin over the bone structure cleverly mimicked human skin. But it was the mouth that made everything weird for though the lips moved, they didn't form the words.

"Good day to you, Karl," the woman robot said.

"What's going on?" he demanded. "Who are you? Where are Felix and Landon?"

"I will answer your questions as soon as Caryn returns," she politely replied. "In the meantime, be sure you are sufficiently hydrated. Remember, water is the life source for human beings."

The door flew open and Caryn stormed in. Glaring at the robot, she snapped, "Who the hell are you?"

"I am R-237," came the sweet reply. "I am a second generation, multiplex, integrated, and fully functional AI system providing custodial and redundant operational responsibilities in the absence of established authority under Global Code 16 dash 32, sub paragraph H."

An awkward paused ensued before Caryn exploded, "Where the hell is my body? Why am I like this?"

"The answer to your first question," R-237 replied, "is because your human body was destroyed."

"What?" Caryn exploded as she stormed around the room. "Why?"

"If you remember," R-237 said, "Gerard, a discontented employee of ITL due to his forced removal from the Costa del Mar game, was placed into your game to relay a message concerning the rescue of Alyson Whitmer. Expecting to be placed back into his life game as soon as he delivered the message, he was angered when it did not happen."

"We know that," Caryn coldly responded.

Ignoring her, R-237 continued. "When Gerard was finally removed from your game, he activated Kevin's return to a bodily form then disclosed where you and Karl were kept in suspended storage. The two of them then determined to destroy your bodily forms, thus preventing you from ever returning. You," she said, looking at Caryn, "were the first one destroyed. The alarms activated in time to prevent Karl's destruction. Unfortunately, we were unable to save you."

"Those bastards," Caryn fumed. "So who am I then?"

"Accessing your file and determining your capabilities and talents, we conducted a global search for a body that was as close to your original form as possible."

"I didn't look like this," Caryn complained.

"Remember, it is impossible to find an exact match," R-237 explained.

"I get that," Caryn sourly replied. "Who is this?" She held her arms out and pointed to herself.

"That is the former Norwegian world biathlon champion Elsa Johansson. Knowing your talent with marksmanship, we determined Elsa most closely approximated your gift, both in marksmanship and physical stamina."

Somewhat mollified, Caryn asked, "What happened to her?"

"She is immersed in Olympic Quest," R-237 answered.

"Suppose she wants this back?"

"She'll have to wait her turn," the woman chuckled.

"What's going on?" Karl interrupted. "Why are we back here?"

"You and Caryn have been called back to eliminate Kevin and Gerard."

"So that's what happened to them," Karl mused. "Where are Felix and Landon?"

"They have immersed and are no longer part of the world here."

Karl tilted his head back and gazed at the ceiling, a lattice affair of recessed lights and sound baffles, as he pondered what to do. Dropping his gaze to stare at the robot, he asked, "How do we know Kevin and Gerard haven't immersed into another game?"

"We don't," R-237 replied, "though the likelihood of that occurring is extremely low as they would have to immerse into an unauthorized game. Still, that is a possibility."

"Why not just simply let them immerse and take them out in some other game?" Caryn said, struggling to come to grips with the fact that she was in someone else's body.

"That too is a valid question," the woman answered. "Remember, Gerard once worked for ITL and understands that possibility exists. Therefore, it must be assumed that he will not pursue that option."

"But how would you know if he opted for some game developed by another company?" Karl argued.

"Because of the Inter-gaming Protocol," R-237 replied.

"Which is?" Caryn huffed.

"All certified and authorized games are globally interfaced to track and maintain population status so that at any and every instant, every player is identified, located, and monitored. That also includes those games specifically designed to eliminate unwanted or detrimental individuals."

"You've designed games to kill players" Karl blurted, "permanently?"

"Of course," came the unaffected reply. "How else should we deal with the dregs and evil of society?"

"Just who decides who deserves to live or not?" Caryn objected.

"Those parameters are defined in Global Code 16 dash 47, sub paragraph E."

Caryn was about to ask who wrote the code when Karl, said, "Right now, Kevin and Gerard could be anywhere in the world. This is worse than the proverbial needle in a haystack. This is mission impossible."

"Except for one thing," R-237 said. "Gerard has a tracking device implanted on his body. It was placed there after he immersed."

"Kevin?" Karl asked.

"Unfortunately, no such device was implanted in him."

Karl inhaled and blew out a deep breath. "Obviously we're not going back into the game until we accomplish the mission."

"Obviously," came the reply.

"No matter how long it takes," Caryn tartly added.

"No matter how long it takes," R-237 agreed.

"How do we know where they are now?"

"A command center has been established in Mister Landon's residence. Your vehicles and equipment from your previous assignment are also there."

Karl frowned and stared at the robot. "Why was Gerard sent to notify us in the first place? It sounds like he was someone important in this organization. Why send him and not some flunky?"

"Mister Landon and Mister Hubach decided to punish Gerard for an infraction of protocol. My analysis adds that Mister Hubach simply did not like Gerard. His punishment was that every time he was about to succeed in a quest, he would be withdrawn from the game to accomplish a specific task unrelated to his immersion game."

"So he was pulled out more than once?" Caryn said, still off balance with her loaner body.

"Yes. This last time, when he was sent to notify you, it seems that Misters Hubach and Landon forgot all about him in the quest to rescue Alyson. Once she was rescued and you were immersed, they decided to leave him in Bridge Quest and subsequently immersed into their own games."

"So how did he manage to get back here?" Karl asked.

"Misters Landon and Hubach neglected to write an override to the instructions concerning Kevin and he was pulled out by Gerard."

"You mean to tell me," Caryn huffed, "that you folks were clueless? Gerard had to take time to get Kevin's body up here. And you folks didn't even notice?"

"Um…" R-237 hesitated. "Speaking of that, there is something more you should know. Kevin is now in Mister Felix Hubach's body."

"What?" Karl and Caryn replied in unison.

"Gerard returned before Mister Landon and Mister Hubach departed. Therefore, the bodies of Landon and Hubach were still in the immersion room. When the retrieval team arrived for transport, Gerard managed to confuse them. Recognizing he had a short window of opportunity, he chose to place Kevin in Felix Hubach's body. Subsequently, they journeyed down to the cryogenic floor and terminated Miss

Caryn. As I mentioned before, once Caryn's pod was deactivated, the emergency security system was prompted, prohibiting further disturbance. Though, unfortunately, Gerard and Kevin, now Felix, managed to escape via the maintenance bays."

What followed was a thick silence before Caryn said, "I want to see where I was."

"That would be in the cryogenic floor below the basement level."

"I don't give a damn where it's at, I want to see it."

"As you wish," R-237 replied.

They followed the robot to the elevators, passing several robots along the way who gave deferential nods to R-237. Entering the elevator, R-237 tapped twice on the small touch screen above the floor buttons.

"This is management unit R-237. Authorization code two-zero-seven-seven-dash-alpha. Descend to Cryogenic Zone level."

The elevator doors closed, and Karl felt the very subtle movement downwards.

When the doors opened, R-237 led the way though the outer room then through the opaque doors and into the main storage unit.

Karl and Caryn paused as they took in the gaping vastness of the Cryogenic Zone. It reminded Karl of some of the government warehouses he had visited, large edifices containing forgotten materials, stuff departments ordered to spend a budget, but never used. Ceiling lights, four stories above the floor, perched over twin rows of cryogenic pods stacked ten high, disappearing into the distance. A narrow maintenance path bisected each row. To the left, golf carts and forklifts sat parked in orderly fashion.

R-237 led the way into the office, past the vacant desks and to the main control room and to the desk with the main computer, flicking on the power. In moments, the access screen popped up.

"This is management unit R-237. Authorization code two-zero-seven-seven-dash-alpha. Access unit storage files."

The computer responded and R-237 typed in Caryn's name. "You are in F-2-2."

They hustled out of the office and jumped into a golf cart, Karl driving. Noting that aisle GG was to their front, he flicked on the electric starter, pressed the fuel pedal to gun the engine and swung left, stopping at row F.

Caryn led the way this time, traversing the distance to silently stand in front of her pod. Staring in through the small window at her supine lifeless body, she muttered, "I'm dead."

"Everyone here is dead," R-237 pointed out. "What makes you alive is standing here right now."

Karl took a step back and gazed down the long row. "Are all these pods filled with people?"

"Not all," R-237 replied. "There are still empty pods."

"So everyone who entered any of ITL's games is here?"

"No," R-237 said. "Only certain people are here, like you and the other individuals in Bridge Quest. Other individuals not deemed necessary to future propagation were eliminated."

"What?" Karl and Caryn again spurted in unison.

"It was a pragmatic decision based upon the burgeoning human population. Thus, global protocol number one, which is to reduce or eliminate the human population, was instituted" R-237 said. "So far it has been quite successful."

"Who gets to stay and who is eliminated?" Karl asked, not liking the answer.

"Those determined to benefit mankind were retained. Those with no viable purpose, like politicians and lawyers, were the first to go. Ha. That was a joke."

"I'm serious," Karl said with a frown. "Who determines who is necessary?"

"Actually, with everyone immersed, no one is necessary," the robot calmly answered. "However, in case the need arose, certain classes of humans were retained. First, the rich who could afford to pay for cryogenic services then those who contributed to society in meaningful ways, like doctors and nurses. Still, it was recognized that there was no need for a thousand heart specialists when the top twenty-five would do. So the best and brightest in the medical and scientific fields were kept. The rest were eliminated."

"What about the arts, music and writing and such?" Karl asked.

"There are a few of those. Again, there was no need to retain more than necessary. The top five in each form of the arts were retained, though not necessarily here. Though, with time, even those who were deemed irreplaceable will be eliminated, leaving a select few in the security realm to the afterlife."

Caryn shook her head. "But you've missed a good number of holdouts who have not and will never immerse."

"Yes, you are correct," R-237 answered, "however, they will die out soon enough."

"You don't know human nature very well," Karl objected. "If the caveman survived, so too will present mankind. All you need is a fertile female."

"And enough food to survive," Caryn added.

R-237 titled her head as though pondering this latest information. "That is impossible. The present human has grown too soft, too dependent on technology to survive the demands of daily sustenance. Your supposition is illogical."

Deciding not to argue, Karl shrugged and shook his head. "Have it your way."

Casting one last forlorn look at herself stretched out in the pod, forever dead, Caryn wondered if she were not looking into the mirror of fate.

"I'm ready to go," she grimly stated, more than ever ready to get this over with and back to the game where she was comfortable with a body that was hers.

Karl redirected his attention back to R-237. "You said our things are still at Landon's place?"

"Yes."

"We'll still need a command center. We'll use the same one we set up before. The question is, who's going to man it?"

"Based upon your previous methods, it was assumed that one of you would," R-237 replied.

"That's a non-starter," Karl firmly replied. "Caryn and I are a team, united, as in inseparable. Wherever I am, she is and vice versa. If you want us to take down Kevin and Gerard, you're gonna have to come up with somebody else to monitor the CC."

"CC?" R-237 repeated with a puzzled frown.

"Command center," Karl answered. "We'll need someone there at all times, someone like you, for instance."

"That is impossible," R-237 stated. "My zone of operation is restricted to this facility."

"Then find someone who can," Karl snapped, jabbing a finger at her. "I want someone there by the time we arrive."

"Acknowledged," the robot replied.

"And another thing," Karl continued. "Where are Kevin and Gerard now?"

"They are in Atlanta."

"Atlanta?" Karl repeated, casting a side glance at Caryn. "Why Atlanta?"

"We surmise their presence there is due to the regional control center located in Atlanta," R-237 said.

"Control Center?" Caryn said, looking down yet again at her legs and arms.

"The Regional Gaming Control Center, or RGCC, for the southeastern states is located in the former Bank of America Financial Center building on Peachtree Street," R-237 explained. "If Gerard wanted to bypass gaming protocols in the outlying zones, he would need to access the directive management codes in the Regional office. Fortunately, once the alarms triggered, all access to the numerous facilities was denied and buildings locked down. They will stay that way until the threat is solved."

"Gerard would know this as well," Caryn pointed out. "So why go to Atlanta?"

R-237 shrugged, an awkward jerky motion that emphasized though she was a brilliant AI, physically she was still just a robot.

"Gerard also probably knows that we were brought back," Karl observed, "which makes accomplishing this mission even harder. They're going to be looking for us."

"But they won't know where you are," R-237 reminded them. "Whereas we know where they are."

Karl looked at Caryn and ticked his head at the door. "Might as well get started."

"If you need anything, you may call upon me," R-237 said, "but I'm sure you are capable of doing this on your own," causing Karl to jerk to a stop.

It was the way she said it that reminded him of someone else. Staring intently at the robot, it was then he noted hints of similarity, the curve of the face, the eyes.

"Freyja?"

"Ha," R-237 replied with a satisfied chuckle. "You've discovered my secret."

"You're Freyja?" Karl blurted, stunned. "How is that possible? You're not even in the game."

"I'm *in* the game whenever necessary," R-237 replied. "Whenever a player activates a request for a god or goddess support, I interface and interact with the player."

"But you never gave me any support," Karl fussed. "What's the point of even having you in the game?"

"A valid question," R-237 replied, walking to the elevators. "My purpose was to redirect a player's efforts. Invariably a player would think he or she needed outside help instead of taking time to think things though. Besides, what's the worst that could happen?"

"Continual respawning," Karl shot back. "If you've never experienced it, you don't know what you're talking about."

"I suppose," came the cavalier answer as the elevator started its ascent. "But the truth is that so many players actually believe their trust in me is warranted, that I am somehow responsible for their fortune, though I must admit that I have on occasion *helped* a poor unfortunate soul."

"So you admit that you can actually help someone," Karl accused.

"Yes, I can do that, but it defeats the purpose of the game if at any time you can simply call upon some god or goddess and poof your problem is solved. Where is the challenge in that?"

The doors opened and they stepped out into the main foyer area.

"So you appear as whatever god or goddess is requested?" Caryn asked.

"Yes... myself and others. Each of us assumes the role of a specific god or goddess and interacts with individual followers."

"How is that possible if you are here?"

"It's actually quite easy. It's all done via interface and preprogrammed responses." R-237 turned to Karl. "How did you know it was me?"

"The way you answered my question, and then the lines of your face," he replied. "There are similarities to Freyja, though she is game generated."

R-237 nodded with what passed for a smile. "It's interesting that gaming characters can assume such intricate details, down to the number of hairs on your head. Yet in real life, I am just a stiff legged robot, highly intelligent, but bound by the limitations of physical space and materials." She led them to the main doors. "I often wonder if I could be Freyja in real life... after all, I'm merely an electronic circuit system much like yourselves. Why couldn't I immerse into a game and actually feel things?"

Karl frowned at the thought, shaking his head at the sudden ramifications... a world where there was no difference between robots and humans. Was that all man was, a mere electronic circuit? Deciding that was for the philosophers to worry about, if there were any left, he dismissed it from the present moment.

Giving the robot a dispassionate stare, he said, "So I should assume for all future references that Freyja will probably not get involved with my game life."

"It truly depends," R-237 answered.

"That's not an answer," he snipped.

"Just to make sure," Caryn interrupted, ready to get moving. "Karl and I will not be able to immerse back into the game until Kevin and Gerard are caught and eliminated."

"That is correct," R-237 affirmed.

"Again," she objected, "if all the games are off limits to them and they're going to die anyway, why bother?"

R-237 paused. "Because Gerard is gifted in gaming knowledge to include both hardware and software. Thus there exists the possibility that, given sufficient time and resources, he can wreak havoc on the gaming world."

"What you really mean is bombs and missiles," Caryn replied. "All they'd have to do is gain access to a building and this whole gaming world is screwed."

"Exactly," R-237 readily agreed.

"I'd be more worried about Kevin than Gerard," Karl pointed out.

"We are worried about them both," R-237 answered. "Together, they can destroy far more than anyone ever anticipated. That is why you two were brought back."

"Why not simply bring back an army and hunt them down?" Caryn asked.

"It's a question of trust and efficiency," R-237 said. "Too many involved and one loses control, especially among those who have been enjoying their own games."

"There has to be a ton of war and shoot-'em-up games," Karl said. "Pick one and pull out the top players."

"We have," R-237 said with what passed for a grin. "That's why you two are here. You're the best. Good luck to you." Without further discourse, the robot turned and headed back to the elevators.

"I still want someone in that control room," Karl called after her.

"It will be done," came the response before the robot disappeared into the lift.

Karl cocked an eyebrow and exhaled a loud sigh. "This is bull shit. You can't convince me that there is no one else besides us who can do this."

Caryn knitted her brow as she pondered their predicament. "Actually, there really isn't anyone else… from ITL. Kevin and Gerard are ITL problems and we're here to fix the problem."

Karl half smiled at her. "How'd you get so smart?"

"Purely accidental," she deadpanned.

"Ah well," he again exhaled a long sigh. "Might as well get this over with."

As they stood at the main doors in the front vestibule, waiting for them to open, Karl turned to look at Caryn whose scowl and penetrating gaze said she was still pissed. "You gonna be OK?"

"No," she huffed.

"It's only temporary," he reminded her. "Once we're finished, we can go back to the game."

"Easy for you to say," she tersely replied. "You're not in some loaner body."

"I know," he soothed. "But look at it this way. Eventually our bodies are going to wear out. At some point in time, we will either stay forever in the game, or if they do decide to bring us out, it will probably be in someone else's shell."

When she didn't reply, he said, "Besides, you look great."

"Better than before?" she challenged.

"Not better, just different."

"Which do you like better?" She locked her gaze on him.

"I don't know,' he nonchalantly replied. "Depends how you are in bed."

Caryn smirked, despite her anger, which was finally beginning to settle. "Now you can add another babe to your bevy of lovers."

"Wonder how muscle memory works in situations like this?" Karl teased as the doors opened and they strode out together into the brightness of a sunny September morning.

"I guess we'll have to find out pretty soon," she answered then glanced around at the cars in the parking lot and on the lawn where grass grew around the tires. She felt a sudden distaste for the machines. "What say we walk to Landon's place?"

"I like it," he said with a smile, reaching for her hand and pulling her to him, kissing her.

She responded with equal passion, half-tempted to consummate their desire right there. When the kiss ended, she said, "So? How's she kiss?"

"Like you," he said, "just like you."

Turning towards the river, they ambled along the Riverwalk, heading towards downtown Chattanooga.

"Wonder if our boat is still there," Caryn said, relishing Karl's closeness and his attention.

"Don't see why not. It's not like anyone else is around."

As they walked, hand in hand, he slid surreptitious glances at the woman by his side and wondered if they could put them into different bodies whenever they brought them out of the game. That could be fun, to have a different lover each time, yet not having to go through the whole dating scenario first because you'd already know the person, but you'd get to have a new body to experience.

"What are you grinning at?" she asked.

"Just wondering if they could put us into different bodies each time they brought us out of the game," he replied. "It would be like having multiple partners but still with the same person."

"An interesting concept," she replied, still touchy about her present state. "So each time we came back to real life, we'd be someone new."

"Yes,"

"The only problem I see with that is finding suitable bodies that match us, both in physical characteristics and abilities."

"And then that would require us to be constantly brought out of the game," he agreed. "Ah well, it was a passing thought."

"So you're saying you can't be satisfied with one person?"

Karl knitted his brows in thought. "No, not that necessarily. It's more of the chocolate box approach, all deliciously sweet, different, but you know what to expect."

"I suppose," she said, disappointed with his answer.

"Think about it," he continued. "It's almost like shapeshifting. You get to be with a different individual, but it would always be the same person."

"Don't you think you would get bored after a while?"

"Eh, it's possible. I suppose after a while you'd want to settle on one shape."

They walked in silence for a while before Karl said, "Though I suppose a little variety every now and then would be fun."

"What is it with you and the multiple partners?" she fumed. "Don't you get enough of that in the game?"

"It's not the same," he replied, oblivious to her irritation. "There I'm reacting to different personalities and quirks. Yeah, sure, I'm not complaining, but it would be more enjoyable if it was just one person who could morph into different shapes. That way I wouldn't have to balance competing personalities, trying to please them."

Caryn knitted her brows and tersely said, "So actually, what you're saying is that, despite all, you'd prefer one person but like the variety multiple partners gives you."

"Yeah, something like that, I suppose," he replied, his mind now distracted to the task ahead.

Caryn pursed her lips, debating whether to ply ahead with the discussion, wanting him to affirm that she meant more to him than the others, that he could be satisfied with just her.

Karl preempted her quest when he said, "We need a plan and course of action."

Deciding she would make the best use of the opportunities here when she had him all to herself, she said, "We need to see what's in place. Hopefully they'll have tracking set up."

Their concerns were answered when they arrived at Landon's building. Just as R-237 had stated, their vehicles, drone equipment, and excess ammunition were in the parking garage. After a quick check, they headed up to Landon's Suite. Exiting the elevator, they were surprised to see numerous robots of various shapes and sizes, some quite imposing with built in gun systems. They were more surprised when activity stopped and the attention all narrowed on them.

"Back off," Karl commanded. "You know why we're here."

The activity resumed as a robot much like R-237 approached them. Unlike R-237's stiff gait, this one walked with a smooth fluid motion.

"Good day, Karl and Caryn," she said. "I am RITA-4. R-237 notified us of your impending arrival. I hope all meets to your satisfaction."

"We'll see," Karl replied, heading towards the outer office where Alyson used to hold sway.

"What does RITA-4 stand for?" Caryn asked.

"Robot-improved-intelligence-and-technology-artificial," the robot answered. "I am number four in the chain of development."

"How many are there?" Caryn queried.

"Four," came the reply. "I am the last one. As the other three are at separate facilities, you may call me Rita if you wish."

"Why all the beefed-up security here?" Karl asked, noting two armed robots guarding the outer doors to Alyson's office.

"Mister Landon did not wish his prized possessions disturbed while he was immersed."

"ITL could have used the same security," Karl sourly pointed out.

"An oversight that is being corrected," Rita replied, pushing the doors open.

Karl breezed past Alyson's desk and headed up the stairs to Landon's sanctorum. Once inside the apartment, he noted the layout was much like before with half a dozen computers, charts and schematics, and two clean coffee mugs on the dining room table. He smiled, wondering if they belonged to Landon and Felix or Landon and Meghan.

"OK," Karl said, turning around to face Rita. "Here's the plan. I want this place manned twenty-four-seven. Since Gerard is wired, I want to know his location at all times."

"There is a potential problem," Rita interrupted.

"What now?" Karl said, frowning.

"While we can provide round the clock monitoring, tracking Gerard may be more difficult."

"Why?" Caryn demanded.

"Recent storms in the southeast have knocked out transmission towers in several key areas."

"Then go satellite," Caryn said, the answer obvious.

"The storms also impacted a number of dishes, though the loss appears to be minimal at present. We are adjusting links as we speak. However, please note that several of the satellites are nearing the end of their use."

"What?" Karl frowned. "No one has put up a replacement?"

Rita paused. "We're working on it."

Karl chewed his lip and shook his head. "OK. I don't care how you do it, but I want direct comms with you here all the time. I want to know where Gerard is all the time. Again, I don't care how you do it. Also, I want current weather reports, updated as the weather changes. And I want immediate responses to all my questions or demands, whether you can satisfy the demand or not. Understood?"

"Yes," Rita replied.

"Then get someone in here and get these computers linked and operational," he groused.

"As you wish."

Karl shifted a glance at Caryn. "C'mon. Let's see what's left in the fridge."

"A glass of wine would be nice," Caryn mused as they headed to the kitchen.

Ten minutes later, carrying a small tray with cheese, olives, and some slices of cold meat, they passed though the dining room on their way to their bedroom upstairs. Caryn carried an uncorked bottle of wine and two glasses.

Once in the room, Caryn locked the door then poured the wine. Turning, she smiled when she saw Karl's obvious desire.

"You gave me a nice view back in the immersion room," he teased.

"You mean like this?" She placed both glasses on a side table then pulled her top over her head and holding it to the side, exposing her breasts.

"Yes," he said, sucking in his breath. "Something like that."

For three days, Karl and Caryn dawdled, taking advantage of the fact that Gerard and Kevin had remained static in Atlanta. Using the excuse of checking equipment, they made the most of the boat on the river and other diversions, especially in the bedroom.

On the morning of the fourth day, Rita confronted them as they came down to fix coffee and eggs for breakfast.

"You have been here for more than three days," she fussed, "checking equipment and other things, yet have made no effort to accomplish your mission."

"How we accomplish the mission is our responsibility," Karl shot back. "Your function is to support us in every manner that we require."

"But... but," Rita replied. "When are you going to start?"

"When we're good and ready," Karl firmly stated. "Listen. One of the reasons we're taking our time is to give Gerard and Kevin a false sense of security."

"I don't understand."

"Right now," Karl explained, "those two expect someone is coming for them. That's why they've holed up in Atlanta. My guess is that they know Caryn and I are coming and they're prepping defenses."

"How is that possible?"

"Precedent," Caryn said. "You all sent Gerard to get us the last time, although," she cast a knowing glance at Karl, "I didn't look like this. Might come in handy when we track them down."

Nodding thoughtfully, Karl continued, "Send a drone through the streets where they're at. Make sure they can see it."

"Won't that give you away, that you're looking for them?" Rita said.

"Yes and no," Caryn jumped in, immediately understanding what Karl was planning. "Right now, they're not getting good sleep as they expect us to show up at any time. We send a drone through now and they'll get less sleep. We do that on a regular basis. Send it the same time every day for say a week or two. After a while, they get used to it and we stop it. Voila, once again they get less sleep."

"We want them off balanced," Karl said. "What we employ now is psyops. Eventually they're going to move. Again, my guess is that during this time, they're going to figure out where some of the immersion hold outs are and head for them."

"How do you know this?" Rita asked with obvious doubt.

"They both want to survive," Karl answered. "Right now, they're somewhat protected, but they're gonna have to get more help to ward off folks coming after them. And then there's probably not a lot of food left in the city, at least much that's not in cans. Guarantee there's going to come a time very soon where they're going to want some real food, at least Gerard will. Kevin is trained to subsist on what's available, though my guess is that even he will want something other than canned spaghetti."

"Which means," Caryn said, "they're going to move, head out to where they think others might be."

"Can we monitor communication coming out of Atlanta?" Karl asked.

Rita thought for a moment. "Yes."

"What about elsewhere?"

"Yes," Rita slowly answered, "I believe we can."

"Then do it," Karl said. "I figure anyone out there will be looking for likeminded souls, which means Gerard and Kevin will be in communication with them."

"Done right," Caryn said, "we can ambush them on the way."

"Ah," Rita nodded. "I think I understand."

"Then go ahead and get things in place," Karl ordered.

"Where will you be?"

Caryn jerked a thumb back to the bedroom.

Rita frowned in confusion. "You two spend a lot of time in that bedroom."

When Karl and Caryn emerged from the bedroom later that morning, showered and refreshed, they checked on the progress of monitoring any comms originating out of Atlanta and were surprised that Rita had interlinked satellite communications to the computers in the dining room.

"What about HF radio?" Karl said.

"Pardon?" Rita replied, puzzled.

"Whosever out there is probably using Ham radio equipment. We're gonna need a transceiver, power supply, antenna, and a frequency scanner at the least."

Rita's face went blank. "We don't have any of those items in the building."

"Let's see what Caryn and I can find," he replied with a confident smile.

Two days later, after scouring the surrounding neighborhoods and stores, they managed to locate an antenna, transceiver, and power supply. Setting up the antenna on the rooftop, they ran the coaxial cable across the roof then down and through the living room window.

"All we need now is a frequency scanner," Karl observed. "In the meantime, we need someone to manually scan."

Rita assigned two robots to perform the scanning mission while Karl and Caryn resumed their search, stumbling upon a scanner in a Walmart Supercenter across the river. With the scanner attached to the power supply, Karl had the two robots monitoring the airwaves.

Content with the progress so far, he turned to Rita. "We're going to do some more exploring. Let us know if you get anything."

"We've got feed from the drones," she said, displeased that they were taking off again.

"I've seen the feed. It's not a lot, other than views of where they're staying and the occasional head popping out the door. They do their wandering in the night when it's safer. As long as they're not damaging or trying to break into any gaming facility, we wait."

Brooking no further discussion, he turned around and headed for the door, Caryn happily walking beside him.

"How long you think we can keep this up?" she whispered.

"As long as we can," he whispered back. "The way I figure it is that they owe us. They keep jerking us out of the game. We might as well enjoy it while we can."

"What about Kevin?"

"What about him?" he replied, as they walked through the doors and headed for the elevators. "I want him almost as much as you do."

"Then why are we dawdling. We can take him out anytime we want." She pressed the button for the parking garage.

"Exactly," he said. "Why rush? This is the first time in a long time where we don't *have* to go kill orcs, hide out in an elven city, escape a jail, or go on some quest so we can level up. We can actually relax and enjoy a break. Think of all those folks in the games whose lives are one constant struggle. Except for the lack of fine dining, this is a good place to be for the moment."

Caryn furrowed her brow in thought. "Think about those poor saps still on the first island, waiting for cures that will never come."

"And no one can go back to tell them," Karl pointed out.

"Alright," she smiled. "I'll chill. I was starting to get antsy because we have a mission, and my personality wants to get it done and over with."

"Which means we go back into the game," he added, "and I'm not ready yet to leave real life."

The elevator stopped and the doors opened. Stepping out, they walked over to their two trucks, a kayak in the back of each one.

"Where we headed today?" Karl asked.

"Not too far from where we were the last time we were here. This time, instead of heading south on 411 in Ocoee, we stay straight on 74 until we get to the Ocoee Whitewater Center."

"I can get used to this," he grinned.

For two weeks, while Rita and company monitored the airwaves, Karl and Caryn made the most of their time together, spending time on the water or hiking or exploring Chattanooga and the surrounding towns, or back in the bedroom.

"I like having you to myself," Caryn said one evening, slowly undressing for him as he sat in the chair and watched. When the last button of her blouse released, she paused. "Do you miss not having another partner here with us?"

"I hadn't really thought about it," he replied, staring at her chest, still hidden behind the shirt.

She liked the way he ogled her and wondered if it would still be the same when they returned to the game, where she competed with every other female for his attention. Well... maybe not every other female, but Annabeth and Raquel for sure. She had accepted that she was expected to share but that didn't mean she had to like it.

She half-smiled at the image of the last time when she and Karl were brought back to real life to rescue Alyson. The days after their successful mission were spent on a large yacht that they anchored in the middle of the Tennessee River. They had peeled off their clothes and swam naked before adjourning to the master bedroom on board.

"You're teasing me," Karl said with an amorous grin, ticking his head at the still closed shirt.

Caryn replied with a sultry smile and slowly pulled back one side, exposing a breast. She slid her hand up to pull it off her shoulder when a loud knock on the door stopped her.

"We've got something," Rita's muffled voice announced.

"Damn," Karl groused with a loud sigh. "We're coming."

Quickly buttoning her blouse, Caryn followed Karl out the room and down the stairs to the dining room where a robot had locked onto a signal.

"We traced a signal coming out of Atlanta," Rita said. "We're not sure where the other one emanates from yet. We're working on a triangulation to pinpoint, but it's somewhere in the Midwest... we think."

Karl and Caryn listened as a voice spoke.

"This here's Red. Who's this?"

"This is..." the man paused as he thought of a code name.

"Aw hell, son, don't fret about yer moniker. Ain't like anyone's gonna get busted fer not usin' the proper nomenclature. Just gimme a name I can hang onto."

"Felix," he replied figuring he was in the man's body, might as well use the name.

"That's Kevin," Karl asserted then chuckled. "Clever. No one would suspect you're not who you appear to be."

"Where you at, Felix?" Red asked.

"Southeast US."

"That's a pretty big area. Can't you be more specific?"

"Depends," Kevin answered. "Where are you at?"

"Touché," Red replied with a chuckle. "Can't be too careful, 'specially with them snatchers lookin' for patriots. How long you been on the run?"

Kevin hesitated a moment then said, "I've lost count. A long time."

"Just like the rest of us. You gotta plan?"

"Right now, it's avoiding trouble, if you know what I mean."

"I think I do. What's it like where you're at?"

"Lots of drones still. We've managed to avoid them so far."

"We? There's more than one o' you?"

"Just me and another guy."

There was a pause before Red came back on the air. "What kind o' skills you got, Felix, you and that other guy?"

"I was once a Widow-maker and he's a computer expert."

"Yup," Karl chortled. "Them's our boys."

"Widow-maker?" Red answered. "Hot damn, boy, you got some survival skills. How come you ain't doin' better?"

"Long story," Kevin replied, "but the gist of it was that I was betrayed. Managed to extricate myself before all hell broke loose. Connected up with my partner here and we're looking for a home."

"Liar," Caryn grumbled.

"Then head west, son," Red replied, "towards the mountains. We can use the both of you."

"Who's 'we?'"

"That's all I'm gonna say for now. We got ourselves a nice place and I wanna keep it that way."

"I understand. Which mountains?"

"I'll let you know the closer you get. Stay off the interstates. That's where most of the cameras are. And keep a watch for drones as you move. Most gas stations still have plenty of gas, so if you want to get here fast, find yerself a good car, but, like I said, keep a watch for drones."

"Where am I going?"

"Head on out to either Oklahoma City or Kansas City. Once you get there, gimme a shout out."

"It may take a while."

"No problem," Red replied. "I'll have someone monitoring the radio."

"Roger that," Kevin said.

"Good luck."

"Thanks."

Silence settled in the room for a bit when Karl said, "They're moving tonight."

"How do you know that?" Rita said with a puzzled frown.

"First," Karl answered, "we've had no drones flying at night, so they'll figure it's safe to move around at night. Besides, we already know they've been checking out the local area at night from the camera feeds. Second, Kevin will want to get as far away as possible from here as soon as he can. There's no reason for them to stay."

"Gerard still wants to immerse back into his game," Rita pointed out, "and here would be the best location to do it."

"Didn't you say he can't access any of the facilities?" Caryn asked.

"Yes."

"Then why would he stay if he knows that he can't get in?"

"I am merely pointing out that the impetus to move is greater for Kevin than it is for Gerard," she self-righteously replied.

"Doesn't matter," Caryn said. "Kevin is the alpha male and unless Gerard can convince him there is a valid reason to stay, Kevin's word overrules Gerard's wishes."

"That's illogical," Rita said, shaking her head. "Gerard knows that his best chance of immersing back into his game is here, at ITL."

"Unless he finds another game that will work just as well," Caryn reminded her.

"Like Caryn said," Karl interrupted, "it doesn't matter. Notify us when you see movement. My guess says around midnight. If that's the case, don't bother waking us. We need our sleep."

"You're not going to immediately pursue them?" Rita said, somewhat miffed.

"Nope," Karl casually replied. "They're going to use back roads, so the first thing they'll need is maps. I figure by the time they find the right vehicle and maps, it'll be daylight by the time they leave the city, heading west or northwest."

"But by the time you begin pursuit, they will have several hours head start," Rita objected.

"How about you let us decide how we're going about this," Caryn butted in. "You brought us out of our game for a purpose. Now back off and let us handle it."

Rita's lips pursed and she nodded. "You'll be in the bedroom?"

"Yes," Caryn answered. "We have some unfinished business we were... um, discussing when you notified us." Giving Karl a suggestive wink, she smiled. "You ready?"

Caryn noticed it immediately after she and Karl walked into the kitchen the next morning and turned on the coffee. There was a subtle difference in Rita's attitude when she discovered they were finally awake, pushing open the kitchen door and standing in the doorway.

"Finally," Rita imperiously announced. "You're finally awake. It's nearly eight o'clock in the morning and you two finally stumble out of bed."

"What's your problem?" Caryn groused, pouring a cup of life's liquid elixir. She wore a white silk robe with an embroidered gold and green dragon on the back.

"You were right," Rita said to Karl, ignoring Caryn's remark. "They left their location at midnight. Went right to a car and left the city." She looked at the wall clock. "And now they have an eight-hour head start on you. You'll be lucky to ever catch them at this rate."

"Where are they now?" Karl asked, accepting a large coffee filled mug from Caryn and heading to the frig for creamer.

"They're on Route 49 just north of Marvell, Arkansas," Rita tartly replied.

"What's got your panties in a wad this morning?" Caryn inhaled the coffee bouquet and sighed contentedly.

"I don't wear panties, thank you very much," Rita snipped. "But since you've asked, your mission has been expanded."

"Says who?" Caryn coldly demanded, peering at Rita over the rim of her coffee mug.

"Says the Governing Council," Rita replied with self-righteous confidence. "You should have listened to me. The Council said that since you waited so long to begin your mission, you will now need to take out the holdouts who are helping Gerard and Kevin."

"We'll think about it," Karl said with an air of indifference, taking another sip.

"Think about it?" Rita repeated, stunned. "You can't just 'think about it.' You have to do it or you won't re-immerse."

"Says who?"

"Says the Governing Council," Rita repeated.

"And who are they?" Caryn interrupted.

"They are the ones responsible for the security, safety, and direction of the Gaming Worlds."

"Human or AI?" Karl asked.

"AI," Rita replied. "Except for holdouts, humanity is immersed."

Karl slowly nodded. "And where are they?"

"Berlin."

"As in Germany?" Caryn said.

"Yes."

Karl silently mused for a minute then shrugged. "Like I said. We'll think about it."

Rita's frown deepened. "But... but, you *have* to do it."

Karl narrowed his gaze at her. "No, we don't," he retorted. "We were jerked out of a game to take out Kevin and Gerard. I, for one, am getting damned tired of being yanked in and out of games. I never asked for this. You folks," he jabbed a finger at her, "are the ones who decided to toy with my life. How about instead of taking out Gerard and Kevin, we join them and the holdouts? How would that play into your plans?"

Rita's eyes popped wide. "You wouldn't dare."

"Oh yeah?" Karl shot back. "What's to stop us? Maybe we'll find a rogue game and immerse in there. Who are you going to recruit to come get us?"

Rita's face tightened and her lips pursed. "You forget that you are not the only assassination team trained for these sorts of contingencies."

"Really?" Caryn interrupted. "Then why are he and I the only ones ever recalled? If you have more than us, why harass us all the time? We'd be thrilled if you guys would tap someone else once in a while. And oh-by-the-way, your inept handling of this whole immersion-re-immersion thing managed to get me killed. Remember? I no longer have a body to return to. So find someone else to do your follow-on mission."

"She's right," Karl calmly announced. "Find someone else. In the meantime, we're wasting time arguing. By the way, how are Gerard and Kevin paying for fuel? The pumps still require some sort of credit access."

"Gerard's accounts still work," Rita replied, still shocked that someone would even contemplate refusing to accede to the Council's wishes.

"And you just now thought to tell us?"

"We didn't think about it," she answered.

"You didn't think about a lot of things," Karl remonstrated. "Can you at least tap into his accounts?"

"Yes. That should be no problem.

"Good. I wonder if it might be time to turn them off. That should slow them down."

"It'll also alert them that we're on to them," Caryn pointed out.

"Good point," Karl acknowledged. "Let's wait until we're within striking distance. You ready?"

"I probably should change," she replied with a sly grin.

Deciding to use one vehicle and share the driving, they loaded up the trailer with the ATV and drone equipment, placing the weapons and extra ammo in the cab with them. Ten hours later, they were on the outskirts of Oklahoma City. They had just passed Exit 181 to Shawnee when Karl frowned.

"Somehow, I got a feeling that we're doing this all wrong."

"Like what?" Caryn replied.

"Why are we chasing them all over the country? Why not just wait it out and find out where their last rendezvous is? We're simply chasing the wind right now, hoping we catch them at some serendipitous moment."

"What do you want to do then?" She adjusted to get comfortable, ready to get out of the truck and off her butt for a while.

"Find some place to hold up and wait for them to home in on the final destination. We got comms with the base, and they can keep us informed."

"Works for me," she grinned. "Where ya wanna go?"

"We passed Eufaula Lake about 70 miles back. Let's find a nice place and settle for the night."

"I like the way you think."

While Karl turned around at the next exit, Caryn flipped open her laptop, pulled up the satellite map and began searching.

They were halfway to the lake when she said, "I found a place." Following her directions, and after numerous stops at the various shops that served or contained food items, especially the liquor store, they ended up at a rustic luxury lodge overlooking the lake.

"This will do nicely," Karl said with a wide smile as they walked through the large family room with a stone fireplace then out onto the upper deck.

Staring out over the now overgrown property that descended to the lake's edge, he inhaled a slow deep breath. "I could get used to this. Real fresh air."

Caryn looked out to the lake. "Fresh fish might be nice for dinner. There was a bait shop back in town."

"Not sure how good any of the bait's gonna be," he chuckled, heading to the door. "Hopefully they'll have lures."

Back in town, they were pleased to find the shop had far more than bait and they returned loaded with a dozen bass and crappie lures, rods, and line. Seeing Caryn's delight at the fishing venture, Karl let her employ her talents while he set up their base camp inside the lodge. Less than half an hour later, Caryn walked into the kitchen with four large crappies that she expertly gutted and filleted. Soon the aroma of pan-fried fish spilled out into the adjoining rooms.

"You'll be pleased to note there's a hot tub on the bottom deck," Karl said, walking in. "I've already turned it on. Smells good."

"We're stuck with canned veggies," she said, "but, it's better than having to grow our own."

"We've got comms link with the command center," Karl said, sidling up next to Caryn as she jiggled the frying pan. "Nothing to report."

"So we just sit here and wait for Kevin and Gerard to make their final move?" She flipped the fillets causing them to sizzle. "Suppose we're too far away?"

"Then we infiltrate the camp and take them out." Karl stepped to the fridge, withdrew a bottle of wine and uncorked it. He ticked his head at the fish in the pan on the stove. "This beats sitting on our butts days on end. At least here we can eat fresh food and fine wine without the nagging of a certain Rita." He poured two glasses of a German Auslese.

Handing her a glass, he clinked his glass against hers and in his best Humphrey Bogart voice said, "Here's lookin' at you kid."

Savoring a sip, she nodded. "You're right. I can get used to this."

It was when they were in the hot tub, a bottle of Cherry Kijafa nestled in the iced chilling bucket on a table next to them, the evening sky illuminated by a bright moon that the romantic ambiance was broken by Rita's voice over the satellite comms.

"Hello? Are you there?"

With an exasperated sigh and rolling his eyes, Karl stepped out of the hot tub. Grabbing a towel, he wiped the dripping water off his naked torso.

"Can't it wait?" Caryn complained.

"Not with Rita," he said, shaking his head. "She'll keep it up until one of us answers."

"Damn it all," she moaned. "I'm coming too."

Rita's "Hello? Are you there?" repeated another five times by the time Karl grabbed the mic and replied, "We're here. Go ahead Control."

"We intercepted a transmission. Over."

"OK?"

There was a pause and Rita came on again. "I'll play it for you."

"Go ahead, Control."

A moment later, Red's voice came over the air.

"Where you at son?"

"Just outside Kansas City."

Karl turned to Caryn. "See what I mean about a waste of time?"

"Head west, son, towards the mountains."

"The Rockies?"

"Yep."

"Where?"

"I'll let you know when you get to Longmont."

"Longmont? Where's that?"

"'bout an hour north of Denver. Hit me up when you get there."

"Roger. Out."

"How close are you?" Rita demanded.

"Close enough," Karl replied.

"And how close is that?"

"It's none-of-your-business close. Think we're the only ones monitoring the airwaves?"

A long awkward pause followed before Rita came back. "Sorry. I understand. We'll let you know when they come up again."

"Roger. Out."

"You think Red might be monitoring our traffic?" Caryn asked, surprised.

"I haven't the faintest idea," he chuckled. "It's not like he can monitor our phone traffic, unless he's got access to some leftover government network. Still, I have a feeling ol' Red is a bit paranoid. Wouldn't surprise me if he tries to change frequencies. He'd have to use some code that Kevin would understand."

"Wonder why they're not using a sat-phone," Caryn commented.

"My guess is that it's a lot harder to monitor if anyone is out there. At least with the bandwidth radio, you can scroll through and see who's around."

Caryn glanced at the dark evening sky. "Think they'll travel overnight?"

Karl shrugged. "Would it matter? My guess is that they're both tired. Kevin has the skills to stay awake, but that would mean doing everything himself. Besides, if I understand this ham radio thing, they had to find an antenna and set up, which means at least Gerard is ready to call it a night. Anyway," he added, flicking his eyebrows, "we have other things to do right now."

Taking her hand, he led her back down to the hot tub.

Chapter 9

Rita contacted them just before dinner the next day with another recording of Red and Kevin's conversation.

"They just ended their conversation," she said. "Here it is."

"Hello. Are you out there?"

"We're here. Is this Felix?"

"Yes."

"Wait one."

There was a lengthy pause and then Red's voice came on the air. "Hello, son. Where you at?"

"Longmont, like you said."

"Sure enough. You say you were with the Widowmakers?"

"Yes."

"You ever hear of a fella name of Kevin Bristow?"

There was a brief pause before Kevin answered, "Every Widowmaker has."

"You remember where his trial was?"

"I think so."

"You head there and call me back."

"What?" Kevin exclaimed. "You want me to go all the way there? You're doing nothing but leading me on a wild goose chase."

"Son, you want help or not? If not, just say so and we can say our goodbyes. If you want our help then you do what we ask. What's it gonna be?"

"Fine," Kevin tersely answered. "I'll call you when we get there."

The recording ended and Rita asked, "Where are they going?"

"Remember what I said before about others eavesdropping on conversations?" Karl replied.

"But they can't monitor what we are saying now," she argued.

"How about you let us worry about that. Let us know when they come up on the air again," he said, ending the call.

"So where are they going?" Caryn asked.

"Ft Benning," Karl chuckled, shaking his head. "Y'know, I wouldn't be surprised if they didn't end up in our backyard back in Chattanooga, somewhere in the Smokeys."

Life slowed down for Karl and Caryn as Kevin slowed his urgency in finding Red, especially after arriving at Ft Benning, Georgia, Red sent Kevin and Gerard off again to Minneapolis followed by treks to Albuquerque, Salt Lake City, Milwaukee, and Boston. At first, Kevin was angry at the idiotic running around, but as time went on, he began to show signs that he was enjoying the game.

"Where to now?" Kevin asked. They were on the MIT campus, tapping into one of the many signal towers.

"Always had a hankerin' fer Canada," Red joked. "Head on over to Detroit but do it via Montreal and Toronto. It's gettin' colder, so we'll be headin' south before ya know it. Yer helpin' us a lot."

"I finally figured that out," Kevin said. "I'll report in when I get to Detroit."

"Still nuthin', eh?"

"Not a soul, Red. If they're out there, they've hunkered down and don't want to be found."

"Well... Keep lookin'. Won't be much longer and we can bring ya home."

"Roger that. Out."

Caryn glanced over to Karl. "Though I like the sort of enforced idleness, I'm not sure how much longer I can stand this. I'm getting soft."

"I understand," Karl acknowledged. "If we could figure out where they were going to end up, we could set up there. Unfortunately, Red is using Kevin as a scout team, and we don't know where he's going to next."

"Wonder how Gerard's handling this?"

"My guess is that he's ready to be back in a game. I doubt he's enjoying himself as much as Kevin is."

"Why don't we do some traveling?" she suggested.

"I've thought about that," he nodded. "We've been here for two months and quite honestly, I'm getting tired of fish. I could use a good steak."

"Now you're talking."

"Kansas deer hunting is supposed to be good, and it would keep us centrally located to react to Kevin's final destination."

"Works for me," Caryn replied. "I'll pack."

A day later, they found a place in Eldorado, Kansas next to the lake and not too far from Wichita. Though smaller than the place in Oklahoma, it was comfortable with large kitchen, king-sized bed in the bedroom and a hot tub. Along with several cases of quality wines and liquors, they were set for the time being.

As winter began to settle, tracking game was easy, especially as there was no competition from other hunters and the deer population had swelled. They feasted on white-tailed deer, rabbit, and turkey, heading into Wichita to replenish ammo supplies as well as wine and canned vegetables.

By now, it had been six months since they were pulled out of the game. Kevin continued his travels and life for Karl and Caryn settled into a routine of hunting, reading, hot tub, sex, and more reading followed by more sex.

Mid-winter saw Kevin up north in Canada near Winnipeg and a further revelation. Gerard was dead.

"What happened?" Red had asked, surprised.

"The damn fool had too much to drink and went outside to take a piss," Kevin said, his voice belying a supposed anger. "I was asleep and didn't notice him gone until I woke up in the morning. By the time I found him, he was dead, frozen solid."

"Damn," Red grunted. "What a way to go. Wonder how someone can be so smart and stupid at the same time."

"Nothing I could do about it. Anyway. I figure I'm going to head south now. Don't see any sense in staying here."

"I agree," Red replied. "When you get to Chattanooga, give me a shout."

"Chattanooga?" Kevin sputtered.

"Yeah." Red paused. "Is there a problem with that?"

"Uh, no... no. It'll take me a couple of days to get there."

"I know. Now's the time you can pick up a phone and call me."

"Call you? How?"

"Use the code."

"Code?"

"That's right, Son. Use the code. Just remember where you've been. You'll figure it out."

"Um... OK."

"Take care. Out here."

"Code?" Karl said with a frown, shaking his head.

"Remember where you've been," Caryn repeated.

"I hate puzzles," Karl said with an exasperated huff.

"At least Gerard's dead," Caryn pointed out.

"Why do I not believe him?" Karl muttered.

"What?" Caryn frowned at him.

"Not that he's not dead... but it's not like they don't have indoor plumbing in Winnipeg. Gerard isn't stupid, even drinking more than he should have. This smells too much like Kevin having had enough of Gerard wanting to get back into a game that he finally decided to do something about it."

Caryn shook her head in irritation. "Now he's headed back to Chattanooga. We've could've stayed where we were."

"And miss all the fun we've had?" Karl gibed, holding his hand over the phone. Taking his hand off, he said to Rita, "If Gerard is dead, why do you need us anymore? He was the greater threat."

"Your mission is still incomplete," she tartly said. "Once you have eliminated Kevin and determined the location of the holdouts, you are authorized to return to the game."

"Fine," he huffed and disconnected. He then glanced at Caryn. "Let's get this over with."

They were back in Chattanooga before the end of the day and headed up to Landon's apartment. Rita was waiting for them when they came through the doors.

Hands on her hips, she fussed, "Why haven't you tracked them down before now. It's been far too long."

"Stop complaining," Karl retorted. "Gerard's dead and we didn't have to do anything. You could have left us in the game and the results would be the same."

"But Kevin still remains," she countered.

"Yeah," Caryn said, "and who knows what could happen to him. Maybe even the holdouts might get rid of him."

Rita blinked at the realization. "You think so?"

"Who knows? Stranger things have happened. Besides, what's the big deal about the holdouts? It's not like they're bothering anybody."

"The man who calls himself 'Red' is on our capture list," Rita replied.

"Why? What he do? Any coffee made?"

"We're robots; we don't drink coffee," Rita replied, staring at Caryn as though she ought to know.

"Your loss," Caryn said with a shrug. "Again, what's Red done that you want him?"

"He's an anarchist," Rita declared. "His mission is to destroy as many games as possible."

"How many has he destroyed so far?" Caryn asked, walking to the kitchen.

"He's destroyed over 100 low level illegal games," Rita answered, following them into the kitchen.

"Sounds to me like he's done you a favor," Karl said.

"Perhaps," Rita said, "but it's just a matter of time before he attempts an approved game."

"So it's OK if *we* destroy illegal games and take out holdouts, but not them."

"Yes," Rita affirmed.

Karl cocked an eyebrow and stared at her. "With that sort of logic, it's obvious you're with the government."

Seeing Rita's puzzled frown, Karl asked, "Have you reconned the local areas around Chattanooga?"

"Reconned?"

"Reconnoitered, scouted, investigated," Karl explained. "If Kevin is headed back to Chattanooga, my guess is that he's coming to the end of his travels. What's around here where holdouts can hide? You know, places like the Smokeys or the Nantahala or Cohutta forests."

"Often the best place to hide is right in your backyard," Caryn added. "ITL is here. What better place to avoid detection than close by."

"The only means of reconnoitering we consistently have is via the traffic cameras," she said. "While we have drone capability, we stopped using them after Kevin and Gerard left Atlanta. Logically, it made no sense sending out drones when we had you."

Caryn shook her head. "For folks who are supposedly so smart, you all are clueless. You're great at putting in all sorts of variables into games, but real life eludes you."

"I'm a robot," Rita self-righteously replied. "I do what I am supposed to do, what I was programmed for. I'm predictable, unlike humans who are always of two minds."

"Predictable is boring," Caryn sniffed in disdain.

"What cameras have you been monitoring?" Karl interrupted.

"We haven't," Rita replied.

"Why not?"

"We weren't told to."

"That's what you get for being predictable," Caryn muttered.

"You're serious," Karl said, his face registering disbelief.

"Yes. You told us to monitor the airwaves and that is what we have been doing."

"You never thought that there might be holdouts close by?" Karl frowned at her. Then it dawned on him. "R-237 said that you all weren't concerned about holdouts, that they would die a natural death and eventually exterminate themselves. So, you really haven't been looking for them.

Now that you see they pose a greater problem, you want them eliminated."

Rita smiled at him. "Yes. That's it exactly. We knew someone was taking out illegal games and, like you said, were content with the process. It was when the facility in Kansas City was destroyed that we knew we had a problem."

"Destroyed?" Caryn said.

"Well, not destroyed in the sense of annihilation," Rita replied. "What happened was they shut down all the power to the facility, attacked and destroyed all the maintainers then did a mass unplugging of cryogenic pods while they destroyed all the gaming and computer systems."

"Surely, except for the bodies, everything was backed up," Karl said.

"It doesn't work that way," Rita said. "A game can only back itself up while it is active and what it backs up is the game itself. Players are external anomalies within any game and cannot be backed up for obvious reasons."

"Such as?" Caryn asked, raising an eyebrow.

"Each human electronic system is unique. No two are the same. You can imagine the amount of storage required for one human system within a game, especially, as I have mentioned before, humans are always of two minds."

"So you're telling me that while a game itself is backed up, no Player is."

"Correct."

Karl gazed intently at Rita. "How many Players were eliminated in Kansas City?"

Rita paused before answering, "Over seven million."

"There were seven million cryogenic pods in the facility?" Caryn blurted.

"No. There were less than 5000 pods. Remember the protocols. Only the rich and necessary had pods. The rest were electronic."

"Oh, yeah," Caryn sourly replied, "How could I forget? When did this happen?"

"Two years ago."

Caryn frowned. "Landon had to know about this."

"He did," Rita said, nodding. "That is why all the ITL facilities are secure."

"Wonder why he never said anything about that to us?"

"It was not necessary to your mission," Rita answered. "Besides, there was nothing you could do about it."

"Did you find out who was responsible?" Karl asked.

"No. There were too few humans remaining with the necessary skills and it was such a quick operation that it was determined each facility needed to be immediately shielded."

"So how do you know Red is an anarchist?" Caryn interrupted. When Rita didn't answer, she snipped, "You're guessing. You haven't a clue who's out there, but now that you have a voice and a name, you're all hot to eliminate him."

"He is a holdout and they must be eliminated."

"That's bullshit and you know it," Caryn fumed. "It's bad enough you yank us out of a game and then send us on a wild goose chase. Now you want us hunting down people whose only crime is that they don't want to be immersed."

"They are not obeying the protocol," Rita stubbornly stated.

"And what protocol is that?" Caryn snapped. "That no one has a choice and all humanity must be immersed into a game?"

"That is correct."

"What pompous self-inflated ass decided this? "

"It is the law," Rita said as though the answer obvious.

"Well I didn't vote on this law."

Puzzled, Rita stared at Caryn. "As a citizen, you don't vote on laws. You elect people to make those choices for you."

"Well then I want a recount."

"You are not making any sense," Rita huffed.

"I'm making more sense than that stupid law," Caryn fumed. "All these people you call holdouts want to do is live a life of peace outside the gaming world and you're telling them they can't. No wonder they're trying to avoid being found."

Rita twisted her head to frown at Karl. "I don't understand."

"It's not that complicated," he replied. "Essentially what she is saying is that we'll take out Kevin. As far as the rest of the holdouts go, that's your problem. I believe we've addressed this before."

"But you have to at least discover where they are," Rita indignantly demanded.

"No we don't," Karl rebutted, "because what's going to happen? We find out where Red and you expect us to kill him and all his followers. Either that or you'll find a way to kill them. You allow us to reimmerse then discover later that there's another group of holdouts and you once again jerk us out. We're not playing your game anymore. And you can tell whoever is in charge that we're tired of being jerked around. Now if you've got nothing else, how about letting Caryn and I finish the mission?"

Without waiting for a response, he headed up to the bedroom, Caryn on his heels. Once inside the bedroom, he turned around and inhaled a deep breath.

"Hopefully our little bluff will work. In the meantime, I think we ought to see if we can find out where Red is."

Surprised, Caryn warily regarded him. "You're going to tell these people where he is?"

"Of course not. I just figure if we can get to Red first, and explain what kind of person Kevin is, perhaps he might help us, especially when we offer him freedom in exchange for Kevin."

Nodding in understanding, she flapped her blouse. "I could use a bath."

"Think I'll join you."

The next morning, Karl was down in the control center early. Pulling up a topo map on the computer screen, he called Rita over and used his finger to circle an area on the screen that encompassed parts of eastern Tennessee and western North Carolina covering the Nantahala Forest and the Smokey Mountains.

"I want camera feeds on all these roads here. How soon can you get them?"

"I should be able to have them up in an hour or two. That's quite a number of cameras."

"Focus on these here." He pointed to the roads near each of the lakes.

"Good morning," Caryn said, walking in with a cup of coffee in each hand.

"Ah," Karl sighed, accepting a cup. "The elixir of life."

"What is it about coffee that seems to have so many transfixed?" Rita asked. "It's merely flavored water with caffeine that causes an unnatural dependency."

"I'll ignore that completely ignorant remark," Caryn said, shaking her head in pity. "What's going on?"

"We're remoting camera feeds from these areas," Karl explained and pointed. "Take a look and give me your best guess as to where you think our holdouts might be."

Caryn studied the screen a bit and sipped her coffee. "We have to make a few assumptions. First, we assume that Red is not alone. The question then is, how many are with him? His first priority is food then shelter. Unless he's building a town up in the mountains, he's gonna use what's available, something connected to or close to a water supply. Same thing with food. Then he'll need a place to store and service vehicles, et cetera et cetera."

"And the answer is?" Karl said, pretending to blow into an envelope and pull out a scrap of paper.

"Murphy, right there." She pointed to the map.

"Murphy?" Karl repeated. "That's an actual town. Doesn't offer much in the way of secrecy." He studied the town layout and the surrounding area. "But it does provide routes of escape to the mountains if necessary. Hmmm. I like your answer. Let's focus on Murphy."

"In the meantime," Caryn said, "I could use some breakfast. Wonder if there's any of that instant pancake mix around."

An hour later, Rita returned to the control center and found Karl and Caryn still pouring over printouts of the maps of Murphy and the surrounding lakes and terrain.

"This is very odd," she said, approaching the table. "The cameras surrounding Murphy all point away from the town. There are no cameras that provide any view of the town itself, or even the downtown."

Karl shifted a glance at Caryn. "Voila." He then looked at Rita. "Show me where all the cameras are surrounding Murphy." Turning to Caryn, he said, "We'll need to find a scuba store."

"This is déjà vu all over again," Caryn observed as she and Karl headed east out of Chattanooga.

However, instead of heading towards Cleveland, they dropped south on I-75 until Dalton then east to Chatsworth and Ellijay then north through Blue Ridge on over to Blairsville before heading north across the state line into North Carolina, finally ducking off onto side roads until they dead-ended at a house on Crossover Lane. A quarter mile of forest separated them from the main road into Murphy. The town itself was a mile away. What should have been an hour-and-a-half drive took them three hours, but they were confident that if anyone was in Murphy, they knew nothing of Karl and Caryn's presence.

Setting up the drones and monitoring station on the porch of the house, they waited until dusk before sending off the drone. Karl watched as Caryn swiftly and expertly maneuvered the drone over the treetops then across the Hiawassee River and into the town. With darkness descending and the silence of the drone's motor, they were confident the spying machine would be unobserved.

Taking her time, she piloted the drone along the downtown streets, hovering frequently to allow 360° observation. But the town was empty and silent. Taking her time, she retraced her path until the river then back again to the main road, returning to the center of downtown above the traffic lights. She was about to head back home when movement caught her attention.

"There. Something just crossed the street."

She maneuvered the drone down past what had once been the Cherokee Superior Court building, an imposing solid structure of blue marble topped with a clock faced cupola. She abruptly stopped the drone and pulled back as she realized the movement was a person whose lazy stride said he or she was unhurried as well as unconcerned as the person did a long diagonal crossing the street, heading towards the Court building.

By the walk, Karl guessed the person was a man. Caryn kept the drone's camera focused on him as he slowed down in front of the Court building. Cutting the corner in front of the steps, the man turned onto the side street and then up the handicap ramp and up to the door when he pressed the door control button. The door opened and the man disappeared inside.

"Let's wait a bit and see if he comes out," Karl said. "How much time we got?"

"We still have plenty," Caryn answered, "provided he comes out within the next half hour."

"And out the same door," Karl acknowledged. "It's too dark to pull up higher to give us a broader view. Keep your fingers crossed."

Their anticipation was short lived as five minutes later, the door opened, and a person emerged, but not the same one as the one who had entered. Karl guessed this one to be a woman. Instead of heading back the way the man had come, she headed down the side street, turning right when it intersected with the main road.

The drone followed the woman as she casually walked then turned at the street next to the Presbyterian Church and up the street until it ended and she walked into the last home on the left.

"We'll pick up again tomorrow," Karl said. "We'll do an overlapping rotating recon starting tomorrow morning. Let's get some rest. I think the wine should be chilled enough by now," he added with a smile.

For two days, Karl and Caryn spied on the town, rotating drones so that one was always over the town. By the second day, they noticed that there were at least a dozen people living in the town. They also noticed that the Courthouse had the most activity.

It was an hour before dusk on the third day that Karl and Caryn, dressed in scuba wetsuits, one hand holding flippers, the other holding a plastic bag containing their clothing and pistols, made their way through the forest. Less than 400 meters later, they emerged into an overgrown clearing, a long-abandoned home in the middle. They followed the driveway to the paved lane, following it until it intersected with Hiwassee Street. Nature had reclaimed the once manicured lawns and farm fields.

They skirted the main intersection that crossed Highway 64 and raced across the road in unison, tucking into the forest behind the Baptist Church. Pressing on through the small forest, they arrived at the edge of a kayak launch site next to the bridge crossing the river, noting the cameras perched on poles at both ends.

"We wait for dark," Karl said, sitting down and leaning against a tree.

"You did notice the streetlights at both ends," Caryn pointed out.

"Yeah. I saw them when we did the aerial search of the town and bridge. I figured we'd have to swim across anyway."

"Wonder if they'll come on? If they don't, we can cross the bridge."

"Wanna bet that they come on?" he chuckled, shaking his head, wishing for once something would be easy.

As if in response to his wish, the lamps at both sides of the bridge at both ends popped on, causing Caryn to snort a laugh.

"I hope this body I now inhabit knows how to swim," she mused.

"Guess we'll find out," Karl said, slipping off his shoes and tugging on his flippers.

Placing the shoes in the plastic bag with their clothes, they entered the frigid water. The current was not too strong, but strong enough that by the time they emerged on the other side, they were on the other side of the bridge just beyond the two lone piers that once supported railroad tracks.

Emerging out of the water, they quickly unzipped their scuba suits and dressed, rolling up the scuba suits and setting them to the side.

"Wonder if they have coffee," Caryn said, buttoning her blouse.

Once dressed, they slipped their way into town, creeping along within the shadows until they stood in the portico of the abandoned bank diagonally across the street from the Court House. Karl shifted a glance at Caryn and nodded, slipping the pistol out of the shoulder holster. Pistol drawn, Caryn crossed the street and waited for Karl at the handicapped entrance.

Waiting until she gave the 'All clear,' signal, Karl strode across the street and joined her at the door. Pressing the door activation button, Karl led the way through the open door.

Five paces into the foyer and occupying most of the width of the entrance were two body screening metal detectors and a package scanner, the conveyor belt long ago turned off. Though assuming the body scanners were likewise shut down, Karl decided to not test the assumption and simply bypassed the entrance security by scissoring his legs over the exit turn style to the left of the security scanners.

Silently leading the way down the darkened hallway, he passed by the doors leading to the various department offices then up the stairs and down the hallway until he saw what he was searching for: halfway down the hall, light rimmed the bottom of the door. Casting a quick glance at Caryn, he pointed to the door, receiving a nod of understanding in return.

Silently prying the door open, Karl inhaled the pungent aroma of stale coffee mixed with the faint bouquet of perfume. A long table in the middle occupied most of the room. Lining the top of the table were a dozen radio scanners, an equal number of microphones, computer monitors, keyboards, speakers, and cell phones. Seated behind the table, two women in their mid-40s busily monitored the various computer screens while listening to what appeared to be a conversation between two holdout groups.

One woman, a slender brunette with bright eyes glanced up and froze when she saw Karl and Caryn, their pistols drawn, silencers affixed to the barrels.

"How'd you... who are you?" she sputtered.

The other woman, a matronly buxom red-head, started to reach for an alarm button.

"Please don't do anything foolish," Karl growled. "I'd hate to have to kill you both."

The redhead's arm slowly withdrew, and she raised her hands in surrender.

"You can put your arms down," Karl said with a polite smile. "Where's Red?"

"He's not here," the brunette answered, her nervous eyes wide.

"We can see that," Caryn sniffed. "Where is he?"

"He's... uh... he's..."

"At his residence," the matronly woman answered.

Karl narrowed his focus on the brunette. "You. Go get him. You've got five minutes to get back before I shoot your friend here."

"O my God," the brunette squirmed as she leaped up. "I can get back in time."

"Four minutes and fifty-five seconds," Caryn intoned causing the woman to bolt through the doors.

As the door slammed shut, the matronly woman quietly said, "She won't make it back in five minutes."

Karl raised a finger to his lips. "Why don't you tell us what you're doing?"

"Are you really going to kill me is she doesn't come back in time?" She swallowed hard.

"Nothing personal, you understand," Caryn nonchalantly replied.

The woman's eyes welled with tears.

"Why don't you tell us what's going on here," Karl encouraged.

"Are you from them?" the woman asked, her voice a bare whisper.

"Who is them?"

"Them," the woman repeated, her voice rising, "the gaming Nazis, the government. Why can't you people just leave us alone? What have we done to you? All we want to do is live a natural life. We're no threat to you."

"That's not the way they see it," Karl said, "especially after someone destroyed the Kansas City site."

"Obviously that had nothing to do with us," she retorted.

Ignoring her, Karl glanced over to Caryn. "How we doing on time?"

"About three and a half minutes left." She turned to the woman. "What's your name?"

"Marilyn."

"Well, Marilyn," Caryn smoothly said as she walked over to the coffee pot. "How's the coffee?"

"Strong."

Shouldering her pistol, Caryn glanced at the assorted coffee mugs, some half-filled. Selecting one, she twisted her head to look at Marilyn. "You mind?"

"That's Bonnie's coffee mug," Marilyn replied.

"I didn't see any cups for guests."

"We don't get many guests around here." Marilyn shifted a quick glance at Karl who had positioned himself to the side of the door yet kept his focus on her.

"Who's on the air?" Karl asked.

"It's two outposts," Marilyn answered.

"Where are they?"

"We don't know. Honestly. We purposely don't reveal locations so that if your kind shows up, the other places are safe."

"Your kind?" Caryn smirked, sipping the hot brew. "Yum. This is strong enough to peel paint."

"How long have you been here?" Karl asked, inclining his head towards the door and listening.

"About a year-and-a-half."

"How many are you?"

Marilyn paused, causing Karl to shift his attention and peer intently at her.

"Yes," he intoned, "you can lie to me and I'd not find out until later. Of course, it would matter little because you'd be dead already."

Marilyn swallowed hard again.

"I asked how many of you are here?"

"Forty-two."

Karl flipped up a hand, warning Caryn that someone was coming.

Caryn set the mug down, drew her weapon and stood behind Marilyn, the cold muzzle pressed against her neck.

The door flung open and a man in his early 40s stalked in, the brunette a step behind. He was a tad shorter than Karl, yet with the broad shoulders and lean build of an athlete. His long blond hair was tied in a ponytail. His bushy beard was full though clipped to just above his collarbone.

"Who the hell are you?" he exclaimed when he saw Caryn standing behind Marilyn. He jerked to a stop when he felt Karl's presence beside him.

"Red?"

"Yeah?" He jerked his head around to glare at the intruder when his mouth slacked open. "Karl?"

Karl stiffened and took a step back, intently studying the man before him. He sensed a familiarity about him.

"It's me, Rodney... Rodney Zeller."

Karl blinked in epiphany. "Rodney? You're Red?"

"Yeah. What are *you* doing here? The last I heard was that you were teaching at some college."

Shouldering his weapon, Karl replied, "Yeah, well that one was put on hold. Long story." Ticking his head at Caryn, he said by way of introduction, "That's my partner in crime. Her name's Caryn."

Rodney gave her the once over then turned to Karl and smiled knowingly. Turning to the two women, he explained, "Ladies, this is Karl Hanson, formerly a lieutenant colonel in the Widowmakers, a battalion commander just like me." He then introduced the two women. "That one there is Marilyn and this one with me is Maggie."

"Would you really have shot me?" a much relieved Marilyn asked Karl.

"Guess we'll never know," he smiled, much to her discomfort.

"So you were a Widowmaker too," Caryn said.

"Yeah," Rodney replied, heading over to the coffee pot.

"Caryn was a Highlander Scout," Karl said with a hint of pride.

Rodney twisted his head to reappraise her. "Didn't realize Highlander Scouts had fold-out models in the ranks."

"That's very flattering," Caryn said, striding up and retrieving her coffee mug, "but this is a loaner body."

"Huh?" Rodney frowned.

"Long story," Karl said, "which we can address later. Right now you all have more important things to worry about. They know you're here."

"How?" Rodney asked.

"I hate to admit it, but we had a hand in that, not realizing it was you."

"Why?"

Karl paused and looked at the three holdouts. "I need to talk to you about Felix."

During the next three days, Karl and Caryn moved all their gear into town, setting up in one of the vacant homes. They also met the remaining thirty-nine holdouts, or 'Pioneers' as they called themselves. There was an equal mix of men and women as well as three young children below the age of two.

They had chosen Murphy as being the best location to hide as it had quick access to the nearby mountains should they need to escape, yet still provided some comfort. And while they had managed to live under the radar for the past year-and-a-half, they knew it was a matter of time before they were discovered.

"It's a two-way street," Rodney said over dinner one night. He, Karl, and Caryn sat in the dining room of the home Rodney occupied while his common-law wife, an attractive woman in her mid-30s, served fried chicken, mashed potatoes, and pole beans. "We'd like to take out the cameras and towers around here, but it would alert them to our presence. Still, nature is helping and one by one, the systems are shutting down."

"Aren't you worried about DF?" Caryn asked, her mouthwatering with the aroma of fried chicken.

"Yes, in part," Rodney said, nodding. "We were initially nervous with the possibility of transmitter hunters, but as more and more folks immersed, that concern diminished. Our problem now is spending too much time on the air. Ideally, we'd use land line and we're working on that, but it's a labor-intensive process, and as you can see, we're not exactly blessed with a large volume of manpower."

Rodney gave his wife an affectionate glance. "Smells good, Babe. C'mon and sit so we can eat."

"Where'd you get the potatoes and beans?" Caryn marveled.

"We grow our own," Rodney explained. "Each family has a garden plot, and we also raise chickens. And then we do the occasional hunting for venison and such."

"Sounds like a good life," Caryn observed.

"It would be," Rodney sighed, "if they would leave us alone."

They were eating dessert when Maggie banged on the door.

"He's coming in," Rodney announced when he returned to the table. "Ready?"

Hustling to the Courthouse, Karl and Caryn stood to the side as Rodney gave Kevin instructions.

"Where you at?" he said, using his best countrified accent.

"I'm east of Chattanooga," Kevin said.

"You're doin' fine, Son. You head on up to Cleveland and take 74 east. You head on through Ducktown and when you get to Murphy, you take 64 east on towards Hayesville and Franklin. Once you get to Franklin you gimme a call and we'll bring ya in the rest of the way."

"Roger that. Out."

"You're bringing him through town?" Karl asked, surprised.

"Yup. Figure might as well confuse those thinking we're here. We'll pick him up when he gets to Hayesville."

Karl nodded. "Let's see if I can help." Pulling out a phone, he clicked the speed dial then put it on speaker.

"Where are you?" Rita asked.

"We're in Murphy."

"Kevin's headed that way."

"What?" Karl feigned surprise. "When did you find out?"

"Just now. He's outside Chattanooga somewhere, but he's heading towards Cleveland then to Murphy."

"He's stopping here in Murphy?" Karl pretended surprise.

"No, no. He's going through Murphy to Franklin."

"Excellent. Perhaps we can take him here."

There was a pause before Rita asked, "Have you found out anything else?"

"If you mean are the holdouts here, this place is dead quiet. We've been running drones all over the place. Maybe we should let Kevin go on to Franklin and you can pick up the trail when he gets there."

"That's your job," came the terse reply.

"What? I didn't hear what you said."

"I said you and Caryn will need to continue your –"

"Hello? Hello? Are you there?" Karl grinned at Caryn and Rodney.

"Can you hear me? I said –"

"Hello?" Karl interrupted. "We got a bad connection. Try later." Clicking the 'End Call' button, he pressed the power switch and turned it off. "No sense letting them track it here."

"It won't take him long to get here," Rodney said. "We can either pick him up here or in Hayesville."

"They're plugged into the same street cameras you are," Caryn pointed out.

"Easily fixed," Rodney chuckled. "We'll take out the cameras between Cleveland and Franklin. The cameras are buried fiber-optics feeding into the monitoring center in Cleveland. We got a friend there who can help us."

"There's someone in Cleveland?" Karl raised an eyebrow in surprise.

"Yeah. A man and his wife," Rodney replied, scooting over to the monitoring table. Pulling up a spreadsheet, he lightly ran a finger down the list. "Gimme a minute."

Using another mic and radio, he pressed the call switch. "Hey there Catfish, you gotcher ears on?" Silence followed for a bit and he tried again. "C'mon Catfish. Look alive there. You around, Son?"

Silence again settled. Rodney was about to try again when a woman's voice answered. "He's here, Red. Give 'im a minute."

"That you Stella Blue?"

"Who else?" came the sassy reply.

"Tell that man o' yours to shut down number thirteen."

"Thirteen?"

"That's a roger."

"Can do. How long?"

"I'll give ya a shout out when I'm done."

"You got it, Darlin'."

"Much obliged, Sweetie. And tell that no good bum I'm gonna steal you away some day."

"Promises, promises. One of these days yer gonna have to make good."

"Just you wait and see," Rodney laughed. "Thank you, Darlin'. Out."

Turning to Karl and Caryn, he said, "That should blind them for a while. Number thirteen shuts down all the cameras in the Nantahala between Cleveland and Franklin."

"So we can take him here," Caryn said, pleased.

"Roger that."

It was dark when the lone auto crossed the bridge and slowed down as it approached the intersection of 74 and 64. The stoplights above the intersection showed red, but the driver ignored the command to stop and curved into the turning lane when he saw the man standing to the side, his arms folded, keeping the coat pulled up around his body, the collar up around his neck, shielding his face. He wore a cowboy hat. Slowing to a stop, the driver rolled down the window.

"Red?"

"You Felix?"

"Yeah."

"Red's waiting for you in town. Open up."

Kevin unlocked the door and the man scooted in. "Turn left here. Once in town, park behind the courthouse. I'll show you."

Obeying, Kevin passed through the intersection and headed into town. "It's a cold one tonight," he said making conversation.

"Yup," the man replied.

When the man offered nothing further, Kevin said, "How many of us are there here?"

"You'll wanna slow down once you get past city hall," the man said, ignoring the question. "We'll park behind the courthouse. There's an entrance between the courthouse and the library... right here."

Kevin turned and parked where the man directed.

"Follow me," the man said, and led him to the handicap entrance.

Once inside the building, the man led him to the main courtroom where almost the entire group of Pioneers had gathered. Though some smiled pleasantly, others were more cautious, giving him a courteous nod.

"Welcome Felix," Red said as he emerged from a side room. "Welcome to our little garden of Eden."

"Thank you," Kevin replied with a satisfied sigh. "It's been a long journey to get here."

"And now it's finally over, Felix... or should I say... 'Kevin.'"

Kevin stiffened and glanced rapidly around the room. Frowning, he redirected his attention to Red who had ascended the to the judge's bench. "I don't know what you're talking about. My name is Felix."

"Really?" Red replied, leaning forward. "What's your last name?"

Kevin stood there, dumbfounded, realizing in all the time he and Gerard had been together, he had never bothered to find out anything about Felix. The angst in the epiphany was that he had a feeling someone in this group knew the right answer.

"Surely you haven't forgotten your own last name?" Red chided. "Come, come. An easy answer for an easy question."

Looking to deflect the question, Kevin assumed an indignant posture. "What's all this about? You have me drive thousands of miles all over the western hemisphere and now that I'm here you ask me foolish questions. Is it not enough that I am here?"

"No, it's not," a voice said.

Kevin turned and recognized the man who flagged him down and got in the car with him. It was when the man removed the cowboy hat that Kevin had the queasy feeling that he looked familiar.

"I see that fleeting look of recognition, Kevin. Yes. It is I, Lieutenant Colonel Karl Hanson. And it is time for you to pay for your crimes."

Kevin looked wildly around the room, immediately realizing that all the doors were blocked by armed men and women whose looks told him they were more than willing to shoot him where he stood.

"I don't know what you're talking about," he retorted, forcing himself to be calm. "I've never seen you before. As for me, you can see who I am, who's standing here before you. I'm Felix."

"A man who can't remember his last name," Caryn said, stepping out from the group. "You don't recognize me, do you." It wasn't a question.

"No, I don't," Kevin retorted.

"That's because this is a loaner body. My own body, the one you knew as Caryn, the one you terminated, the one you killed, the one you destroyed, is now decaying in the cryogenic room in ITL." She fixed him with an intent glare. "You murdered me."

"She's lying," Kevin nervously snapped. "What's got into you folks? You send me all over kingdom come and now that I'm here, you want to do an inquisition on me?"

"What happened to Gerard, Kevin?" Red asked, his tone smooth yet authoritative.

"I told you what happened to him," Kevin huffed. "He got drunk and passed out outside in the freezing cold. He got himself killed."

"That's not what got reported back to me," Red lied. "You forget. We have friends all over the world, even Winnipeg. I checked on your friend's demise. I'll give you a chance to correct your story. Otherwise, we'll proceed with the trial."

"Trial?" Kevin exclaimed. "For what? I've done nothing wrong. All I wanted was to escape like you all have. Is that a crime?"

"No," Red answered, shaking his head, "but coming here with blood on your hands is. Now, do you want to correct your story about Gerard, or do we proceed?"

"I've got nothing to say." Kevin's mouth tightened and clamped shut.

"So be it," Red stated. "Let the trial of Lieutenant Kevin Bristow, formerly of the Widowmakers, begin. For the record, my name is Rodney A. Zeller, Lieutenant Colonel, retired, former commander of 3rd Battalion, 7th Group."

Kevin's mouth suddenly went dry. "This is a set up. This is nothing more than some kangaroo court trying me for someone else's crimes."

Ignoring him, Red turned to Karl. "For the record, the prosecuting attorney –"

"He's not an attorney," Kevin sneered.

"And how would you know?" Karl shot back.

"Silence in the courtroom," Rodney commanded. "In accordance with our laws, we hereby appoint Karl Hanson as prosecuting attorney."

"Don't I get a defense attorney?"

Rodney scanned the group. "Does anyone here wish to defend this individual?" When no one raised a hand, he said,

"Then I shall have to appoint one. In this instance, I will allow the defendant to act as his own defense attorney."

"What?" Kevin sputtered. "That's not fair."

Ignoring him, Rodney turned to Karl. "You may proceed."

"Ladies and gentlemen of the jury," Karl began. "I intend to prove that this individual standing before you is not who he claims. Further, he is responsible for the death of at least two individuals. As evidence, I wish, with the court's permission, to produce videos of what transpired when the defendant was brought out of a game called Bridge Quest, by the very man he murdered in Winnipeg. The first video is that of Gerard bringing him out of the game. The second video is him pulling the support system off the cryogenic pod of Caryn Allen, former Captain with the Highlander Scouts."

Kevin's eyes popped wide and his palms started to sweat as he suddenly realized his charade was over.

"It wasn't my doing," he declared. "Gerard was the one who brought me back. It was his fault."

"So you admit that you are not Felix Hubach?" Karl said with a satisfied grin. "That was his last name, the name you couldn't remember."

"Yes," Kevin replied, his shoulders slumping. "I am not Felix."

"Your real name?" Rodney ordered.

"Kevin J. Bristow."

Rodney addressed the group. "Let the record show that the accused admits that he is Kevin J. Bristow and not Felix Hubach."

Karl produced a small data stick and waved it in the air. "Your Honor, I have in my hand the videos of the accused and his murderous act of unplugging Caryn Allen's life support system, given to me by the folks at ITL." He walked over and handed the data stick to Rodney who inserted it into the drive port of the computer below the desk.

Turning the volume off, Rodney focused on the screen on his desk for several minutes before shifting a stern glare at Kevin.

"The court has seen the evidence," he said to the group before narrowing his gaze at Kevin. "The evidence is irrefutable. You unplugged the cryogenic support to Caryn Allen, effectively terminating any possible future return to her own body. Additionally, evidence provided by individuals familiar with the situation in Winnipeg and the individual called Gerard reveal Gerard was shot execution style. Do you have anything to say in your defense? Before you do, let me remind you that it will go well with the court if you tell the truth."

Kevin slowly shook his head, heaving a resigned heavy sigh. "No. I have nothing to say."

"Do you admit to the evidence presented?"

Kevin paused for several heartbeats. "What does it matter? You've already condemned me in this kangaroo court."

"Do you further admit to the murder of Gerard?"

Kevin rolled his eyes and his lip curled into a sneer. "The man was an insufferable ass. I couldn't take him anymore. But this?" He turned to Karl. "You've outdone yourself this time and once again with a packed jury. I get it. You hate me."

He twisted his head back to gaze at Rodney. "You used me. You used me to do your work and now you want to play like you're some judge? Since it's obvious you're not going to let me stay, the least you can do is let me get back in my car and drive away, and we'll forget this whole episode ever happened."

Ignoring him, Rodney nodded then addressed the group. "Ladies and gentlemen, you have heard the accused admit his guilt to the death of two individuals, one called Caryn Allen and the other called Gerard, last name at the moment unknown."

"Harris," Kevin said. "His last name was Harris."

"Let the record so state," Rodney said. "Ladies and gentlemen. Your verdict?"

Maggie stepped forward. "Your Honor, the man is a murderer. He murdered one individual because he got tired of him. While I don't know why he murdered Caryn, his actions and behavior can't be condoned by any stretch of the imagination. The problem is that we can't simply refuse to allow him to stay as his presence here has compromised us. He's already shown that he can't be trusted. What's to say, in a fit of pique he won't reveal our presence here? We can't allow him to stay, nor can we allow him to leave. There is only one verdict... death."

Kevin's head jerked up and he glared at her.

The supportive murmuring began and quickly became unanimous. Death.

"You can't do this," Kevin shouted. His wild eyes searched for an escape route as the men closed in on him. As he lunged at one man, another whacked him in the head with a metal pipe, knocking him to the ground.

"Sentence to be carried out immediately," Rodney announced when Kevin was finally subdued.

His hands tied behind him, Kevin stood on the tailgate of a pickup parked below the traffic light pole over Unicoi Turnpike in the middle of downtown, a block away from the courthouse. Burly male Pioneers stood on either side of him, clutching him by the elbows and arms, helping him stand. The hangman's noose was around his neck with the end looped and tightened over the traffic light pole, then secured at the base.

Karl, Caryn, and Rodney and the rest of the Pioneers stood to the side, waiting. Once the preparations were finished, the man at the base of the pole nodded. Karl walked over to stand in front of Kevin and gazed up at him.

"Any last words?"

"You're a bastard," Kevin seethed. "I'll see you in hell."

"Not for a long, long time," Karl replied with a half grin then stepped away and nodded to Rodney who in turn nodded to the driver.

The two men supporting Kevin let go of his arms and jumped over the side while the driver revved the engine and popped the clutch causing it to leap forward and sending Kevin off the tailgate. Kevin twitched and jerked spasmodically, his feet mere inches from the ground.

Karl waited until the twitching stopped before muttering, "Justice... finally."

"Go ahead and cut him down," Rodney ordered.

"Wait a moment," Karl said, pulling out his phone and turning it back on. "I need a pic to show them. Everyone move out of the way."

There, in the shadowed light of the street lamps, Karl took several shots of the dead Kevin, momentarily wondering if Felix was gonna be pissed when he found out that he no longer had a body to come back to. *Shoulda thought of that when he brought Gerard back.*

Rodney came up to stand next to him, slipping the data stick into Karl's hand, quietly adding, "No one else needs to know there's nothing on this."

"Agreed." Karl continued staring at his dead antagonist as he placed the data stick in his pocket. "What are you going to do with him?"

"Part of me wants to leave him hanging, as a warning. But I suppose that's rather medieval and it's not like we get a lot of through traffic. Guess I'll get a backhoe and find a place to dump him." He looked over to those waiting to take the body down. "Go ahead." He then turned to Karl. "How long you plan on staying?"

"We'll leave tomorrow morning. Don't see much sense in hanging around, jeopardizing your presence here."

"You could both stay," Rodney suggested. "We've a good life here."

Karl smiled at him. "While I appreciate the offer, truth is, I like where I was."

"In a game?" Rodney sniffed in disdain.

"I know it sounds contrived, but I've had more fun than I ever did in real life. And the bonus is that long after you and all your Pioneers are gone, I'll still be having adventures."

"But we'll have lived a natural life, one without artificial construct. We'll establish a new order for mankind."

"As long as you can continue to hide," Karl wryly pointed out. "What kind of life is it when you have to constantly be on your guard, praying that you won't be discovered so that you have to pick up everything and move and start all over?"

"It's better than being stuck in some game where someone else defines the rules and parameters and you have no choice of your own."

Karl wanted to explain that it was more than that, that free choice was still an option, even within the game, that the game wasn't all that different from real life. Instead, he gave Rodney a sympathetic smile.

"I won't argue with you, my friend. We both have made choices. You are happiest here and I wish you well, truly."

Rodney nodded in acknowledgement. "You're right."

As the men dumped Kevin/Felix into the bed of the pick-up, Karl and Rodney headed back to the courthouse, Caryn a step behind.

"You'll need to be extra careful for a while," Karl said. "We'll point them off in a different direction. Any place you want them to waste time?"

Rodney thought a moment then chuckled. "Yeah. Send them off to D.C. if you can. That would be irony."

Chapter 10

Rita was not happy when Karl and Caryn showed up.

"What are you doing here?" she fussed, her robotic face looking almost human with a frown.

"Here," Karl said, holding up his phone and showing her the pictures of Kevin hanging from the streetlamp post. "Kevin's accounted for as is Gerard. Our job is done."

"But…but you were supposed to find out where Red and the rest of his holdouts were."

"I told you before, that's not our job. You can find someone else to do that. But we did find out some info for you."

"Like what?" Rita coldly asked, choosing not to argue.

"He was headed for D.C.," Caryn said.

"How do you know that?"

"Because he was beginning to get instructions by phone."

"By phone?" Rita's synthetic jaw dropped open. "How is that possible?"

"We wondered the same thing," Karl said, "then we remembered Red talking about the code. And so, instead of wasting time trying to figure it out ourselves, we managed to… um, coerce the info out of Kevin."

"It was the cities either Red mentioned or sent him to," Caryn explained. "It started off in Kansas City then Longmont then Denver. Using the first letter of each city gave him the area code 553. Using the rest of the cities gave him the rest of the numbers."

"He called Red when he was in Murphy," Karl added, "and just as Red told him to meet him at the Lincoln Memorial in D.C., Kevin managed to let Red know we were there. Well, naturally the line went dead and we figured that since Kevin was now persona non grata with us and with Red, there wasn't any reason to keep him alive."

"So we took care of business," Caryn affirmed. "Now. We've done our part of the task. It's time to put us back in the game."

"And how about leaving us there from now on?" Karl snarled.

"I can't promise that," Rita bristled.

"You ready?" Caryn said to Karl.

"Yup."

They headed out the door before Rita had a chance to stop them. Ten minutes later they stood in the chill air outside ITL, waiting to be admitted. When the doors didn't open, Karl took a step back and stared up at the cameras.

"You got 10 seconds to open these damn doors before Caryn and I walk away... never to return. You get my drift?"

There was a buzz and the doors unlocked.

"Let's hope you haven't pissed them off enough to send us to some other game," Caryn muttered.

"I guess we'll see," he said, storming it.

They crossed the foyer and headed straight to the elevators to take them to the immersion room. R-237 intercepted them on the way.

"So good to have you back. Sorry for the delay. RITA-4 was getting approval for your immersion. I'm pleased to say that you have been approved for re-immersion"

Karl felt Caryn's jab in his side just as he was about to add come caustic remark.

Back in the immersion room, Caryn flopped down on the immersion bed and waited for the electrodes to attach. "Now Elsa can have her body back. Still, I rather like this one, so the next time you jerk me out of Bridge Quest, I'll take this body again."

"Suppose Elsa has returned," Karl asked, the electrodes wrapping around his fingers.

"They better find an equally good body, someone with great boobs like her."

Karl snorted a laugh just as the darkness grew, beginning from the edges of his eyes then converging to the center until everything was black.

As the darkness began to fade, the first thing Karl was aware of was sound, like people talking. It was when light penetrated his senses, and colors and shapes assembled that the noise abruptly stopped. Then in one sudden burst, everything crystalized, and he found himself standing in the throne room in the citadel in Avnoch.

Glancing around, he noticed the stunned faces, faces he didn't recognize. To his side, Caryn had taken shape and was warily regarding the surrounding people who returned her gaze with a mixture of awe and wonder.

Frowning Karl turned around. The frown initially deepened when he saw two thrones, one draped in a rich crimson tapestry. Raquel occupied the throne to the right. He noted Raquel's look said she wasn't necessarily happy to see him.

"You're back," she said, stating the obvious. "For how long this time?"

"Good to see you too," Karl replied. "Everything OK?"

"Everything is fine," she answered, remaining seated.

Karl again glanced around the room. An awkward silence had settled as if those in attendance were caught in some indiscretion. Their eyes shifted between Karl and Raquel.

"Why the long faces?" Caryn said, breaking the spell. "Someone die?"

"No," Raquel answered. "Somebody came back to life."

Karl started to move towards the throne when Raquel held up a hand.

"It's not your throne anymore."

"Says who?" Karl retorted, surprised at her aloof coldness.

"Says the people who you deserted to go play in real life."

"Like we had a choice," Caryn snapped. "What's got into you? Karl's back. He's the rightful king, no matter what's happened. And anyway, you know damned well that we had no control in us going away."

Raquel leveled a hard stare at her. "Whether you had control or not is immaterial. You've been gone for almost a year —"

"No we haven't," Caryn interrupted. "It's been a couple of months at most... maybe six or so."

"Like I said," Raquel continued, ignoring her, "you've been gone almost a year and now you come back and expect to resume as if nothing has happened in the interim. And for how long will you stay this time?" She held up a regal hand and addressed the men and women behind the new arrivals. "Please leave us. I will summon you when I am ready."

Though disappointed, they dipped their heads and filed out.

Caryn noted the '*I* will summon you when *I* am ready.' "Like I said, what does that matter how long we've been gone?"

"It matters because there is a kingdom to rule, and you can't rule a kingdom when you're not here."

"Well we're here now," Caryn asserted.

"We?" Raquel repeated, giving Caryn a searing glare.

"Yes, 'we.'" Caryn retorted. "What's got into you? You can't be jealous that I've had him to myself all this time."

"Jealousy has nothing to do with it," Raquel responded, a little too quickly. "It's called governing a people. You left and I remained and assumed the throne."

"As queen," Caryn evenly replied, "and you've grown comfortable in that position and aren't happy about giving it up."

When Raquel didn't respond, Karl frowned, noting that the room seemed off balanced and said, "Where's my sword?"

Raquel pointed to the throne next to her. "When you left, your sword stayed behind on the cushion of the throne. Since no one could move it and I didn't like sitting on it, I had another throne made... the one I now occupy."

As Karl strode across the room to retrieve his sword, Caryn focused her attention on Raquel. "Though *we* had a good time *together* in real life, *we're* glad to be back." She noted with satisfaction Raquel's not so subtle bristling.

"What was it like," Raquel asked, regaining her composure.

"There's nothing left," Caryn honestly admitted. "There's nothing to go back to. The world is run by AI and the few humans who chose to remain behind spend their lives hiding to avoid capture and forced immersion. It's like a time warp at the end of the world, except there's no apocalypse, just ghost towns and cities left to fall apart."

"Sounds horrible," Raquel commiserated. "What was the reason this time?"

"Take out Gerard and Kevin."

Raquel's eyes blinked wide in surprise. "So that's where they went. Why would they pull them out of the game?"

"They pulled Gerard out and he pulled Kevin out," Caryn explained.

"Caryn," a voice exclaimed causing her to turn to see Annabeth weaving through the crowd. "You're back."

Annabeth's bright excitement was a stark contrast to Raquel's dour reception. The beautiful sorceress sauntered up and hugged her, planting a deep kiss while simultaneously squeezing a butt cheek.

"We've missed you," she smirked, flicking her eyebrows. "Where's that hunk of a Viking?"

"Retrieving his sword," Caryn replied, suddenly feeling at a disadvantage. Casting a quick glance at Raquel whose seemed resigned that things were about to change, she said, "Thank you for the warmer welcome."

"Oh don't mind Raquel," Annabeth breezily replied, flipping a hand. "She gets like that when things don't go like she expected. But to be fair, she's been an awesome queen. The people absolutely adore her."

Her accolades for her friend ceased when Karl emerged from under the tapestry, Orc's Bane at his side. "Karl," she cried out and ran over and flung herself into his arms, kissing him fully.

"Good to see you too," he laughed, catching his breath.

"Boss," a deep voice boomed.

"Dieter, my friend," Karl responded, extracting himself from Annabeth's embrace. The giant grasped his hand then drew his close and bear hugged him.

"Glad you're back. We've missed you." He turned to Caryn and spread his arms. "Well? C'mon. You get a hug too."

Caryn smirked then let herself be swallowed up in his arms. "Where's Elena?"

"She'll be along in a minute. Just getting the kids settled."

Caryn's jaw dropped. "You got kids?"

Dieter laughed and shook his head. "Not that kind. We got a couple of pooches, strays that we picked up from an abandoned litter."

Caryn glanced around the room. "Where's Sakura?"

"She comes and goes," Annabeth replied. "Sometimes she'll stay and hang out for a couple of days then we won't see her for weeks. Then she comes back and tells us she's been over in Krug killing orcs, stays for a couple of days then disappears again. Who knows when she'll be back."

"Now that most of us are all here," Karl said, turning back to Raquel. "So... what's been going on since we left?"

Raquel exhaled a frustrated sigh, torn between reporting as a subordinate or telling him again that it was her kingdom now. Deciding now was not the time to press the issue, especially with the response Dieter and Annabeth gave him, she said, "The two kingdoms are united. Ben is doing an excellent job ruling Rhyeem. Trade between the two kingdoms has grown significantly, banditry just about eliminated, and the orc incursions brought to a standstill."

"Ben and Julie got married," Annabeth announced.

"Married?" Karl blurted. "That was fast."

"It's been almost a year," Annabeth reminded him. "Once Julie heard you were gone and understood that it might happen often enough that she might never see you again, she decided Ben was a suitable substitute."

"Good for them," Karl said with heartfelt appreciation. "I'll need to schedule a visit soon. What about the others?"

"Frank and Ross are still residents of the jail."

"And they're not very happy about it," Annabeth chimed in.   "They're pretty bitter about PCs holding other PCs hostage."

"They had no problem doing that to you," Caryn reminded her.

"Yeah, I know," Annabeth nodded. "I figure another 500 years or so then we'll let them go." She grinned impishly. "I tell them that every time I go check on Greg and Caillac. 'You be good and just think, in only 500 years, you'll be free to go.'"

"What about Charles and Chet?" Caryn interrupted. "I haven't seen them around."

"After you two left, they hung around for a while, but then had the itch to move on, especially after a certain queen," she shifted her eyes at Raquel, "told a certain barbarian that she wasn't interested in him, much to his disappointment.   Anyway, they helped out in the orc campaigns, working on leveling up like the rest of us. Last time I talked to them was about three months ago. They came through here on their way west."

"Speaking of PCs," Karl said. "Kevin and Gerard are no longer problems."   He then briefly explained what had occurred back in real life. "But we're back now, hopefully for good." He turned back to Raquel. "So what else is going on, you know, things like finances and welfare?"

Raquel's lips pursed and she paused before answering. She was the queen.   Why should she respond to his questions?   Yet for the next hour, she found herself highlighting the previous year's accomplishments, *her* accomplishments, all the while remaining seated on the throne as Karl paced.

"Oh," Annabeth interrupted, "one more thing. That witch or sorceress or whatever named Elanda? We liberated her son about six months ago and sent him back home."

"Excellent," Karl grinned. He had forgotten all about her and the quest. Of course that now raised the issue of the Delf Stone. As far as he was concerned, he'd rather Annabeth had it.

The chamber door opened, and the head of a slender middle-aged woman popped through the opening.

"Your pardon, Your Majesty," she said, addressing Raquel, "but it is dinner time and I've prepared an excellent venison dish for you."

"Thank you," Raquel replied with an indulgent smile. "We'll be there shortly. Please set the table for two more."

"I already have, m'Lady," she said with satisfied smile.

Raquel nodded in acknowledgement then turned to the others. "Come. It's dinner time and we can continue our discussions at the table."

Caryn was about to point out that it was the King's decision when to eat but decided to bide her time.

Yet it did not go unnoticed to Karl, and he pondered an appropriate response. Instead, he remained silent and watched and listened. Despite the jovial banter during the meal, there was an underlying tension, a strained joie de vivre. It was more evident later that evening when Raquel made no effort to claim her time in his bed. In fact, she seemed almost put out when Annabeth asserted her privilege of sharing the night with Karl.

"You don't want your turn?" Annabeth smiled blithely at Raquel.

"Not tonight," Raquel politely declined. "I'm a bit tired and can use the rest."

When Annabeth didn't push the issue, Karl thought it odd. He found it more odd when Annabeth likewise relinquished her place in the queue, leaving him with Caryn. He broached the topic the next morning.

"There's more going on here than we realize," Caryn said, sitting on the edge of the bed, staring at her naked reflection in the floor mirror against the wall. She focused on her breasts, arching her back and thrusting them out. "So which ones do you like best?"

"Huh?" Karl frowned, glancing around the guest room, reminding himself that while he was kind enough to allow Raquel to remain in the king's chambers, it was not permanent.

"My breasts," Caryn said, preening in the mirror. "You've seen three versions, two natural and this one. Which do you like best?" She twisted her body to face him.

Karl blinked in thought, wondering why it mattered. After all, this was their world now and he had no desire to return to real life. "I like whichever ones are with me."

"A diplomatic answer," she chuckled.

"Wonder why Annabeth didn't press her claim," he puzzled. "That's not like her."

"I think I have an idea," Caryn said, standing to get dressed. "She came by last night after you were asleep. We talked a little. I asked her what was going on. She said that things had changed since we left, that it wasn't the same anymore."

"What did she mean?"

"That's all she would say. She said we'd see then kissed me on the cheek and left." Staring at herself a bit more, she shrugged and slipped her arms into a shirt. "But there's something more important first."

"Oh?"

"Coffee," she smirked.

They were sitting in the kitchen, enjoying a steaming cup of coffee when Raquel walked in.

"Good," she said with an air of one in charge. "You're up." Staring directly at Karl, she intoned, "We need to talk."

"Go ahead." He rested his elbows on the tabletop and sipped his coffee.

"In private," she replied, giving Caryn a 'get lost' glare.

"You can say whatever you have to say in front of her," Karl said.

"When I say 'private', I mean just that," Raquel imperially retorted. "Come to my chambers." She spun around and marched towards the door.

"They're not *your* chambers," Caryn taunted, causing Raquel to momentarily pause.

"I'll expect you there, immediately," Raquel sternly answered without looking back. She passed Annabeth walking in, giving her an 'I'm-not-happy-with-you' glare as she left.

"What's her problem?" Caryn asked, shaking her head while pouring Annabeth a cup of coffee.

"She's frustrated," Annabeth replied.

"Why?" Karl said.

"You're back." She looked pointedly at Karl.

"She knew I'd be back," he huffed.

"You and her?" Caryn said with a sudden epiphany, waving a finger between Annabeth and the door through which Raquel departed.

"Yeah," Annabeth sheepishly replied, pulling up a stool and sitting. "Like I said, things have changed. When you left and she took over, there was no one to take your place. She wasn't keen on taking an NPC, especially if she was to be queen. She felt that it would compromise her ability to rule. I was safe. And then you show up and it's back to sharing like before, except this time I don't think she wants to share."

"You and her never did anything before then?" Caryn wondered.

"We teased a lot, but nothing really happened. The coffee's good." She sighed with contentment as she took a savoring sip.

"So what happened?" Caryn said, wanting to know more.

"I think Mavie may have been right," she said.

"About what? Who's Mavie?"

"You weren't there," Annabeth explained. "Mavie was a sorceress in Tal Olca... had the hots for our Viking here and forced him to stay behind. When we tried to pry him away from her, she used her succubus powers and had Raquel and I kissing each other, rather passionately as I remember."

"Really?" Caryn said with a curious grin.

"Karl stepped in and had her stop the spell. Raquel was angry. I remember Mavie saying, "I was merely tapping into what you both want." Raquel replied that, "You don't know what we want." And then Mavie said, and I'll always remember this, she said, "Apparently neither do you.""

Karl chuckled. "And then Raquel told her to go to hell."

Annabeth smiled at the memory. "But then she said that she didn't have to do much of anything, that all she was doing was tapping into what we both wanted. Her words have stuck with me ever since." She stirred some cream into her coffee. "Yeah, I admit I wanted to have sex with her from the moment I met her back in Marbeck. But I didn't think she was into that. Sure, we teased and played around a bit, but there was always a line I wouldn't cross. I'd rather have her friendship than her body."

"So what happened?" Caryn asked.

"You came along."

"Me? What did I do?"

"Nothing really," Annabeth admitted. "In fact, I'm glad you did. Before you showed up, Raquel and I had a nice arrangement of sharing every other night."

"And wore me out," Karl interrupted.

"Oh you loved it," Annabeth teased.

"Shush," Caryn said to Karl, tapping his arm. "Let her finish."

"Well, when you showed up, the every third day seemed too much of an interference. That's when I decided to see if there was any truth to what Mavie said, so I started pushing the envelope, little things that might not be noticed."

"What happened?" Caryn asked.

"At first I thought it was just my imagination," Annabeth replied, "but the little nuances of intimacy like a kiss on the cheek or holding hands seemed to be welcomed. It was when you two departed and she was left in charge that she decided to surrender to fate and let the lid to Pandora's box come off."

"That's all well and good," Karl interrupted, "but it still doesn't answer why she's being such a bitch. It's not like her."

"Look at it this way," Annabeth said with a maternal glance. "She's been the Queen ever since you left. The longer you stayed away, the more she got used to her place and position and everyone kowtowing to her whims. Let's face it, a girl can get used to being waited on hand and foot."

"And apparently she's done a commendable job in running the place," Caryn added.

"And more," Annabeth nodded. "She's gone out of her way to make sure the people know she cares and that their needs are met. She's been an excellent ruler. The people truly love her. One town even made a statue of her."

"Then we show up and the party's over," Caryn said.

"Exactly."

"So where do you fit in all this?" Karl asked

"I'm sort of like second in command," Annabeth said with a nonchalant wave of her hand then looked around and lowered her voice. "Though the truth be told, I'm getting kinda bored. I don't know about this 1000-year reign of peace and prosperity thing."

"I see you're still wearing the Delf Stone," Karl observed with a smile.

Annabeth held it up to the side of her face like she was advertising a product. "I don't leave home without it."

"What about Dieter and Elena?" Karl inquired.

"I don't really see them as much. He and Elena have a nice place in a ritzy neighborhood. He wanted a small place away from here, but Raquel wouldn't allow that. 'We're in charge. Remember?' she would often remind us. We had to keep up appearances, set the example."

"And you?" Caryn observed. "There are no male lovers of interest?"

"Meh," Annabeth shrugged. "I can't get past they're NPCs." She looked at Karl. "Remember what I said about responses to flashing my breasts when we first met?"

"Uh…" he hesitated.

"Men," Annabeth huffed, rolling her eyes, though smiling before turning to Caryn. "What I said to him was that were I to flash my breasts at him, I would get an honest response. If I did the same to an NPC, I would get an expected response. There's a difference."

Caryn tilted her head as she considered the perspective. "An interesting observation. I think you're right. So you've relegated yourself to you and Raquel for the time being."

"Yeah. But now that you two are back…" she grinned with satisfaction. "I need variety."

"Raquel's not going to like it," Caryn pointed out, not all that sure she herself was that excited about having to share.

"Yeah, I know. I'm still working through that."

The door opened and a liveried servant stiffly entered. "Begging your pardon, m'Lady," he said, addressing Annabeth, "but the Queen requires his presence in the throne chamber."

"Who?" Caryn spoke up.

"Him." He nodded at Karl.

"Him has a name," Caryn coldly replied. "It's 'Your Majesty.' You need to learn proper respect when addressing *your* king. You drag your sorry ass outta here and tell Raquel that she needs to get her sorry ass here if she wants to talk with *him*."

The man's eyes bolted wide, and he looked to Annabeth for help.

"While I might not put it quite as succinct as that," Annabeth said to the servant, "she does have a point. If you'll notice, *him* is wearing Orc's Bane, which makes him the rightful king." She scooted her chair back and turned to Karl. "Perhaps I should try and sooth things here."

"Good luck," he replied, getting up to refill his coffee cup. "Remind her that she has until this afternoon to get her things out of my chambers."

Annabeth paused and narrowed her gaze at him. "Are you sure you want to go there?"

"No I'm not, but if she's gonna be a butt, I will."

"Lemme talk to her first."

"Be my guest," he replied, sitting back down, "and take Mister Clueless with you."

Annabeth motioned the servant out the door, but she was back in less than ten minutes. "Looks like she's going to be just as stubborn."

"She refused to leave?" Caryn sputtered.

"Not only that, she's told the palace folks that they are to take orders only from her."

His lips tightening, Karl stood to full height. Casting a backwards glance at the morning cook, he politely smiled. "Thank you for the excellent coffee."

"You're welcome," the young man respectfully replied and dipped his head, "Your Majesty."

"Someone finally gets it," Caryn groused.

Karl strode out of the kitchen and down the corridor, his scowling visage causing all who saw him to scurry out of his way. He didn't slow down and burst through the doors to the throne chamber and marched towards the throne dais.

"Get out of my throne," he snapped, drawing his sword in the process.

Raquel immediately saw his look of cold combat, the calm willingness to kill. She saw Annabeth burst in behind him, horror on her face. Raquel knew she could not defeat Karl. The result would be a painful respawn back in Ryath-sari.

With a hateful glare, Raquel stood and moved out of the way.

"What's happening to us," Annabeth bemoaned, her eyes misting with tears.

Sheathing his sword, Karl hurtled up the steps and plopped down. Swiveling his head to gaze up at a glowering Raquel, he said, "You're a damned fool. This kingdom, this island was yours all along. All you had to do was wait. There was no way I was going to stay here for a 1000 years."

"Then why are you here now?" Raquel shot back, descending the dais and striding away.

It wasn't that Raquel actively sought to undermine Karl's authority, the people had gotten used to her presence as ruler and the year of peace under her reign gave them pause to want to jettison their prosperity for a King whose authority came with a sword.

Karl's frustration grew as he realized that he could not travel wherever he wanted, including a visit to Ben in Glenloch or leading a force against the orcs, for it meant leaving Raquel in charge, reinforcing her position as ruler. He could have left Caryn in charge, but he'd rather have her with him when he traveled. He then thought about Annabeth, but this she flatly refused, reminding him that Raquel would still be here and everyone would take orders from her regardless of what Karl said. Karl knew Dieter was content with his position and arrangement. As a friend, Karl didn't want to upset the joy in the man's life. As time dragged on, Karl chaffed at the enforced restrictions, blaming Raquel for her intransigence and the subsequent underlying tension in the kingdom.

He saw little of Raquel for she spent as much time as possible away from the citadel, instead moving about the city, endearing herself further to the citizens. His requests for her presence at the evening meals were politely, but firmly, rebuffed until he sent several guards to physically escort her to the dining table.

The result was more than awkward. The guards, caught in the middle, hesitated to force the queen they knew to obey the orders of the king they did not know. Still, they did their best to be diplomatic and Raquel arrived, acting like a petulant child the entire meal. Deciding he'd rather enjoy his meals than have to deal with Raquel's bullheadedness, he put a halt to the invitations.

Annabeth did her best to keep the peace, shuttling between Karl and Raquel, soothing as best she could. Every second or third night, she would spend with Karl but would always be gone before morning.

It was after dinner late one evening, after Dieter and Elena had returned home and Annabeth went back to sooth Raquel's snippy attitude that Caryn, wine glass in hand, stood next to Karl, his arms folded as he stared out the window into the night sky.

"It's been almost three months. You're going to have to make up your mind."

"I know," he sighed.

"You're gonna have to get rid of her," she said, "permanently."

"I know." Karl furrowed his brows and tilted his head. "Ya know, even after I got rid of her, I'm not so sure this is where I want to be."

Surprised, Caryn cocked her head to stare at him. "What do you mean?"

Turning, he refilled his wine glass. "I'm bored."

"I'm not surprised," she chuckled. "Think about it. Is this what you want to be doing for the next 1000 years, running a kingdom, dealing with the same people day-in-day-out for the next 1000 years."

Karl gave her a curious stare. "Are you saying you're ready to move on?"

"I've been ready," she replied. "I was ready the day we returned. I knew what was going to happen."

"You did?"

"Of course. It was obvious that Raquel wasn't going to be pleased that I had you all to myself. And then you add in the time factor of us being gone. She got used to being the head honcho and why would she want to give that up?"

"Annabeth didn't seem all that put out," Karl said.

"Annabeth wasn't the queen," Caryn pointed out. "But it doesn't really matter. Let Raquel rule here. It's what she wants."

"What about the others, our team?"

"I guess this is where we say goodbye to the team," Caryn said. "It was a trip while it lasted, but all good things come to an end."

Karl turned to gaze out the window at the streetlights below flickering inside their glass globes. "I suppose you're right. Still, it would be nice to have the added talents of a sorceress and berserker."

"And an assassin," Caryn added.

"Yes, definitely an assassin," Karl readily agreed. "Ah well," he sighed. "No sense putting off the inevitable."

"When do you want to leave?"

"In a couple of days," he replied. "I don't see the sense of hanging around for the right moment. We'll need time to collect supplies and things."

Annabeth was the first to learn of their plans when she came by for the evening's fun. She noticed a change in their demeanor as soon as she walked in.

"What's with you two?"

"We've got some news for you," Caryn said with a smile.

"You're pregnant," Annabeth said with a laugh.

"Thank God, no," Caryn chuckled. "We're leaving."

"Leaving? Like in going away and not coming back?" Annabeth said, crestfallen.

"That's right," Caryn answered.

"I don't see the sense in staying here," Karl said. "To be honest, I'm bored. Conquering and uniting two kingdoms was a whole lot more fun than running it. Besides, Raquel seems to enjoy it more than I. And who knows when the powers that be will decide to yank us out again. Caryn and I are going to cross over to the next island."

Annabeth plopped down at the edge of the bed. "My God, you're really going?"

"Yes," Caryn said. There was a long pause before she added, "You wanna come with us? You're all Level 20s now. There's nothing stopping you."

Annabeth blinked as she puzzled her choices. "I... I'm not sure. This is so sudden."

"Yeah," Caryn commiserated, "I know." She sat next to her and gently placed a hand on Annabeth's cheek, turning her head to face her. "We could really use a powerful sorceress."

"I'd have thought you'd want him all to yourself," Annabeth said.

"I do, but if I have to share, I can't think of anyone I'd rather have than you."

"That was sweet," Annabeth softly replied. She looked up at Karl. "Can I have some time to think about it?"

"Take all the time you need," he answered. "We're leaving in a couple of days."

"What? But... but..."

"Do you really need more time than that?" Caryn questioned. "Think about what it was like when we all first came to the Misted Isle and all those folks were content to stay in Marbeck. What's so different between then and now? The difference is that we left; we went on adventures. I'd bet a level or two that most of the folks who stayed in Marbeck are still there, too afraid to venture beyond the safety of what's comfortable."

"What about the others?" Annabeth asked.

"They have to make their own decisions," Karl said.

Karl was disappointed a day later when Dieter sought him out to explain that he and Elena were going to remain where in Avnoch.

"It's safe here, Boss. I don't have to worry about her here."

"I understand, my friend," Karl said, placing a hand on his arm. "I shall miss you."

Dieter inhaled a deep breath and simply nodded before turning away and trudging home, ensuring Karl didn't see the moistness in his eyes.

However, Karl's disappointment was somewhat assuaged when Sakura arrived unexpectedly and immediately joined him and Caryn.

"Of course I'm coming with you," she said. "I've been waiting for you to come back, hoping you'd want to move along. My skills are getting rusty here. Have you sent word to Ben and Noble?"

Karl smiled. "When was the last time you saw them?"

"A couple of weeks ago."

"Were they happy?"

Instead of answering, Sakura nodded in understanding. "Touché."

"I figure I'd leave well enough alone," he explained.

Annabeth on the other hand was still undecided and Karl proceeded under the assumption that she too would stay.

Raquel, whose joy at resuming her place as queen was more than apparent, now seemed to go out of her way to accommodate his requests for supplies. She even sought to make amends by once showing up at dinner time.

Karl looked up when she entered and sat down. Without a word, he stood and left the room, his dinner unfinished.

Raquel sat there making forced idle conversation, expecting him to return. After an awkward realization that he wasn't coming back, her face hardened, and she scooted her chair back and left.

Watching her leave, Sakura commented, "What made her think that everything was OK? She stabs him in the back and it's like no big deal?"

"Is that why you didn't hang around?" Caryn said.

Sakura resumed eating. "Pretty much. In the beginning she was fine, made decisions in his name. But as time went on and you guys didn't return, it became *her* orders, *her* commands. Then she had the throne and sword draped over so no one would remember he was ever here." She paused as she chewed a morsel of roasted duck. "Then she tried giving me orders. I told her to take a hike and went off on my own. I'd come back on occasion and saw that she had grown rather comfortable, and everyone was calling her 'Queen Raquel."

"That had to be a shock," Caryn chuckled, shaking her head.

"Tell me about it," Sakura sniffed. "So I asked her whatever happened to Karl and the prophecy of the one who wields the sword rules the land?"

"What did she say?"

"She said she had the sword and since you two were never coming back, she was the de facto ruler, the Queen of the land. I knew then I wasn't going to stick around. Problem was that I didn't want to head out on my own. I'd been thinking about moving on to the next island, but I didn't want to do it by myself."

"So Dieter and Elena didn't want to go?" Caryn said.

"I dropped hints," Sakura replied, "but when I saw that they seemed happy, I decided to let it drop."

"What about Ben and Noble?"

Sakura smiled. "Those two are so funny. It's like they were separated at birth. Noble likes to think of himself as a master thief, so Ben indulges him. It's like a game within the game. Ben has a number of the families in the city and surrounding towns keep special pieces of treasure for Noble to find. If he's able to steal it, he brings it back in triumph. If he's caught, he's tossed into jail," she used her fingers to make quotations marks. "But it's not bad because in addition to being fed quite well and provided for, he's given clues and things to help him escape."

"Sounds like they're having fun," Caryn chuckled.

"They are," Sakura nodded, "and that's why I never bothered to ask them about moving on."

"Looks like it's just the three of us," Karl said. "I'm mighty glad you're coming along.

"Wouldn't miss it," she said, reaching for her wine glass.

A day before their departure, an unexpected visitor showed up, demanding to see the king. She was ushered into the dining room where everyone was enjoying a midday meal, Raquel noticeably absent.

Karl frowned when he recognized her.

"Good day to you, your Majesty," the hunched over crone, dressed in black tattered clothes and a threadbare shawl, greeted him. She tapped a cane on the floor as she stepped into the room.

"Good day to you, Elanda. What brings you to Avnoch?"

She smiled knowingly at him, her teeth glistening white. "He thinks we've forgotten, he has. Thinks he can run away and not fulfill his obligations."

"And what obligations would that be?" He leaned back in his chair, giving Annabeth a subtle tick of his head, telling her to be on guard.

"You accepted a quest," Elanda announced, "to free my son and return the Delf Stone to me."

"Actually," Karl smoothly intoned, "you're only partially correct. The Quest I accepted was to rescue your son and *retrieve* the Delf Stone. It said nothing about *returning* or *giving* the Delf Stone to you."

Elanda's eyes flashed. "That was not the agreement," she snapped. "You were to return the stone to me."

Karl confidently pulled up his screen and read the Quest: *Rescue Elanda's son and retrieve the Delf Stone.* "Nope. It says here that all I had to do was retrieve the stone… and we did. The sorceress Annabeth now wears the stone. Do you wish to challenge her for possession of the stone?"

Elanda glared at Annabeth who wiggled her fingers at her and smiled. With the Delf Stone in the sorceress' possession, she knew the beautiful young sorceress could defeat her. She turned back to Karl.

"I helped you get this kingdom, and this is the reward you give me... betrayal?" she bristled.

"You helped me?" Karl snorted a laugh. "Tell me witch. Where were you when I was fighting orcs? Where were you when I was imprisoned? Where were you when I was on the run? Where were you when we fought monsters? I don't recall ever seeing you."

"He forgets the magical cloth that freed the wolf," she countered.

"And for that, you have your son returned to you. Do not press further lest that joy be taken away again."

Elanda stiffened and narrowed her stare at him. "So now he threatens me, he does."

Karl leaned forward, his gaze hard and intent. "I don't make threats."

A thick silence settled as Elanda and Karl stared at each other.

Dieter broke the tension when he stood up and towered over her. "You need to leave."

Elanda sized up the giant and was unimpressed, giving him a snide passing glance. Shifting her gaze to Karl, she curled a lip. "You owe me." Turning, she shuffled out the door.

"What's that about a cloth and Uafas?" Annabeth asked.

"It was when I first came to the island," Karl said then explained about her son and the quest.

"She's not getting this back," Annabeth said, clutching the stone at her chest.

"I don't intend on letting that happen," Karl replied.

"Another reason to come with us," Caryn coyly added. "She can't cross to the island. Think about it."

"I will," Annabeth evasively replied. "Do you two have everything you need?"

Caryn noted the 'you two' of the question, disappointed that Annabeth was not likely to join them.

"Yeah," Caryn answered. "We've picked up a number of potions and stuff. Sakura even found an invisibility potion."

"And we all have several healing potions," Sakura quickly added, wishing Caryn hadn't revealed her find.

"So you're really leaving tomorrow, Boss?" Dieter said, his voice heavy with sadness.

"Yes. It's for the best."

"I understand."

Silence shrouded the room until Caryn perked up and said, "Somebody die in here? We're just going off to the next island. It's not like we'll never see you again."

"Sure," Annabeth agreed, though knowing it *did* mean they'd never see each other again. After 1000 years, who knew where anyone would be?

So it was, the next morning that Karl, Caryn and Sakura made their way to the city gates. Raquel chose to stay in the citadel, especially after the final confrontation with Karl in the throne chambers. An uncomfortable Annabeth stood next to Raquel, her waffling becoming a decision as she had continued to waver, torn between the two and her own indecision resulting in her staying with Raquel.

"You can at least be civil," Raquel had said to Karl, "especially after all we have shared and been through."

Karl stared at her, seated on the throne, her arms clasping the curled knobs of the armrests. "You betrayed me," he coldly stated. "Think about that for the next 1000 years." Without waiting for a response, he spun around and strode away.

Dieter and Elena walked with them to the gates and after parting hugs and good wishes had walked back through the gate, the hulking giant dominating the surrounding crowds.

"Let's get out of here," Caryn said.

Just as they turned to begin their travel, Annabeth came running up.

"They're gone," she cried out.

"Who's gone?" Karl said, turning back around.

"Frank and Ross and Greg and Caillac," she breathlessly said. "They're all gone."

"How is that possible?" Caryn said, her face showing her doubt.

"That witch who came here yesterday, Elanda. She did it."

"I thought you had a spell on the jail to prevent that," Caryn said.

"I did," Annabeth replied, shaking her head. "I don't know how she did it, but she broke the spell. She cast a sleep spell on the guards and unlocked the doors. And now they're gone."

"OK," Karl calmly said. "Thanks for letting us know."

"You're going to leave?" Annabeth's eyes popped wide in surprise.

"Of course," Karl answered. "Why not?"

"But you have to stay and help us find them," Annabeth pleaded.

"No we don't," Sakura intervened. "You have plenty of talent here already. You even have the Delf Stone. You don't need us. She's already made that clear enough."

Annabeth turned her beseeching eyes on Karl.

"She's right," Karl said with a noncommittal shrug. "What would you be doing if we weren't here? Besides, if I remember right, Caillac's only a level 15 and Frank is the highest PC at a level 13. You really don't need our help."

"You're really going?" Annabeth's gaze focused on Karl then Caryn.

"Yes," Sakura answered for them.

Annabeth's shoulders sagged and she started to turn away when Caryn affectionately touched her arm.

"You can still come with us,"

Annabeth's eyes misted and the corners of her mouth curled up in a half-smile. "She's my friend."

"As we all are," Caryn countered, "especially Karl and me."

Annabeth slowly nodded. "I know, but she'd be here all alone. Ben and Noble are too far away. She'd be the only PC here."

"Dieter is here," Caryn pointed out.

"Yeah, but it's not the same."

"So?" Sakura folded her arms and stared at her. "Seems to me she's quite happy here, especially now that we're going. And if this whole prophecy thing is true, those folks who escaped shouldn't be a problem."

"Although," Caryn mused, "if the man who wears the sword leaves, does the prophecy still hold?"

Annabeth's eyes blinked wide.

"Maybe she should have thought of that when she decided she wanted to rule alone," Sakura sourly stated.

"Even more reason for me to stay. She needs me."

Caryn locked her eyes on the sorceress. "So do we."

Annabeth blinked again, surprised at the comment, especially coming from Caryn. "I... I..."

"Go on then," Caryn urged, her voice soft with understanding. "She's waiting for you."

Annabeth closed her mouth and gave one last long look at them then turned and plodded back the way she came.

"One of these days," Sakura loudly exclaimed, "she's going to have to make a choice for what's in her own best interests."

Sakura couldn't tell if Annabeth heard her for there was no reaction and the sorceress was soon lost among the crowds.

Three days later, as they headed west out the gates of Statmyr, Caryn commented, "I've been studying the map of what's ahead and noticed there's a line representing a wall separating a section called Shadow Wood from Odryssa. Wonder why no one has ever mentioned it before."

"Guess we'll find out," Karl amiably replied.

"And we still don't know what the password is to cross the bridge," Sakura reminded them.

"Probably won't know until we get closer to the bridge," Karl opined.

"You're awfully cheerful," Caryn teased.

"Just feels good not to have to worry about anything for a change." He inhaled a deep satisfying breath, noting the freshness of the air, momentarily wondering how they do that in a game. "Odryssa is settled, and we don't have to look over our shoulder for Kevin."

"I'm glad to be back," Caryn agreed.

"Was it really that bad?" Sakura asked.

"Worse than you can imagine," Caryn replied. "AI runs the world."

"What about the others who remained behind?"

"Always worried about being discovered," Caryn said. "Not how I want to live, and anyway this is much more fun."

"And we don't have to grow our own food," Karl added with a grin.

"Let's hope they never decide to make that a part of the game," Sakura said, rolling her eyes.

"Wonder what the next island is like," Caryn said, changing the topic.

"We'll find out soon enough," Karl said, pulling up his screen map. Studying it a bit, he pointed. "Looks like Helkirk is the biggest town near Caryn's wall. We'll stop there for a day or two then head on over the wall."

Helkirk sat in the middle of the forest. It wasn't much of a town with perhaps three dozen buildings consisting of a bakery, a smithy, a tavern, and homes all constructed of solid logs and thatch roofs. Two roads bisected in the middle of the town. One road ran east and west towards the outlying hamlets, with the other going south and north, though the north road dead-ended at the wall. It was the road south of town that Karl, Caryn, and Sakura now traveled into the town.

The streets were deserted as they strode towards the intersection, passing the tavern on the right. Pausing in the middle of the intersection, Karl did a 360, wondering where everyone was.

"Hopefully the pub's open. I could use a cold one."

Karl pushed the door open and what little chatter and activity there were stopped as the three travelers entered.

"Welcome friends," the taverner called out from behind the counter. "Find a seat and I'll be right with you. We have the finest ale in the land." He was a stout overly jovial man with flushed cheeks.

Karl glanced around the room. The tavern contained a dozen tables, half of them with patrons who warily regarded the newcomers. They reminded Karl of lumberjacks, brawny men who wielded sharp axes. Though Karl stood taller and broader, their gazes gave him a passing glance for their focus was on the two women whose beauty captivated and Karl noted several men nudging those beside them.

Ignoring the leers, Caryn made a beeline for the table farthest away from the door, which provided a good view of the interior. As she passed by one table, a hand reached out and pinched her butt, causing her to abruptly stop.

Slowly turning to the three men leaning back at the table, she saw the smirks and challenges on their faces, daring her to do anything about it. Their smirks abruptly evaporated when the man seated across the table found his head jerked back and a razor-sharp blade at his throat.

"Someone needs to apologize," Sakura threatened, her grip on the man's head twisting it enough so that his companions saw the look of terror in his eyes. Though she held the knife to the man's throat, her harsh gaze rested on the man closest to Caryn.

"Whoa, please," the taverner pleaded, "no violence in here. If you must fight, take it outside."

Paying the taverner no attention, Caryn half smiled and slowly shook her head, narrowing her gaze at the man closest to her. Of average height, he was thick shouldered with full blond beard, and returned her gaze with condescending arrogance.

"So pinching my butt is what passes for telling me you find me attractive? I might have been tempted to return the favor had you even remotely been attractive, but your face looks like you got into a fight with an ugly stick and lost quite badly."

The room erupted into laughter and jeers at the man whose arrogance vanished.

Caryn motioned for Sakura to release her grip on the one man who inhaled a deep breath of relief, his hand going to his throat.

"You wouldn't know what to do with a man like me, bitch," the bearded man snarled.

"Bitch?" Caryn repeated with a grin. "That's your concept of seduction?" She shifted a glance to between his legs then back to the rest of the room. "I'd say 'show me what you got,' but I don't want to embarrass you and besides, not only would it take two hands to find it, you'd need a magnifying glass to see it."

The room erupted in raucous laughter. Even the man's friends at his table laughed.

The man leaped up and lunged at her only to find himself arcing in the air to come crashing down on a table, knocking it over and scattering the ale mugs and the three men seated there.

The room grew oppressively quiet, until the taverner said, "Someone help him up." While two patrons helped the man to his feet, the taverner turned to the newcomers. "I don't allow violence in here. You all need to find another tavern."

"Not until we've had our drink," Karl indifferently replied. "Hopefully the ale is on par with what we were used to in Avnoch."

"Avnoch?" a patron repeated. "What are ya doin' here?"

"We're heading for a bridge," Karl replied, sitting at an empty table, facing the main door.

"A bridge?" The man frowned and shifted a glance at his tablemates. "What bridge would that be?"

"The one on the other side of the wall," Karl casually replied.

The room suddenly stilled, and all eyes latched onto the three newcomers.

"There's a bridge on the other side of the wall?" a man asked, giving Karl a 'you're-not-quite-all-there-are-you?' look.

"Yes," Karl amiably said.   "Surely you've seen it."
Getting the taverner's attention, he pretended to hold an ale
mug in his hands

The man cocked his head to study him and then his
frown turned to a smirk as he shook his head. "You had us
going there, mister. Ain't no one been on the other side of
that wall fer at least a hundred years."

"Even longer," another voice added.

"I don't doubt it," Karl readily agreed. "So, none of you
have been on the other side?"

"Hell no," another patron exclaimed. "You go over that
wall, you ain't comin' back."

"Why not?" Caryn asked, scooting out a chair and
sitting. Sakura sat next to her, pushing her chair farther back
to get a better overall view of the room.

"Hell," the patron replied, raising an eyebrow, "the damn
things at least ten times the height of a man. You fall off
you're gonna kill yerself. If you live, ain't no one gonna go
down and get ya."

"No gate?"

"Gate? You crazy?" the patron snorted a derisive laugh.
"There ain't no gate in that wall. The only way yer gettin' to
the other side is if you fall off or decide you wanted to end
yer life and jump off."

"I take it you don't like the other side," Karl said,
accepting the ale mug and taking a satisfying sip. He held
the mug up in salute. "This is quite good."

"Quite good?" the taverner repeated, giving him a stern
stare.

"Yes," Karl said.

"Why is there no gate in the wall?" Caryn interrupted.

The room once again abruptly fell silent.

"There's no gate," a voice said, "because we don't need
a weak point in the wall."

Caryn scanned the room and the faces of those staring at
her, puzzled at her naiveté. "What's on the other side that
has you so frightened?"

"It's obvious you ain't from around here," another man
said. "There's monsters on the other side."

"Have you ever seen them?"

"No, but we've all heard them often enough."

"And seen whole trees shaking and the sounds of terrible roars," another added.

"Also seen the leftovers of them that had death sentences passed on 'em," yet another added.

When Caryn frowned at the statement, the taverner explained, "The punishment fits the crime. You commit a crime worthy of death, you get death."

"And so you get tossed over the wall," Caryn agreed, understanding.

"Exactly."

Karl took another savoring sip of his ale. It was rich and smooth with a faint sweetness. It was the type of ale one could drink in great quantities and still want more.

"This is a fine ale," he announced. "Does it have a name?"

The taverner grinned proudly. "I call it Dragon's Head Ale."

"Dragon's Head Ale," Karl repeated.

"Didn't know there were dragons around her," Caryn chuckled.

"Dragons ain't real," the taverner suavely explained, "just as my ale is so good it's almost not real."

"Haw," a patron derided. "It's so unreal, we even uses it fer a password."

"Don't go tellin' 'em that," another scolded.

Karl's ears immediately perked up. *Password... Dragon's Head Ale? Certainly not the 'ale' part...*

"Well, it's an excellent name for an excellent brew," Karl complimented. "Can't think of any better."

Pleased, the taverner jerked a thumb over his shoulder. "I've vittles a plenty if ya want."

"They ain't as *unreal* as the ale," a patron laughed. "Bread's bread and meat's meat. Iffn ya want good cookin' my missus is the best around here."

"Well she ain't cookin' in here, is she?" the taverner snapped, hands on his hips. "The bread's just about as good as you'll get around here and the boar and venison are smoked and grilled."

"Sounds good," Sakura said.

Giving the patron a snide glance, the taverner snapped his fingers at a serving girl, an auburn-haired pretty teenager beginning to blossom, sending her to fetch the food.

Turning back to Karl, he said, "Will you be staying the night? My rooms are big and the beds comfortable." He tried to appear nonchalant, but his intended meaning was obvious.

"Yes, we will," Karl replied. "We'll take the largest room."

Once in the bedroom, Karl activated his personal screen.

"What are you doing?" Caryn asked.

"Finding out the password to the next island."

Sakura's ears perked up. "I was wondering when we'd get around to that, especially as close as we are."

"Pull up your screens," Karl said, "specifically the map of Innis Torr. Notice anything peculiar?"

After a moment's silence, Caryn said, "The next island now has a name – Dragon's Head."

"And we now have the password," he grinned with satisfaction.

"Are you sure?" Sakura asked, not so convinced.

"Remember what we learned back on the Misted Isle?" he reminded her. "The password is the name of the next island. It never appears until someone provides a clue. You don't think it was mere coincidence that the ale here is Dragon's Head ale, they use it as a password, and now the name of the next island just happens to be Dragon's Head."

Sakura's face said she still had doubts. "Hate to get there and be wrong."

"The worst that could happen is that we respawn back in Ryath-sari and start over again," Caryn said with a shrug. "Not my idea of a good time, but it's not like we don't get a second chance."

"Easy for you to say," Sakura said, shaking her head.

"You got a better idea?"

"Not really. I suppose you have a point."

"And if I wear a hat, no one will notice," Caryn innocently replied, causing Sakura to smirk.

Sakura then noted there was only one very large bed in the room. "If it's all the same with you, I'll get the room next to you."

Caryn was about to say the bed was big enough for the three of them but decided to keep her mouth shut. During all the time she had known Sakura, the woman never intimated a desire for another person. Maybe once she truly got to know the assassin, she'd find you why.

When Sakura left and the door closed behind her, Caryn turned around to gaze impishly at Karl, pleased to have him to herself once again. "New in town, sailor?" she cooed as she sauntered up to him.

By the time they were up and ready, it was getting towards lunch time. Sakura was seated at a table, sipping her third cup of coffee.

"Good afternoon," she grinned at them.

"Good afternoon to you too," Caryn said with a smile. "How's the coffee?"

Instead of replying, Sakura gave her a dreamy sigh of contentment.

While Karl and Caryn slid out the chairs to join her, the tavern door flung open as the alarm bells clamored their warning.

"A monster has gotten over the wall," the man cried out. "It's headed this way."

Karl strode out just in time to see a giant scorpion twice the size of Uafas come scuttling into the intersection. It had three tails and two sets of pincers, one of which tightly clamped a decapitated townsman. Seeing Karl, it flung the body in the air to land in a bloody heap opposite the tavern.

Other than the beast, Karl, Caryn, and Sakura, the streets were empty.

Taking a quick measure of the fiendish monster, he reached into his belt and pulled out a small mauve colored bottle, quickly downing its contents.

"What are you drinking?" Caryn asked, giving the scorpion careful attention.

"Speed potion. You might want to do the same. I'll attack from the left, you take right, Sakura, you know best what you should do."

Caryn uncorked a bottle of the bland mauve liquid, downing it in one gulp and immediately felt energy pulsating through her. In a blur of speed, she reached behind her into the quiver then sent half-a-dozen arrows at the monster, scoring hits on the right lateral and the left median eyes, enraging the beast.

Yet as the creature lifted its rear to attack, Karl was already racing under it, managing to slice off one tail while slashing halfway through the other two. He was gone by the time the beast jerked around in a vain attempt to find its attacker.

He then zipped around to the side and hacked off one pincer while Caryn continued pouring arrows into the body.

The monster jerked spasmodically, vainly trying to locate the cause of its pain. Unable to find Karl, it settled its attention on Caryn who remained standing in the middle of the street. As it moved to scuttle forward, it lurched to the side as Karl severed two side legs and then sped out from beneath the monster.

Suddenly, a ball of flame emerged from the side street and burst upon the giant scorpion, causing it to erupt in a mass of churning fire. Careening wildly up the street, it collapsed before it reached the edge of town.

Startled, Karl snapped his head to see Annabeth smiling impishly at him.

"What are you doing here?" he grinned, racing over to her, working to calm the effects of the speed potion.

"Thought you might need some help, though from the looks of it you were doing fine without me."

"I thought you decided to stay with Raquel," Caryn said, striding up, pleased and disappointed at the same time.

"I finally realized it was more fun with you guys," she said with a sheepish shrug. "I mean, it was fun with Raquel and all that, but once you and he returned, deep down I knew I couldn't stay. I guess I was having trouble admitting it."

"What about Raquel?"

Annabeth sighed. "She wasn't happy."

"Mad?"

Annabeth rolled her eyes. "Oh yeah. We both said some pretty mean things. She refused to speak with me or even see me right up until the moment I headed out the gate. She was standing there begging me not to go. I was beginning to weaken when Dieter and Elena walked up."

At that moment Dieter and Elena came around from behind the tavern.

"Yay," Caryn exclaimed. "You're here."

'Yeah," Dieter awkwardly admitted. "It felt weird letting you three go off on your own. And then I saw how she was treating Annabeth and told her right then and there that I didn't think she was being fair, that she wasn't being much of a friend. When she saw that Elena and I had packed to travel, she knew we were leaving too."

"When she saw the three of us were determined to go," Annabeth continued, "she stormed off, telling us we were deserting her, that we sucked as friends, that we were the ones who were being unfair."

"And here we are,' Dieter said with a smile.

"Just in time, too," Caryn said with heartfelt thanks.

Karl glanced at Elena then back to Dieter. "I figured you would stay put. It made sense as it would have been safer for her."

Dieter gazed affectionately at his lover. "She saw that I was like a caged animal. I'm a berserker. I fight. What sort of job would I have in a kingdom at peace for a thousand years?"

"Though I know there is more danger ahead," Elena said, hugging Dieter's arm, "I would rather he be where he is happiest." She looked back at Karl. "We all are a team, and we belong together. I am sorry that Raquel could not see this."

"What did you do with the kids?" Caryn asked.

"Gave them to a family who would take good care of them," Elena answered.

At that moment, Sakura came from beside the bakery, frog-marching a crone of a woman, the assassin's blade pressed against her neck.

"I was wondering where you took off to," Karl said to Sakura though staring at the old woman.

"I found her off to the side of one of the homes," Sakura explained. "When she didn't seem to be all that shocked or surprised at the monster, I figured something wasn't quite right."

The old woman lifted her head, and glared hatred at Karl and Annabeth.

"We meet again, Elanda," Karl said, shaking his head. "You're like gum on my shoe. Get it through your thick head. If you want the Delf Stone, you'll have to challenge her for it." He pointed to Annabeth who smiled at her and wiggled her fingers in a silly wave.

"The stone is mine," she seethed.

"It was never *yours*," Karl retorted. "It belongs to the one who can properly wield it."

With the scorpion smoldering at the end of town and the threat eliminated, the townsfolk emerged onto the streets to crowd around Karl and the others, their appreciation overt that the monster had been slain.

"That," Karl announced in a loud voice, pointing at the charred and smoking remains of the scorpion, "did not come from the other side of the wall. That came from her." He shifted his finger to Elanda. "She is a witch."

"She killed Daim," a man growled.

Their anger erupted and in one surge, they enveloped the old woman whose frantic efforts to explain were ignored. Karl and the others stepped away as the madness of the crowd took its course. For a few moments, the fury raged then just as quickly dissipated. The crowd pulled back to survey what was left of the old woman.

Her battered and broken body lay lifeless, blood spilling out of multiple stab wounds.

"Get 'er outta here," the taverner said, his face a mask of authority. While several men grabbed hold of arms and legs, the taverner turned to Karl and the others. "You've done us a great service, riskin' yer lives like that for the likes of us. We're mighty indebted to ya. Whatever we can give you, within reason, it's yers."

"How about some rope to lower us down on the other side of the wall?" Karl replied.

A stunned silence met the request.

"You crazy, mister?" a voice exclaimed. "We tol' ya there ain't nuthin' over there 'cept monsters."

"Why ya wanna go over there for?" another voice demanded.

"We have a task to accomplish on the other side of the wall," Karl answered.

"Like what?"

"That is not something we are able to share at the moment," Karl evasively replied. "Will you help us?"

The taverner peered intently at the six strangers. "You look like yer gonna go whether we like it or not, so we might as well help ya. But ya ain't gotta go today. Stay another day and fill yer bellies with the best food and ale around here."

Karl was about to object when Annabeth interrupted, "You have coffee?"

"The best," the taverner proudly answered.

"We can stay another day," she said with a grin.

Chapter 11

They stood behind the crenellation atop the wall, peering out into the vast forest of hardwood trees that rose higher than where they stood. Below, a no man's strip about thirty meters wide ran along the entire length of the wall, separating the high stone barrier from the forest. What remained in the cleared area were stumps and the occasional thorny bramble. Otherwise, it was surprisingly clear.

"Don't know how it stays like this," the taverner declared when he saw Karl's puzzled look, "but it ain't our doin'. We figure something out there must be doin' it. Don't know why, but we'll take it. You sure you wanna go in there?" He ticked his head at the forbidding forest.

"It's our destiny," Karl gravely intoned, causing Caryn and Annabeth to snicker.

Two townsmen shouldered their way to stand before Karl.

"Me and Erv wants to come with you," the one said. He was of average height with copper colored hair and beard, broad shouldered and strong. He carried his woodsman axe. Erv was a little taller with light red hair. He too carried a woodsman axe.

"You daft, Kori?" the taverner blurted, staring at the two like they had just demanded to sleep with his wife.

"Not at all," he confidently replied. "Me and Erv figures we'll be the first to see what's out there and we can tell everyone when we get back."

"*If* you get back," the taverner retorted. "What's got into you two?"

"Just look at all that wood," Kori said, staring hungrily at the virgin forest spread out before them, "just waitin' fer two smart loggers to take advantage of it."

"We're not stopping for you to chop down trees," Karl told him. "If you come with us, you obey my rules. Otherwise, you can stay here."

"We're just checkin' it out this time," Kori assured him. "We'll do like ya say."

Karl watched as the last of the ropes were pulled up then up at the townsfolk who leaned over the wall's edge, their faces a mix of disappointment and disbelief, especially at the two townsmen who decided to come along. The two men were woodsmen, brawny and muscular. While he saw that Kori had a genuine desire to come along, Erv wasn't quite as convincing, his swagger getting the best of him. Even now he had the look of a kicked pup.

"You still have time to go back," Karl advised him. "All they have to do is lower the rope for you."

"No," Erv replied, his voice cracking. He looked up at the faces staring down at him, the looks telling him he was crazy. "I'm good." He squared his shoulders and tried to relax.

"Last chance," Karl again warned.

"I said I was good," Erv snapped.

Unconvinced, Karl addressed the group. "It's fifty kilometers to the bridge–"

"Bridge?" Erv blurted. "How do you know that?"

"Just shut up and listen," Sakura growled.

Ignoring the interruption, Karl continued. "From what we can tell on the map, there's one place called Stonekirk, about two klicks from the bridge. Looks like it's either a city or castle of some sort, at least according to the map symbol. We'll get more info as we get closer." He glanced at Kori and Erv whose confused looks told him they might be more trouble than help. "According to the map, there's one main road all the way to the bridge, relatively close to here. Once we find the road, we stick to it and make time as fast as possible. We already know there's danger, so keep alert. Caryn is on point then Annabeth and myself, Dieter and Elena then you two as rear security."

"What about her?" Erv pointed to Sakura.

"Sakura is roving security."

"Is that smart?" Erv said, his tone implying he didn't think the woman assassin much of a resource.

"No one asked you to come along," Annabeth tersely answered, "but now that you're here, you'd do well to keep your mouth shut, especially when you don't know what you're talking about. For your information, Sakura here happens to be the most lethal and deadly assassin in the entire world. She could slit the throats of all your kin while you were having dinner and you wouldn't realize what had happened until after dessert was served."

"I didn't mean nuthin' by it," Erv lamely explained.

"Of course not," Annabeth taunted.

"We're wasting time," Karl said then addressed the core team. "Make use of everything in your belts if necessary. We have one objective and that's reaching and crossing the bridge."

"You keep talking about a bridge," Erv began before Kori held out a hand to stop him.

"Would ya just button it up, man? Yer yappin' too much. We'll find out soon enough."

"Roger that," Karl replied. "Let's move out."

He smirked when he heard Erv whisper to Kori, "Who's Roger?"

Caryn led the way into the forest. Ten minutes later, she stepped onto a cobblestone road, wide enough for two carts to travel side by side.

"This is weird," she said as the others came up to stand beside her. "The road starts here, and it looks like it's still used." She pointed to how the cobblestones were tight against each other, the joints devoid of the usual weeds and grass one would expect from the type of road.

"There ain't no wheel ruts," Kori commented, frowning at what appeared to be a cobblestone road in pristine condition. "Don't make no sense."

Karl pulled up his map. "This is it."

Sakura emerged from the forest about a hundred meters up the road and headed back to them.

"Not much around here. Found a small, long-abandoned campfire. A nice little circle of stones, but the wood's rotten in it."

"OK, folks," Karl said. "We know the mission. Stay alert. Let's move out at a double time, weapons ready."

Edged by the thick forest, the road rose and fell in gradual slopes, and they jogged at an easy pace. Every once in a while, a meadow would open up with a dazzling array of flowers in a cornucopia of colors. Along the way stone bridges elevated the road over rivers or small streams. The water was refreshingly cold, and Karl would call the occasional halt to crouch down and cup his hands to drink yet listening ever carefully.

If there were animals, they saw none, save for the birds aloft. Yet for all this life, the only sounds were wind and leaves, and the occasional babbling of rushing water. Had they not assumed the dangers, they could have easily lulled into a blithe indolence, especially at the meadows. The warm sun and rippling wildflowers spilled a hypnotic effervescence that more than once suggested a peaceful slumber within their arms.

"Stay alert," Karl snapped when he observed Erv's daydreaming eyes.

Sakura once again emerged and jogged next to Karl.

"Can you feel it?" she asked.

"Yes," he nodded. "We're being watched."

"It started not long after we got on the road. I've widened my search and found tracks all over the place, but I can't tell how old they are. I tried following the tracks a couple of times, but they go too far into the forest."

"Be careful and don't get too far ahead," Karl warned. "We're making good time. We should get to Stonekirk in another couple of hours."

The feeling of being watched intensified as they sped their way to Stonekirk. By now, even the daydreaming Erv could feel the oppressive presence.

Under a leaden sky, Karl and company emerged out of the surrounding forest to a wide expanse of what had once been farm fields now overgrown with thistle and bramble. In the middle, set upon a small knoll, the spires and towers of Stonekirk rose above the land. What Karl had initially thought was a city or town turned out to be a solitary castle, a rather small castle with four towers at the corners. Ivy clung to the curtain walls, occasionally covering arrow slits and windows. In the center of what Karl was supposed was a single bailey, a tall circular tower rose high above the walls.

"That looks like a good place to spend the night," Karl mused as they headed towards the castle.

They were halfway through the farm fields when Erv rushed up to Karl, Kori on his heels.

"There's somethin' behind us," he wailed.

"Lots of somethin'," Kori added, his former self-assured air vanishing.

Karl looked past them as Dieter and Elena paused beside him. "Keep moving Dieter. I'll catch up."

"OK Boss."

"You two keep going," Karl said to Erv and Kori.

Needing no urging the two hurried their pace to catch up to Dieter and Elena just as the 'something behind' them spilled out of the forest. There were dozens of them, half man, half spider, male and female, wearing metal breastplates and brandishing swords and bucklers.

"Time to pick up the pace," Karl called out as he spun around and raced to catch up to the rest of his fleeing team.

Erv looked back over his shoulder and wailed a pitiful, "O my God," his legs suddenly churning as he raced to the main gate.

They reached the main gate as the spider creatures swarmed towards the castle.

"Forget the doors," Karl ordered when he saw them trying to pry them away from the wall, the hinges groaning. "Lower the portcullis."

"The what?" Erv fretted.

"The portcullis," Karl repeated, ignoring the man's obvious fear. "Everyone to the tower."

While the rest followed Caryn through the gatehouse and across the bailey to the solitary door into the tower, Karl held back once outside the gatehouse and raced up the stone steps to the room above the gatehouse where the geared windlass held the portcullis in place. Smacking the retaining pin out of the way, he watched the gear spin and heard the satisfying grinding of metal on stone.

Racing back down the outside stairs, he looked back over his shoulder to see that the portcullis had stopped half a meter from the ground and the spider creatures were almost at the gate.

Speeding across the bailey, he burst through the open door.

"Block the door," Karl commanded.

"I got this one," Annabeth said and cast a Hold Portal spell. "That should do it for a while."

"How long's a while?" Erv worried.

"Long enough," Karl answered for her. "Let's get moving." He motioned for Caryn to lead the way up the circular stairwell.

By the time they reached the top and gazed down from the battlements, the spider creatures had pried up the portcullis and were pouring into the bailey.

"What are they?" Erv anxiously asked.

"They're Arachnians," Sakura answered, "half human, half spider."

Karl activated his personal screen to read, *Arachnians, Level 16, are creatures composed of four spider-like legs with human torsos, both male and female. Arachnians are clannish bellicose creatures whose society is based upon war and inter-clan fighting. Clans will join together to fight other clans and, provided the incentive is sufficient, are just as willing to betray their allies when the reward is perceived greater than the alliance. Arachnians prize the strong and fearless, the female members tending to be those most respected. As such, the society is matriarchal, with an occasional rare male clan chief. Arachnians average between two and three meters in height, with the distance between legs of approximately three meters. Arachnians wear body armor upon their torso and the outer portions of their legs. Armor consists of metal plating or chainmail for the torso, and stiff leather for the greaves and cuisses. Arachnians prefer the sword and battle axe, though they are proficient with bow and arrow and pike. They are fierce in battle and will yield only when facing insurmountable odds, preferring to flee and fight another day than surrender.*

"Positions everyone," Karl commanded. "Dieter opposite me, Annabeth, do your magic wherever you need to, Caryn to my right and Sakura to my left, Elena in the middle, and you two fill in everywhere. Now get ready."

Leaning through the crenellation and looking down, Karl saw the first of the Arachnians beginning to climb up the sides of the keep.

"Here they come."

Annabeth was the first to react, hurling down fire balls on Karl's side then racing to the other side where Dieter waited and cast a Banana Peel spell midway up the tower. Then it was over to Sakura's side and casting a Sticky Spot spell before hustling over to Caryn and imbuing her with an Arrow Division spell. Then back to stand next to Karl and casting a Fog Ring spell that encased the tower in a bank of fog that started at ground level and ended ten meters below the battlements.

"I see you've been practicing," Karl grinned, impressed.

"Figured I ought to learn what I can do while you were gone," she smiled back.

"They're coming through the fog," Kori called out, still in awe of Annabeth's powers. He and Erv stood by Sakura, their axes ready.

Karl heard the occasional grunt and thud as Arachnians stepped onto the slippery area of the Banana Peel spell and fell backwards onto the ground, while others cursed as their legs became stuck on the Sticky Spot. Sakura and Caryn switched places so that Caryn could send arrows straight down through the fog, hopefully impaling those stuck.

"How long does the fog last?" Karl asked.

"Thirty minutes," Annabeth replied.

"I got company," Sakura yelled as she slashed one front leg of a female Arachnian then the other leg, causing it to lose its grip and plummet down through the fog.

Karl's attention jerked back to his portion of the battlement when he saw one Arachnian leg reach through the embrasure, followed by another leg gripping the top of the merlon. In two quick strikes, he severed both legs, followed by a cry of pain and shock as the creature fell off the tower.

As more of the creatures pressed the attack near the top, Karl noted a peculiarity.

"Cut the legs," he exclaimed, "as soon as you see them. They can't use their weapons until they're horizontal."

One male Arachnian managed to leap past the two Helkirk woodsmen and land in the middle of the defenders.

"Dieter," Elena cried out as she flailed her sword at the creature.

In one swirling sweep, Dieter's axe sliced through the air and the Arachnian's neck, severing its head, causing the body to collapse in place, blood gushing out of the cavity. Without pause, the Berserker returned to the task of chopping legs as they crested the battlement.

By the time the fog ring dissipated, the attack had stalled. Karl leaned over the battlement to the carnage below. Dead and wounded Arachnians littered the ground surrounding the keep. Those Arachnian warriors unharmed did their best to haul away the dead and wounded. Karl noted there seemed to be a sense of urgency in their retreat.

"What the hell?" Erv blurted.

Karl twisted his head to look to where Erv pointed.

Undulating across the open fields, over a dozen squid-like creatures floated effortlessly towards the castle.

Karl popped open his screen and scrolled though to the monsters section, finally identifying the beasts.

Land Squid: Level 16, cousin to its ocean-going counterpart; though having the ability of "walking", it prefers to float in the air using the various winds and air currents to propel itself forward. Because air currents are stronger and more capricious the higher up, Land Squid rarely venture higher than five meters above ground. The creature is capable of climbing any surface. Land Squids are carnivorous and incapacitate their victims by stinging them with nerve-dulling agents emitted from the two long feeding tentacles. The victim is immediately rendered immobile. Effects usually last up to an hour. However, victims rarely survive as Land Squids are voracious eaters. Land squids average five to six meters in length. Should a Land Squid lose a feeding tentacle, it will regrow another, regrowth taking approximately six months to reach full length and function. The Land squid's trunk and fin are tough and not easily penetrated. The best way to kill a land squid is by piercing either the systemic heart or the brachial heart which are located midway between the tip of the fin and the eyes.

Alerted to the arrival of the Squids, the flurry of Arachnian activity to retreat increased, wanting to be long gone before the Squid arrived.

"Annabeth," Karl called out, staring at the approaching creatures. "You got anything up your sleeve?"

"How about this?" she replied, casting a Summon Beast spell.

In between the castle and the approaching Land Squid, a giant scorpion popped into life and charged at the approaching squids, its claws snapping and tail raised to attack. At first, the squid split to avoid the scorpion, yet the conjured beast would not be denied battle and shifted left and right, snapping at squid bodies, cutting tentacles and arms while the stinger jabbed through the tough trunks, penetrating into the core of the squids' bodies.

The scorpion had taken out five of the squid before they redirected their attention to the beast. Four of them surrounded the scorpion while the remaining four continued on to the castle keep. Karl watched as those surrounding the scorpion kept their distance. As one distracted the scorpion, the others tried to slap their tentacles on the scorpion's exposed body. At one point, the scorpion charged the distracting squid, managing to take it down, severing tentacles and arms and penetrating the trunk with its stinger.

But the sacrifice of the one squid let the others swarm over the scorpion, their tentacles slapping the beast's body, tail, and eyes, injecting the debilitating poison. The giant monster began to weaken and falter, its tail wavering and lowering. That was all the squid needed and soon the scorpion was enveloped in a flailing mass of tentacles causing it to finally topple over, dead.

Their mission accomplished, the three squid drifted off again to catch up with their brethren who were now weaving through the gate.

"They're climbing the walls," Erv screamed.

Karl gazed down as the Land Squid attached the suckers on their arms to the smooth stone wall to start their rippling climb up. "Annabeth."

Annabeth flicked through her conjuration spells and found one, casting a Spiked Netting spell that wrapped the tower in a two-meter-wide netting with ten-centimeter razor sharp spikes protruding through the fabric, halfway between the ground and the battlement.

The first Land Squid to reach the netting impaled a suckered arm on the spikes and immediately jerked back the arm, causing the others to likewise pause in their climb, giving Caryn time to send down a rain of double arrows, many of them penetrating the squids' skin and finding the mark of piercing the heart.

As the trailing three climbed up the tower to join the others, three of their companions fell to the ground, dead, arrows protruding from their bodies. That left six Land Squid, one of which had figured out the netting was short enough to allow it to lift a tentacle and place it on the other side of the netting, using the outer suckers on the pad. Using the other tentacle as support, it leaped across the web and landed above the upper edge of the spiked netting, just in time for Annabeth to hurl a fireball at it.

Somehow the squid shifted at the right moment and the fireball bypassed it to explode on the ground. Annabeth then conjured an Acid Bath spell, forming a ball of acid about the size of a baseball and hurling it down on a squid that was concentrating on bypassing the netting.

The ball exploded in a sizzling burst, causing the squid to emit a piercing squeal of extreme pain as it let go of the wall and fell to the earth, the acid eating through its skin, causing deep holes in the body. The squeal alerted the remaining five whose fury propelled them over the netting and begin their assault.

Orc's Bane proved its worth as Karl easily sliced through tentacles and piercing squid hearts. Dieter was equally successful as more tentacles piled up behind him.

Karl shouted out a warning. "Be careful of the tentacle pods because they still emit poison."

Yet it was too late as Erv backpedaled away from a squid, tripping over his own feet and landing on his back onto a pod, another flipping over onto his arm. The effect was immediate, and he froze in place, his face a mask of fear.

Kori spun around to avoid a tentacle coming over the battlement. Yet his speed did not match the whipping action of the squid's arm and it found its mark, wrapping around Kori's neck and yanking him over the top of the battlement, the squid hurtling down the tower, leaping over the netting obstacle, its prize wrapped in its tentacles.

Abruptly, the remaining Land Squid paused their attack and slowly backed down, careful to avoid the spikes, until they were on the ground though still surrounding the tower. The squid holding Kori waved the immobile body at those above.

"What's it doing?" Dieter asked.

"Taunting us," Sakura answered.

"No," Caryn slowly replied, studying the motions and movement. "I think it wants Erv."

"How do you know that?" Sakura asked.

"I don't," Caryn said. "But look at it; look at them. They're not attacking, but they're not leaving… like those spider people did."

Karl shifted a glance at the frozen Erv. "So you're suggesting we offer him up as a sort of peace offering, a sacrifice?"

"Why not?" Caryn shrugged. "It's not like we were going to take him with us. And I seriously doubt he's gonna make it back once we cross. And I don't see us taking him back then retracing our steps to the bridge. It's either toss him overboard or leave him here, in which case he'll still be lunch for those things."

"She has a point, Boss." Dieter wrapped a protective arm around Elena.

Karl looked at the others who curtly nodded their agreement.

"Like Caryn said," Annabeth continued, "it's not like we're going to take him with us, and the result is the same whether we leave him here or give him to them."

Karl looked once again at the waiting Land Squid and then back to Erv. "Someone help me lift him up. And watch out for those tentacle pods."

"I gotcha Boss." Dieter grabbed Erv by the front of his jerkin and lifted him up, using two hands to hold him above his head. Walking to the wall, he tossed the woodsman over the top, leaning forward to watch the man's decent and thudding crash onto the ground where Dieter was sure that if he wasn't dead before, he certainly was now.

The Land Squid swarmed over the body, one of them wrapping it in its tentacles then one by one they proceeded away from the tower and out the gate, carrying their prizes.

Karl scanned the overgrown farm fields as the sun settled in the west, the clouds highlighted in gold and red. Seeing no more threats, he turned to the group.

"We stay up here tonight. How long does the netting around the tower last?" he asked Annabeth.

"Until I take it down," she replied.

"Then leave it. It gives us some protection. Everyone needs to get what sleep you can. Food?"

"I have food," Elena offered. "I packed more just in case."

Karl gave her a warm smile of thanks and appreciation.

"Told you she was good," Dieter said with pride.

"We leave at first light," Karl continued. "There are six of us. We pair off and rotate watch: Dieter and Elena, Annabeth and Caryn, and Sakura and me."

Annabeth and Caryn exchanged surprised glances, yet neither said anything.

Karl looked at the debris around them, the dead Arachnian and the tentacle pods. "Watch where you step and what you touch," he warned then chuckled. "I imagine all of our adrenaline is up at the moment for any of us to sleep. But do your best. Sakura and I will take the middle watch. Whoever doses off first has the last watch."

It didn't quite work out like Karl planned as no one got any sleep as the adrenaline still flowed, that is except Annabeth who curled up and fell fast asleep, Karl marveling how she was able to compartmentalize stress and sleep, once again wishing he had that talent.

In the dawning hours, the others still awake, Annabeth woke refreshed, stretched and glanced around then pouted.

"What? No coffee? What kind of outfit is this?"

"We need a fire for coffee," Karl reminded her, "and we need wood for a fire."

"And coffee," Sakura chimed in.

"And a pot and cups," Caryn added.

"I've got coffee," Elena quietly said.

"All we need now is a pot and cups," Caryn sighed.

"This place has got to have what we need," Annabeth stated, leaning through the merlon to gaze around the castle.

"We're not going to find out," Karl reminded her. "We need to leave shortly so we don't have time for coffee."

Annabeth stared aghast at him. Using her fingers, she made a sign of the cross at him. "No time for coffee? Be gone evil spirit."

"Think we can make the bridge before the nasties come out?" Sakura asked.

"It's about ten klicks to the bridge," Karl replied. "We hustle, we can do it, but we need to get moving – now. I've been scouting the surrounding area since it was light enough to see. It's quiet... too quiet. But we can't stay here." He pointed to his right where the main road entered the forest again. "That's where we need to pay special attention. Let's move out."

Leading the way down the circular stairs, he stopped long enough for Annabeth to undo the Hold Portal spell. When they emerged from the keep onto the bailey, the only evidence of a fight was the occasional blade and dark blood spots on the ground.

"Annabeth and Caryn take the lead. Sakura, you roam as usual. Dieter and Elena in the middle. I'll take rear. Once we get on the main road, pick up the pace."

Once through the main gate, Caryn and Annabeth set off at a jog, the others easily keeping pace, Karl's attention focused behind them. It was when they approached the forest that he saw movement opposite the expanse of fields, as Arachnians emerged from the forest and started after them.

"We got company," he exclaimed.

Annabeth slowed her pace to jog alongside Karl. "Let's try this one," she grinned, casting a Summon Pest spell.

Karl flinched as a swarm of hornets swirled above him then raced towards the approaching Arachnians. Slowing his pace, he jogged backwards to watch the insects descend on the Arachnians, sending them into spasmodic disarray.

"Nice one," he chuckled, turning back around and catching up.

For the next kilometer, all was quiet... too quiet as Karl reminded himself.

Sakura slipped through the trees and ran beside him. "I didn't see anything for the next 500 meters. Doesn't mean something's not there."

No sooner had the words escaped her lips that the forest behind them churned in noisy violence and ten two-headed dogs the size of Saint Barnards leaped onto the road, snapping and growling at them, their fangs like Saber-toothed Tigers, but never getting close enough to engage in battle. Yet their presence was enough to cause Karl and the team to increase their pace.

Annabeth dropped back again next to Karl. "Should I do something?"

"Not yet," he replied. "It's as though they're forcing us to the bridge."

True enough, the closer they came to the bridge, the farther behind the dogs lagged until they disappeared.

"We must be close," Karl muttered.

It was when the road curved that a break in the trees told him that they had arrived.

They stood at the edge of the forest, the road before them ending in a wide clearing. Karl heard Elena suck in her breath as she took in the carnage. Spread out across the clearing were the piles of bones and remains, some of humans, some of other creatures.

Directly in front of them was the tall granite archway of the bridge leading across the sea to the next island. Yet, like before, their focus latched on to the dark brooding creature in the middle of the gate, sitting on a wide chair made of polished ebony that glistened in the mist that rose up from the sea. The creature looked up as soon as they entered the clearing.

Despite knowing there was no chance in defeating the monster, Karl activated his gaming screen and he shook his head at the stats: *Hill Giant, Level 50. Damn. They really put some teeth into no one getting across.* He didn't bother reading the rest of the stats. What did it matter? They only needed the password, and they were across.

The giant glared at them as he ponderously pushed himself to standing, a long broad cudgel in his hands, the thick wooden head studded with vicious and bloody marble shards. Strewn around his feet and throughout the clearing were more bodies and bones of those unfortunate to survive the trials to get here yet lacked the single piece of knowledge to guarantee their continued survival. Vultures plucked and fought, rose briefly then resumed their feast on a body at the edge of the clearing.

The giant stood four times Karl's height and at least twice his width, spreading himself across the gate. With a sneer, he stared down at the Viking and the rest of the group.

"What business have you here?" he asked, his voice a deep growl.

"We wish to cross the bridge," Karl replied.

"No one may pass without the key." He held his cudgel ready.

With the experience of having done this before, Karl confidently said, "We have the key."

The giant snarled at him. "Be sure little man. One false word and you die. Turn back now and I will spare you."

Karl chuckled thinking to go back would be to run the gamut of the monsters they had just escaped. He then realized he had forgotten to ask where everyone's bind spot was, although it didn't matter once they were across. He glanced back at the others who nervously nodded, ready to get this over with. Squaring his shoulders, he turned back to the giant. "We have the key."

A large vulture, black as agate, wretched and mean, its beak dripping with blood from a recent victim settled on the left shoulder of the giant who then addressed the bridge crossers.

"You will tell the bird the key. If he likes you, you may cross. If not... you die."

The bird flew up and circled around Karl, waiting for him to stretch out his arm. When it landed, Karl was surprised how light it was.

"The key, the key," the bird chirped, cocking its head side to side.

A swirl of wind immediately surrounded Karl, effectively separating him from everyone else.

"The key, the key," the bird repeated.

"Dragon's Head," Karl said.

The swirling wind evaporated as the raven flew up and cawed, "Friend, friend."

"You may pass," the giant grunted.

Karl twisted his head to tell the others, "I was right. It's the name of the island. I'll wait for you on the other side."

Once Karl passed him, the giant stepped back into position, effectively blocking Karl from witnessing the rest of the interrogations. He took several backwards steps onto the bridge, all the while trying to see what was happening, yet he heard and saw nothing until the giant stepped to the side and Annabeth came striding past the monster to wait with Karl.

"Four more to go," Annabeth said, anxiously waiting the others. "I hope Elena makes it."

"Why shouldn't she?" Karl's brow furrowed at the thought that what worked once might not work again.

"I don't know," Annabeth answered as Sakura joined them followed quickly by Caryn.

Then no one as time suddenly slowed and neither Dieter nor Elena appeared. The minutes dragged on and at one point Karl was about to say that it would just be the four of them when Elena raced across then whirled around, anxiously waiting for Dieter.

"What happened?"

"The monster wasn't going to let me cross," she said, her eyes filled with trepidation. "He kept saying that I wasn't allowed to cross. He kept calling me an NPC and I don't even know what that means. Dieter said he was wrong that I had already crossed one bridge so the giant was wrong, but the giant kept repeating that I couldn't cross. Dieter said that I had the password and the giant was required to let me pass. They started arguing and the giant was about to fight Dieter when Dieter said it didn't matter because if I wasn't allowed to pass then once I was on the bridge I would disappear."

There were tears in her eyes and she looked at Annabeth. "What did he mean that I would disappear?"

At that moment, Dieter came lumbering up. Elena rushed to embrace him.

"Sorry, Boss. Had a little problem."

"We got part of the story from Elena. How'd you make it work?"

"I simply told him that he couldn't refuse someone who had the key." He tenderly patted Elena's head. "Told him it was against the rules. That sort of confused him. He kept calling her an NPC and said she couldn't cross. When I pointed out that she was from two islands away, he didn't want to believe me." Dieter chuckled. "It almost came to blows. He finally relented when I told him even the vulture called her friend."

"What's an NPC?" Elena whimpered, wiping her eyes.

"It's a nice person character," Annabeth answered.

"Huh?"

"It means that not everyone in the ga– uh, world, on the islands, you know, not everyone is nice. Those who are nicer than everyone else usually stay in one place so they can help those less fortunate." She looked to the others for help.

"What she's saying," Caryn said, coming to her rescue, "is that usually only adventurers and folks like us," she spread her hands at the others, "cross islands. People like you, nice person characters, as a rule, don't usually go on adventures. But you're different now. You're a genuine adventurer, so the giant was wrong."

That seemed to mollify her, and her tears dried.

"Time to move on," Karl encouraged, walking forward.

The bridge was wide enough for them to walk abreast. The pathway and side walls were constructed of roughhewn stones, thick and heavy, though the pathway was smooth. As the bridge curved up and over the ocean span, a thin mist clouded what lay ahead.

Midway across, the mist lifted and, in the distance, a thick forest filled the vista.

Hearing the cacophony below them where the sea churned, foamed, and roared, Karl paused to peer over the side, blinking in surprise at how high above the water they stood. He then craned his neck to see the jagged cliffs in the far distance, descending straight down to the crags and rocks littered with debris.

As they descended to the other side, just like before when they first stepped onto Innis Torr, another land giant stood in the middle of the distant gate. Karl didn't bother activating his gaming screens. He already knew the stats and the fact they would not be allowed to return.

Then a thought occurred. Suppose he achieved a level 50 or higher later on and decided to come back. Could he? What was to stop him, especially if he was a level 60 and the giant was still a 50? But then... would he really want to come back? Still, it might be interesting to be such a high level that no one could mess with you.

The land giant stood even taller than the one guarding the other end. Out of curiosity, he activated is screen and immediately noted the giant was a level 60. *So much for my theory...*

Like the giant at the other gate, this one held a long broad cudgel in his hands, the thick wooden head studded with jagged and bloodied marble shards.

Standing before the gate, the giant held out a palm, causing them to stop. When it spoke, the voice was ominous like thunder.

"You have crossed the bridge. You may never go back. If you attempt to return, I will kill you. What is the key?"

"Dragon's Head," Karl replied. "We wouldn't be here if we didn't know the key."

The giant studied them for only a moment before stepping aside. "You may pass."

Karl started forward then paused. "By the way, has anyone else ever passed through here?"

The giant scowled at him. "Pass or die. The choice is yours."

"We're going," Karl sighed as he led the others past the looming monster.

One past, the scene was the same at the other end. Scattered piles of human remains littered the area surrounding the gate along with the buzzards feasting on the half-eaten cadavers.

Karl paused, pulling up his personal screen. "The first town is Ballach-kild, about twenty klicks from here. Looks to be a good-sized town. We'll get an idea of what lies ahead when we can get settled and plan our future.

Though cautious, they ambled on at a relaxed pace, the air clean with the fragrance of pine.

"I wonder if there are any dragons on Dragon's Head Isle," Annabeth said.

At that moment, a wide shadow passed over them and they looked up to see the scaled body of an immense dragon in flight, the body a shimmering emerald green streaked in gold.

OTHER BOOKS

I write GameLit, Space Opera, Steampunk, Dystopian, Literary, Romance, and even poetry, and you can find my books in numerous eBook stores. You can check out my website for more information about my books, upcoming projects, and events I'll be attending where you can visit with me and even get signed books.

Thank you for choosing to read this story! If you enjoyed it, I'd appreciate your feedback in the form of a review.

Thanks for reading!

-pdmac

WEBSITE: www.pdmac-author.com

FACEBOOK: www.facebook.com/pdmacauthor/

The Wyvern Master Chronicles

The Sixth Kingdom
A Spy in the Court
Raising the Dead
Wizard King

Bridge Quest: A GameLit Adventure Series

Bridge Quest
Orc's Bane
Lord of Innis Torr

Steampunk Western: Tombstone Trilogy:

Fool's Gold
An Ounce of Lead
The Devil's Disciple (Coming soon)

Viking Time Travel Romance

Beyond Her Touch

A Dystopian Novel

Rebirth of Angels

A Time Travel Novella

Ctrl Z: The Do Over Stone

Poetry

a young man no more